Shaded Canvas

Shaded Canvas

Isis I

Shaded Canvas
Copyright © *2008* by Isis I

Book Design and Printing by Falcon Books

San Ramon, California

ISBN: 978-1-4343-4450-2 *(sc)*
ISBN: 978-1-4343-4451-9 *(hc)*

Library of Congress Control Number: 2007907837

Published by
ISIS I, LLC
361 17 th St. NW Suite 924
Atlanta, GA 30363
www.isisprivatestock.com
Email: isis@isisprivatestock.com

PRINTED IN THE UNITED STATES OF AMERICA

ACKNOWLEDGMENTS

For any accomplishment there are always persons to thank:

For Nylah Isis—just in case you needed the footprints. Thank you for the joy that you always bring—every time! Welcome Hannibal Carter Navies II.

I bow deeply to Clifton Summerise Sr., the devotee who has been invaluable. I am eternally grateful for the strength you have shown and for all the sacrifices you've made (too many to count). Without you, this book would not exist. You made the difference!

My extreme gratitude goes to my editor, Kaye Washington. Thank you so much for your eloquent and passionate editing of the manuscript for *Shaded Canvas*. Your insights and expertise added much to bring about a fuller understanding of this book to readers. Thank you for seeing this challenge through.

To my publicist, Wendy M. Welch. I recognize and appreciate the strength you have shown. Thank you so much for being on point with *Shaded Canvas*.

To my two sons, Robert Uhuru Greene and Hannibal Carter Navies, each whom I deeply love in a unique way. Thank God for making me special that way, to be able to love so differently, yet equally. Having you two as sons has made me stronger as a woman and a mother. Yes, sometimes it was hard and things might have seemed unfair, but consider this: You all were only my first and second experiment with motherhood! Being a mother to you two has been the greatest joy of my life. Your understanding and patience with me is noted; I was allowed to write *Shaded Canvas* without distraction. I hope this book brings more understanding to each of your lives so that your light will shine even brighter.

Thank you also to Tagiri The Memphite and Kelly Navies, two stepchildren whom I helped to raise. I learned so many wonderful lessons from each of you and I hope that this book will assist each of you on your chosen paths.

I send my love and appreciation to all of my phenomenal nieces and nephews throughout the country. To Shelia Wiggins and Amanda Wiggins—we are family.

I thank my daughters-in-law, Simone Greene and Teresa Navies, for being great daughters.

Thank you, Rodney Cook, for those long, intellectual conversations.

I embrace my tireless and patient advisors, Deborah McFadden, Sandra W. Williams and Sheila Williams for their immense encouragement.

To Nia Elaine Marie Alsop, thank you for showing off your talents.

To my treasured friends—Charlie Smith, Jackie Buist, Willie Cook, Bertha Kelly, Ayinka Robinson and Alice Turner—It was Grace that placed people like you in my life.

Thank you to every child that I had an opportunity to teach and to learn from. Thank you to all of the Summerise children (Jackie, Robert, Clifton) and to Stephanie Whitehead, Jason Smith, Monica Saunders, Stacie Watson, Stephen Gregory, Terrance Gregory, Camilo Casey and Joseph Austin.

To the memory of my wonderful parents,
William and Ruth Wiggins.

An eternal light shines on Mr. Harrison Summerise, Sr.
and Mrs. Clara Summerise.

1

One can easily imagine what your childhood was like, but when you are all grown up, well, no dream could have portrayed the crush of reality that trampled upon my family's bond. My family's bond was unbreakable, but as my siblings and I grew to adulthood, now I must accept otherwise. Our once protective and comforting walls that created a haven and refuge have been breached by not so quiet storms in the personal lives of siblings. Where once I could count on reassuring hugs, it seems now those arms have become brittle, thorny, hurtful. This is my story:

My mother ran a tight ship at home. The girls in our family were mildly calm while the boys were so-so, but whenever we got out of line, and Mama had to call punishment upon my siblings and me, well, let's just suffice it to say, we all but knew the difference between heaven and hell. Still, no matter the punishment, it never included spanking or whipping. Mother said a parent would have to be downright angry or uneducated to beat on a child or even yell, for that matter. She would never discipline in any fashion to mirror techniques from days of old. But whenever she imposed strict discipline, it often surfaced when my brothers acted up, hurried and confused with their manhood under siege of a female's dictatorship.

My eldest brother E.J. often tried branding an image-ego for the younger brothers by mouthing back in his boyish-man voice with words that were so predictable, "But, Mom, that's not fair."

Mother replied in her stern yet gracious voice, "Son, how many times must I tell you that there is no such thing as a democracy in this home. It only happens after you've reached eighteen and are out of this household." We all knew that, for it was my daddy's favorite saying.

When I was thirteen, my daddy died from a rare form of leukemia, so Mom had no choice but to step in and become a true matriarch over three boys and two girls. Mom would acquiesce in her role as the matriarch, however, whenever my grandma on my father's side was around, Mom never negotiated. Even so, she managed a balancing act out of this world. None of us felt slighted or thought she had a favorite, even with my being the youngest and baby girl of the family. We were a structured family and did not show any signs of being dysfunctional. Mommy says she never dropped any of us on our heads even if the thought occurred.

The clock strikes another tick for Mom. I graduated from high school at age sixteen and was the last one away at college, but leaving Mom was not so easy. It was often harder on Mom's psyche than mine and not because she was going to miss me either. That was not even close to a reason. Mom had prepared for my leaving ever since my second eldest brother Rodney had gone away to college, which gave her the opportunity to turn his bedroom into a meditation chamber. Mother thought it was a reward from God with the extra space, peace and calm to figure out how to get the rest of her three children to the next level—into college. Joey's bedroom was turned into a sitting room. Mom said that she did not want any grand babies moving in on her space even though she was not likely to become a grandmother anytime soon. We all knew that about Mom, she was not going to be a second-time-around mother. Her mantra is You make babies; You provide the clothing, food and shelter for them, period. Babysitting was never a subject to arise. Maria was the older of us two girls. Her bedroom had been turned into an office, while my space was turned into a state-of-the-art fitness room. Mother was all the way into herself—making her karma right, mind, body and soul. She's a youthful Mom, yet educated and beautiful for if not because of her age, always responsible and appropriate in her actions. All of her children love her so much. Mother says that the love from her children is her sole reward for childbearing although she always expected expensive gifts; even for holidays she did not celebrate, she expected gifts.

Mainly through Dad's annuities and pensions, Mother successfully sent all of her children into college; however, she suffered two side effects, one mild and the other major. The mild effect was that I attended a black college and graduated summa cum laude from Tuskegee University, while my brother E.J. graduated from a white Ivy League university magna cum laude. Even so, Mother still expresses that black colleges just do not exude, in today's time, any real university clout or reflection of esteemed intellectualism. She senses that since Carver's era, very few great scientists or inventors have come out of black colleges.

The major side effect Mom suffered was from my brother Joey, who attended Tuskegee several years before I did. He majored in African Development and minored in African American Studies, only to drop out at the end of his sophomore year. Mother's older sister Roselyn graduated from Tuskegee, but Mother did not get along with her too well. My siblings and I thought that perhaps it just did not sit well with Mom that her own children should attend her sister's alma mater. But Mother held firmly to the opinion that black colleges did not demonstrate that they are as good as white colleges.

Mother said that black colleges do not seem to aspire to get up on their feet enough to compete with white colleges and that not enough research is coming out of those institutions. With one hundred or so black universities, she wonders what it is the schools produce that they can boast about.

She does not like the slogan, "A mind is a terrible thing to waste." She says the whole slogan wastes one's time when reading. She often said, "Even those without thought could be put into a mode to see in their mind's eye if they could read 'A mind is a wonderful tool to imagine.'" She thought, Why not occupy that space with something positive, with impact, instead of the two negative words "terrible" and "waste"? Mom believes that the black colleges need to come into a twenty-first century mindset. By now the college buildings should have had attractive facelifts, and in some cities she often wonders why the schools never became business-minded enough to buy up all of those blocks of uninhabitable houses or old vacant buildings and make them useful and attractive for the colleges' and universities' use. "Why should African American kids have to go to schools that look inferior?" she would ask. "Certainly that must have something to do with their drop in enrollment."

Mom still takes high school kids on her Path to Success college tours. She makes about five trips a year, taking black children from all over the West Coast to tour colleges in the South, most of them being black colleges. Mom takes a lot of Mexican American students on tours, too. She says with Historical Black Colleges and Universities (HBCUs) doing more recruitment of Mexican students, maybe black students will embrace the challenges and opportunities now being afforded to Mexicans by the government and HBCUs.

When Mom took me along on tours to Howard University, I was small, but I will always remember as a special part of that tour—the United States Capitol. It was there that I saw the bust of Reverend Dr. Martin Luther King, Jr., the first bust of an African American to go on display in the Capitol. Included on that tour was the Smithsonian National Museum of African Art. I had never before seen such beautiful African art. In Atlanta we visited Spelman, Clark, Morris Brown, Morehouse, Atlanta University, the home of Martin Luther King, Jr. and his gravesite. In Tuskegee we visited Tuskegee University and saw the works of George Washington Carver and also toured Booker T. Washington's home. That's when I fell in love with Tuskegee University. It was quiet, clean, very green and small compared with Ivy League schools. All in all, that was the school that had stolen my heart. It was the right place for me because I did not need all of the hoopla found at bigger colleges or white colleges. With its poignant history, the school just demanded that serious learning take place.

All of the kids wanted to go on Path to Success Tours led by my mother, educator Brenda Navies, because she had celebrities that came in to talk and interact with her students. I even got to see Janet Jackson on one of the tours. She was on a national tour promoting her latest record. I think she was the best of all the celebrities I had an opportunity to see.

It is a little hard even today to understand why Mother still takes students on black college tours when she does not think the schools good enough for her own children to attend. I did not argue with my mother about our different views on black colleges. I saw the colleges before enrolling, liked what I saw and chose the best learning environment for myself. Principally, I thought that African American students came out of the black colleges with their morals more intact and held a better image of what their purpose should be as individuals and as African Americans.

Ever since we were little kids, we all knew that after high school was college life. College was an automatic next level. It was not as if we had a choice in the matter, plus each of us knew we would get a car at the end of our sophomore year in college. Each of us embraced Mother's philosophy, "Freedom is yours to choose, and what you do with it determines how well you will enjoy the next level." Although I did not really understand much of that until I got older, right away I at least realized that education was my freedom.

All five of us being grown and earning our own money, we knew Mother's rule of not lending money and our not being able to return home to live. She believes when a child leaves home and returns, that is likened unto trespassing. So Mom took every step to help each of her children own homes, using President Bush's Minority Home Ownership Initiatives. In 2006 Mom listened to President Bush during his first address to the NAACP which, by the way, did not come to pass until he was in office as U.S. President for five and a half years. He said, "And we want more people owning their own homes. I like the idea of home ownership, and I hope you do, as well. Three years ago, I set a goal of creating 5.5 million new minority homeowners by the end of this decade. And we're getting results. We've already added 2.3 million new homeowners, minority homeowners, putting us ahead of schedule. Today, nearly half of all African Americans own their own homes."

The part of the president's speech that resonated throughout Mother's six-bedroom home was when he said, "We're going to provide down payment assistance for families; counseling for new home buyers. I don't know if you've ever seen one of those contracts, but the print is really small. We need to help people. Perhaps a good project for Black Expo is to join with Alphonso Jackson and the Housing and Urban Development to help people understand what's in the print so it doesn't—that small print doesn't frighten them off from becoming a first-time home buyer. I believe we ought to have tax credits to encourage construction of more affordable housing in low-income areas. See, what I want is more and more people from all walks of life, including our African Americans, opening up the door where they live and saying, welcome to my home; welcome to my piece of property." Mom stated there was no reason for her own children not to be included in that 5.5 million number of homeownership.

Mom said that if she needed to make a personal call to Mr. Alphonso Jackson, by phone or face-to-face, in order for her children to benefit from those housing programs, she would do just that. She felt that her own children must be able to benefit from such programs, and if not then she would not allow the programs to masquerade, to front for being something they are not, something for which her kids could qualify, but end up as something of which they could not take advantage because it was all really just talk without earnest intent. That's how Mom is; she's going to make sure her children receive their fair share. Her children should fit into one of such programs that the Administration has proposed. There was the American Dream Down Payment Fund to help low-and moderate-income families overcome the threshold problems of down payment and closing costs on a home, often the greatest barriers to homeownership. "The SHOP Program." That was the Self-Help Homeownership Opportunity Program that offered home purchasing opportunities to families willing to contribute their own "sweat equity." But Mom knew her children well, that they were not willing to give sweat that way.

"All I need," Mom said, "is an incentive to ensure my children never return home to reclaim citizenship in their old bedrooms." Mom works assiduously to make sure that each time she takes one of her children through the process of securing a piece of property that after that process, each child will be able to make other moves in buying property without her due diligence. We are taught to make sure we stay on top of things and learn for ourselves how the workings of the government should benefit us as individuals first.

Mom constantly tries to get Uncle BeBe's kids to take advantage of the program, but Uncle BeBe said that his kids aren't disciplined enough to pay a mortgage note on time. He said that he has to meet all three of his children at their jobs just to collect rent money that is owed him before they go and gamble it away. His stepdaughter Monica is the only one who had enough sense to buy a home with her new husband.

Mother then offered to help one of her church member's friends take advantage of the homeownership program, but the woman said that she does not like to stay in one place very long. That woman, along with three other women, rented rooms from a Mexican couple that had been in the country for only two years. Mom even picked up the paperwork for the young woman and planned to drive her back and forth until everything was completed. Sometimes Mother feels it is very challenging to help black people because if it takes ten steps to make something happen, they want you to take all ten of the steps for them.

Mom wondered why the NAACP did not do more to make known the benefits that blacks could take advantage of from this present administration. She did not think it fair that blacks should have to wait eight years for progress because partisan was the mindset of such an organization. Mom wondered, too, how the oldest black organization in America could claim to represent the whole of African Americans and be out of contact with a superpower, the Oval Office, the head of the country, for five and a half years! At least, there should have been someone in the organization who employed astute diplomacy and abilities to host a conference meeting with President George W. Bush sooner than 2006.

Mom was excited that Bruce S. Gordon came aboard as president of the NAACP. She also expressed regret of his too soon departure. Mom said that since the NAACP is one of the oldest organizations still around, it should be doing more in the twenty-first century than works accomplished in the twentieth century. Mom felt here would be a most fitting philosophy of Jesus, "and greater works shall you do." She said Grandma is a member of the organization, and maybe that is the mindset of the leaders—dated.

Mom is in no way, shape or form a Republican, but that is not why she would never in no shape, form or fashion agree with former Republican Representative J. C. Watts, who blasted the NAACP and some of the folk, calling them "race-baiting poverty pimps." But she became most incensed about how the NAACP handled the senatorial candidacy in Maryland in the 2006 election, allowing a white man to take office over two qualified black men who ran for the nomination. Mom said it could have been a great opportunity for African Americans to unite, but rather what happened was despicable; she thought it scandalous that the NAACP did not support Michael Steele as the African American senator from Maryland, knowing that there was only one black in the Senate. She said if they could have done that, African Americans would have two black senators sitting today instead of one. In her opinion the NAACP no longer holds the "master key to substance" for future generations. She wondered whether the organization should be looked upon as full representation for the Black Diaspora in America any more. Mom said it was just as disheartening to accept that Kweisi Mfume served as president of the NAACP for almost a decade, yet he did not qualify for the "full support and backing" of the NAACP as its choice for senator from Maryland. Mom thinks Barack Obama had better not count on the NAACP either. Mom mentioned her concern to several officers with high ranking as she is outspoken on every issue, but her heart is rock solid as a Democrat. That fact about Mother is hardest to comprehend: What if the Republican ticket ran John McCain and Condoleezza Rice, and the Democrats ran no African American? Would Mother remain as a sacrifice to the Democratic Party to keep hope alive for the next generation?

We should try to know as much as possible about the people we hire and put into political office was something else we learned from Mom. She instilled in us that the people we vote into office are the ones who could affect the status of our lives for good or bad. She kept up my father's tradition, taking us to the polls on Election Days. We all had to sit in the family room as Dad went over candidates and their previous performance in the political arena. Dad did not vote for anyone he did not like, no matter how popular the candidate.

Mother made her children pay particular attention to propositions on ballots and encouraged us to be participants and not just observers of others' voting practices and habits. Mom said many black people are poor because they will not take the time to be good stewards for understanding what their own voting habits should be. She says our people understand voting about as much as they understand the Bible.

Mother never could understand how a person could go to church Sunday after Sunday for twenty to thirty some odd years and not, at some point, understand the Bible personally if, indeed, one professes that is the guide to be used in life. It really irks her when folk try to tell her what God would do for her when she sees no proof of God having worked in their own lives. She says it is comfortless that a person should give reference to someone they themselves do not know about. Mom says one should study everything to show one's self approved. Her favorite story is that of King Solomon. He experienced all things to know for himself.

Our family system as we knew it felt happy and secure. Mother was still involved in our lives even when we became grown ups; she was always available to give advice when asked. She talked to us once a week, keeping in touch more with her sons. We children all tried to meet at Mother's house when possible once a month, usually on Sundays. It was clear to us that Mother kept in touch to receive a progress report of our states of mind. We did have a regular, everyday life growing up, but it just seemed that Mother expected more from her children than what she herself had been able to accomplish. Her children should do better in life than she did because more pathways had been created for her children than had been laid by her parents. I did not know if anything greater than what Mother had done in life would occur but felt something greater, indeed, should be the course. My other siblings being older, well, it's just hard to know what they will act upon. My brothers are all self-employed. I expect to be so, too, one day soon. I was able to save a little money from my job and took a sabbatical to attend Stanford University to receive a doctorate in political theory. My dissertation was Next Level: *Why the Party of Booker T. Washington—for African American Women.*

When I enrolled at Stanford, Mother had admonished me neither to emulate any aspects of white culture that were of a negative façade nor to experiment in their world in order to fit. Rather, I should master the study of knowledge. She said it is not that those people and students were any smarter, but it was the opportunities that flowed through those types of institutions. Mother tried hard to balance the critical view held by my dad—that whenever blacks excelled at white universities, those were the graduates sought out for the advancement of whites rather than for concentration upon their own race. Mother was not so thrilled about the content of my thesis and nor about seeing me with the book in hand, *Condi vs. Hillary* by Dick Morris; she wondered if I had selected the school based on the fact that Condoleezza Rice was Provost of Stanford. Regardless, Mother could not contain her joy when boasting of her daughter's degree received from a white institution, though she always failed to mention the content of my thesis. Whenever Mother would see me and every time she called, whether or not I answered the telephone, the tone was always the same. She delighted in saying, "Dr. Zemi Navies—such strength in the name."

Everybody was calling me before I could make room for any mellowness. All of a sudden, requests for interviews were coming in from all parts of the country. Cal Berkeley's African American Studies Department called. Berkeley High School was looking for someone to chair an African American Studies Department. Hampton University in Virginia, Morgan State University in Maryland and Johnson C. Smith University in Charlotte, North Carolina also contacted me. It was good to know that I was slightly in demand, but I needed more, something that could radically advance my career. Calls kept coming mostly from academia, but I just did not have a full sense that my talents could be further developed, expanded or be shown as top-notch in what I viewed as a passive posture. I was certain my talents would be easily overlooked. Academia was not where I was to be. I had exited that stage, and my passion sought other venues, other challenges, indeed, other stages, as it were. The publish or perish thing did not intimidate me. To be frank, I wondered whether I was preoccupied with plotting my ascent to wealth. *Psaphonic?* Humph! But yes!

I thought about using my education in the marketing and advertising world. My actress sister Maria said that I would be lucky to get on with a multicultural company, Burrell Communications Group, based in Chicago. She says the company has a strategic understanding of the African American community but also adds a breakthrough style in everything they create. Maria knew so much history about the company that I thought she must have had a way in, perhaps knew someone specifically who worked there in a high place. So naturally, I asked Maria the approach for employment since my experience in marketing was next to nonexistent. Her heady advice was to tell the company that I ate a lot of General Mills foods, maybe that I drove a Toyota or used Verizon Wireless. And to think, I'm the younger of the two of us. Oh, well, yet another dream deferred.

* * * * *

Just as I had finished contemplating career paths, Shauna, my brother E.J.'s fiancée, called and invited me to see the play, *The Color Purple*, in New York. She encouraged me to take some time out, to cool down, and accept her gift for earning my graduate degree. Shauna pressed, "I have purchased the tickets already and let me tell you, Missy, you cannot step out of this engagement because I have the most expensive and best seats in the house. And besides, you and I need to spend some quality time together, and we are staying in a five-star. So what do you say, Missy? Do you want to indulge yourself and sashay down the jet set carpet next weekend?"

Before I could really think about my answer, I blurted out, "Thank you, Sis. Count me in."

We flew into LaGuardia Airport—first class. The play was amazing. The songs and voices in the play were riveting, just awesome. We spent two wonderful days in New York, staying in a hotel right there in Times Square. I loved New York but wouldn't actually want to live there. Maybe the toughness needed to survive on Wall Street wasn't in the genes.

We walked back to our hotel since it was only two blocks from the theater. The walk seemed just the right moment to express my gratitude: "Shauna, it was very thoughtful of you to invite me to something so grand." I stopped for a second to lift my heel from the crease in the sidewalk. "It did me good to change pace a little bit. Studying was interesting, but it's good to be able to close the books for a while. It seems like eons since I have been out. I cannot remember the last time I have been to see a play, maybe *The Wiz* or *Wine in the Wilderness.*"

It was mid-September and the weather was a little bit on the cool side, a surprise for New York. A light rain began to fall. As Shauna tied her scarf around her shoulders and muffled, "Girl, I hope it was not *The Wiz*. That has been so long ago—the yellow brick road has all but turned to dirt, and the scarecrow, well, he is just not that recognizable today."

The bottom of my feet felt a bit sensitive. "These two blocks seem like two miles, walking in heels. Stilettos aren't made for walking."

"I feel you on that," Shauna agreed, stopping on the second step of the hotel and breathing heavily. "And not to mention, it was nippy and the nerve of us walking and just singing in the rain as if we had the type of hair that wouldn't roll up like tweed when water hits it."

"Be careful. The steps are a little slippery," a pleasant male voice took care to caution.

"Thank you, sir," Shauna said, addressing the doorman as he opened the door.

We went into the Jazz Parlor inside of the hotel. "Where would you two ladies like to sit?" we were asked.

"Right up front," Shauna answered, tailing the waiter. Turning to me, she whispered over her shoulder, "I want to be able to look right into the faces of those handsome musicians."

After we were seated, I leaned toward Shauna and said so that only she could hear me, "I don't see why you had to sit so close to the front. It's not like these guys look like athletes, all handsome and muscular. Really, Shauna, these musicians look old enough to be my daddy. Don't you have any standards?"

"Yes. I do have a standard," said Shauna. She untied her scarf and let it rest across the back of the chair.

"And school me?" I asked.

"You're not listening," responded Shauna in a sing-song voice. "I said 'standard' without the 's.'"

"Okay, then what is your standard?"

"Male is my standard."

"Come on, Shauna. I know you have high standards. What are they?"

"I am kidding," Shauna smiled. "I do have standards but, no lie, it is difficult for black women to find the right mates nowadays. Either we are competing with men who date black men, with white women who date them, or with Asian and maybe Mexican women who date our men. I'll tell you something else, too, that folk don't like to admit. Black men like to pretend that they do not know why white men don't like them enough to have them merge into their social club world."

"Ohhh! Enlighten my world on the matter," I urged.

Shauna leaned in closer. "It is not difficult to discern that white men resent black men always chasing after their white women and daughters. White men don't really like that all that much."

"How do you know that to be the case with white men when they are the ones to allow and perpetuate the mixing most often seen on the big screen?" I asked.

"Because I don't like it, and a whole bunch of other sisters out there don't like their black men chasing after white women either," Shauna explained, squirming around in her seat.

"Are you sure it is black men doing all of the chasing and not the white women being the aggressors?" I huffed.

"Let the truth be known," said Shauna. "I think those daddies had better get it through their hard hearts that their little girls just can't stay away from the chocolate. You know, Zemi, until now, I never really thought to ask why white women don't chase after their own white men the way they are all enthralled with ours. Hmm, I guess, too, white men on the QT must be wondering why their own women are so preoccupied with our men. Surely, as a black woman I wonder that about black men."

"You ever dated a white man, Shauna?"

Shauna rubbed her forehead. "Well-l, being an event planner, I sometimes like to flatter myself by flirting every now and then with them, but other than business meeting dates I don't venture on that playing field. What about you, Zemi? What little secret have you held back from your experience at Stanford?"

"Well, I had some pizza and movie dates, but I never allowed anything serious to occur. I never thought of dating a white man seriously. In the back of my mind was always the lingering thought that they only wanted to find out what it was like being with a black woman, and I knew I was not up for the experiment." I threw up my hands and accidentally knocked my purse to the floor, "Besides that, my family would explode if I brought home a white guy!"

"Zemi, your family will explode once they truly know that you are turning Republican."

I was putting back the articles that had fallen out of my purse. "I know one thing for sure, be it a black or a white man, my standards list will not change. But now the order of requirements might have rearranged themselves."

"Oh, yeah." Shauna put her hand under her chin and with a smirk on her beautiful face, asked, "From your list, supposing it's a white guy, what's the number one requirement?"

"That he be well endowed."

"Okay, now girl. I didn't expect you to trade in the graduation gown so quickly for that negligee."

I stared hard at Shauna. "Oh, I am so sorry, Shauna, to have presented that impression of my priorities."

"What are you saying, Zemi?"

"When I used the words 'well endowed,' they referred to a man who was expertly accomplished."

Shauna's smile was disarming. "I, too, am sorry—for you. But anyway, Dr. Zemi Navies, if you would, please give me a glimpse of what coincides with well endowed." Shauna maintained an innocent curiosity on her face. I could not be sure whether it was sincere.

"Of course, Shauna. My pleasure to do so." I set sail upon a stream of future projection and brought Shauna along for her delight. "My own fulfillment would be accomplished, nevertheless, completed with the regimen of the man who gains his enjoyment from the fullness of his duties as king to my queenship."

Shauna smiled. "All right, now. It's your world and I'm just visiting in it."

Shauna and I were both feeling quite humorous. Shauna seemed especially glad about the weekend and to see that I was unwinding.

"My friend Amy, who shared an apartment with me in Palo Alto and also attended Stanford, said that white men are easier to date than black men. She said white men are more giving as well as more respectful. Now and then, she would date a black man but said she would never marry one because they are too quick to run off and leave their children with the mother. Her biggest turn off to black men was that they stayed broke all of the time and always wanted her to foot the bill for everything. Amy summed up her opinion of them as being too selfish and the competition being too fierce and not worth the toil."

"That is not surprising coming from Amy. She is the product of a white mother and a black father but hates the fact that society regards her as an African American woman," said Shauna. "Amy has a whole list of dramas."

"All Amy is trying to do is to let America know that freedom does not exist in its own society while they speak of bringing freedom to Iraq. Amy feels that she has as a right to be categorized as a white woman, disregarding society's one-drop-of-blood rule that makes her an African American woman. And with that right she chooses to be a white woman. The point itself holds logic. Amy's mother is a white woman, and she wants to be what her mother is. Really, Shauna, I don't see what is so unconscionable about Amy's request. She wants to change the rule so that if you have one drop of white blood, you may also be considered Caucasian."

"White Society is never going to accept that, so Amy might as well cash in the ticket she pulled and enjoy being black." Shauna popped a mint into her mouth. "There is much excitement to the rule; she just needs to explore it." Shauna's metamorphosis was as much too sudden as too abstract. "Maybe you don't know this, Zemi, but on several occasions Amy boldly stated that America framed the term African American because some mixed kids were so awfully close to looking Caucasian that it was difficult to even say that some were black. She felt the term African American was firmly incorporated to keep the Caucasian race from being mixed, thus reinforcing the rule that one-drop of black blood is a covert enforcement of the real definition of white supremacy."

"I am fully aware of her sentiments as well as her soon-to-be published book, *Blood of Fury and Consequences*." I really wanted to drop this subject, but Shauna persisted.

"Zemi, aren't you a bit annoyed having a friend who exhibits such an open discomfort in having to be an African American? Maybe I could understand if she was fighting for an inheritance as a kinship to Thomas Jefferson, but she is too vocal on something that seems to be a slap in the face to blacks."

"Ah, Shauna, Amy herself meant nothing bad toward African Americans. She is just calling America out, on the state of its pretense of virtue—as if race is not an issue in this country—and America's shallow display of justice."

Shauna tucked her hair behind her ear. "You can try and dress it up using fine words, Zemi, but of Amy's own volition came the statement that African American is the throw-away race—if you can't recognize to which race one belongs, then just tack it on to the African American race."

I pressed my ears as the music grew louder. "But, Shauna, try and understand why Amy says such things. One day when Amy and other mixed friends of extremely light complexions were around some 'real' black folk, they made it known they were blacks. Unfortunately, the 'real' black folk did not accept them as blacks. Amy said they were looked upon as if they were something other than black but were just trying to fit in comfortably. When they were around white people, Amy says the whites knew that those in the group held some white blood but still made them feel tainted because of the drop of black running through their veins."

Shauna raised an eyebrow. "Sounds like Amy is stuck in purgatory."

"Amy is searching, as we all are, for one thing or another," was my retort to that.

Shauna continued, "I know that you love Amy dearly, but I am not all that fond of her. She is in denial. Amy has expressed to me that it was easier for society to place people like her into the 'lower' race classification, to her meaning African American."

"Still, Shauna, what you are unable to internalize for yourself should not in turn be considered peripheral or nonessential as it relates to Amy's true concern." A certain emotion rushed my heart. The need to protect and support Amy's belief was of the essence. Her mixed bloodline was not a violation upon the genuineness she and I had cemented; that was a bond like real blood sisters. Maybe Shauna was a bit jealous that my love for Amy was equal to the love I held for her. Perchance Shauna thought that her lineage from two African American parents should have placed our relationship above that of my tie with Amy.

I knew my face gave me away. I chose my words carefully so as not to further offend Shauna. "But Amy truly loves black people. I know that about her."

"You and I are never going to feel the same way about Amy." Shauna tapped her fingers on the table. "Do you share Amy's sentiments about black men, Zemi?"

"Not fully. Not so much her concern of black men and competition."

"Hmm-m." Shauna nodded her head.

"What's so wrong with competition?" I asked. "If it's a man I wanted, I wouldn't mind the competition it takes to get him because he would have to do likewise to get my attention."

Shauna turned her head to look for the waiter.

"What can I do for you ladies?" The waiter seemed to appear from nowhere.

"I'll have a Long Island, please," Shauna requested.

"And you, miss?"

"I'll have the same." I removed the light jacket I was wearing even though the air conditioner seemed to be running full blast. The music started up again. Engaged in intense conversation, we had not noticed when the band took its break.

"Competition isn't bad, but you just have to work so hard for a black man because he has so many choices in his selection-pool of women," said Shauna, squeezing lemon into her drink.

I thought just then about how my dad used to say that if you use your head the right way, everything else has to follow accordingly. My words escaped without the benefit of my thinking much about them. "I do not believe in any type of hard work to get a man, it doesn't matter if the guy was that tall, distinguished and handsome

Congressman Harold Ford." Dang it! Just that quickly I had forgotten the scandal that surrounded the congressman during the 2006 election. I did not catch my own words in time and knew right away that Shauna was going to say something not so pleasing.

"Honey, dear, I would not hold my breath waiting on Harold Ford. You just might have been molded out of too dark a hue for him." Shauna raised her hand for the waiter. "I am not feeling it with this drink. As a wine connoisseur, it might be best if I just stick to my wine list."

"Yes, miss."

"Could you please bring us a bottle of red Chateau Margaux, and you'd better bring two new glasses. Zemi, you might want to try a glass."

The music was pleasant, soft jazz. Shauna and I were both quiet for a few minutes, soaking up the ambience. The waiter returned.

"Oh, thank you," said Shauna.

"Certainly, ma'am."

Shauna sipped her wine. "Hey, Missy, oh, excuse me, Dr. Navies," Shauna said, employing an elegant if mock refinement.

I smiled, trying to get used to the title. "Oh, come on, Shauna. You don't have to call me that when it's just the two of us."

Shauna said, "No way, girl. I am going to give you your props. You've earned the kudos." Shauna raised her glass and toasted, "So tell me, Dr. Navies, what's stirring on the horizon for the lady who's moving and shaking with ideas?"

A joy rippled through my being. I am feeling Shauna's love and pride and joy for my accomplishment. Shauna and I are close like sisters though she is not my sister-in law yet. She has been around forever and a day, waiting for my brother E.J. to set a wedding date. I cherish the relationship that Shauna and I share. She is an extraordinary woman whose opinions I have respected and valued since knowing her and not because she is ten years older.

This trip is nice. Shauna obviously knew that I needed to exhale, as in waiting to.

"First, I want to express my sincere thanks for such an impressive and unforgettable evening. This weekend was just what the doctor ordered," I began….

"Well, you are welcome." Shauna's head bobbed to the beat of the jazz. "There was no one else I would have wanted to see this play with besides you—unless your brother E.J. would have come. Then we are talking a different story." She rolled her eyes.

I continued where I had left off. (If Shauna really wanted to make E.J. an agenda item, she would.) "You know how it goes, Shauna, when you go deep, but your thoughts are still on the track of an instructive journey, but you are not quite certain of how to switch tracks. To be honest, I have given my next step a little consideration but have not had the time to do any more than that. Sometimes when you have so many choices, you look up and find out that you really have none any longer; the choices were not the things you thought you wanted to do in life," I explained.

Shauna glanced up, her eyes dancing with the vibe of the music. Her voice grew louder over the music. "Well, exactly what is it that you want to do with all of the intensity, Zemi? You are sitting on a build-up in more ways than one, if you know what I mean."

I looked at Shauna with my mouth slightly open.

She plunged into the issue as she saw things. "I'll tell you what I think the problem is. You are too close to being a perfectionist. You are very young and yet, you're trying to come up with a life endeavor that will carry you through age ninety."

I gently twirled a lock of my hair. "Gee, Shauna, I have not even gotten into planning my life for next year," I answered defensively.

"Zemi, there is too much stomachache in trying to eat the whole pie all at once. When you make a plan for your life, sometimes you just need to take that blueprint and see how well you've already laid the foundation before attempting the next level. It is also good to include in your chart the breaks it takes to smell success so that you can get used to the many 'fragrances of success.'"

Shauna studied my face to see if I was feeling her philosophical mood. I must admit I was being tantalized with her 'fragrance of success' cliché. She made the journey ahead an endeavor worth defining.

"Some steps have a 'romantic scent.'" Shauna's eyes seemed to reflect such an occasion. 'A time in her own life?' She went on. "That's when you allow a god to imagine what it is like to enchant a goddess. And an evening of enchantment is not some guy taking you up to Lake Tahoe or Las Vegas because most times that is for his enjoyment. There is not enough seduction in the world to compete with the roll of the dice. You got that, Zemi?"

I snapped my fingers and chuckled. "Now that registered just like an eight-point earthquake!"

"Good," said Shauna. "Now you cannot get anywhere if you leave out the 'toilsome scent.'" She adjusted the scooped neck of her blouse. "That's the drippings of all the sweat and grind it takes to make something grandiose happen beyond your greatest expectation! Keep in mind, with that scent you should not be too prissy to be perspiring a little bit. Some of my greatest works have been performed while sweating. Are you still taking all of this to heart, Zemi?"

I looked at her squarely and assured her. "You have an Einstein at your feet," I confessed.

"Good. Moving along to the 'spoil me scent,' which is when you take your credit cards or whatever cards, and you don't have to look for the sale racks when shopping."

The talk was making my temperature rise. I have often wondered what types of things I would purchase whenever that day should present itself. How would I spend as an African American woman? I love shoes and purses but after that would spend to buy a luxury home and lots of land. Bling-blings were neither me nor for me. Grandma said that bling-blings were for those who weren't taught how to wear wealth as class but more as a way for them to be identified and then classified.

"And at last, Zemi." Shauna put her hand to her waist and lowered her head. "There is the 'take your bow scent' when you know you have performed a job well to climax with true celebratory moments." Shauna took her napkin to fan her flushed face. "That's when you take yourself to the island of Punta Cana, and you stay at the Paradisus Resort in the $1600-a-night room with a god who is deserving of you because he knows your magnificence. See, Zemi, those are the kinds of scents that help to take some of the spinning off the spin. They help you enjoy what it is that you do."

"You've got me ready to do my own thing," I had to tell her.

Shauna jerked her head. "Oh, but I forgot to mention all of that is not easy to obtain with a nine-to-five. Okay?"

Shauna had me going, ready to embark upon my own business. I had figured out that a nine-to-five would be slavery all over again. Now I just needed to figure out what I was to do and where I was to go exactly.

Shauna asked, "If you could do anything that you wanted with your life right now with no impediments, and everything that you needed to make it happen was at your fingertips, what direction would you take?"

I had been so absorbed with just trying to perfect my thesis and had not really settled upon a specific direction in which to take my education, but I do possess some understanding of the direction in which not to head. Shauna's portrayal of a nine-to-five did not smell of those scents mentioned, so I seemed to be taking a push in the direction of self-employment.

I tendered a shy grin. "Well, there are two things. I wouldn't mind owning my own business, a Writer's Palace. I would like to run a retreat sort of place where female writers, artists and speakers could come and produce their life's works. It would have to be on spacious land, a soothing, temperate spot that would be the next thing to heaven, providing all of the amenities for ultimate creativity. Of course, such would occur with no obstacles. A second ambition would probably be a lobbyist."

"A lobbyist!" Shauna said with her mouth wide open. "I would never have pictured you in that role."

"Why is that?" I asked.

"Well, we never see African Americans portrayed in that role, be it real life or big screen. We have so few black lobbyists in real life that it would be strange to see them in that role on television. It would be nice, though, if those few African Americans who are in the field could be more active in teaching others the ropes," said Shauna.

"Give me irony or give me definitiveness," I answered back. Now I am in a conversation with another, but talking privately to myself at the same time: To all appearances, I had left the school of formalities and was saturated in an ambience of freedom. More ironic was the iteration of my talk about becoming a lobbyist or that I would even make such a desire known to anyone. That one was so far on a back burner that I was shocked it came out. Especially since I thought of myself as the type of person who likes to make things happen before letting others know of my plans.

"As I said, Shauna, thoughts of my next move haven't been formulated or cemented, but no matter which door it is, I will greet it with a ready-to-forge-ahead passion and energy."

Shauna got up and gave me quite an embrace. "Oh, I am so proud of you," she gushed. "Nothing, and I mean nothing, compares to that type confidence. I believe in you, and your presence epitomizes the kind of energy that no matter what you decide to do in life and whenever you set your mind to accomplish it, any business would do well to have you aboard."

The thought circled aimlessly. Wouldn't that be just great if I could muster the confidence to make all of my wishes come true? Confidence is easy to acquire but it takes more. It's all the other things that don't seem easy to come by. After contemplating Donald Trump's and Robert Kiyosaki's book *Why We Want You to Be Rich*, maybe I spoke too soon of my ambition. I don't want to be a lobbyist. I don't even have a passion for such a thing. Though I haven't actually verbalized it, my body, mind and cells, everything, feel unified and synergized around the idea that I want to be rich, not just rich but filthy rich, disgustingly wealthy. I want to own a business and know what it would be like to become wealthy from my passion as opposed to a nine-to-five, six-figure paycheck, especially with the middle class slipping and getting squeezed, as they say.

Soon I hope to be in pursuit of discovering, "Where my heart lies, therein, would be found my treasure." Maybe I had used up too much time and energy pursuing that Ph.D.

"Shauna, that all sounds good, but getting into that kind of position in life as a lobbyist is not based so much on what you know but whom you know. That's a tough thing to do. I'd have to have a lot of genie power to make that one jump out of the bottle."

Shauna was not having the back peddling. I had told her I was forging ahead.

"The competition may be stiff, but I do know you are prepared for the competitive game. Excuse me." Shauna pushed away from the table. "I'll be back in a minute," she said.

I drew a deep breath. I felt assured that I had done my share of studying. Now out from a shadow comes an urging for my next move. I am but the age of twenty-three. Perchance purpose should have flung itself at my knees, and I could be its mistress. But no, purpose came seeking to rule what I wanted to imagine was my realm. It was true that opportunity doesn't knock, opportunity waits. All the things that I was told to do in life were done—stay in school, get that big degree, buy a home, don't get married too soon and don't start off too quickly having babies before building a secure foundation. Why such a long and arduous path of preparation and foundation building when there was a short cut? You have folk who are cashing in making rhyme and rhythm when others try to make do from paycheck to paycheck even though they have mastered the cadence of the King's language. Did I make a wrong turn somewhere?

Shauna returned and pulled her chair up to the table. I rested my arm on her chair. "You certainly took a long time. I thought I was going to have to come and find you."

"Oh, I was fine. I just didn't know that they had a dance floor in the other room," said Shauna.

"Do you want to move over to the other side?"

"Oh, no, this is fine until I finish sipping my wine. Then we can go and sit in the lobby. It's more of a scene out there." Shauna winked.

"Besides, I wanted us to do some intellectual bonding, Dr. Navies."

"Shauna, I was just sitting here thinking of all those years spent in school and how all I have to show is debt for a student loan, while rappers show how smart they are with time by building a stockpile. Now, they are your smart folk even though some of them don't even take the time to finish high school. Yet they know how to handle business and get endorsements."

"Yeah, but with your education you have built a foundation, Zemi," said Shauna.

She used the same word from my thought, foundation. "Maybe. But I wish my parents had taught more the philosophy from the book *Rich Dad, Poor Dad*, but choosing the rich dad's philosophy. Even the co-author of the book said that traditional schooling, while very important, is no longer enough. We all need to understand money and how it works."

"I still say that you are young enough and smart enough to make your education work for you. You have to spend out of what you have been given. Besides, you haven't spent the kind of life that most rappers have to survive in that world, which is almost from another planet," said Shauna.

"I have an education from one of the most prestigious schools in the country, and yet I do not believe that America really values education. Oh, yes, America talks a good game. She upholds education, but good teachers really have to struggle and make a sacrifice to go into the teaching arena because the salary seems to be just a tiny bit more than a Wal-Mart paycheck. They want teachers to produce Socrates off of welfare checks. Obviously, rappers did not buy into the hype of the education game."

Shauna stood. "Dang, just a little bit of alcohol really becomes a downer for you, huh, Zemi? Let's go and sit in the lobby."

The lobby had a plush atmosphere in which beautiful people passed. The couches were snug and cozy.

Shauna's tone had become more earnest. "Zemi, you need to make your presence known by doing something big, something different with your intellectual savvy. I'd write a book of substance to get folks' attention, dealing with something that is polemic in nature. Go on some of those TV shows, but don't waste time trying to get on CNN. Outside of Jesse, Al, J.C. Watts, Roland Martin and Donna Brazile, that pretty much covers the faces of blacks on that network. Maybe Lou Dobbs would have you on, but then again, you're not Mexican. Blacks' issues aren't being discussed."

I humored myself with the notion. "Maybe I'll do a piece or something on the narrow-mindedness of a superpower and see if newscaster Paula Zahn would go for that since she's left Fox News for CNN. She's one of the few from that station starting to deal with things that are of discord. Oh, but I just remembered, she's no longer at CNN. But I am glad that I caught one of her town hall meetings on the topic, 'Confronting Racism.'"

"Yes, I saw that one, too. I was glad to see her deal with the subject because a lot of talk shows want folk just to pretend and act as if we live in a color blind society," Shauna rejoined.

"Yeah, but why do we have to be color blind when God took the time and made so many beautiful colors and races of people so we could see different kinds of beauty?" I answered, patting Shauna's cheeks to demonstrate my point. "For me to be color blind would be to pretend I did not exist because my color is an important part of my being." Then I patted my own cheeks. "I am not about to deny this beautiful dark hue, just as white people have no need to deny their color of white."

Shauna furthered her point. "Even with that attitude, I still think O'Reilly certainly would have you on his show. Maybe some daytime talk shows. I don't know. If it is polemic in nature, talk show hosts might shy away from anything that is too contentious. And, God knows, just about anything you say nowadays could be construed in a way you don't mean it."

"Though important, that might be the reason so many shows shy away from controversy," I said quickly.

Shauna tapped my shoulder. "Do you remember Governor Arnold Schwarzenegger's remark that was subject to controversy? He said Mexicans and Puerto Ricans are hot, and it must be that they have some black blood in them. Now it appears that some Mexicans got upset over his words. For the life of me I cannot understand why. I mean, really, is it the black blood relation that upsets them? Somebody needs to tell me something because I could say some things myself that could get some people even more upset than what Schwarzenegger was able to do," said Shauna.

"Okay," I agreed, adding, "Even after that remark, Governor Schwarzenegger said something else that Mexicans took offense to. He said that Mexicans needed to learn English and learn how to assimilate better in America. Mexicans had the nerve to really be upset over that! But let's hope all of that is more about political hoopla than anything else."

Shauna frowned. "Whatever the reason, I have for a long time and forever will be upset with the former president in Mexico. While they are crossing the borders illegally, I wonder if they bring with them the racist views of former Mexican President Vicente Fox."

"What do you mean?"

"Now check this out," said Shauna. "In my opinion the Mexicans here in America are not upset nearly enough over the overt racist wickedness that their own President Fox expressed towards African Americans. What Schwarzenegger has said, well, it's just nowhere close to the mean-spiritedness President Vicente Fox of Mexico showed when the government issued a series of five stamps depicting a dark-skinned Jim Crow-era cartoon character with exceedingly popping eyes and super big lips."

"Yeah, now that really offended black folk, those with any sense of pride," I said.

"The curator of a Michigan museum who collects Jim Crow memorabilia confirmed Memin Pinguin's caricature was a classic 'pickaninny,' all right. Given all of that, here is what I would like to discern before fair play: The Mexicans here in America like holding up their Mexican flag, and by holding up that flag, are they also holding up the racist's words of their own President Vicente Fox? As an African American, I would need to have some things clarified before I jump on any Mexican bandwagon." The more Shauna talked about this subject the more headstrong she appeared to become.

"Well, you know the National Urban League and Jesse were terribly upset over Fox's remarks," I said.

Shauna nodded her head and said slowly, "Yeah, I know. I know. Jesse was outraged, and he should have been on this one, but you know, as always, when Jesse gets upset somebody better start apologizing. What Fox did was something that's just unforgivable coming from one who was the president of a country. My heart is hard against a person like that Fox because what he said was just too hard a pill to swallow. I think that a whole lot of Mexicans opt for America because they obviously know that their President Fox is about the nature of his name. Nope, a mere apology just won't suffice this time. The way I see it, blacks need to counteract in a way where they won't see it coming."

"But, Shauna, we have to be careful, all brown people in this country are not Mexican. Some who can trace their ancestry to Mexico, those who were born here consider themselves Chicano, and it is usually PC to refer to brown, Spanish-speaking people as Latinos," I cautioned. "Besides, not all brown people have the views of Vincente. That's a slippery slope."

"Zemi, when I say, 'Mexicans,' I am talking about those crossing the border, and the illegals are those coming across illegally."

The conversation made me very uncomfortable, for I knew that brown, Mexican, Latino or Hispanic unfairly and erroneously portrayed the face of "illegal aliens," conveniently leaving out all the illegals who were here from Europe and other parts of the world. I became distracted from heady thoughts when I looked over to a table nearby—and smiled. "Shauna, did you see those two guys staring at us? One of them, the hunkier guy, looks like a football player, the cute one."

"The other one is cuter," said Shauna, eyeing the pair.

"Okay, then I will order them both."

Under the table, Shauna's knee hit against mine. "We are going to have to bring you out on more dates." She passed me a napkin. "Here, take my napkin."

"What for?"

"You are dribbling from the mouth with desperation for a man to show you some attention," Shauna jibed.

"I am not! And you should not talk, Shauna, Miss too-hot-to-trot, wanting to sit at the front and stargaze at some old, out-of date musicians. Every one of those guys appeared over forty."

Ignoring me, Shauna revisited Fox. "As I was saying, maybe Fox needs somebody else to belittle so that his own people won't think and feel that he as a leader was to blame for their seemingly forever poor conditions in Mexico. Or maybe this act could be some kind of esoteric code he's sending to his people here in America—that the way for all other immigrants and minorities to get ahead in America is over the backs of blacks. I know our folk are going to do something about those images found on Mexico's stamps. It just takes us so long to move." Shauna poured another glass of wine from the bottle the waiter had brought from our other table. "We are slowly waking up and getting the hang of things," she went on. "So this just is not a good time to mess with black folk because they are already over-the-hill stressed. Indisputably, our folk are on short circuit. But I keep telling myself that they are waking up and when they are completely awake, then they need to blow a fuse at the voting polls. Jesse swore that he would lead a demonstration if Fox did not apologize. See, I am not at all for demonstrations and apology rhetoric." She nudged me with her elbow. "Zemi, do you want to know the side effects of political apologies?"

"I am listening." I cuffed my ear with my hand and turned in her direction.

"Apologies are just words, just another way of spinning. Apologies are like, well, it is the same as when a man cheats on a woman and apologizes but does the same thing over and over. An apology is like hot air; you don't have to do anything extra since every time you open your mouth it's there," Shauna explained.

I knew about the Fox issue before Shauna brought up the subject, but I was not as much upset about it until now, hearing Shauna talk about it. Although a couple of days ago when I discussed the Fox incident with Kaye, a close attorney friend of the family, she expressed the same type of exasperation in an e-mail. I told Shauna of the e-mail and Kaye's take on Fox and the stamps.

Kaye had written me on the subject. She admittedly was in some stream of consciousness, if not irritation. She wrote: Black Memorabilia is a hard swallow; I know I could not get it down when I first saw it. My friend Lauren and I went to such a show in Berkeley twenty years ago; I did not take my son Camilo as I wanted to preview it. I am glad I did! I never took Camilo to see the show although I did buy the book on the collection. I am sure I still have that book somewhere. It was so difficult to see such objects. Talk about visceral reaction! I actually get a bad taste in the mouth now as I think of that show. Some Japanese have been big time BM collectors. My feelings about the issuance of the stamps by the Mexican government are hard to express; I am not certain I even know what those feelings are. I suppose that if in this country we attempted a "Truth" dialogue as was attempted in South Africa after apartheid was illegalized, this would be quite appropriate, for this U.S. government, which has never apologized for genocide of the native people of this soil or for U.S. slavery, to speak on the issuance these stamps. An apology for slavery goes against the ill-advised opinion of a single black American. How in the heck can one black person speak for millions of us? We need to stare this ugliness in the face—every American. There are some sores in this country that need to be lanced. I am just not sure how to do it!

While I say these things, I do understand the protest against the issuance of the stamps with no explanation of why and how widespread distribution of them would help to "stamp out" racism, sexism, imperialism, radical religiosity, self-destructive nationalism, ethnosuperiorty-ism, homophobia, anti-child-ism, and the destruction of the planet's ecosystems and systemic poverty, e.g., the policies of the World Bank and the International Monetary Fund (IMF). In the final analysis, we humans seem to find every way to destroy other humans and humanity and the only planet we have to live on. Of course, every "anti-ism" is not for everyone—we have our pet picks and actually rank the importance of the anti-isms. I just do not like to see people wounded, especially the innocent, the defenseless, the poor, and the meek. The uncanny thing about the stamps is that big lips are "in" (were they ever "out?"). Every other celebrity you see today looks like she or he was punched in the mouth by a prizefighter. I and millions like me are blessed with natural, full lips, but there is nothing beautiful about the depictions of the stamps that make the subjects appear crazed, fearful, weak, "male ego-busting" or totally nonchalant about their circumstances.

Shauna raised her hand and said, "Right on, Kaye, let's hear it for the girls with the big lips."

Puckering my lips, I said, "Finally, now I have something that is sporty. I was wondering when the broadcast was going to resonate to other black women that full lips are not a trend; they are a part of women's charm appeal."

Shauna did not take any humor from the joke; in fact, her face contorted in a display of frowns, one after the other. "I say the backlash to Fox's remark should still be brewing," she said. "Just because apologies were offered…well, that's not good enough for us, not for the young in today's time. Young people aren't into the pacifier motif this time around. As far as I am concerned, our folk deal with feelings just a little bit too much. That's why people do not keep promises made to our folk. Our folk would rather feel something than deal with some things."

Although Shauna's profession is event planning, sometimes she talks more like a social scientist. And her passion for our folk is greater than that of many friends that we have in common. Shauna was really into the subject. The focus of a couple of gentlemen was directed in our direction, but Shauna ignored their attention. When the guys' attention then zoomed in on me, my facial expression sought Shauna's approval, but she ignored me, too.

Crossing her legs, Shauna said, "All one has to do to appease our folk is to play to their feelings the way Bill Clinton has done. He has not hesitated to play it to his advantage, for he knows all too well the psychology of our folk."

I had to tell her. "I just don't understand why blacks love Bill Clinton so much. Now that I find to be the $365,000 question."

"Zemi, you probably don't remember, the time Clinton played the saxophone on Arsenio Hall's show. I was younger then, but it was a cool thing, and I enjoyed watching him because you just don't get to see a president doing anything so unusual. It was just a rare moment."

"Anything Bill Clinton did, blacks just ate it up. He was there breakfast, lunch and dinner," I retorted.

Shauna turned in her seat. "Ah, come on, Zemi. You know that you love Bill, too. How could you live in America, be black and not love Bill Clinton?"

"Humph. It was easy for me."

"And, Zemi, Bill touched the hearts and feelings of blacks again when he apologized by acknowledging the evils of slavery. Those were the jingles that made Bill the first black President. Many blacks thought that Clinton had shared the same type of pains as they had, growing up without his biological father, taking on another man's last name and having a stepfather who was an alcoholic, a gambler and abusive to his mother. That was the feel-feel stuff that made blacks fall in love with Bill. They simply felt he could relate, could feel our pain."

"I don't guess Bill Clinton relayed to blacks that a black person who had an alcoholic as a daddy could never become president in the twenty-first century."

Shauna wiggled away from my point. "Toni Morrison is well liked as an author, and she sort of put her thumbprint on the verbiage that Bill Clinton was our first black President. That kind of made it a favorable adaptation by our folk," said Shauna.

"I am against such propaganda," I snapped.

"Why? I kind of liked old Bill myself," said Shauna.

"Because it endorses a propaganda to the next generations that blacks could be satisfied by pretending that they have had a black President rather than place an authentic breed in the Oval Office. It's such a degrading footnote, and it adds to the image of blacks' inferiority and their sense of somebody having ownership over them." I pushed my empty glass into the center of the table. "I really detest it when blacks make that statement because it helps to engrain the thinking that a President of the United States can only look white. It sends out a defeatist signal to blacks that it is almost futile for them to attempt the presidency. How did our leaders let that get a passing voice anyway?"

"It was all just make-believe, Zemi."

"Black people pretend too much already," I answered angrily.

"Yeah, but I guess all of our folk pretend in some way or another."

"I do not pretend!" I barked. "Maybe you do, Shauna, but my dad taught me to have a thorough sense of self," I said, sitting up proudly.

"Zemi, I am not saying that your dad didn't give you a strong sense of self. But we could take something as small or as big as black women straightening their hair-dos as an example. Nearly all black women straighten their hair. Master hair stylists nowadays, can hook a sister up so, she walks out of a beauty salon believing she was born with her hair that way. Another thing, consider cosmetic surgery for people who want thinner noses, or women who get implants for bigger breasts. We, too, pretend." Shauna fixed her face in an unwavering stare. I did not see, but felt a mocking grin. "Now tell me, Dr. Navies, why does that not shatter the facades of pretense?"

There was nothing to say. All I could do was to bite my bottom lip, for I had no recourse to offer. I thought to myself that white folks never had to pretend that they had a white president.

"Chill a little, Zemi. You are reading way too much into Bill as a black president. Much of that was just a political ploy," said Shauna as she lowered her hands.

"We are too fragile to be duped with so much nonsense. I am offended by the statement, 'Bill Clinton, the first black president.' We are confused enough as it is with our bloodline."

"Ah, whoo, whoo, whooo." Shauna patted my cheeks with both hands. "I am going to have Bill offer a personal apology as soon as we get a black president in the Oval Office," said Shauna.

"Clinton can keep his apology," I said, feeling a bit toxic. "I feel deep down in my heart—the stained and wounded part,—that bloodstain should forever follow Bill Clinton for allowing the destruction of my kind—the machete-chopping of 800,000 Rwandans. His hand is scripted in the written Rwandan Genocide." I spit on his apology. Is that apology a pass for Hillary Clinton to receive African American votes come '08? Yes—It takes a village? And whose policies stood by while a Village got taken? Are African Americans having a memory lapse? Does lost of memory ease the pain? Should God be the only one keeping tally? This peculiar pain I could not share with Shauna. "And anyway, I think President Bush offered a more touching, warm, distinct and heartfelt apology than President Clinton when he visited Goree Island, where slaves were actually captured and held until it was time to take them away from Africa to foreign lands. Bush went to the root, a place that operated as the loading dock for slaves, a base where my ancestors were first shipped into an open sea, bound for the journey of slavery. As President of the United States, Bush openly admitted the tyrannical wrongdoings, atrocities and injustices decreed upon my kind by small men who took on the powers and airs of tyrants and masters. And I championed the sensitivity with fire in my heart."

"Zemi, how you and other folk, including a lot of black Republicans, seem to want to give that man a conscience is more than a mystery to me—it is straight up Twilight Zone. Goree Island? That was a speech somebody wrote for Bush! All he had to do was recite it. And why do you think Bush's response to Rwanda would have been any different from Bill Clinton's? Can you cite anything to demonstrate that? When I look at Bush, I just do not see a man of conscience; I see someone put in office by the U.S. Supreme Court after Al Gore actually won the election. As far as I am concerned, it was like a junta, and the Supreme Court had no business in the matter. I just needed to put another view on the record, as it were, okay? And, Zemi, one day you and I will compare those two men's apologies of slavery and see which one imparted the most earnest words. Okay? Now, we are going to do that soon but not on your first weekend out of the book hole. For right now, no more Clinton and Bush stories." Shauna pulled my chin down. "Now do you promise?" she teased. "And let us just pray to God that the 2008 U.S. Presidential election is not highjacked!"

"Okay, but I just wanted to ask you this one question."

"Is it important, Zemi?"

"Well, I want to know if I can sue somebody."

"Oh, goody. My ears are perked for a suit because California is the land of opportunities and legal suits." Shauna put both elbows on the table and cupped her chin. "Go on, tell me."

"Hmmm, maybe I had better not say because it is somebody you admire a lot," I said.

"Oh, my! Does it have anything to do with E.J.? Tell me, girl. Don't have me waiting in suspense any longer." Shauna's voice was trembling.

"Well, I have received several phone calls from a guy lately, and, you know, I don't know the man, have heard of him but never met him personally to have given him my phone number. So my question, isn't it illegal for him to harass me, calling every other day, asking the same question over and over?"

"Oooh. That sounds serious. Maybe you can sue. But how do you think the guy got your number in the first place? And what is the question that he keeps asking you?"

"I am a little embarrassed to tell you," I said with a look of mock innocence.

"Now, Zemi." Shauna spoke slowly and held up her smallest finger, the "pinky"?

"Now you give me your finger."

I connected my "pinky" with Shauna's.

"Okay, I promise not to tell a soul," said Shauna as she almost crushed her face against mine in her hurry to hear what she figured for salacious.

"Well-ll," I started with a lack of conviction, "the person was Bill Clinton, asking me to vote for Proposition 87, 88 or 89? I don't know which one, but I wonder if I can sue for invasion of privacy? How do you suppose he got my home number? I am not listed. I don't have his home number."

Shauna's mouth was wide open. "No, you didn't do that to me, Zemi. You are going to pay for that sin. I will get you back when you least expect it. I promise you. You are so wro-o-o-ng."

Just then, the two young men approached our table. One stood on Shauna's side of the table and the other on my side, as if they were ready to be our escorts.

"Good evening, ladies," said the one standing nearer to me. "I am Uhuru and this is my friend Carter. We would like to know if we could interest you young ladies in drinks at the bar."

Shauna smiled alluringly, "I am so sorry. We are leaving soon, but thank you for asking."

The two gentlemen walked away.

"Why did you tell them no, Shauna?" I asked with disappointment. "You were rude, and that is exactly the reason why black men say we are mean women. It's women like you giving good women like me a bad rap. They were so polite, well-dressed, and the one with the name Uhuru has the sweetest dimples."

"He only had one dimple," Shauna retorted. "Why get so excited over dimples when you and your whole family are known for hauling potholes in the cheekbones?"

"See, you have E.J. at home so you don't care if I meet someone—and I thought you wanted me to enjoy myself."

"First off, I was not rude to those guys. And I do want you to have a nice time, Zemi," Shauna said, patting my hand. "The brother was handsome, but what were you going to do with a man with a name like Uhuru? And he was stuck on himself. I was surprised he didn't come off saying he was an Aries or some other astrological sign as an opener. You know that old song that goes, 'Hi my name is Larry and I am an Aries.' Anyway, you and I were having a very intellectual conversation."

I protested still. "I don't care about his sign. He was handsome and looked to be a very intelligent guy."

Shauna seemed to want to put all of thirty-four years of her smarts on the table at once. She was so lucid in expressing herself. In a grand debate on black people's state of emergency, Shauna was lead debater. "You see what I mean, Zemi, when I say our folk are too sensitive about things. Their asses need to be more businesslike and start signing contracts, learn to put things in writing like documenting that forty acres and a mule. Then we wouldn't have to go around saying what's owed today. If I were around then, I would have made President Lincoln, Frederick Douglass or somebody write that forty acres into the Constitution or amend the mule or something."

I felt my cheeks getting warm. "I think you are being a little bit too incensed over the struggles that black folk were up against back then, Shauna. They were not even allowed to read if they could, and if they were caught reading, they were beaten badly with whips. This might account psychologically for some people's lack of interest in reading today."

Shauna ignored what was meant as an incendiary remark. Her heart was feeling the words she uttered. "I am just saying, Zemi," said Shauna softly, "we take all day long to explain an excuse for not doing some things. At some point our folk must buckle down and learn things, things to catapult the masses. See, sister girl Oprah knows what it is to do a contract. The sister is dealing. XM Satellite Radio has signed our TV talk show goddess to a three-year, $55 million deal to work her media magic on the radio. Okay? The black women in Hollywood must be sleeping because they should have been able to pick up something from the woman. I mean, they are right there in the Hollywood industry, where if one wants to know something, the how-to is all around."

"Shauna, Oprah is on a serious and global mission beyond what the minds of the masses can comprehend and realize at this moment. You see what type of school she has opened in South Africa, an Oprah Winfrey Leadership Academy for Girls."

Shauna twirled her glass and smiled. "Oprah's work is headed in the direction of nature's true call. Women must be prepared, and, when you are one of the ones to prepare, well, you cannot waste time explaining to those who are not a part of making things happen on their ends. Things are much bigger than Oprah than those who have eyes to see."

I took the extra glass of wine, "Let's make a toast to the golden goddess." Shauna and I held up our glasses and saluted Oprah. Shauna elucidated her point about serious business. "But no, really, when I do business, I need contracts. I have to have all of my business work in writing as a real business deal. It just won't hold up in a court of law if it's not written or on a video camera like Rodney King's scenario. See, that's why I'm marrying your brother. I need an attorney in my household, working pro bono for me 24/7, and of course, I'll do my pro bono, too, in the home, just not 24/7. A girl's got to keep something in reserve while keeping it preserved. A woman's got to always be able to reach back in the pack and bring out a new flavored Tic-Tac to ignite new sparks!"

Shauna and I laughed giddily on that note. It was a good thing that neither of us had to drive. We only had to ride the elevator upstairs to our suite. Shauna plans things to the letter.

*   *   *   *   *

On the flight back to California, Shauna and I were able to sit in first class together this time. Though it wasn't Air Force One, it was close enough, better than flying coach again. I'm musing about taking on Shauna's mindset and upgrading my lifestyle.

Shauna pushed the button above her seat. "I don't know what class I fit into in the black race, be it lower, middle or upper class. Mainly, I'm not really concerned about that type of class thing, but let's not get it twisted. I mean, whatever it takes to be in first class flying, I am going to be sitting in first. Make no mistake about me in that class. And if you're putting me in a hotel, I don't count less than five—and no matter who's counting for that matter. And I am keeping it real light."

"What can I get for you?" The flight attendant was at my elbow.

"I'll have coffee. Black, please," Shauna answered.

"And how about you, miss?"

"Coca-Cola, please."

Shauna began to harass me about working on a plan. "Really, Zemi, you should give serious thinking to becoming a talk show host. You are smart, young and beautiful, and no one can argue the fact that there are not enough black women represented on television to do some serious speaking to their own kind. You need to go on the chitlin' circuit."

"Huh? What's that?" I know that *chit-ter-lings* are filth, the small intestines of a pig, and found it despicable that they are categorized as anything edible for human consumption. "Shauna, I wonder if any other race of people eat *chit-ter-lings*. Maybe our folk should think more on the cliché, You are what you eat. And with God's magnificent bounty, why must my folk always indulge beneath His grace?"

"Zemi, do you know people who eat turkey?"

"Yes, of course."

"Well, are all those people dumb? 'Cause turkeys sure are stupid, and pigs are said to be smart."

I sat there, speechless looking dumb. She had me.

"Oh, Zemi! Forget about that. I'm just pulling your pigtail. What I really want to say, Zemi, is that you are a tiny bit younger than I am. Well, anyway, what I meant was you should consider building your platform around something that you are passionate about and tour the country talking about it."

"Like what?"

"Well, bring to the attention of the entertainment, media world and political parties that not enough African American women are being included in positions in those three arenas. Make an issue out of why it would benefit them to consider using more African American women who look like the masses of women in our race. Hell, make that an issue!" she exclaimed.

"I don't understand." I relaxed into my soft, cushy seat. "Could you be more specific?"

"As you have so often stated yourself, even when you were in high school, it was hard to identify the voices of African American females on television networks and in political parties mainly because you don't see them. Today, Zemi, aren't you even a bit curious as to why that's still the case?"

"Of course, I am even more concerned about that today."

"All black women should be asking why are we so underrepresented in those arenas. Black women should continue to reap their overdue benefits, and we must become more knowledgeable of our social roles."

Yawning, I asked, "Haven't Jesse and the Rainbow Coalition already done precisely what you are suggesting?"

"It is a different time, though."

"Yeah, Shauna, but the agendas are still the same."

"No, not really. Don't you see, Zemi? The Civil Rights Era of the 50s and 60s made great strides in getting certain doors opened for blacks, but those strategies allowed for only one in a field at a time to go through. The Civil Rights Movement did what it was supposed to do then."

The flight attendant came by and took our meal orders. I wasn't really that hungry but had requested a vegetarian meal when Shauna first booked the reservations.

"Look at Doug Wilder," said Shauna with a smirk. "When he was elected the country's first African American governor, this was in the 90s. He stood alone in the arena as an only governor of our race," said Shauna.

"That is so shameful of the country," I tsk-tsked. I kind of wanted to add more to the dialogue, but I was tired now and only allowed myself to follow where Shauna threatened to lead.

"No. The shame is that we sat back sixteen years celebrating, basking in the sun to wait for the opportunity to occur a second time until Deval Patrick was elected in 2006 as the first African American governor of Massachusetts," said Shauna. "What blacks accomplish as milestones are set in cement, only softening up enough to occur every two decades."

"So, what is your point?" It was an effort not to sound impatient.

"My point is that the Civil Rights folk did their job and very well for that time. Never can we do other than to give them high praise and great marks." Shauna's expression was unsettling. "With that said, it means that we, the young of today, should be able to take the experience from the greats of yesterday and couple it with the speed of youth at this opportune time."

"But Shauna, unfortunately, when some of the few got through, they became cowards or greedy and did not widen the doors. That's exactly what did not happen. Those who got through off of the backs of the many who struggled were too selfish to pull others through. Our folk and leaders have a hard time passing the baton," I said.

"Ooooh. Ummm! This smells delicious. Even the food smells better in first class." Shauna was pleased. She clasped her hands together in prayer. I watched Shauna pray, thinking it inappropriate for people to pray in public. Praying done, Shauna removed the cover from her dish, and revisited our conversation. "But keep talking. I understand what you are saying, Zemi. Those who got through doors did not prop them open for others, huh? And that would have been a fair way to give back and pay tribute to our ancestors."

I reflected on what Shauna was saying. "You know it should not have taken almost twenty years before another African American was elected governor in this country."

"California Democrats didn't even have guts enough to do succession planning and get ready for an African American for governor before an immigrant was able to just waltz in. They should have done whatever was necessary to get an African American in that office," said Shauna.

I agreed. "That's right. Californians had a recall election to get rid of Gray Davis, didn't they? They will put in the weak, feeble at heart in office before a minority is in as governor."

"Zemi, I think that you had better start smoking your peace pipe because our color in California has already gotten as close to governorship as it's going to get when Mervyn Dymally became the first foreign-born African American to be elected lieutenant governor of California. It is too late for our kind to be elected governor of that state. And on the quiet side of things, the definition of an African American is precarious at best. A *foreign*-born and at the same time an African *American?* Yeah. Okay."

"O-okay. So you had an immigrant before an African American become governor. Might I presume that what you're thinking is that there will be a Mexican as governor of California before an African American?" I asked.

"Exactly. You heard the Mexicans say they did not cross the border but the border crossed them. Blacks had their chance in California, and they blew it because they shouted 'Hallelujah' with a tiny milestone thrown," said Shauna. "And how long ago was it that Dymally was even lieutenant governor?" she wondered aloud.

"They will probably want to change the Constitution to allow an immigrant to become president before an African American becomes president," I speculated.

"Well, I don't think the Mexicans need get too happy too soon just because they voted Arnold in as governor," Shauna said, making her point. "Remember, I said it won't be soon, but a Mexican will happen in that office before an African American is governor," she went on. "Plus, the Democrats would rather put up for governor one who showed all of the signs of impeachment before ever putting in a qualified Mexican or an African American."

"See, that stinks, too," I intoned. California has never had an African American as governor. Barack Obama is the only African American member of the Senate today and only the third elected since Reconstruction. I mean blacks are acting as if Reconstruction was just yesterday."

"And things will continue to stink," said Shauna, "until African Americans stop using out-of-date strategy to solve today's situations."

"The way I see it things definitely will not change with the out-of step leaders we have in leadership," I said.

"That is exactly what I am talking about," Shauna agreed. "Until more of us are on stage representing our folks in an uplifting fashion, that will continue to be the case. Now a person like you, Zemi, has education as a backup that allows you to play around with so many other options."

I had another view I wanted to get across. "We like keeping the same old leaders out in public view even though they are not about winning the race because they are so old; they crawl at the pace of snails. Such leaders present a mindset to the young, 'Don't move so fast' or 'Now is not the time.'"

Seeing things a lot differently, Shauna cautioned, "It is foolish to think that a leader is too old to get a job done the same as it is to think one too young. Trust me, the leaders out there today are not too old to get the job done. Now, if you had said that they were too comfortable in their positions and with the lifestyles to which they have become accustomed, then I could agree."

I couldn't agree with that. "I still think that they are too old."

"Zemi, you mustn't continue to think just because a person has passed the twenties, he or she is old."

As I bit into a bread stick, I pondered my true feelings and allowed my maturity to take a stand. "I just think that the old have done about all that they can do and they should now be ready to pass the baton. Our black leaders don't seem to have brought many young people along in terms of leadership, and that is why their art of old has gone by the wayside."

"Let's see," said Shauna. "Do you think I am old?"

"Of course not. I do not consider anyone in the thirty's age bracket old."

"What about Oprah? You know she is fiftyish, so do you consider her old?"

"Nah! Not Oprah. She acts young, at least her clothing style and the six-inch high heels make her seem youthful. But a lot of people her age act old."

"So then we are talking mindset making the difference and not necessarily a set of numbers."

"All right, all right, you've made your point."

Shauna patted herself on the chest.

"But before you become too cocky, your point was not all that great," I told her.

"As long as you concede that it is not about age, then I am cool with just making the point." Shauna took note of my plate. "Okay, let's put the old folk to bed so that we will not have to talk about them again. I see you didn't eat your strawberry cheesecake."

"Do you want it?"

Shauna reached over and took the cheesecake, placing its saucer before her. "I know that I do not need any more sweets in my system, but this piece is irresistible. Maybe I'll just eat half of it."

"Shauna, who would have guessed after completing school that the decision of what to do with one's life would have been so difficult to figure out? I thought that school would have made the process easier, but it seems more burdensome than ever before."

"It's not that hard, Zemi. Just think about what it is that you like doing and call somebody's attention to what should be happening. I keep saying: go back to the passion you have always held since your youth. It's still there, sizzling."

"How do you know what that is, Shauna?"

"Because you keep talking about it. Simply stated, our women do not have any type of platform out there to make their voices known. You make the point that not one solitary television show is about our kind, and that the black men's agendas don't truly address the situation of our women. You even thought that the Million Man March should have at least included their women. I disagree with you a lot on that, but it is, nevertheless, a worthwhile debate. Shucks, you might open up a whole can of worms, verbalizing just ways in which some black men have ignored their women."

Just then Shauna rubbed her stomach and lay her head on my shoulder. I pushed Shauna's head away.

"Oh, God, I shouldn't have eaten both pieces of cheesecake. Oh, Lordy, why hast thou forsaken me? Why didn't you hold my lips together? You knew eating two pieces was too much for me to bear."

"Suck it up, Shauna," I said. "We have more important things to ask of God."

"Well, if God wants me to be the one answering your questions, He's got to offer some relief."

I removed my purse from under the seat. "Here, this is from God." I offered Shauna some Rolaids.

Shauna then pushed the light to summon the flight attendant. "Would you please bring me another bottle of water?" she asked. After a couple of minutes, Shauna was back to her train of thought.

I said a silent prayer, Thank you, God, for speedy miracles.

Shauna unfastened her seat belt and turned to face me. "Provide black women with a platform to speak to America, and you would score big. As quiet as it's kept, if you air the dirty laundry of some men out there for public discussion and show how they have ignored their women—girl, they would rise up like Lazarus but with scorn in mind."

"I wouldn't let that bother me."

"I know," said Shauna, "but why not take the path of least resistance?"

"Earlier, Shauna, you said yourself that anything polemic in nature does the most selling."

"Yeah, but I don't know if you would want to go out and conquer without having support in your corner," said Shauna.

"See, that's just the thing. The truth is that our men don't act as if they are in the corner of our women. These men want to get theirs first. Black women cannot wait for black men to stand up and lead in positions of power. Already they'd rather play third tier to their own status of patriarchy—runner-up to the white woman as a possibility in the Oval Office before truly feeling equitable enough to step in, at least, after the white patriarch," I said. "Such a portrait helps to make our women feel some shame for our black men, not to mention stuck."

"So you think our men should be better leaders by now, huh?"

"Black men should be thinking that of themselves, too," I said.

"Do you think possibly the black man wants a white woman to be president, thinking she may soften steps—the path for his steps as the third watchman?" asked Shauna.

"Of course, the white woman and black man have saddled up as partners to make the white patriarch relinquish some of that power. White women it appears, more than black men, are the ones benefiting from affirmative action. When huge corporations had to hire minorities in top executive positions, most conveniently white women were coded fast, quick and in a hurry as a minority group, also becoming senators and governors along the way. I have a couple riddles for you, Shauna."

"I am listening," said Shauna.

"What is the race of the female co-host seated next to the black male newscaster? When a black man has a leading role in movies, always, what is the race of the female sharing as co-star?" I asked.

"Girl, those riddles were too easy," said Shauna.

"And I would have thought that after Sidney Poitier, the first African American man received his Oscar, Hollywood should have by now come to the realization that black actors can be great, too, given fitting roles and scripts. Too, some speedy influence should have been used to see that a black woman could follow before having to wait almost forty years. Am I right or wrong?"

Just then, the captain announced that we were about to hit some turbulent pockets and should fasten our seat belts. Shauna became a bit fearful and began to talk even more. I remained calm.

"It is not a matter of you being right or wrong. It is the question of what measure will get the attention through the door," said Shauna, pulling her seatbelt tight.

"I don't have any fears about doing any issues." I fastened my seatbelt.

"Oh, God, sometimes it takes so much energy to just get through to you, Zemi."

"Shauna, you are on an airplane. There are not so many other things to do right now. You can either talk to me or go to sleep, and I know which one you are going to do."

Shauna's face lit up.

"I saw that light bulb come on. What are you thinking?" I asked hopefully.

"The spirit told me to tell you to walk in the light of a television talk show as the way," said Shauna.

"What spirit are you talking about?" I was ahead of Shauna's game, and knew that she was trying to pay me back for the joke I played on her earlier.

Shauna shrugged her shoulders. "Ummm. Just a spirit. You know the kind of spirit that old folk say speaks to them, and they just submit and obey."

"Then maybe that spirit meant for you to give it to some old folk, or maybe you didn't understand it clearly. What kind of voice was it?" I asked.

"I don't know. It spoke in tongues," said Shauna.

"Was it a Swahili or Spanish tongue?"

"Okay, now. Don't you know that you are not supposed to mess with Mother Nature?"

The captain announced that we had passed through the turbulence.

Shauna got up to stretch her legs. "Okay. I am still going to get you for what you did earlier," she threatened as she stood in the aisle.

"Face it, Shauna; your wits are no match for mine."

Shauna leaned over towards me. "We'll just see about that at another time. But Zemi, be honest, don't you just hate when people come up to you and tell you God gave them a message for you? I find it annoying that God should give out my business to someone before letting me know about my own stuff."

"I feel you on that, Shauna."

"Usually when someone tells you something in the spirit, soon to follow is a request for a donation," said Shauna.

"How do you deal with them?"

"I tell them in return, the spirit told me 'to trust not every spirit.'"

Though full of humor, I gave Shauna's prodding some thought. Hosting a talk show had never occurred to me. No reason it should have. Phil Donahue is no longer around. Who would I mimic? Oprah? Nah! I don't have any toys to give away. Many talk shows are for the most part pure sit-down-and-share- personal-stories entertainment. I would like to have serious dialogues with black women. Yes, I would. Whenever our folk are on talk shows, they are positioned to look and act so ineffectively until they are just ignored by the media and politicians. It would have helped if I had studied journalism. The search of what to do in life continues.

Shauna climbed back into her seat. "I don't suppose the talk show idea grabbed you all that much. I don't think that you want to go the book route either, right, Zemi?"

"Right. I am all tired out with writing." Now I stood up to stretch my legs.

"I can tell you this much, Zemi, with much of what you are considering, a lot of people who are not in that egghead world won't know why and what you are saying, that is if your topics are too serious. Whether it is a talk show or book, you have to put stuff in the syntax to match with black women's timely passion. Okay, I don't know what I intended for the message to be in that statement." Shauna yawned.

"Hmm." I shook my head in disagreement. "I think that the need and aptitude of black women are thought to be too borderline and are underestimated," I said, not realizing that my voice carried a bit more since I was standing.

Shauna moved into my aisle seat. "Everyday black women cannot, perhaps, perceive what your studies have offered and all that you have learned and know already. They do not have the same reference to process things the same way, Zemi. But now you can break it down to them in a way that's easier to understand and digest. It might be a little difficult at first, but I believe you can get the women involved to the point of listening and participating if you talk about things they are passionate about. The open space is there for new sponsors to grab and unveil things that are of special interest to our women. To tell the story, you must be innovative, provide true context-images of African American women and not be afraid to conjure up that thought-provoking zone with concerns as you see them."

"It is time for African American women to take the lead too, so that black women around the world can take notice on the global stage. I really do feel movement for us, Shauna. It's nice today to hear from some new women movers and shakers like Prophetess Juanita Bynum, but at the same time, you've got to pay homage to Bishop Ernestine Cleveland Reems for making that door known to our women. Politically there is outspoken Congresswoman Barbara Jean Lee and Congresswoman Sheila Jackson-Lee, I wonder whom they're grooming—no matter, still tough shoes to fill. There is Kaye Washington, rising on the scene as one of the foremost African American writers and editors in the country. There is Queen

Latifah, who has also crafted an increasingly successful screen, music and savvy business presence. Everything she's touching is turning gold. Beyonce, a savvy business woman is steadily demonstrating what a force she is; Linda Johnson Rice, the new President and CEO took over the helm of affairs of Johnson Publishing Company; Harvard University for the first time named an African American woman, legal scholar Patricia A. King, to serve on its governing corporation." I looked at Shauna with a heartfelt appeal, "I just wish people could see black, positive female on a more frequent basis, for younger ones to observe who's out there to aspire to. The time is ripe," I said. "I truly feel it!"

"Well, let's just hope that the women won't be like the character Hem in the book *Who Moved My Cheese?*"

"I am going to call Les Brown and tell him to move on over 'cause Shauna, the new motivator, is in town," I said.

"Are you being sarcastic here with me, Zemi? I might not have a Ph.D., but I know sarcasm when I hear it. But I'll tell you one thing, girl. You had better pay me some sound mind because I am probably going to be your first convert to your program before a lot of our women can catch on."

"Ah, come on, Shauna, you know the women will love me on stage."

"Right. You know, if one is not talking to our women about how to find a man or about suffering and drama, then it's really hard to know if they will listen. So often black women act stuck; they'd rather stay in their places of familiarity than to try to make something better happen. Our women wear a badge of suffering as though it's an honor. And it really irks me when they say, 'Well, God will make a way.' And I am wondering, what is wrong with you making a way for yourself and your children to live a better life? What was the point of God giving you two legs when you won't walk, two arms when you won't do anything, two eyes and you refuse to see light, a brain but you won't study to know anything? It appears as though God's made a way already. You know what I mean?"

I did not want Shauna to lose her train of thought, but I was tired of standing and wanted my seat back. I prodded her by the arm. "Move over to your seat."

"Be creative with topics and issues, Zemi."

"Creative how?" I asked.

"Well-ll," Shauna began. "Select distinct topics that are controversial in nature, but you do not want people who are looking for their 15 minutes to act out with fussing and cussing and fighting and yelling. People who want to act a fool can go on the Maury Povich or Jerry Springer show, but they definitely will not appear on your platform. There are not enough psychologists in the world who would know how to handle the pathetic women who stoop so low on some of those shows. But you should set and showcase a platform that's intellectual, but has a homey-like touch to draw the women, the audience, into you and your sphere of thinking." Shauna placed her hands up under the air current.

Just then the flight attendant passed by.

"Could you bring me some Kleenex please?" Shauna requested.

"The temperature does feel as though it dropped a bit, huh?" I said.

"Make your talk show vogue but not with a bling-bling agenda," said Shauna. "I think the public has had an overkill of ghetto fabulosity. You want your show to appear down to earth but nothing to distract from the subject matter at hand. You want to bring about change, not a stage for the aggrandizement of those with starlit careers to magnify their own ego and showcase their vanity."

"Shauna, you talk as if I could just step up to the plate and do a talk show."

"You can. You might think that you will have a lot of competition, but you won't. Folk are doing talk shows, but substance is missing in most of them. Mind you, they know the substance has escaped but haven't a clue as how to create a needed platform, so a lot of talk shows are on their way to becoming dated. Talk show hosts can only tell the people for just so long who's getting divorced four and five times and who's up for an Oscar nomination for a picture many did not see anyway and who got arrested driving drunk. And, for goodness sake, never stoop to anything that would make you come out of orbit. Never repeat the overkill that has taken place on some other talk show." Shauna ripped open the package of tissues the attendant handed her. "Now Zemi, you see why I say, 'Strike while the iron's hot.' People want to talk to each other, not feud. There is already enough war going on around the world. You would put the people at peace while igniting thought. That's what time it is. Take the hate, anger and yelling out of the talk shows today. People need to listen but can't hear, let alone comprehend, given the earsplitting matches on shows nowadays."

"Shauna, I don't want you to think I'm not paying attention to you because I have been, but I am still clueless as to where and how to begin a talk show."

"Pick your subject area and know where any competition might be lurking." Shauna held my hand as if she were a tutor and I the student. "Look, Zemi, you have four siblings, a mama and a grandma and all of them are in the Democratic Party. Hmmm, I forgot, you're still a registered Democrat yourself."

"Please make your point."

"Start off with a topic that is smoking! Now you know that I'm a Democrat and my sister is a Democrat, Mama, my daddy and his daddy and everybody that you know personally is the same," said Shauna.

"Everybody except for Amy."

"Come on, Zemi. Amy is a little different, and we all know why that is the case."

"Amy is my friend. Don't talk about her that way."

"I won't mention her again. Now let's move on. Everybody and their mamas who are black and disenfranchised are with the Democratic Party. Disenfranchised, yet we all remain with that Party. It is as if African Americans and the Democratic Party are conjoined twins. More than likely at the feet, which is why our folk are unable to walk away from a Party that treats them like scumbags."

"I definitely agree."

"Of course, you would because I have touched upon something which you feel deeply about, and you would know best yourself why that is the case," said Shauna. "Frankly, we could end up with something big here because the Democrats are not going to treat our folk any better, and I don't think the feelings you have are going anywhere either. You are much too passionate about the matter for the feelings to disappear."

I sat straight up in my seat. "I am passionate, but that alone is not enough to move our women onward. However, I remain of the opinion that staying with the Democratic Party obstructs a heightened change for African Americans, especially the women," I said.

"See, Zemi, you can feel a change coming on, you can taste and almost touch that change."

"What do you mean?"

"You don't know your role to be in this universal change taking place." Shauna took off of her high-heeled boots and pulled on some thick woolies she'd taken from her oversized bag. "Take me, for instance. I'm the kind of woman where all you have to do is break something down to me once, and if it makes sense the first time, then bam! I'm on the scene. And I mean that sincerely, not sarcastically. It will be interesting to see how your main focus group of women will take to the notion of a young sister dissecting the political canvas that's been hanging in the homes of black folk almost as long as DaVinci's *Last Supper*. And you know they are not about to mess with a DaVinci family heirloom. Girl, our folk will fight over that picture when a grandma passes on."

"I have a tall order ahead, huh?"

"That is your mission, Zemi, should you accept it—to help our women rethink for greater actions and better results. Now, I'm not saying that they won't stare at you with both crossed eyes at first and that all kinds of stuff won't come at you. But that's expected because change is never easy."

"I am glad it's just the women. At least, they're easier to deal with than the men," I said.

"The types of men that some black women deal with probably don't even vote," said Shauna, as she folded over the top portion of her boots and slid them under the seat in front. "But, girl, the moment you start to speak on the subject that women should open up their minds politically, then just watch those brothers come from cyberspace to tell black women how to vote, knowing that they themselves cannot vote because they have felonies—and even that law needs changing. But keep in mind that the men will be a bit con-temptuous. You'll hear the M.C. Hammer come out of them then, 'U Can't Touch This! It's a hot topic. Almost too hot to touch.' But I'll tell you this much, in all honesty, if anyone, and I do mean anyone, can hold on to that torch, it's you, Zemi."

Shauna has given me a lot to think about. Every time she says 'Zemi' this or 'Zemi' that, there is something else Shauna thinks 'Zemi' should consider. I know she means well, but I feel now that 'Zemi' needed to rest her eyes. 'Zemi' had a lot to think about. Shauna was trying to put a burden on me, and 'Zemi' needed to think. 'Zemi' had spent years to earn a doctorate and now Shauna was trying to re-school 'Zemi' during a mere five and a half hour plane ride to take on something 'Zemi' had not even studied! A talk show? Ostensibly, the purpose of a talk show would be to present the interests of African American women. Change happens, but could a talk show really be a significant enough strategy to make a difference?

Shauna nudged me. "Are you sleeping on me?" she asked. "This is free counseling for your next level in life. Take the shame out of your game! Create your platform. Then use it to talk about the inept-ness of some black men to act as leaders here in America. Talk about the inappropriate behavior of some rappers. And remember, I am talking about some black men and some rappers. Don't get it twisted! Talk about black actresses and how the roles they accept are mediocre and betray their own consciences. The public is on overkill with black female comedic roles. Ask why aren't they performing in more roles of substance to come up to par with that of white women's roles in their field? We'd like to see them acting more in roles of senators, governors, church ministers, renowned psychia-trists and CEO's of mega-conglomerates, to name a few. Talk about black politicians who are without strategy and how they've failed to keep their constituents informed. Talk about black female politi-cians and how they've failed to do succession planning to get other black women in as senators and governors. Ask why white women are stampeding in the Democratic Party and why black women are not? Talk about black organizations and how they've received donations to lobby for causes unfamiliar to their base." Shauna paused as if gasping for air.

"Talk about the black churches and their inability to get the message across to the black men who have abandoned their children and families, not all of them, that would be unfair to typecast anyone, but the church leaders need to advise some black men about their spiritual calling to heed their duties and uphold their responsibilities as fathers, as Dads. Did God just give these ministers—male and female—words only to make some of female congregants get up and shout in happy, near hypnotic ritual? Have black preachers become intimidated and isolated from the flock described in the Bible? Is the human nature of the flock so much different than the flock during the days when Jesus walked the earth? Are preachers getting paid to stay in ivory towers and pray for the choir? Do politicians rather than God own black churches? Has the church failed to make the talk of Jesus pertinent for today? Has His way become prehistoric?"

"If I came out with just those topics, at least everybody would get a piece of the action and have something to discuss," I remarked. "But now Shauna, Grandma wouldn't want anything mentioned unsaintly about the church. No matter what. In a public forum the church is untouchable. When you talk about the church in that way, to Grandma that's the same as blaspheme."

Shauna sat up straight in her seat and with a tone intent on educating me, she said, "Zemi, the thing is, no matter the topic, you must be balanced and show your connection to the subject matter at hand and that's especially when discussing church. There will be nothing untoward about your topics. Let your audience know that although not every church has grown and risen to shine on 'high-beam' in the community, nevertheless, there are countless church edifices that stand to deliver Jesus' messages about living life more abundantly."

I nodded; I got it, and told her, "The balance would be to offer some 'faint praise' about the church then."

Seemingly a bit annoyed, Shauna shrunk back in her seat. "Zemi," she said after a moment, "don't stay narrowly focused. Elaborate on the issues and show a willingness to help resolve them.

Otherwise, what is the point of bringing up a subject? And when speaking to audiences, always show that you have done your homework. Jesus Christ!"

"Okay," I said. Looking to hear more, I challenged her. "And what's the rest, Shauna?

Shauna cried out, "Clearly the conventional wisdom among us is not divided evenly. If you went to church more often you would know to take notice, that no matter how we might complain, the church is the foundation of much of the progress taking place in our communities because the government has gone to sleep. There is nothing meriting mere 'faint praise' about the works of churches like The Potter's House; they have all kinds of businesses going on like beauty supply stores, barbershops, football teams and schools; University Park Baptist Church in Charlotte, NC. All one has to do is just look at that church to see progress going on all around. There is City of Refugee and Noel Jones Ministries, Center of Hope, Allen Temple Baptist Church with outreaches of scholarship, senior and disabled housing and social services. One has to rate highly what Glide Memorial United Methodist Church does for the out-of-luck and downtrodden homeless population of San Francisco's notably affluent and prosperous city. New Birth Missionary Baptist Church in Lithonia, Georgia, is another church doing great works for the community and the same can be said of Zion Baptist Church, Minneapolis' largest black congregation. Rev. Jeremiah A. Wright Jr., of Trinity United Church of Christ in Chicago has to stand out as a congregation committed to the Historical Education of African People in Diaspora." Shauna patted my shoulder, "Now Zemi, you have to say high praise is due when you have churches committed to these types of missions. Girl, you just have to give it up."

I looked at Shauna, my ego slightly bruised. "Okay," was all I would give her right now.

"Don't be afraid to deal with the black churches. You'll be all right giving up the goods on them too," said Shauna.

"Well-l," I said slowly, "its just that we said so much other stuff about the church and now it seems if though we've done a 360 turnabout without even going to church. And earlier you said…"

Shauna interrupted, "Stay with outside-the-box thinking, Zemi. The role of the black minister has been dualistic, and the black Church, well, don't even try to pinpoint its role because the people's needs are so great."

"All right," I told her.

"Just remember, God is the God of redemption not the God of condemnation." Shauna smiled at me. "You can always make things right with God, and instantly too."

"It seems easy now to sum up Shauna, given your information about churches, that many that are worthy of emulation and recognition." I said this as much to myself as to Shauna.

"Have a talk show that expresses concerns about governmental intrusion into religion," said Shauna.

"Well that topic can make for a very provocative segment, a shift to discussion of the churches' impediments to fulfill their missions as they see them. Yeah. Yeah," I nodded. That would be a great topic on "unjust," "intrusive," and "an attack on our religious freedom and privacy rights, I thought to myself.

"Make even the President come to know who you are, Zemi. Tell the Republican Party to stop shucking and jiving and that if they want black folk to come into that party, then make them feel like it is their party also."

Shauna's portrayal was unfamiliar, and there was no stopping her from holding forth. "Show them how they, too, need to open up black platforms to compete with those platforms that the Democrats have in place to attract our type of voters. How else do they plan on bringing black women into their party? Through Ann Coulter?"

"I don't think black women are listening that way."

"And that is exactly why they are behind," said Shauna. "You need to just come straight out and ask black women what is wrong that they feel they cannot compete."

I brought my seat forward and felt my face transform from high to low beam. "Shauna, are you crazy? Black folk will kick me into high hell with so much negative, high-charged blasting. And as far as black men are concerned, Mother says you have to be very careful when discussing them. She says that in recent decades black men were made the poster symbols for everything wrong with this country. Mother says, and these are her words—not mine, that somebody campaigning was pandering to the worst in people so shamelessly he stooped to put a black man on his anti-crime campaign poster. Mother says it was straight, plain racism, and I had to agree with her on that. Mother also said that at the very same time black men were labeled 'endangered,' just like they were a plant or animal species, and she hated that term, how could they be responsible for so much that was wrong if they were disappearing? America is all messed up Mother said and needed a scapegoat; and the face of a black man was such an opportunistic move. But she said that the media focus on crime in America has been forced to change with white kids shooting up school campuses and malls, white female teachers preying sexually on boys, alleged stalking for the sake of love in the space program, and 9-1-1. So America has had to find another bogeyman—but America did not pick the white face!"

"Well, it sounds like your Mother needs to be a guest speaker on your show, Zemi. I agree with her, you know, about those whack portrayals of black men and crime. E.J. says that when he was going to New York all the time, he almost had to put his body in front of a taxi to get it to stop, and you know how he guaranteed that he would be picked up? He had to say he was going to the bank!"

I moaned.

"So, there is a lot of truth in your Mother's words, and she is a lot older than we are and would know. I mean E.J. has talked about how hard it is to be a black man and just leave the house. Walking down the street, and he is looked upon like a suspect. Going through a parking lot and he hears car doors locking. It has not been easy for him—and he's a lawyer!"

I was hurt to hear that my brother had had those experiences. "Well, that's awful."

"Remember Zemi, your topics must be balanced. There are a lot of black men, including many who were raised by single mothers, who are taking care of their families. They are older than you Zemi; a lot of them are in their early to mid 30s now. They are not leaving their children, and they are staying married. It is a beautiful picture, and we know these young men, and the list is long. If only they were a stereotype...."

I nodded in agreement.

"Yeah, for black men and white men, too; those wonderful black men could be role models for all men who choose to bring children into the world," Shauna added. "Zemi, when you know something different, put it out there. Even if just for argument. Put it on the table, Zemi. Showcase the men you are talking about, these men who belie crime posters and portrayals of black men in media and entertainment. And if what you say is truth, then that is God's way of making a people move into action. You know God said He was coming with fire next time. Maybe that's what you have to be with our people in this day and time. Since the Flood, they've seemed drunk off of too much watered down Kool-Aid."

"I know that controversy sells, but I am not that kind of person. I don't really like being confrontational all that much," I said, backing off.

Shauna hiked her shoulders up. "Girl, you must not be a true Navies because your mama, all of your siblings and your grandma never back down from anything. Even the family dog goes all up and down the street, bossing other dogs. You just haven't used it yet, but that ingredient is in your make up, too, Zemi. It's a family trait. That which you feel most passionate and hotheaded about will make that ingredient come out. Just keep yourself under close observation, and I promise you will see that side manifest."

"Hmmm, hmmm." I agonized quietly. According to Shauna, the usual roundup of black leaders no longer had black women in their back pockets. We were up for grabs but not necessarily to the same bidders. Was Shauna saying that Al, Jesse, black churches, the NAACP, the Congressional Black Caucus, or the Urban League no longer could spend black women's votes frivolously? Could it be true that black women were ready to stand up and be leaders to negotiate their votes themselves? Can black women break free for self-preservation—a better future for the granddaughters and grandsons yet to be born?

Shauna nudged me again. "And when you are on your platform, Zemi, interview Condoleezza. Bring some sincerity and recognition onto your stage. And let Condi know from me, that she is not the only woman who can show some legs and wear a red dress, either."

Shauna looked down at her legs. "The Party needs to know that when they invite some of these black and brown sisters in, they are not going to be dressed like Mother Teresa. The Republicans need to look at a new image, or they will not be in control again for a long time."

I yawned. "Hmmm. Maybe I could get Angela Bassett to speak on the future of black women in Hollywood. But Diana Ross is really the one to take the lid off. She summed it up best at the BET awards."

"This is a grave and heavy time for the Republican Party, and they need to do some serious facelifting because all the scandals going on in their front and backyard are disgusting, just too much government and political indulgence in bad behavior. With the corruption and series of backroom scandals surrounding disgraced lobbyist Jack Abramoff, the Party is looking like the Wild West gone completely out of control. This Party alone is beginning to make rappers and boys in the 'hood look like angels. There was the bombardment of the media about Republican Congressman Mark Foley's hypocrisy. He moralized about family values while he headed the Committee to Protect Children from Exploitation, only to be later tagged with complaints about inappropriate behavior toward teenage male pages. Next was that guy who represented nearly 30 million evangelical Christians, and he had to resign after a man claimed to have had a drug-fueled rendezvous with him."

"You are speaking of Ted Haggard, who was president of the National Association of Evangelicals. Goodness gracious, Shauna, I must say that you are really up on the mission of Republican Party's self-destruction."

"And it's harder today to be exact, even about Scooter Libby's behavior with President Bush having commuted his sentence. But see, Zemi, Republicans think that black and brown folk don't know enough about the naughtiness of Republican elected officials and that somehow their regular voters' memory will be at the amnesia stage, come 2008. And though black people have not voted in any great numbers for the Republican Party, they still need to know where they are most needed politically. People do much to recover their needs," said Shauna. "Think about it. Given that most black people are Democrats, young and old, current and future voters, then this is a political party that holds almost 12 percent of a specific voting population in its fold who now could be up for grabs by another party. That is a lot of people who could make cool Republicans sweat come 2008. Now I ask you, do you think the Republican Party can afford to ignore blacks?"

"I suppose not. Sounds like the black women have an announcement to make to the Democratic Party."

"What's that?" asked Shauna.

"No more back door thrills."

"Okay now, girl, we all understand that."

"Black women must make a bold statement because the question can no longer be asked, 'What do you want, Jesse?' Because black women are not to defer to him on everything this time around." Shauna had me pumped up. Perhaps she and I could co-host a talk show.

"You got that right," said Shauna. "Black women will frame the question for themselves this time. Depending on who's asking determines which question is under consideration. If it's the Republican Party that's asking, then the question becomes 'What's the Republican Party truly willing to do to get African American women into its party?' And if it's the Democratic Party that's asking, the question becomes 'What must the Democratic Party do to keep African American women in their party'?"

Was Shauna serious about such strategies? She was breeding a new kind of confidence. Could it become easily spread, though? Shauna observes my twists and turns and studies me pensively.

"What if neither of the two parties is listening to black women?"

"Good. You are thinking," she told me. "Convince black women that we are not afraid to go Independent. God did not make us beggars. We will just have to do a flip and follow in the footsteps of New York's Mayor, Michael Bloomberg. He switched from the Democratic Party to the Republican Party. And now he grandstands as non-partisan. Remember, Zemi, you are to help black women take the shame out of the game."

"So the slogan goes, 'No more guarantee on black women's votes.'"

"Yup. I am not sure if blacks should negotiate their votes and accept a check made payable to them for just minimum wages because minimum wage cannot put a roof over black folks' or any folks' heads, no matter how many hours they work. Since Congress thinks black and brown can live off of the low minimum wages placed on the tables in a superpower, then Congress should give themselves minimum wage instead of the 23 percent being asked."

"Hmmm." I reached up to turn off my air.

"Heck, everybody can see, even if blind, that both parties have screwed over African Americans. But at the same time, our folk might need to be made more aware that they can pull out just as many screws from the Democratic Party as those they can pull out belonging to Republicans. Both parties had better use the time before the 2008 election to persuade the voters they most need to woo. Seriously though, the Republican Party needs to make more than manna fall from heaven upon some folk to make more things right." Shauna stood up. "Excuse me, Zemi. Can you lift your tray up for just a second?"

I thought maybe next time I should let Shauna have the aisle seat. Shauna crawled over me and pulled a blanket from the overhead compartment. "Thank you, Zemi." She started in again, hardly missing a beat. "Black and brown folk should go to whichever party will make something happen for those still left in the ghettoes. Those are your new voters because down in the ghettoes they haven't really voted for either party. One of those parties has got to use something to bring them out. And you know you cannot go into the ghettoes selling those people hot air in their present conditions. They know a game when they see it 'cause they live it everyday. But with those voters, you've got to give them something in order to get something. Maybe a preacher man can work with those in the ghettoes."

My eyes were closed, so maybe Shauna thought I was asleep. But, oh, I felt a sneeze coming on. "Aaah-choo!"

"Bless you," said Shauna.

"Thank you." "It seems as though political leaders and ministers have taken up the same plights and causes today."

Shauna lifted her blanket. "Whatever the case, Zemi, something has made the females appear to be the least in leadership."

"Are you saying that the Bible teaches us to be docile followers, rather than assertive and effective leaders, I mean, for women?" I asked.

"Well, maybe not the Bible as much as some interpreting it that way. But ask yourself, Zemi, do our churches produce more male leaders in our society and more female as followers? Sometimes the proof is in the pudding. Otherwise, why would a congregation with attendance of mostly women and a lot fewer men make the men the leaders, the decision-makers? Somebody has to follow and somebody has to lead."

"Unmistakably, not much leadership is coming from women. That is a sad thing," I said.

"Blacks are mostly followers anyway. Probably a real reason some blacks don't read books other than the Bible is that many ministers have them believing that is the best and only way to learn. They believe that the Bible is a one-stop for all understanding or ailments. And if another book is recommended, it is usually one written by that pastor or it is usually another religious book. If you tell the people that God said something or gave a word, then followers tend not to do much in examination. Our folk think they need to have pictures in their books to understand. They do not want to think, and that is why they will buy magazines but not books," said Shauna in an accusing tone.

I sat in silence, mulling over her words.

"Zemi, have you ever paid any attention to churchgoing people's home libraries, that is if they have a library at all? And I am talking about blacks."

"No, I must say that I have never taken much care to focus on other people's books. In our home we had an enormous and widespread library with some books related to religion," I answered.

"Yeah, I know, but I think that in some respects your household was not average. Like in my household growing up, we did not have a library of books, but we had plenty of Bibles lying around as if they were centerpieces. Now you understand what I am saying to you?"

"Sure, I get what you are saying," I said, envisioning the books in my childhood home.

"But nowadays when you walk in the houses of folks who have children and they don't have a library or books, then it's obvious that not a lot of reading, teaching or learning is going on. Really, if you don't see any books and you see four televisions in a three-bedroom house, what could the family possibly be reading? Sometimes you might see an *Essence* magazine on the table, and that's all the credit due to the family. Zemi, your family dealt with books as though your home was a clearinghouse for a publication company, but that is not the norm for a lot of other households. When parents of these households want to entertain their children or offer quiet times, it is the TV. Heck, you can even go to some childcare centers in the ghettoes, and the kids are watching television—as if *Everybody Loves Raymond* is a special alert or breaking news story that they need to catch," said Shauna.

"Geez, I am out of touch. I thought that was an evening program," I said.

"See what I am saying. Teachers must be bringing their own tapes or DVDs. Now you know, that is sad."

"I think when people are really hungry enough, they will use whatever it takes in the universe to do what they want to do to find their way, with or without all of the necessities in the home," I remarked.

"That may or may not be true, but the question should arise, Why don't parents feel that they need to get off their butts to ensure that, at least, the children they gave birth to have a head start? I think that is near criminal and at least sinful for parents to raise illiterate children when there is so much learning available. Hell, they have cable to watch rap videos. Let them turn to cable news channels to learn some things. I also think it's criminal if a school district receives money to teach children and no improvement is made." Shauna signaled to the flight attendant passing by.

"Yes, what would you like?" The flight attendant flashed a smile. "I wanted to offer you some things out of the basket, but you were so engrossed in your conversation that I didn't interrupt."

"Oh, that's okay," said Shauna, smiling back. "But I will take a bag of those Captain Chips and two of those butter cookies."

"Can I get you anything to drink?" asked the attendant, handing Shauna the snacks. "Yes. I'll have a Sprite, please," said Shauna.

"And what would you like, miss?"

"I'll take everything that she is having," I said, "except for the Sprite. I'll have another Coke."

"I'll be right back with your ice," the flight attendant said, passing us the drinks.

Something inside of me could not fully accept that the responsibility should sit solely with the parents for the conditions of their lives and the lives of their children. Shauna seems to think it is time out for excuses and that every African American should be held accountable for the situation he or she stands in. But if our folk believe in God so much the way Shauna says, then why won't God reward them for their belief? I know works without faith are dead. We are not a bad people, but we seem to catch God's entire wrath. Does God extend His mercy to blacks? Perhaps they have been worshiping some other god. Maybe our folk expect too much from God. Maybe they could reward themselves better by grasping the teachings of life and studying more tenaciously, with greater concentration and precision to see a thing through and not wait for God so much. But my people's goals are so small, so local, for them to truly understand what is, in fact, at work.

Shauna seemed comfy with her seat laid back and her head snuggled against two pillows. I started not to bother her, but I placed my hand on her shoulder. She didn't move. I shook her gently. "Shauna, are you asleep? Huh?"

"Not really."

"I was just wondering, what do you suppose our folk are doing wrong?"

"Wrong how?" Shauna mumbled.

"Why is it that black people don't enjoy God's abundance? Grandma says there are thousands and thousands of promises in the Bible. You think maybe some black people don't pray enough?" I asked.

Shauna yawned, covering her mouth. "Zemi, have you seen how black and blue some of our folks' knees are? Why, there is little doubt that black folk have a habit of praying. But there must be more than what meets the eye. Maybe they got what they prayed for. Could it be they are asking for such a small-ticket item that they received it but just did not know it came from God. When you already have a used, beat-up Toyota in your possession, you don't have to take up so much of God's time to get yourself a used Honda. God gives that to just about anybody who has to make it to work and back. Besides, our folk don't know how to feel deserving of much. And that is probably due to the output of their deeds. That is why there has never been a black in the Oval Office because they don't feel they deserve that spot since the DNA keeps reading 'children of slaves.' It is hard for some who have just physically come out of slavery to rethink in terms of ruling."

"Your thoughts are interesting and at the same time quite amusing, Shauna. But what happens if you want something better and grander than a used Honda, something like a Rolls Royce?"

"Well, now, we are talking super faith if you want that Rolls-Royce, you know. You just feel like God wants you to do a little more than a nine-to-five to obtain that and all the trimmings that go along with owning a Rolls-Royce. You do not see any schoolteachers, mailmen, store clerks, people who play the lottery or those dancers in rap videos, for that matter, driving Rolls. So you sort of make a covenant with God because you do not feel it's all that easy to obtain that Rolls on your own. Yet, you believe it is obtainable, and you believe you have whatever it takes to see yourself in that Rolls."

For a while I was following, Shauna, but then she lost me somewhere between reward and covenant. I leaned closer to Shauna, looking straight into her face.

"What?" she asked.

"Hah! You did not make any sense," I said in accusation. "Are you trying to tell me that you have to do more or believe more to get more?"

Shauna paused for a moment and then spoke slowly. "See, even you have the formula. Added to that is to know the strength of your God."

"Don't we all serve the same God?"

"In a way we do, but the strength of God really depends on your battery charge and output. Our folk love to say that they are waiting on God. That is why they stayed in slavery so long. They were way too patient in a hostile, killing environment, waiting on God to hear their plea. What? Was their god deaf at the time? Waiting on God is why our people did not get an Oscar for another forty years, again, being too patient. That is why they let other immigrants come over and do better than themselves in this country and in their neighbor-hoods because they are waiting for God to stand up and speak out against injustice. But, you see, God has already done His work. God is never going to come and put more brains into one's head or more diamonds into the earth. He's already God, so one does not have to wait on God to do a thing but, rather, when you as the actor are ready, God and the stage are in place for you. You know, I like it when God says, 'I will go before you and make the crooked places straight.' That tells me that God knew you would have challenges and even in that has taken care to keep you going to get to the main point where everything is straightened out. Even if you have trepi-dation, that doesn't mean you don't keep going. Action requires you to be a steadfast participant in your own destiny," said Shauna, her eyes beaming.

"So, really, God is whoever or whatever a person believes Him to be?" I know I sounded skeptical.

"Basically, because in God there is no compulsion; one has free will to be whatever one believes. One can climb Mt. Everest, or one can work in the coal mine. One can be a president or rule an empire because he believes he can do that and convinces others that he can; or one can work in the fields obediently because he or she believes that is the will of the God to serve that way. It all boils down to one's belief system. Of course, this is strictly my interpretation, and I'm not sure how much of this stuff I understand myself, but it sounds right to me. I mean, I might wake up in the morning and this could all seem like Greek." Shauna smiled brightly.

For a moment I thought that I was in some "science of mind" class. Shauna was talking so abstractly that I wondered who had the Ph.D.

"So, Shauna, do you think I would need such a powerful spiritual footing to do something grand or so worthwhile?"

"It depends on what you perceived as your part and portion in life. I mean, I don't know offhand what you could do without being spiritual. If you wanted to just sit at home and get fat, I am pretty sure you don't need to be spiritual for that. But, on the other hand, if you want to lead black women into becoming independent thinkers to live a better way, then you are going to need a firm spiritual foundation, grounding. You will need a spiritual army and some spiritual angels for the mission."

As close as Shauna and I are, I had never experienced this spiritual side of her. Perhaps it is hard to judge one's spirituality, but I don't believe that I am as spiritual as Shauna. In my age group, I don't know anyone else who is, either. One would imagine that ministers would be spiritual, but most appear more religious than spiritual. Sometimes I've wondered about black ministers. Many of them are without a specialty, a line of work, a thorough educational background, and no significant business acumen, without funds or strategy—and yet they say God called them to lead. Do they know what God's requirements are to lead a people? What are the requirements to be a minister of a church? The ministry seems it has become a traditional stepping stone to enter politics, for black and white preachers alike. It's just hard nowadays to pinpoint someone's ministry although self-aggrandizing stands tall. I think good stewards would question exactly what God called these ministers to do if they themselves are going to be followers. That's a sensible thing to do. Some of those ministers inherited a pulpit, and unfortunately experiment at the cost of those who follow. If a minister cannot make things happen in his own life, what then is the evidence for his calling? Congregations have failed to hold ministers accountable for showing the church, the people, and the community how to walk in the ways of Jesus and not to theorize Jesus so much (and that, only on Sundays) that one is remiss in actually applying His teachings. Walking the walk to show people in need how to live life more abundantly, according to God's Word and will.

My family went to church every Sunday when we were children, but to be honest, I did not like church at all. Out of sixty-six books in the

Bible, only two books were about females—Esther and Ruth. I thought as short as Ruth's book was, why did they even bother to print her story? The Bible was taught to me in such a way that I wasn't feeling all that good about women. There was obviously a boys' club going on back then, and they must have paid dues. How else would Judas have been able to embezzle some type of means from Jesus' bag? Maybe the men weren't playing golf, but one could certainly tell it was a club, all right, with board members of about twelve getting together all of the time over wine and brunch—how else could it be the *Last* Supper? The men in the Bible had all of the time in the world to bond with each other. I wondered too, what would a picture of a group of women's Last Supper depict them doing?

Maybe I am missing something from the Old Testament because mom just loves the story of King Solomon. I wonder whether other people can see a connection between the historical sexism from the old, old, old days and women's relatively slight gains today. In the Old Testament the women showed too much dislike for each other. I could not have been born back then because the women seemed to be around merely for procreation, sex on demand, getting whipped for somebody's problems, getting stoned even if her brother-in-law forced himself on her, forced marriage to the brother-in-law even, if the same killed the husband, fanning some queen or king, washing clothes in the river, raising babies, cooking, cleaning, taking care of the sick, more cooking and cleaning, delivering somebody's babies, housework and field work. Hey! Let's do a Venn diagram and compare today's female roles with female roles a few centuries ago. Now check out that picture! If we indeed have come such a long way (baby), our destination must be light years away!

In all honesty, today I might even have some fears just to speak freely of these thoughts. It is difficult to admit that some of the men of the Bible yesterday and still some of today do not place much value upon women. When will women change that? The Bible yet today is the reference most quoted by sexists—why won't ministers, especially women ministers debate the roles of women in the Bible? I understand why men do not preach upon such topics, while there are several reasons why women ministers might not discuss the low posture of women found in the Bible. I believe fear to be the first, and secondly, women don't cite enough readings from the Bible to make significant points for a debate. Many women ministers have not been stellar in church-business, quite like the male ministers might be; the women in ministry do not seem primed to make grandiose, and I don't think that they believe women should be catalysts for big change. So the question to ask is, from where will women leaders originate? Women in the church have already been indoctrinated to feel less than what they are. I don't believe true empowerment for women can come from the church as it is presently structured. Shauna once asked the question, But from what other source would such power evolve?

When ministers begin to face that piece of darkness and bring it into the light, then maybe the church will be a place for me. It would be interesting, though, to see how sexism would be settled through the church. It is not going to be an easy thing to have happen because most women have somehow bought into their low status in the church as the command of God. Well, for me, anyway, to accept that thesis would be accepting an inferiority complex, and I just couldn't do that. It would not be Godlike.

Yes, I am thinking that it is interesting, too, to hear, when people ask the question, What would Jesus say? I am totally off with that question because Jesus already said what he needed to say and then some. Why try and reinvent Jesus' words? He has done his works as have Martin Luther King, Jr., Rosa Parks and Malcolm. It is folly to ask such a question because all have indicated that greater works shall the coming generations do, not lesser works and not less work, not work to tear down what those notables built up. It is up to us now. This generation must be accountable, at least, in thought, and more so in deeds—no more excuses! The role of this generation is to lay bare to the rest of the world the great possibilities within this superpower.

I was pretty quiet, listening more than talking, but Shauna's philosophies about everything kept popping off, inducing odd thoughts. Each time she finished one statement I seemed to have more questions to ask, like what black leaders offered our people as progress. Their leadership is in serious questioning, and the mistrust is so thick in the ghettoes that the people can only go for so long hearing about celestial streets paved with gold while they almost sink in potholes in their neighborhoods. Obviously, something is wrong. I guess some of those ministers are already maneuvering to the beat of a different drummer. Their message is rather convoluted and confusing, especially to those in the ghettoes whereas middle-class folk have more of an option in interpreting the Bible.

Shauna's head appeared from under her blanket. She whispered, "Zemi, I can just hear those wheels of yours turning now. Tell me what's going on inside."

I took a short pause from my thoughts. I looked Shauna directly in the eyes and said, "I was thinking back when I went to bed one night and there were nine planets in the sky, and when I woke up the next morning, there were only eight. It's amazing, though, how mathematical formulas are used to establish a truism, and centuries later a different formula proves that scientific formula fallible. I mean, Pluto was just thrown out—no more a planet. Other scientists came up with their own formula and used it to justify making truth whatever they wanted it to be. Think about it. Pluto did not change, but astronomers' definition of what a word did. All of a sudden, Pluto is, in some sense, no longer what it used to be. That's weird—language, communication."

Shauna looked shocked. She acted as if I couldn't possibly know what I was talking about. Clutching her blanket, she asked anxiously, "And where did you get that information?"

"Astronomers were all over the media waves with their new findings. But here's my point. Black people in the twenty-first century find themselves much like the ex-planet Pluto. With each new election and each new political party, African Americans have lost much of the ground and many privileges that were extended to them through the Civil Rights Acts of 1964. Those losses may have occurred through re-interpretation from Supreme Court Justices, and even those interpretations depend on the political makeup of the decision-making body, whether it is a liberal or conservative court. Or it may be that both parties compromise too many bills and initiatives in a stalemate, negating any benefits to African Americans and Mexicans or other minorities."

"You might as well admit that is the strategy used by both the House and Senate to do nothing for the people. Both parties also are sitting on their butts doing absolutely nothing and getting nothing accomplished except for their paychecks raised," said Shauna.

"I think the government is a rip-off. But I am not willing to go as far as not paying income taxes to prove my point," I said.

Shauna hugged the blanket to her waist. "The government is a rip-off, any way you look at it. The ones in office should be the ones getting minimum wage. You know, the way people used the Bible to make folk believe in something is the way leaders use partisan politics to make black and poor people think that there is a distinct difference between either party or that either party is really trying to help them. I just feel sad for my folk. One day the people are fed the Bible to believe in man and woman as marriage; then the next decade that same Bible is used to justify same-sex marriage. People are confused."

"Now that was my point about Pluto: Depending on who's in office determines what stays status quo, or what goes and comes," I said.

"I think about preachers telling women a couple of decades ago not to dye their hair red or wear red lipstick and make-up. Now those same preachers are putting on more make-up than women right before they preach their sermons on television. But I guess what you are saying, Zemi, since the scientific field is constantly changing, is that black people ought to be even more about change. I think that is why folk are found in the condition that they are in because they don't apply spirituality as a science," said Shauna.

"A lot of folk don't know things because they are too afraid to test anything. They lack confidence and don't know how to process and modify data to accommodate personal situations in life. I think that's part of the real problem, and they act too much being other than themselves," I said, between nibbling on my chips.

Shauna seconded, "Black leaders are the ones putting on airs. Check out those who head non-profit organizations, and then compare their millionaire status to the output of their missions in the communities they left. What do you get? I'll tell what you get. You get millionaire leaders who got paid for not accomplishing a damn thing worth noting in black communities. On the QT, those leaders don't even make appearances in the ghettoes anymore. No sightings of famous black leaders in the ghettoes since James Brown last held one of his performances in black communities. That's why in one of his songs, James Brown begged Santa Claus to go straight to the ghettoes. I think Santa Claus was the code word being used to ask black leaders to show up at least sometimes in the ghettoes even if just once a year at Christmas time. When those leaders make speeches and appearances before an audience of African Americans, check out the venue, Zemi. There are big trees around, Mexicans making beautiful landscapes of flowers, valet parking in nice, tall, clean, air-conditioned buildings with a front door attendant and concierge, too."

"That's probably because their audiences are made up of middle-class African Americans," I said.

"I know this based upon first-hand experiences. As a PR and event planner, I host events at plush places where the kinds of people who come through those doors are in tailor-made suits and preachers wearing Rolexes." Shauna began to stand, and signaled toward the restroom.

"Do you want to switch seats?" I asked.

"No. No. But five and a half hours on an airplane is a long time."

I got a respite from so much thinking. My head seemed heavier now. For a few minutes I figured I could lighten up.

But when Shauna returned, she missed nary a beat. "Girl, I am not mad at them either because I will not do any event planning in the ghettoes myself. You can't even hold prayer meetings today in the ghettoes without drive-by shootings occurring." So much for a respite. "Remember how it used to be when those old sisters in the church, one by one, would get up from their bench, walk up to the front altar and drop down on their knees to pray with their eyes closed? And then one sister would 'break out' and get happy, which was a signal for all of them. They'd get up shouting, all sanctified and filled with the Holy Spirit. Remember those days, girl?"

"Kinda," I remarked.

"Newsflash," Shauna said laughing. "It's just not happening that way today. Those sisters have stopped dropping it like it's hot.

They've stopped doing all of that jitterbuggin', too, from one side of the church to the other. They've stopped making those James Brown movements with their feet, and they've stopped running down the aisles, throwing their purses every which way, because they know that those gangbangers might be right there snatching those purses up like hotcakes."

"I never could comprehend why the women always got 'happy' and the men never did," I observed.

"Well, you know," said Shauna, "my dad used to be an usher in the church on Sundays, and he didn't mind catching those small, cute sisters who got 'happy' every once in a while. But Dad said with him being a small man that whenever those heavyweight sisters, the big mamas over two hundred pounds, got 'happy,' he himself would pretend to be happy and run his behind to the back of the church out of view. He said that he never could figure out why the big mamas got 'happy' more so than the cute little mamas. He said that maybe God was chastising those big mamas for coveting the Big Macs, Whoppers and then lusting after their children's Happy Meals!"

Shauna and I laughed so loud that some of the people in first class gave us a not-so-friendly look. We made a rapid return to sophisticated comportment.

"See, I can't talk about those sisters anymore because I crack up whenever I think about them. The pilots will have to make an emergency landing, believing that you and I have both lost our minds," Shauna chuckled.

"Okay. Let's pull ourselves together here because Dr. Zemi Navies is never to act out of character in public," I said in jest.

"I feel you, girl," said Shauna.

"Then get back to the point you were making earlier so that I can take my mind off of those sisters," I said, still laughing.

Shauna turned off the light above us, toning down the mood. I sat up, more poised in my seat.

"I need some coffee to remember where I left off," said Shauna.

I signaled for the flight attendant to bring us each a cup of coffee.

Shauna sipped her coffee. "Ah, yes, this is the way that I like my coffee. Okay, I was talking about black leaders having pulled the wool over the eyes of folk. In private gatherings folk speak of the betrayal they sense from their leadership. I'm not so sure that those in the ghettoes aren't tête-à-tête either, though it might not be expressed the same as the middle class, but keep in mind they're feeling ignored mostly, and that more than likely accounts for them not voting. Like you alluded to earlier, our leaders are going to have to swim through the most deep and turbulent waters ever to make an impact like they did in the '60s and '70s with African Americans. Honestly, I don't think that type of leadership will ever come from African Americans again."

"Why not?" I asked.

"Black leaders cannot sell their ways of old material to the middle class, and they cannot sell that non-working preaching in the ghettoes either. That's like singing to the choir if all they came to do was solve problems as an oratorical smoothie. It's just never going to happen again," said Shauna.

"Then who's listening to those leaders today?"

"That has a simple answer. Why do you think rappers have become so widespread and masters of the ghettoes? It is because those other leaders left a big old void in leadership. They went from wearing jumpsuits to tailored suits. Now they've forgotten how to relate. The present leaders can go under in baptism every day of their lives to be born again and they won't have the kind of power to shake, rattle and roll the masses," Shauna lamented.

"Much of what you say is obvious. The leaders, just about all of them, have been ineffective or unjust with our folk, and today's circumstances demonstrate just how ineffective or unjust they have been," I agreed.

As she spoke, Shauna's face was covered with a hardness I did not remember ever seeing. "I think if every pretending black leader across America would vanish from the speaking circuit, because talking is all that they are doing anyway, our folk today would be better off without them because then they would study more to find out for themselves what is going on. They would not wait for someone to come by and give them fake IDs. Folk need to be just like those handling cash at the casinos. They protect their interests by checking for counterfeit dollars. That's exactly what our folk need to awaken to—learn how to spot a counterfeit leader."

"Oooo-wheeee. Black leaders are going to be very mad at you, Shauna."

Shauna rolled her eyes. "Please! No, they won't. They are already hearing it for themselves. Bill Cosby has been talking about black leaders and preachers quite a bit lately. But the funny part about that is just the other day when I was in Barnes & Noble, I was reading through this book by…um…what's that author's name?" Shauna hesitated. "You know, the nice-looking, kind of pudgy author who likes using those multi-syllabic words that make ten and twenty sounds at a time. And I thought Cornel West was bad. Jesus! I tell you, I have never had to go to the dictionary so much until I started digging into their stuff. I'm trying to call his name. Dang it!" Shauna snapped her fingers. "It's right on the tip of my tongue. "Girl, doesn't that just make you mad when you are trying to think of something important, and it won't come to mind. Here I am in my early thirties and shucks, I'm acting like Ronald Reagan now."

She was hissing and still snapping her fingers. "He wears glasses and wrote the book, *Is Bill Cosby Right? Or Has The Black Middle Class Lost Its Mind?*"

"Yes, of course. Michael Eric Dyson. I definitely read that book, and I've read most of his books. In fact, he and Bill O'Reilly are two on my intellectual people's list right now."

"Yeah, that's right. That's him," said Shauna. "But tell me how you come up with two favorite people on a list that are direct opposites of each other?"

"Well, they are both substantive," I said, "and aside from one being black and the other one white, they both demonstrate superb intellect and logic. In their interview exchanges they give viewers something to listen to or something to listen for. The talk you hear from them makes you want to go and research further."

"Well, I guess, sometimes you may find that people seem more alike than not," said Shauna.

"True. Take persons like Democrat Reverend Al Sharpton or a Republican like Reverend Jesse L. Peterson. They are very different b-but…"

Shauna interrupted me. "Well, I don't know who that Peterson guy is, but I don't think Al's intention is to speak for the African American middle class, not when he goes around trying to take up the banner for some of those 'causes.' Please, give me a break."

"Yeah, but his latest march in D.C. made sense to me."

"Zemi, I don't believe folk in the lower class are even watching *The O'Reilly Factor* and probably don't know who Dyson is either, even though he might be writing on their behalf."

"Shauna, again, I don't think that you give folk in the ghettoes enough credit for grasping certain concepts."

"We might have to wait and see, Zemi, who has the most insight on those in the ghettoes."

"The way they vote in 2008 may give us a better clue," I said.

"You know both political parties are flashing their handpicked blacks as bait, but neither party has a clue as to what it's going to take to galvanize African American support for their candidates come 2008. They can hold Cosby up, Al or whomever as leaders, but black folk aren't laughing at the tickle. Folk know what they need, and they know those who have not delivered for them."

"Well, you know, uh...."

"With Dyson and his book" Shauna started. "First thing that came to mind, though, about his book was, dang, if Bill Cosby is considered middle class with all of his dough and degrees, and I have a master's degree and making $175 thousand a year, what class am I in? I am going to have to ask Dyson about that because I would sure hate to have to come to grips with being in the lower class. I've just worked too hard not to be at least somewhere in the middle. You know what I mean, girl? Let's see, even with my parents' inheritance, I am still hoping for at least middle class. And if I don't share that with my siblings, still no budge. I've got to go over this class thing because that is really scary to me, and now there is talk about the black middle class's numbers slipping. Here again, I am so worried, and isn't that a blip? I may not even be enrolled in the class."

I chuckled. At first, I thought Shauna was playing, but her face showed otherwise.

"It was a fortuitous encounter. Maria and I met Dr. Dyson on a flight from Chicago to San Francisco. He invited us to come and hear him speak at UC Berkeley's Black Commencement a couple of years ago. He kept the audience going up and down all throughout his speech with standing ovations. He's really good, I think, one of the best authors out there for today."

Shauna removed her diamond clip-on earrings. One ear had turned red. "Well, I've never met the guy, but your brother told me to go and pick up his book *Why I Love Black Women.*"

"Um-um. Maybe E.J. is getting ready to set a marriage date," I said.

Shauna ignored *that*. Never certain of E.J.'s intentions, a discussion about him and marriage was probably unnerving. "I think that Dyson wrote *Why I Love Black Women* a couple of years ago. It was interesting to see the women Dyson had chosen to be on his front cover. Hmm…but it was healthy to see a black man who has a stage and is very confident with a black woman on his arm."

"Yeah, I liked the title of that book myself," I said.

"But now that more recent book on Bill Cosby was quite a piece of controversy." Shauna jingled her earrings in her hand. "The NAACP was commemorating the 50th Anniversary of the *Brown v. Board of Education* desegregation decision when Cosby made some of his comments that the African American race was not holding up its end of the deal," said Shauna. "His comment was intended for folk on the lower economic rung of the ladder and given the occasion, he probably thought that it was okay to make mention at such a gathering."

"Gee, give Cosby a break. He made the statement among his peers because he felt comfortable and cozy with the NAACP," I said.

"Cosby might have felt comfortable, but Dyson did not like his choice of words. At that gathering, Cosby said that people marched and were hit in the face with rocks to get an education, and that now we have knuckleheads walking around." Shauna shook a finger, saying, "No, no, no. Now, Bill should have known that his remark was too much of a hit below the belt," said Shauna.

I begged to differ. "My goodness, that part was not so bad."

Shauna begged to differ right back. "It's not necessarily a bad thing, but when you start saying such things as these people are not parenting and are buying things for kids—$500 sneakers for what?

And won't spend $200 for *Hooked on Phonics*. Then you are asking for a slap from your audience." Shauna jerked her head back and winced, feigning taking a slap herself.

"I am not so sure that Dyson was any more polite when he said Cosby should explore his gifts for comedy and leave the social analysis and race leadership to those better suited to the task," I said, fanning with my napkin. "Now that was a really barbed dagger thrown at Cosby, and if he didn't feel the sharpness, then a dagger does nothing to cause pain."

"You know, it used to be that our folk didn't criticize one another in a public forum to the extent they do, but now give them a platform, and they'll tell you exactly what everything is all boiling down to," said Shauna.

"Who would have thought that Dyson would have come out so bold and so strong against Bill Cosby, especially with them both being in the same political party?"

"Maybe they just don't like each other," said Shauna.

"Which one do you agree with? What Cosby said or what Dr. Dyson said about Cosby?" I asked.

Shauna said, "I more agree with Cosby on some things but not every point. But then I do not agree with Cosby when he ridiculed the names of African American children 'with names like Shaniqua, Taliqua and Mohammed' and calls it all that crap, and saying all of them are in jail. Now, I've got problems with Cosby because my name Shauna is the root sound of Shaniqua. So when you smirk at those types of names, you are in a way, 'playing the dozens' because the children did not name themselves. And you know black folk don't like anyone talking about their mamas and, in essence, that is what Cosby does. Maybe he should have started a while ago and upstaged actors for their menacing portrayal of the Shaniquas and the Sha-nay-nays on television."

"Speaking of portrayals, I take personal offense to the portrayal of black women by black men in drag. But more to your point. Many of our people were more upset with Cosby and thought that he was wrong to air our folks' dirty laundry in public. That might have been the thing that most fueled Dyson," I said.

"Cosby scored points with me," said Shauna, "when he talked of our folk speaking in the vernacular of 'why you ain't,' 'where you is' and saying that one cannot be a doctor with that kind of crap coming out of one's mouth. And I am with Brother Cosby on the Ebonics issue. I cannot speak the way those people do, either, and as an African American woman, I strive very hard to be the best I can be in this society. It would be too much for black women to accept such a low standard. Black women are about self-empowering, and Ebonics is just not acceptable. Sometimes you can teach in a nice way like Dyson, and sometimes you have to be just downright real like Cosby," said Shauna.

"Who made the most valid points then?"

Shauna stretched her legs. "Dyson said Cosby has famously demurred in his duties as a racial representative. He also stated in his book that Cosby has flatly refused over the years to deal with blackness and color in his comedy. Cosby was defensive, even defiant, in his views, as prickly a racial avoider as one might imagine for a man who traded so brilliantly on black culture in his comedy. While Cosby took full advantage of the Civil Rights struggle, he resolutely denied it a seat at his artistic table. Thus, it's hard to swallow Cosby's flailing away at youth for neglecting their history and overlooking the gains paid for by the blood of their ancestors; he passed on "representing" when service long ago beckoned at his door, at least, according to Dyson. It is ironic that Cosby has finally answered the call to racial leadership forty years after it might have made a constructive difference. But it is downright tragic that he should use his perch to lob rhetorical bombs at the poor." Shauna made a shaky gesture with her hand. "If I had to really vote between the two, that decision would be a toughie."

"I am assuming now that you are in Cosby's corner as much as Dyson's," I said.

Shauna replied quickly. "If Cosby can help to make black men better for black women by speaking of them in that fashion, then more power to him. If Dyson can get our men to learn with his style, then bring it on, too. The black race is so far behind—and our women and their children need so much help right now. It is going to take a thousand different approaches and techniques just to make a noticeable dent."

I shared many of Shauna's sentiments. But I hope the African American race won't have to experience the saga of W.E.B. DuBois and Booker T. Washington again through the dissension between Bill Cosby and Dr. Michael Dyson. I believed that if DuBois and Washington could have found a way to work together, African Americans would be further along now in understanding their position on the world's stage. From where I sit, I don't see either man as wrong but, rather, the benefit of two different types of tonics to continue to uplift a race. God would be the best Knower—"He sees not as man sees."

I thought perhaps both men's contents, as contrasting as they were, could still get ready that distinct group for a specific moment in time. Malcolm and Martin had different religious beliefs with different philosophies on achieving the same thing, an end to racism, and each had a hand in bringing about equality for blacks and the poor. Maybe soon the proper settings at the table will appear enticing for the palates of both Bill and Michael—to break bread together as Jesus did, perhaps over some chilled wine. Perhaps together their great minds will be able to effect change for a greater move in the political direction for poor and black people in America. Nothing and no one will be perfect, but as African American leaders, may we take the good from the bad. We are already divided on so many other things that something like this should not even be considered a divisive factor. I felt that both men were sincere in the expression of their views, and that has to measure volumes.

"Zemi," said Shauna, "you know what I was thinking?"

"Huh-uh."

"Cosby and Dyson should be influential enough to use their platforms to address Congress and political parties on behalf of the people in Louisiana and other states who were hurt so badly by Katrina. They could influence Congress to come up with a more workable plan to actually bring the Katrina people back home into rebuilt developments—and jobs for the rebuilding of New Orleans. These people are wandering around in the wilderness as black folk did after slavery—but only this time with more psychological illnesses inflicted on an already disenfranchised group. They could persuade government to stop the window dressing and create a solid plan to jumpstart those poor people out of their hellhole conditions and into a new life."

"Or they could address the issue of African American women who are afflicted with AIDS," I added.

"I agree," said Shauna. "Again, whichever party answers the call and participates in these endeavors before the 2008 elections, then that could be the political party that should get the votes of African Americans. There is just no other way to do it. Cosby and Dyson could be the ones to help implement such a blueprint. Both are great men, just hopefully their egos won't get in the way of the progress, true progress they can jumpstart."

I nodded my head in acknowledgment, but reminded myself that neither man should encourage black people to give their votes to a party if our people are not satisfied with its actions. Neither man should advocate for a party if the party has not done the job sufficiently for the people. I wondered why neither Cosby nor Dyson would lay some blame on the political party they serve. I almost felt like jumping on a bandwagon myself, but I had to do some serious destination checking. Again, isn't it time out for black people giving their votes away, just because somebody got a talk show or a Rolex? A time out needs to be called for mothers living in a superpower, begging like dogs beneath the table, scratching for bones. And it is definitely time out for all black people giving their loyalty to one political party. Darn it! Don't we as a people know how to be creative enough to bring into being some competition among political parties? Black folk need to be like professional athletes: Seek out agents before setting up for a field goal. Instead of our folk being loyalists, devotees to just one party, we should seek out experienced negotiators before simply casting votes. Forget about black leaders, about orators and preachers. For Samuel L. Jackson could rise to the occasion as an experienced negotiator and effect changes that our leaders have not been able to effect thus far. Call to the table those who know best how to present the deal on behalf of the African Americans.

Earlier, Shauna recited, "A huge question on the table is what black people will get if they should help to put Hillary in the Big House. The Democratic Party cannot win the Oval Office without the support of African Americans. Are black folk in on the tidbit of that specific data? Will blacks accept the crumb in the hoopla that Barack Obama could possibly serve as Hillary's VP running mate? Howard Dean said that the Democratic Party had taken the African American vote for granted. Will Dean's pronouncement of what people already know help to make his party take a turn and do the right thing in '08? Dean says if Clinton were in office that he would have cleaned up New Orleans by now."

I couldn't help but wonder if perhaps former President Clinton had performed his job sufficiently and dealt with more priorities, perhaps this country might have survived Hurricane Katrina with fewer casualties and catastrophes. If the Democrats should get into office, come '08, by the hands of African Americans, do they swear to make Katrina a top priority? Or will illegal immigration or perhaps same-sex marriage trump the list of priorities after Iraq? Anyhow, since this is a superpower, is it really the case that the country can only handle one thing at a time? Cosby and Dyson. Perhaps they can help to make the real culprits now become accountable, or tell them we will punish them at the poll in 2008. Whatever to do with minds of giants?

"Zemi," Shauna whispered.

I did not respond.

"Zemi, are you daydreaming?"

"Huh?"

"Zemi, get ready," said Shauna softly.

"Get ready for what?"

"The challenge at hand. If something of tradition isn't working anymore for black women, help them to see another way. We know that our folk have not gotten their fair due from the Democratic Party, but what would it take for a Republican switch? Our women are hurting, and they don't have it in them to keep struggling so hard and keep hope alive at the same time. How long must one hope before they see results? I keep thinking about an Independent Party for blacks." Shauna nodded pensively.

"Hmmm," I mumbled. "Shauna, I don't think you can draw a fair measurement between the two parties because on a whole, blacks don't vote the Republican ticket to really hold the party accountable enough."

"Zemi, neither you nor other women of your kind can afford to put so much energy into something for promises—we women have to get ours first this time—that's the new New Deal. The Republicans helped the Democrats to screw over us by their own party denying the values of blacks. Republicans were just as negligent as the Democrats have been, and now they both need the support of African Americans. I tell you, girl, our women had better find out for themselves and stop being the victims of some feel-good orator. If the Republican Party is shopping to get more black women's votes, then they had better find out today what it is these women will demand. They need to provide platforms for black women in America to showcase who they are and what they are doing. These black women can't come out looking like post-Katrina victims because, should the truth be told, nobody had done anything for those people way before there was a Hurricane Katrina. Leaders won't address that now, will they? And especially not black leaders because the portrait would show those leaders missing in action. Of the African American race, black women are the larger voting constituency. This is what we need to leverage with the Democratic Party and the Republicans. Zemi, if you can pull the black women in, these women with all this voting power, and become a voice for them, then we might be on to something."

"Well, at least we have Condoleezza out there as an African American woman who is not afraid to look at the other side." I flexed my feet to get the circulation going, the way those in-flight magazines tell you to do.

"Yeah, but we women need to see more than her looks or her features on platforms. You have no black women out there with the mantra of the Republican Party. On the real side, what African American woman does the Republican Party have that would chant Republican the way Ann Coulter does for the Party? Again, she is a die-hard Republican and there is no shame in her game. Where is there a black woman who could be as cogent? Nada. They do not have one on main circuits. Ann Coulter might be great for attracting all the white women they need, but she would not be successful with black women even if she tried," said Shauna.

"Why do you think that is?" I asked.

"Well, the Republican Party up until recently did not care to take much notice of color missing in their Party. And this is a personal opinion, but the agenda of white women in the Party seems such a contrast to what black women need and want to be about. It is hard to see black and white women bonding in the Republican Party. It appears more a challenge for white women to convince black women, whereas it has been almost an effortless thing to do with black men," said Shauna.

My spirit was lifted. "I have a difficult time seeing how black women can relate to Democratic women such as Barbara Boxer or a Nancy Pelosi as opposed to white Republican women. When I think of the statement Boxer once made to Condi, I think women of all color should take offense to her insinuation that because Condi does not have children or anyone in her immediate family in the military, this makes her noncaring and non-sensitive to our soldiers in Iraq."

"There could be a little sense to Boxer's way of thinking," said Shauna.

I shook my head. "May I remind you that past secretaries of state from both parties have mostly been men, and have sent many soldiers to war—and who has said anything about their not having family in the war? The wars, rather."

Shauna rubbed her nose. "I can't argue with you there. But Boxer's comment begs the question of whether a person in political office should have a vote on sending our sons and daughters unless they themselves have a family member in the military. But I guess one could be wondering, too, whether Boxer's memory still functions adequately. Maybe Boxer should begin with self-criticism since she signed a blank check for President Bush to go to war. Okay, Zemi, maybe I can't touch that one because I did not like the blank check from Boxer either."

I wanted to go back to talking about the power black women voters needed to wield. "Anyway Shauna, it is acknowledged that more African American women are registered voters than black men. But I see what you are saying, that the Republican Party needs to make things happen that are well supported by the masses of blacks and formulate a program to keep them on task. Hopefully, now they will understand how to do the things that need doing."

"That's a close enough wrap," Shauna intoned. "Still, I do believe the Republican Party scores higher in turns of what they have done as a government in favor of African Americans during the last term and a half over the measure of the Democrats," I said.

"Well, now, I would not run buck wild with that tally Zemi, because the doings of the Republican Party are minuscule to faint. Whatever the Republican Party has done, they do not have any notable media where blacks can feel encouraged to attend programs or call up to discuss issues. Blacks just have not been shown in mainstream media expressing themselves with any modicum of presence. How will African Americans know how or whether black Republicans or other blacks have benefitted from this administration if those beneficiaries are not seen anywhere championing the Republican cause? You know what I am saying, don't you, Zemi?"

"Yeah, but again, you do have *The O'Reilly Factor* where blacks feel at ease interacting even if in opposition, which is most often the case. Juan Williams is always on and Al, too. Has Al turned Republican? And the same goes for *The Hannity and Colmes Show,* but after that it becomes rather scant on any station for African Americans."

"I knew that's where you were going to go, Zemi. You are so predictable."

"But, really, it is just so strange to me that black Democrats can only appear on the Fox channels with their polemic concerns and issues, while a liberal channel like CNN has totally obliterated black Democrats from its screen-except during election time. And, Shauna, for your information, I am not so predictable."

"If you say so, girl. E.J. makes no bones about his favorite news shows. Surprisingly, Chris Matthews With Hardball heads his list followed by Michael Baisden. But still the question that needs answering is how does the Republican Party intend to compete for black listeners and audiences with Democratic black radio and talk show hosts?"

"They do have a few black Republican radio talk show host on the scene," I said.

"Plain and simple, Zemi, the reason Republicans are being ignored by African Americans is because they totally ignore black women, and that is a fact. More and more black women championing and embracing the Democratic Party are popping up fast on the media scene. There is Whoopi Goldberg with a new radio show and, of course, Oprah's sweet radio deal. Now, also there's former talk show host Rolanda Watts, who will appear as a host of GreenStone's talk radio network being backed by Fonda, Gloria Steinem and Rosie O'Donnell." Holding her hand over her mouth, Shauna sneezed.

Wake Up With Whoopi? Hmmm. Has her morning radio show been canceled? I started to ask Shauna. But she would know if that was the case. I am glad though, to see Whoopi on *The View*, she is a great addition to the show.

"The appeal of the new left wing radio network is to target women listeners and to confront the dominance of conservative talk radio that their network says is bulldozed by a male point of view. The GreenStone describes itself as a clear alternative to the polarizing, highly political talk commonly heard on AM radio. One thing the network has made clear is that they are at war with Rush Limbaugh, Bill O'Reilly, Michael Savage and dozens of other hosts whom they claim dominate the airwaves."

I wanted to ask Shauna why does Liberal Talk radio fail so miserably? But I didn't ask. Radio? Out of my league. "Sounds like the Democrats are getting serious with a plan," I said.

"Girl, these women are serious. They've got game and they've got strategy. The women said that they know what women want, and GreenStone says that they have the entertainment, political, social and business connections to deliver it. They said their goal is to build the leading brand for women's talk programming."

"Is it predominantly an African American station?"

"No, no, no," said Shauna, "not with topics such as plastic surgery and Feng Shui. But they do claim it will deliver de-politicized, depolarized talk radio by women hosts for many female listeners.

Whatever they do, they think that women like things delivered with amusement, something lighter to respond to."

"I don't know about that, but it is interesting that the different stations chose those three types of black women—Oprah, Whoopi and Rolanda. They are so diverse in appeal," I said. "I don't know anything about the radio playing field. I mean, I can discern the obvious—all three are black women and all with Hollywood ties and are baby boomers, all Democrats, each very articulate, each assertive with strong opinions."

"What it boils down to, and make no mistake about it, Zemi, though these are opinionated women, they, nevertheless, exist on stations to influence audiences for the left wing and to bring people into their fold of thinking. When it comes to politics, I don't really think that the left or right wing will present a balanced forum. It is all about the art of persuasion and who can draw in the most folk for sponsors."

"One thing I know for sure," I said, "Rosie O'Donnell just does not have what it takes to influence African American women in any form or fashion."

"And I do not think that she is trying to, either. She is just who she is, a very strong woman who is passionate about her beliefs," Shauna observed.

"Okay, Shauna, here is our goal: To find ourselves a platform." I turned off my overhead light. "We have time for a good nap before we land."

2

S hauna and I returned three days before the entire family was to meet at Mom's house. It was a celebration for Dad's ascension twelve years ago. Dad was stricken at age forty-six with leukemia, then the worst cancer of its kind. He fought that battle for two years. Dad's roots started in St. Louis, and his mother left him there with his Aunt Annette for three years until she got herself situated in Detroit with a new husband. Dad grew up in a household of jazz in St. Louis, and in the Motown Era in Detroit.

When Dad first found out he had leukemia, drives were held throughout the country in search of matching bone marrow donors. The bone marrow had to be race specific, meaning that only blacks could match with blacks, Asians with Asians, Caucasians with Caucasians; Dad's chances of a successful match were less than slim since African Americans did not usually respond to blood drives, and therefore, were not usually bone marrow donors. Dad's only chance for life was a possible match from his biological father. Everyone else in the family had been tested but showed no match. After Dad was born his father professed adamantly and vociferously that he was not the father and had walked away from any parental accountability. And that was the reason my dad refused an offer from his biological father to be tested as a possible match. Mom said sometimes that Dad could be a very stubborn man.

Dad was well known as an educator and scholar around the country. He was a professor of and expert in African American History. His position as head of the African American Studies Department at Berkeley High School, Laney College and DeAnza College, all in California, afforded him the opportunity to write many articles for newspapers and magazines. Many of those articles were controversial. Since blacks were the only group of people brought to this country involuntarily, Dad passionately fought for black and white students to learn African American History as a required course of study. Just like American History was a graduation requirement. Dad said that the will to survive the ghettoes of Detroit prepared him for the many challenges and the opposition he faced with school and city officials in both Berkeley and Oakland.

Realizing that he could have been fired from his job at any given moment and believing that taking care of his family in a gracious manner was always his main responsibility and concern, Dad supplemented his school teacher's compensation by preparing taxes for small businesses and individuals. Prior to his work as an educator, Dad earned a Bachelor degree in American History and a Master degree in business finance from Wayne State University. That education helped Dad with his investments in the stock market.

Since Dad's death, each of us has contributed $2,000 a year to host a dinner party in Dad's memory. I started donating when I became twenty-one. It was Grandma's idea to start a scholarship in her son's name three years after his ascension. Most of the money collected for the dinner party really goes towards the scholarship fund. My family has been hosting the celebration ever since Dad died. This year, Grandma wanted to give the money to Fatimah Gilliam for The Leukemia and Lymphoma Society. Miss Gilliam ran in the Honolulu Marathon, racing in memory of Mr. Richard Navies, racing to save lives. My dad was her professor in school.

When I was in high school, friends used to think the idea of celebrating Dad's ascension was a bit eerie. Mom schools anyone who questions these celebrations, by imparting a bit of her personal philosophy: "I celebrate Martin Luther King's birthday every year and watched President Kennedy's burial on television. Though these are great men, I never met them personally; nevertheless, it is considered an expectation, if not a duty, to commemorate their legacies. Surely, a man—who was my best friend and husband, who gave me five beautiful babies and made it possible even after his ascension for his own children to eat and be clothed and further their education—should be worthy of remembrance. Then Mom would say, "With that said, how could I do other than celebrate a man who paid such a contribution?" Mom said that Dad's influence on their children and his involvement in their lives made life easier for her and parenting easier all around. She told my friends that a celebration was such a small thing for one who was so wonderful in her life and the lives of her children. Mom always ended on the (gratuitous) note, "Perhaps there are those who might feel that their husband or their children's father is not worthy of holding up. But then, whose influence would those children deem noteworthy and worthy of honoring?"

This is a big deal to my family, so everyone dresses up and usually each sibling brings several guests to attend what we called "an ascension fit for a king." I was on my way out to shop for something to wear when my brother Joey phoned and said that he was bringing someone special to the celebration for me to meet.

"Look prettier than you normally look," Joey said. "Of course, for you, Baby Sis, that just might be an impossible task."

"Is something going on that I don't know about?"

"Why do you ask, Sis?"

"Well, first Mother calls and says she has someone special for me to meet, and right after she hangs up, Maria called to say that she was bringing a beau for me—and now you. Did I hit the lottery and no one told me?"

"I don't know about what those guys have set up for you, but the guy I have set is the jackpot and more, and that's no joke," Joey assured me.

"What's wrong with him, Joey?"

"What do you mean what is wrong with him?"

"What does he look like?"

"That question shows immaturity on your part, Zemi."

"Don't dodge the question."

"See, that's what's wrong with you black women. Kimora didn't ask what Russell Simmons looked like, and Virginia Lamp didn't ask that about Clarence Thomas."

"I'll tell you what, Joey, since Mother and Maria each has some one for me to meet, why don't I bring my friend Amy to meet your friend?"

"No. Hell, no! Amy is out to lunch. No real black man wants to deal with Amy's drama."

"Amy does not do drama."

"Okay, maybe they have a new name for her issues. But tell me, how do you call a woman who has a white mother and a black father anything other than a black woman? Huh?"

I said nothing. 'Here he goes again,' was what I was thinking.

"I didn't hear your answer, Zemi. Amy's just a shade and a half from being as dark as you. The girl took her color bloodline more from the dark side of the DNA, and in her view that's both the unfortunate and rebellious side of her genes. She calls herself a white woman just because she has very keen facial features. Even white people think Amy is crazy when she tells them she is white."

"She has a right to define herself as she pleases—in whatever way works for her best."

"Well, her forefathers—meaning the white ones—did not see it that way when some of the fledgling states wrote their constitutions. The woman is legally black."

"No law in America can enforce such a rule," I said.

"Well, Hollywood's surely enforcing that rule," said Joey.

"How?"

"Don't act as if you don't know. The girl is a best friend of yours. Amy is trying to become an actress, but she can't get parts because she wants to be cast as a white woman. She can speak with a white southern accent all day long but will always be looked upon as black," Joey answered flatly.

"Amy's just trying to get America to see the psychological preposterousness that's associated with its intolerance for people of mixed parentage. Besides, Joey, in a lot of ways, Amy looks like a white woman."

"Why can't Amy just accept that she is black?"

"Amy says in most situations people can't tell whether she is black or white."

"Amy is the only one who's thinking that," Joey shouted.

"Joey, you don't even want to understand why all of this is so important to Amy, do you?"

"This situation is not going to change for her," Joey said, ignoring my question.

"Okay, Joey, okay. How about my girl friend Jawana?" I asked. "Your friend can be her escort?"

"No. And a thousand times no. Jawana's got a pretty face, but she just returned from Iraq. She needs time to cool off. In her mind, she still needs to boss everything in sight. She did not learn anything from Iraqi women. In the few times that I have talked to her she has wanted to dominate the conversation. No doubt about it, she wants to be the boss. She might have ruled some soldiers over there, but it ain't happenin' here, not on American soil. That woman is definitely going to need to be self-employed."

I sighed. "Okay, Joey. I give up. I'll meet your friend. What's his name?"

"His name is Zeth. He's a cool guy."

"I am still going to ask Amy to come to the celebration."

Joey said, "I am bringing my girlfriend Natasha. We have an announcement to make to the family tomorrow."

"Oh my! Are you two tying the knot?"

"Hmm...no," Joey answered ponderously. "You know I am already tied to my restaurant, and there is no love greater than business love! If I do my business right, we will always be together. But a woman? A man can do the right things for her all day long, and she will never be satisfied. It's just in a woman's nature to complain and whimper. Now with my business, I serve it right and it rewards me back. But a woman? God knows, she will try to break a man's back to make him love her."

"Joey, what on earth are you talking about?"

"I'm saying that marriage thing isn't for me."

We both grew quiet, then Joey said, "But guess again, Zemi."

My brother Joey is a really gregarious, tall, handsome man, but all of my brothers are "tall, dark and handsome." Joey owns a very posh vegetarian restaurant in Atlanta. He has had a few side jobs, but he never saw himself working for anyone for long because he always said that he wanted to work for himself. His girlfriend works for the airlines, and Joey flies to California often, mainly to see Mom. He only stays at Mother's home and usually it's just for a very few days. Joey is fun loving, but I really didn't have the time right now for his guessing game.

"Okay. Joey, that is the last guess that I am going to make. Let's see, I can't really think of anything else. Just tell me. I'm in a hurry because I have to go shopping for something to wear."

"Come on, Zemi, I am so excited. Just one more guess, I promise," he pleaded. "I don't know, boy. Okay, I am going to say something stupid and ask if she's pregnant. I know that's crazy, Joey, but I've just run out of guesses."

"Why do you think that would be so crazy?" he asked.

"Maybe it's that Natasha just does not appear like the baby-mama drama type. Anyway, I am done guessing. I've got to go shopping. Everyone is telling me to look extra nice tomorrow, so will your surprise secret hold until tomorrow? Can you just save your surprise until tomorrow, please, and I'll get the scoop with the rest of the family? Love you. Bye."

* * * * *

Everyone has arrived at the celebration except for Shauna. E.J. told her to bring the wine and champagne since she is the family connoisseur and is in charge of everything posh. I had dates all over the place, so I decided to let all these prospects check me out before I met any of them. Ah! Shauna finally arrived with the wine and champagne.

My brother E.J. walked up to Shauna, took a bag from her hand and called out to the server, "Go out to the car and get the cases of wine." E.J. gave Shauna a kiss.

Shauna walked into the large entertainment room, and greeting all at once, asked, "How are all the favorite people doing on this auspicious occasion?" she asked.

Everyone answered her at once, creating a din of light conversation.

"Gosh, everyone is looking exquisite," Shauna said playfully, affecting high class and decorum.

Whenever Shauna is around E.J., she is always proper and loves to impress. She is so forward with everybody else, but around E.J. she acts differently, more passive than when around her girlfriends. She doesn't use slang or profanity around him either.

The server, back with champagne and wine, asked, "Which bottle should I open first?"

"One moment," E.J. signaled to the server. He took Shauna's hands and placed them on his chest, then asked her, "So what kinds of wines did you get for our most favorite occasion, honey?"

Shauna was happy to tell him. She just loved being part of E.J.'s showing off, but mostly his showing her off. "Six bottles of your mom's favorite Riesling and two cases of Caymus red and one case of Krug Champagne and a surprise," she answered smiling sweetly at her man. Having played the role for E.J. dutifully, Shauna walked over to the server and whispered something to him.

The server returned with a bottle of champagne wrapped in a white cloth and handed it to Shauna. "Sweetheart," Shauna said as she held out the bottle of champagne, "look at what else the woman of your dreams has come upon. I did an event this afternoon for one of my clients who won this bottle of Cristal off a $50 raffle ticket. He doesn't drink, so here's looking at you, babe."

Shauna was standing in the middle of the floor in the entertainment room and had everyone's attention. "Really, can you believe how lucky it was to win the bottle of Cristal?"

Everyone seemed delighted to hear about Shauna's luck and eagerly awaiting for champagne glasses. I doubted that anyone in the room other than E.J. had ever tasted Cristal.

E.J. accepted the Cristal from Shauna and to her surprise said, "We are not going to drink the bottle of Cristal. What other kinds of wine and champagne did you say that you brought?"

Everyone around was waiting for the punch line, thinking that E.J. was playing around. It had to be a joke of some sort.

Shauna spoke mildly, "Excuse me, did someone just turn off a hearing aid?" She put her arm around E.J.'s waist and with her eyes searching his face told him, "Honey, I could see you being upset if I had paid our own money for the Cristal. But weren't you listening? The person who gave me this bottle only paid $50 so money could be raised for charity. Read my lips, the bottle of Cristal is free. You are an attorney, so I'm sure that you know the meaning of the word free."

E.J.'s face grew stern. He did not look pleased about Shauna's words.

Shauna surveyed the room, apparently searching for anyone who might have a clue. "Help me out here, folk." She held her arms out. "I am clueless. What's going on with your brother?"

Joey lowered his head and glanced down at his shoes, but then in his compunction addressed E.J. "Hey, Big Bro, bring it down a notch. It's not like we're going to drink this one bottle and get hooked on it or anything. I mean, it may be good, E.J., but I doubt if it's it all that we have been missing in life."

"Thank you, Joey," Shauna said gratefully.

"It all boils down to this story," said E.J.

"Wait, stop rolling the camera," Maria said holding up her hand. Maria was a professional actress and the fourth youngest out of the five siblings. "I just love hearing fables and all, and while we do not want to be kept in suspense, E.J., I believe the rest of us would like to start drinking some of the other wines that Shauna bought unless you have fables about those wines, too. Come on, this is a celebration, and I don't know about the rest of you guys, but I am ready to slake my thirst." Maria removed a glass from one of the server's trays.

E.J. stepped over to the servers and told them to pour red wine for everybody and a white for his mother and Grandma.

"Okay," Maria said, sipping her glass of wine, "now that you have taken us off of the forsaken desert, spill the beans, Big Brother."

E.J. said, "Okay, Maria, I see you got game early on in the celebration. Well, anyway, the story goes that rapper Jay-Z announced that he would be boycotting Cristal champagne in reply to racist remarks made by an executive of the company that produced the wine. The question was asked whether hip-hop artists' fondness for the champagne might be hurting the Cristal brand, and the answer given was fatally candid: 'That's a good question, but what can we do? We can't forbid people from buying it.' So the Def Jam Recording's president and CEO has stopped selling Cristal at his 40/40 night-clubs and apparently plans to pull it from his lyrics, too. It is also said that Jay-Z intends to omit all references to Cristal when he performs in concert."

Maria, standing with one leg forward and her foot slanted, in a model-like pose and holding her glass, turned to E.J and said, "Now let me get this straight. The man you are talking about is the second wealthiest rapper in the world, worth approximately $340 million dollars, and you held up our finest drinking moment for this 'nothing to do with us' speech? I mean, E.J., do you have an affinity for Jay-Z just because you guys share an alphabet in common?"

People in the room began to laugh, even the servers.

"All right, Maria, there is no end to your plenty and pitiful jokes, huh? I see that we are going to have to let you take Arsenio Hall's place," E.J. said with a broad smile.

"Arsenio." Maria's tone was laced with concern. "But he is not even on television any more. He is out of the picture."

"That's exactly my point, Maria," said E.J., rubbing Shauna's shoulder. "And if you keep those awful jokes coming, we are going to throw you out of the picture, too." As E.J. headed out towards the pool room, he turned and asked, "Who wants to lose at a game of pool with the pro here?"

Maria hurried behind E.J. "I'll play with you, E.J., but don't get upset when I win now. You know how you get when you lose at anything. I am serious, E.J., because you are a very sore loser." The dueling duo had a queue of people who followed them into the pool room, Shauna and I included. E.J. stepped over to the pool rack and took out his favorite cue stick, chalked it up and then walked over to the pool table.

Just then, Amy, who had gotten to the party, entered the poolroom with her mother. She was dressed in a very elegant strapless dress. Amy's hair was a little more blonde than usual. She left her mother's side and pranced over to E.J. Amy touched his elbow, and said with a sultry voice, "I would just love to play with you when you're finished playing pool with Maria."

E.J. smiled. "You're really dressed nicely, Amy."

Amy pulled her hair from her face as she offered an alluring smile.

Maria held her pool stick by her side as she waited for her next shot. "I am going to make you a boy today when I beat you, E.J.," Maria threatened."

E.J. frowned, "Please. Be serious, Maria. I guess Hollywood has kept the doors to reality shut tight."

"You know the word is out that you hold a called-for slip for bad sportsmanship, especially when it comes to pool," Maria shot back.

"How would you know that I am a sore loser?" E.J. smiled. "You've never been the one to beat me at pool. Dad played pool like it was a science. He mastered the game, and I am the next person to fill those shoes in this home. So Maria, you will need to apologize to me after I whip your butt."

Joey yelled, "Hey, E.J., I'll take you on after you whip Maria. Call me when you're done."

"All right, Joey," Maria called. "You are going to owe me an apology for assuming too much."

"Nothing comes from an apology, Maria. You should know that about now," said Joey as he walked into the room.

Following Joey was his girlfriend, Grandma, Mother and some of the guests.

Talk had begun. Shauna was saying, "Maybe Jesse should stop asking for apologies and take a strategy hint from Jay-Z."

Joey held up his glass of wine, "Now, why do you have to throw a curve in the mix like that?"

Everyone in the family knows that no matter the discussion, Joey is Mr. Debater to the rescue.

"I'm just saying Jesse should see that apologies don't work. When some of these folks apologize, they are not thinking about right, wrong, morals or how they hurt a person or disrespect a race. Many times these people are thinking about how they might look bad in the media, and about their careers or profits. I mean the next thing we know even some mega corporation is going to be saying the corporation itself is going to rehab or get counseling after spewing some racist vermin. But of course, the company would apologize first. Now isn't that crazy?" asked Shauna.

Natasha piped in, "Well, the rehab thing wouldn't work for media-exposed sex piccadilloes of high-profilers. That much I know."

Joey snickered, "But going to counseling might work, huh? 'Sides, a man's gotta do what a man's gotta do," said Joey.

Natasha frowned. "And what's that, Joey—bring shame to the wife and family?" she said.

"Come on. Who's playing dumb here? Women know that a man of high stature is going to play around. Politicians do it, athletes do it, Hollywood folk do it, rappers do it, ministers do it, and ah, yes, don't leave out the guys wearing those long robes either. It's just in a man's nature to do so," said Joey.

Natasha was aghast. She stood looking at Joey, her mouth partly open. Natasha is a beautiful young woman, but looked sad today without her usual smile. She and Joey seemed to be at odds.

"You know, Joey," said Natasha, "you always want to make excuses for black men not doing the right thing. Even if it is in a man's nature, when a man makes a commitment, it should not be turned around and made into a lie. Because then that man becomes, at best, a liar, and his integrity is a falsehood." No one apparently knew why Natasha had an attitude with Joey.

"Wait just a minute." Joey walked from Natasha and stood by Grandma. "Do I need to remind you of your dearly beloved president, Billy Boy, and his chicks on the side? Now you may think Ole Billy Boy was a black man because he played a saxophone, but I've got a newsflash for you: That man was a white man who made that spill in the Oval Office. Need I remind y'all? Now, just because he says, 'I did not have sexual relations with that woman' does not mean that he can just arbitrarily change what the definition of sex was for men. Why, that is just like throwing Pluto out as a planet because some scientists used different instruments to measure the size of Pluto in a different fashion. Now, don't get me wrong, I don't think that Bill did anything wrong in that Oval Office, either. He was just taking care of political business the old fashioned way and was the only one to get caught that way." Joey twitched his head and rubbed his throat. "Ump, ump. Bill was taking care of a man's call to duty."

Natasha rolled her eyes at Joey and walked over to join the group sitting near Grandma.

"Where Bill went wrong, his only sin," said Joey, "was in trying to change what the definition of sex was for guys. Any man, when he is not fronting, will tell you emphatically, that the magnitude of what Bill did still registers on the Richter Scale today as sexual relations. Besides, old Bill admitted just the other day, 'I tried and I failed. But at least I tried.' So there, I don't see why all of you women are being so hard on Jesse. At least, he is not messing around with pages like some of your Republicans. Men have affairs all the time outside of their marriages. Again, it's in our nature."

Joey's diatribe about the Clinton case caught E.J.'s ear.

E.J. put down his cue stick to render his opinion on the matter, and he got everyone's attention, saying, "Where the prosecution went wrong was to permit Bill to ask and answer his own question at a deposition. He answered truthfully when he said that he did not have "sexual relations" in the Oval Office because, by definition "sexual relations," the operative word being "relations" and not sex, means intercourse, which is what did *not* take place. In other words, what happened between the two would not have consummated a marriage."

The server passed around stuffed mushrooms with a cheesy spinach dip.

Natasha took eight mushrooms off the platter at one time. "Joey," she whined, "I need a stool to sit on."

"Okay, baby, but let me say this one thing first," said Joey. "Thank you for the education, E.J.," Joey yelled over to E.J., "but you must know you did not change my thinking on the matter. Next subject: Just as some people say they were born gay and y'all women are so eager to accept that as truth, then we real men were just born with our nature in high gear. Come on, women," Joey rubbed his hands together as if to reward himself with kudos, "you cannot have it both ways. Obviously, that's the way God intended it. He made us, too—God did. It's not like a man can go against what he is. Ain't that right, Mom?"

Mom, apparently wishing to stay out of this, said, "It is proper to say, isn't that right."

"Ah, yes! And thank you, Mom, for concurring," said Joey, as he hugged Mom and went to get a stool for Natasha.

"Dog it! I missed my shot." E.J. yelled from the pool room. "All right, that's it. Who put Paul Robeson music on? Who is trying to throw my game to Maria?"

"Grandma did," I told him. "Grandma, would you like for me to get you anything?"

"No, sweetie," Grandma answered.

"I know you, Zemi," said E.J. "You are the one who put that record on and made me miss my shot." E.J. walked over to Grandma and rubbed her back. "Grandma, do you want Paul to keep singing because if you're not the one who put that record on, I am going to take it off. I love Robeson's music, but his singing mood messes with my concentration when I am playing pool. Do you mind?"

"This is your mama's household." Grandma patted E.J.'s arm. "Son, I can't tell you young folk what to do in your mama's space." Grandma was diplomatically staying away from the friction.

E.J. looked at me and charged, "Zemi, Grandma did not put that record on, so I am going to take it off right now. Don't put Robeson on again!"

"Tone it down, E.J.," I said, rubbing his bald head, "don't you see all the men checking me out? Everybody seemed to have picked tonight for me to meet guys. I wanted the guy most interested in me to know what I liked in a man. I thought Paul Robeson's rich baritone voice and deep interpretative sense would be my process of elimination."

E.J. tilted his head and gave me a look that showed his chagrin.

"I played Paul Robeson so that the right guy would be attracted to me, and the others would fall into the pit of omission."

"Zemi," E.J. whispered giving me a hug, "I don't want to hurt your feelings, but it's sad to say that you are the one who has fallen somewhere and that is off the planet Earth. I don't know what it is, Sis, but you are missing something. What is it that we did not teach you? No man here in his right mind would be impressed with you just because you played 'Ol' Man River.' And here your family has been trying to pinpoint why it is that you don't have a boyfriend, and the answer has been right under our noses since you were born."

I went over and put on some Ella.

When Ella's voice of crystal began wafting through the entertainment hall, E.J. yelled out, "Would someone else please take charge over Zemi's assignment to play the music?"

"What did I do wrong now?" I asked him.

E.J. left his pool game, came into the other room and walked defiantly over to the turntable. He took Ella off the turntable. "Zemi, what's really going on? Is this a feminist thing between you and Maria? Otherwise, why are you doing everything to aid Maria in winning at pool?"

"I am just trying to pay tribute to Ella Fitzgerald because she has been honored with a United States postal stamp to keep her legacy alive as part of the black History series."

"I am glad to be informed Zemi, b-but..."

I interrupted. "E.J., did you know that Paul Robeson, Marian Anderson, and Hattie McDaniel were also previous honorees on postal stamps?"

"Zemi, I am sorry as I see this is very important to you. And I don't want to dismiss you again, so is this the last of your retrospection?"

"Yes. It just seemed that Dad's celebration was a most fitting occasion to acknowledge such artists by playing some of the old records he liked."

After beginning and ending dinner with a prayer, everyone retired to the living room. The server poured champagne into everyone's glass except Rodney's. He was served sparkling cider. Rodney put on John Coltrane's, "A Love Supreme" and made a toast to the painting on the wall of John Coltrane and Duke Ellington.

"Yeah, those two guys made an indelible mark in jazz. They were two of Dad's favorite jazz artists, and he took his last money to acquire that painting some forty years ago," said Rodney.

"That's true." Grandma said, wiping her eyes. "And I remember every detail of your father's send-off as if it was yesterday. The band from Berkeley High School played Coltrane at Allen Temple Baptist Church when your father was all put out to rest in his white suit with his Kente cloth scarf that he loved wearing so much. Your father's send-off was held at one of the largest churches in Oakland where the very prominent Rev. Dr. J. Alfred Smith has served as Pastor. He and Reverend Robert McKnight preached a well-deserved send-off for your dad."

Maria held Grandma's hand.

Grandma folded her hands in her lap as she looked up at Maria. "Did our family ever thank Pastor Smith, those good members of the church, Reverend McKnight? What about all of his good friends and neighbors and the entire Berkeley High School family, including Gail Whittle?"

"Of course we did, Grandma. The Richard Navies Family let them all know that we appreciated everything they did for us," said Maria, stroking Grandma's hand.

"Did we thank all of his friends, especially Charlie Smith? You know that Charlie was like a brother to your father. And what about all of his college and high school students? You know your dad loved his students; he felt like they were his family, too. Your dad did not like for anybody to call his students Afro-Americans and he did not like for anyone to call his department the Afro-American Department. To him it was always the African American Studies Department. Your father's was the very first African American studies department in any high school around the country."

"Yes, we know, Grandma, our dad was great," said Maria, "and we are all so fortunate to have had him for a father."

"You know a lot of people loved your dad; the National Marrow Donors and the Judy Davis African American Marrow Donors were so very helpful. They really helped us to make it through those difficult times." Grandma placed her hand under her chin. "I never got to thank that rap group called Digital Underground. The leader Humpty gave us so much money to get people tested. He had a friend named Nzazi. Did we thank him and all of the community folk, did we thank them too? There was really a wonderful lady who helped with all of the printing. She was the owner of Marcus Bookstore in Oakland. I wish I could remember her name." Grandma looked worried.

I felt my eyes welling up as I looked over at Grandma. "Her name was Blanche Richardson," I told her.

"Yeah, that's her name all right. Did we thank her, too?"

"Yes, Grandma. Don't you worry about that now. Over the last twelve years we have tried to thank just about everybody. Jeff Harrison, then the program manager of KDIA radio, represented the Navies family and publicly made an announcement of our sincere gratitude over the airwaves to organizations and communities around the country," said Maria. She sighed heavily as tears spilled upon her dress.

Grandma said, "So many people showed such a tremendous outpouring of love for your father. That really helped ease the family's pain."

The server filled our glasses again. Everybody in the room held up a glass for the main toast of the hour to the painting of Dad that hung on the wall, bathed in a delicate and complimentary light.

"Maybe your father is having a good time up there in heaven somewhere, listening and playing with those other two fellas. Your father had a great singing voice, you know. It sounded similar to Robeson's voice," said Grandma.

"Grandma" Rodney began gingerly. He had to tell his grandmother what he believed. "Heaven is here on earth. It is what you make it to be right here in America or wherever you travel on this planet, but when you leave this earth your spirit is the only thing left, Grandma. Your flesh returns to the earth and becomes a part of things that spring from the earth, the dirt. Black folk have to learn to enjoy heaven here while they know what's going on now and not use a later life, another life, as a reason for not doing their best."

All my siblings appeared stunned by this talk coming from Rodney. Although we were always taught to speak our minds, Rodney was composed and silent on most things. Never before had Rodney a point of view that he so boldly expressed. I would not dare speak in opposition to Grandma, but I agreed with Rodney. I think that when one's physical body is no longer with us, then all we have is the spirit that stays alive if another living chooses to have it around. The rest of my siblings held fast to Grandma's belief.

Grandma shook her head, "I hope God forgives you for that, Rodney, and I am going to pray for you tonight because I do not want your body burning in hell." Grandma put her hands together, "God, forgive this child." Grandma murmured underneath her breath, "I wonder if that ganja smoke has taken that boy's mind?"

"Um-um. And moving the family right along," E.J. said. "You know, Mother, being that I am the eldest, you should let me hang that picture in my new home now, this year, he asked fashioning his request with a touch of witticism.

Just then the server brought in tea and desserts.

E.J. gestured towards where Grandma and Mom were sitting. "It would be nice for you to serve Grandma and Mother first," said E.J.

Mother answered E.J.'s request for the painting, telling him, "Well, E.J., when I have made my ascension, maybe that will be the case."

Putting his arms around his mother, E.J. said, "You see, Mom, that's what black families need to change. We don't always have to wait until someone dies to pass on a family heirloom. If a parent knows what gift they want to give to a child, then let that child be able to enjoy some childhood memories while the parent is living. I would really love to host Dad's celebration at my home next year, and we can move this picture to my place. That way, something of Dad's is at each of our homes as we each take a year to host his celebration."

Rodney, whose disagreement was so obvious, said mockingly, "Say, E.J., maybe now you want the family to address you as Edward John since you are taking on the statesmanship role in the family."

"Well now, that is my name," said E.J., his face inscrutable.

Rodney said, "Just because you were the first born does not mean that you should necessarily get the painting."

"Why not?" asked E.J. "I did ask for it first. I made it known several years ago that I would like to have that picture hanging in my home." E.J. set his cake plate clattering on the table. "Tell me something, Brother Rodney, had you ever asked for the picture?" Once E.J. gets into his cross-examination mode, it is hard for him to come out of it.

"No, I mean, who was I going to ask for the picture? Mom is still alive, for heaven's sakes," said Rodney.

"But would you like to have the picture, Rodney?" asked E.J.

"Well, I really never gave it any thought."

E.J. shrugged his shoulders and shook his head. "Now, isn't that something? If you never gave any thought to obtaining the picture, and obviously I gave it a great deal of thought, then I should have the picture since I am the one who has put the energy out there with specific intent to acquire the picture," said E.J.

Rodney withdrew in his behavior. "I really don't know why we are talking about this subject as if it's an issue anyway."

Obviously annoyed, E.J. clenched his hands and glared at his brother. "Just so it doesn't turn into an issue," said E.J. "Watch yourself, my man, to make sure you don't turn into one of those crabs-in-the-barrel type blacks. Our folk are suffering enough from that already."

I was not sure why Rodney made an issue of the painting. It's not like he really wanted the picture anyway. There was something different about my brother Rodney.

Rodney returned E.J.'s stare. The other guests were very quiet.

"Well," I said, "everyone knows that I am getting Dad's library, and since E.J. is getting his picture now, well, Mom, I would like to have the library, those books, in my home now. After all, I am the only intellectual in the family."

"And where did you find that information?" asked Maria. "Just because you have three alphabets following your name, there are still twenty-three of those bad boys left, you know."

"Maria!" I exclaimed. "I thought you were on my side."

Maria held up her glass and gave me a kiss on the cheek. "All jokes aside, I personally think you would be the one who would most appreciate the books. But since I do photography on the side, I would like to have those books from the Gordon Parks' collection," said Maria, "but only if that's okay with you, Mother."

Joey did not want to be left out. "And ah-ah," Joey stuttered. "I would -ah- like to have those old *Jet* and *Ebony* magazines and the *Ebony Jr.* for my child that's in the oven baking. And I know, no one wants those old *Playboy* magazines that date back to 1963. I mean, there are even better-looking bunnies out here today."

Everyone ignored Joey's "bun in the oven" comment and I was wondering why did Joey want to take so much from the library and expect it to stay intact?

I cried out, "If the library is going to be broken up like that, then I don't want it. Everything that you guys are asking for, Joey and Maria, helps to makes the library unique."

Joey said, "Oh, Baby Sis, it's okay. I'll just come over to your house to read through the magazines. But just remember, when I have children, don't say a word when I bring the village to your home and tear it up."

Maria said stubbornly, "I still want those photography books."

Rodney walked slowly in the center of the room, looking rather sweaty and nervous. "Well, I think it's a good time for me to let you know, Mom, Grandma and the rest of the family, what's going on in my life."

Everyone's eyes were on Rodney. He's always been the most secretive of the family members. "I-uh, gee, I'm a little nervous here, mainly because I don't know how you guys are going to accept what it is that I have to say."

"Oh, Rodney, oh, man, not you, too," said Joey sarcastically. "Is she under eighteen? If she's under eighteen, brother, you might as well enlist yourself in the pedophile camp for therapy."

"No. No. It's nothing like that," said Rodney rubbing his palms together nervously. "Actually, my news is that I have changed my name. I had not told anyone yet because I was waiting for the legal process to be completed, and I did not want anyone to try to dissuade me. I first had to run my name in the newspaper, and I was kind of hoping you guys would have noticed it that way. So it would have saved me this difficult moment. But now that I have received my papers from the courts with the name change, and—well, my new name is legal through the court system."

Everyone's mouth dropped opened because Rodney was not the joking type. Whenever Rodney said something, one could take it to the bank.

Rodney wiped his forehead. "I have also changed my faith, my religion."

"Rodney…." Joey started.

"Please let me finish before any of you ask questions. For the last two years, I have been studying Islam, and it has been fulfilling for me. I have converted to that religion. I have changed my lifestyle." Rodney loosened his tie. "And uh, I uh-have changed my name to Ishmael Muhammad. Now what this whole transformation means to me is that I have changed my life to submit to the will of Allah. I don't drink alcohol anymore, and I don't smoke marijuana anymore either. I don't eat any meat, I don't chase women anymore and I don't gamble. Well, really, I've never been much of a gambler to speak of anyway. I know this is all a lot for the family to digest, but I have one more surprise for the family. Nadir, the woman I have been courting for about two years…well, I have asked Nadir to marry me, and her answer has made me a very happy man," said Rodney. Holding his shoulders straight, Rodney looked around at each family member's expression. "I want you guys to meet her, so she will be coming by here later tonight. She had to work late at the hospital."

Mother looked spellbound. "Why, I just do not know what to think or say," she said quietly. Her eyes upon her son were sad.

"Well, the floor is open for questions, and I hope that they won't be too hard for me to answer," said Rodney.

Joey jumped up first. "Okay, Rodney," Joey seemed very uncomfortable with Rodney's news. "I am just going to be straight up on this thing." Joey spoke a mile a minute. "Congratulations on the marriage thing. But this other stuff is kind of scary. I mean with terrorists on the loose in America and each one of them carrying their weird or long-ass names, Akmed or every other one is called Mohammed. I mean, how could you pick their side and their religion? How do you just…like that, go and give up your father's name. There is strength in the name Navies."

Natasha pulled Joey's jacket.

Joey leaned down. "What is it, baby?"

"Honey," whispered Natasha, "you shouldn't be so hard on your brother. He has a right to do whatever he wants with his name."

Joey snapped at Natasha, "Finish eating your ice cream and stay out of this because it's not your business anyway. You are not in our family that way."

Natasha got up and excused herself from the room, teary eyed.

Joey went on. "Give a sensible reason why you would go and do something so not you, Rodney. Please don't try to go in the zone and tell us that your birth-given last name was a slave master's name. You do know, Rodney, that Arabs had blacks enslaved, right? You do know that much about them, don't you? And just because they can roll off twenty-six alphabets in one word as in 'As-sa-laam-alaikum' and whatever else they add on to it, don't misinterpret that 'Peace be unto you' as real peace either. What they mean is that my piece's aimed right at you. That's what that means. And their piece is as long as their names. You've seen them pull a piece from under the counter in the liquor stores." Joey frowned and waved his hand back and forth. "Nah, they ain't scared to show them to you either. That's one thing they picked up on fast, quick and in a hurry when they came into this country—their right to bear some arms. Yeah, some arms. Those jokers use their basements as ammunition depots."

"Joey, lighten up with that drama," Rodney cautioned. He seemed disappointed and certainly not amused.

"It's true," said Joey. "Those dudes are loaded down and stockpiled up to the ceiling. You see how they are killing our soldiers over there as if they were nothing. Those Arabs don't care anything about you, just as they didn't care about your ancestors."

Rodney said, "If you are going to continue to use that as an attack—that Arabs had our ancestors as slaves, too—then what would be the big deal of me choosing one former slave master's name over the other? You do remember that blacks were slaves here, too, in America? You do know that, don't you, Joey?"

Joey raised his voice. "Well, at least I know the white man over here. I know him well, I know how he has been, and I know he wore sheets to do his mischief. But tell me what black person in America doesn't know that? I know that, Rodney, but I am not trying to learn how to live through another ex-slave master's mentality—and especially not a foreign one at that." In a show of defiance, Joey glowered at Rodney and paced backwards, away from Rodney, his angry eyes locked into his brother's.

My heart dropped. I do not recall any such demonstration of rancor in our family, let alone disrespect.

Rodney addresses his angry brother. "You are too emotional over this matter of my name change, and I also must say there's not much sense to your rambling," he said.

Joey walked hurriedly over to the server and picked up a glass. "You're damn right I am emotional that you want to give up our father's name as if it means nothing." He walked over by Grandma and set his glass down.

"Joey is right," said Grandma. "Black folk always want to mix and take on the heritage of another group without accepting what is theirs to appreciate. I don't see Arabs trying to own any culture that blacks have embraced. The Navies family means something, and we don't need anyone validating our name for us to appreciate its value."

"You see, Rodney," said Joey, "you don't make sense to anybody. Ever since slavery was abolished in 1865 by the 13th Amendment to the Constitution, blacks in America have been trying to untwist the twist that had twisted our minds. Tell me this, Rodney, what, just what, have those Arabs ever done for black folk except sell us some alcohol and Hershey bars from their 7-Eleven stores?"

"What do you mean, what have they done?" Rodney asked, frowning. "Exactly what kind of question is that?"

"What, you speaking Arabic now?" asked Joey. "Because I know I am speaking English to you. All the Arabs have done in this country is to come and enjoy the comforts of America. They don't assimilate. They wear their turbans and stay in those long shirts and drawers as if they don't like the culture of America. It makes one wonder why they continue coming into our country if they do not like us. But they seem to be able to enjoy an awful lot off of our labor without their due diligence. They don't even interact with any other group of people here, not even white folk, and you know something is wrong with that picture."

Rodney shook his head. "Why are you ranting without the facts? I think you are a little over the line with your prejudice. Arabs haven't done anything to you. What? Are you upset because you aren't the darling minority in this country any more?"

Joey walked over and faced Rodney. "Man, you are crazy. What would it matter if a black man were prejudiced in the face of America? In this day and age what could have possibly clicked in your mind, Rodney, to make you find an answer in their way with all of the havoc they've caused upon America? Better yet, explain to me how does a man with a good life, a black man, a banker in the United States in the twenty-first century, go and do something so off the wall like this? And, Mama, you know that kind of fundamental stuff is just going to upset her so much! And, man, I hope to God that you're spelling your last name with a 'u' in it. Please tell me, it is Muhammad and not that Arabic spelling 'Mohammed.' At least, offer some saving grace. Tell me, what's going to be your next move? Are you going to live in Detroit, hoping to fit in with the large Arab population there?"

"Some of this is just too asinine to dignify," said Rodney.

"What does Ishmael mean?" I asked.

"It means 'God hears,'" said Rodney.

As Amy sat next to Mother, she blurted out, "Islam must be becoming infected with black men." Whenever Amy is around, she naturally feels a part of my family. Amy targeted Joey to say, "The United States now has its first Muslim Congressman, Keith Ellison. He took his oath of office by swearing on a Holy Qur'an."

"See what I mean. Black men are losing it," Joey said.

Maria asked with some trepidation, "Say Rodney, it is spelled M-u-h-a-m-m-a-d, isn't it? I mean, I could live with that name change. You know, a person like Muhammad Ali, people with names like that. Are you that kind of Muslim? We know who they are and why they are. I am going to be honest with you, Rodney. If it is something other than being that kind of Muslim, then I am going to have to look your moves over when you are around me! Now I am not trying to be cynical or anything like that, but there's just no sense in me lying about it. What is with you? Do you mean it is not enough being profiled as a black male while driving? Now are you trying to be noticed so that they can start profiling you now as black and terrorist? I am telling you, Rodney, you are staring right at

Guantanamo Bay, and you saw those pictures for yourself. E.J. is a great attorney—but to help you out in a mess like that—I don't kno-o-o-o-ow." Maria caught herself, putting her hand to her mouth. "I'm sorry Mother, Grandma," she said apologizing for saying "mess," which to many elders is the same as saying the "s" word. Maria acknowledged Grandma's and Mother's smiles, their acceptances of her apology, and then went back to Rodney. "Why couldn't you pick a name like Memphite, Mutabaruka or Kujichaqulia— something that has a beat?"

Shauna walked over to Maria and whispered in her ear, "I don't like to interfere in close-knit family matters, but you do know that Kujichaqulia is one of the seven principles of Kwanzaa?"

Predictably, questioning E.J.'s lawyering skills did not pass unnoticed. And predictably, E.J. said something. "Watch it now, Maria," E.J. warned. "Don't step on my greatness in order to make and inflate your own small points. I am what I am as an attorney. No matter the facts or situation, I am still a great attorney. Now all of y'all need to let go and loosen up your harness on what Ishmael's name and religion mean to him. This is your brother here that we are talking about. He is family and he is our blood. We have never known him to be anything other than a logical thinker. A successful man, a banker. It is mighty strange that all of y'all in the family knew who and what your brother was when you needed a mortgage financed."

"All I am saying, E.J., is that we don't know who Rodney is anymore," Maria responded.

Her comment got E.J. talking. "How can we not know our brother? We know what he is. We know who he is. Your brother does not believe in any of that suicide fanaticism." E.J. gestured to Grandma. "You just saw for yourself that Grandma cannot even get him to believe in life after death, a heaven or a hell, unless he is experiencing it right here on planet Earth. Our brother has proven himself in life as each of us has. Nine-eleven, of course, was a terrible, terrible thing to happen to America, but we are a family. So let's not go over the top because of how this country profiles us. So what? Ishmael may be a Muslim name, but lots of people change their names and for all sorts of reasons. Whenever young folks say

Bow-Wow's name, they say it with a smile because they associate his name with great entertainment. And you guys didn't have a problem when Master P, Diddy or Kweisi Mfume changed their names. What? You think their mamas gave them those names from birth? You don't fret at the name Barack Obama, and he has Hussein as a middle name. Obama is a household name now and is as American as Johnny Appleseed! Today's Americans are used to hearing uncommon names, and they love saying such names, as well, like 'Schwarzenegger.' He is an immigrant and yet able to become the governor of California. So, cut your own black brother—and I am talking about blood brother—some slack, too."

"Hm-m." Joey scratched his chin. "You know, the defeat that Kweisi Mfume experienced at the polls in Maryland to become the senatorial candidate for the Democratic Party did not just happen." Joey cleared his throat loudly. "Maryland, a state with approximately 30 percent African Americans, Kweisi, the former and recent President of the NAACP, one of the oldest black organizations in America too—and he lost to a white guy. Why, for all we know…" Joey began. Treading lightly, he continued, "…well, just maybe, Mfume might have done better at the polls had he changed back to his old name. Joey nodded his head, convinced of his own point. "Yep! I think it was his name, all right. And, by the way," Joey added, "even Kweisi's son went over to the other side to cast his vote after his father lost the Democratic nomination to a white candidate. Then after that, Kweisi's son backed black Republican senatorial candidate Michael Steele. As it turned out, Steele was later defeated by the white Democrat who first defeated Kweisi."

E.J. rubbed his hands together. "Lordy! Lordy! Why is it so hard for black folk to let a black man be an individual and define himself for himself? Kweisi Mfume's name is what makes the man alive, and he has stated publicly that everything that made up his old name, Frizzell Gray, is dead. How does it benefit you, Joey, to unbury Frizzell Gray?" asked E.J.

"Well, I'm just saying that he might have had a shot at winning in Maryland had he used his real name. White folk ain't trying to hear much of that African drum calling in names—it's too different from what folk feel comfortable with. Besides, black people seem to go back and forth when they use names other than their real names. Look at Prince. One day he is Prince, next day The Artist and the next day Prince again," said Joey.

E.J. shook his head "Well, I don't know Prince's reasons for going back and forth. Whatever the reason, it seems to still be working for him. But Kweisi Mfume has been a steady rock in his public service and African Americans tend to love him. Anybody that is into politics knows that Kweisi Mfume cares about black folk, be they in Maryland or anywhere else in America. And speaking of Obama, he is the only front-runner whose name even *rhymes* with America. America! Obama! See what I mean?" E.J. sat grinning proudly, knowing he had scored a point or two.

Maria, removing her scarf from her shoulders, piped in. "Okay, E.J., your reputation as a great debater remains intact. Anyway, I really think Kweisi lost in the primary because he had too many mama-baby-dramas going on. The man had too many babies with two many different mamas."

Joey, taken aback, screeched, "So what, Maria? Those babies were born when Kweisi was very, very young. Plus, the babies had mamas, like you say. What about the mamas and their parts in having the babies? Maybe they could have seen to some of that; it's their bodies as you women like to remind us. And at least, Kweisi acknowledges that they are all his children. Maria, I think that you have a serious problem with black men having babies. You need to turn the page on that sister, and move on." Joey flipped his hand. "Just turn the page. Can you do that for me on this mama-baby-drama thing?"

E.J. directed his comment to Maria, "This conversation right here and right now is not about Mfume or his life, but is about your brother's name. Now your brother's name might be Muslim, and his face is black, but when I look at him, I see my brother, an educated man with a Ph.D. in economics, an African American man who is a citizen of this country, who has something to live for. Daddy taught us to want to learn, get an education and gain knowledge. And when you do that, it sometimes puts you on a different journey, on a different path, and in directions that might not be familiar to others." E.J. paused, and after studying the faces of each of his family members, went on. "Some of the journeys we begin take us places either for a temporary time and some take us places to stay permanently. When you gain an understanding of something for yourself, it makes you look at situations and people differently. To be true to one's self, the perception should always be through the study of our own eyes and mind, and not through someone else's perceived fear or perspective."

Still maintaining everyone's rapt attention, E.J. went over and sat between Mother and Grandma. He placed one hand on Mother's knee and the other on Grandma's, and continued his speech. "Now, the man said that he was getting married. I am more concerned about that. I want to know who is this woman? What kind of family does she come from? Is she educated? Is she a widow or divorced? Or does the woman have any babies' daddies whose butts we might have to kick? You know, stuff like that the family can handle, but this terrorist stuff—Bush and Condoleezza—that's what they get paid to do. Now, as far as 9-11 goes, your brother wasn't the terrorist then and he is not now. Bush and the billionaires, those kinds of folk, got more money tied up in this country to protect than you or I do. Bush and those guys, they know what they're doing, and if not, we now have a Democratic House and Senate, so let those folk do their jobs. And you best believe that those folk in Washington cannot hijack the country, cannot try to fool and make the people feel safe, by locking up some black Muslims in America because they don't eat pork, or like saying 'Alhamdulillah' or like eating bean pies. Hell, I like eating bean pies myself, and no one in this family eats pork, so what does that make us?"

Rodney looked at E.J. and gave a warm smile.

E.J. continued, "On the whole and relative to the rest of the population, you really don't see devout black Muslims breaking the law in America. I am not saying devout black Muslims are crime-free and I am not saying that there have not been aberrations. What I am saying is that individuals who are devout black Muslim tend to be more law-abiding. If you think differently, then you need to study more about these people and who they are and what they tell you that they believe."

Grandma wiped more tears from her eyes.

"Freedom of religion is a given in the Constitution." 'Lordy!" a seemingly exasperated E.J. said, signing off and rubbing his forehead, "please don't let my family try and be the one taking that freedom back from us. Now, Mother, Ishmael and I are going to have to sit down and discuss this further with you. We know it might be difficult for you that your son is no longer Christian, but let's sit down and see exactly what that means for the rest of the family."

"And I agree," I said, starting to cough.

"Here, Zemi," Grandma passed me a glass of water. "This lemon water should help."

E.J. stood up. "Mother and Grandma, we know we are your grown children now, but we still owe you the respect to let you know what brought about these changes in our lives. Because I think that if you know what thinking has gone into making these transformations, you will be able to deal with the changes a little better. And with that said, I think the family is going to be all right. Yes, indeed. I think we'll have that bottle of Cristal now."

Ishmael walked over to E.J., and whispered, "Your words are priceless. Thanks for having my back, man."

Sitting attentively nearby, Grandma listened to the brothers talk.

E.J. regarded Ishmael and smiled. "What do you mean, your back?" he asked Ishmael. "You're a piece of the love. You're a part of the family; therefore, I had the family's back. Family is my life first, and it is always going to be that first because I am a reflection of my family. And by the way, are we cool with the Duke-Coltrane painting, huh? Because make no mistake about that, it's coming to my home." E.J. smiled broadly.

"Do you want me to pay to have it shipped to your home? Ishmael asked, sighing as if a burden had been lifted, as if his offer to pay the shipping was a wee gesture compared to E.J.'s huge demonstration of love, faith, unity and support.

Already, E.J.'s attention was focused elsewhere. "C'mon, Grandma." E.J. took Grandma's hands and gently coaxed her to stand. "I want my first dance to be with my favorite girl."

"Ah, boy, can't you do any better than me for a dance partner?" Grandma fussed.

"No, I cannot do any better than you," E.J. answered with a wink. "You are the best."

"Hey, Grandma, can I cut in?" asked Joey.

In an unanticipated move, Grandma paired Joey's and E.J.'s hands, and teased, "Why don't you two dance together while I rest a while?"

Joey pulled his hand away from Grandma and wiggled his finger. "Oh, nooo, nooo!," he answered. "But I picked up on your drift, Grandma. You want your grandsons to leave you alone. Am I right?"

As if to answer, Grandma walked back to her chair.

As Amy walked past E.J., she whispered softly, "If you can't find a dance partner for the rest of the evening, then I'll be your partner." With her drink in her hand, Amy then made her way over closer to me. "Zemi, does E.J. date white girls?" she asked.

I didn't know what to make of the question at the time. I hunched my shoulders. "Hmm. I don't think so. Or at least I've never seen him with one. Why do you ask?"

Amy lowered her eyes and answered, "Ah, no real reason."

When Amy left my side, Joey replaced her. I thought that Joey's talk was for my benefit, but E.J. joined us just in time to catch the tail end: "…Amy appears to be getting blonder by the second. She is going to kill herself trying to be a white woman. I guess when her mother is in town, and she brings her along, it helps Amy to believe that the public sees her blond hair as natural, too."

"I think the hair color goes well with her shade of skin," E.J. commented.

Joey leaned towards E.J. and asked, "Hey, who is the 'border dude' your sister Maria's dancing with? I mean, it's nothing we need to worry about, is it?"

"Well, he could be the dude who fixed her car, or he could be the actor she played opposite in the movie," said E.J., shaking his head as his eyes followed his sister.

Joey folded his arms. "Yeah, that would be the movie which the family has not seen yet. She better not let Mama see that movie, either."

E.J. added his admonishment of Maria: "I have already told Maria not to speak to Mother or Grandma about the nudity role she played in the movie."

Joey eyed the Mexican guy. "He looks fishy to me."

"Hum." E.J. tilted his head up.

"He looks like he just came over. What's his name?" asked Joey.

"José, Jésus, Chico. Heck, I don't know," said E.J. nastily.

"I am going over there to see who he is," Joey said, and walked in Maria's direction.

Just then, Maria's friend left Maria's side and moved away from her and from Joey. It appeared that he was seeking to avoid friction with Joey. Joey followed Maria. She walked out onto the side terrace and Joey followed her there.

"Hey, Maria, you never introduced me to your friend. How come?"

Maria shrugged. "Ah, he's nobody special."

Joey's expression showed that he was not convinced.

Maria turned her head away from Joey as if to ignore his probing.

"I was just curious, Maria, why you would show up here with not one Mexican but two Gonzaleses," Joey told her. "Was one of your border dudes supposed to be for Zemi?"

"I happen to have Mexicans as friends. Is something wrong with that, Joey?"

"Why did your Mexican friend run away when I approached?" asked Joey. "Does he feel that he does not belong—I mean here in this country?"

Maria was aghast and could not believe this talk from her brother. "Not every Mexican is illegal, Joey." She started to walk away, but Joey pulled her elbow.

"Yeah, just like not every Mexican you see is legal either. I am just looking out for you because Mexicans are on the lookout for citizenship. And you know black women sport their brand of naïveté all too well. They will be the first ones sought as clearance cards for Mexicans under the pretense that love's got something to do with it."

To Maria, Joey's comment was from inane to toxic. Maria pulled her arm away from Joey. "You know what, Joey, you are seriously tripping. If I needed any help on the matter, I would definitely know to skip over you and call 911 first." Maria stomped into the next room. "Oooooh," she cried out.

"Hey, Maria," Joey yelled after her, "no matter what you may think about me, I don't want to be an uncle to any mixture of brown and black nieces and nephews. There is nothing worse than two poor races mixing."

Maria turned her head back. "You know what, Joey, you are so prejudiced."

"I just factor in the facts about things." Then Joey said in a louder voice, "That seems to be something I am able to do which you are not." Joey followed Maria back into the room, but happened upon Ishmael before he could reach her. Concern covered his face for the second time that night.

"What'd you do to get Maria so worked up?" Ishmael asked Joey.

"I am trying to preserve the reputation of the family. But I don't think that would be much interest to you now would it, Rodney? Pardon me, I mean Ishmael," Joey said with a nasty smirk.

"Tell me something, Joey," Ishmael asked. He took a step back, as if trying to temper his anger. "Who made you the policeman of the family? And why are you so sour against other races of people? Does that make you feel a bigger man? Why are you such a racist, man?

"Let's see now," Joey held up his glass and with it tapped Ishmael's shoulder. "I wonder if Caucasian governor George Wallace, who blocked two African American students, Vivian Malone and James Hood, from entering the University of Alabama, felt bigger? I wonder if the folk who put the signs up that read Balconies for Colored or signs on water fountains that read For Whites Only, if those people felt bigger? I wonder if those who dressed in white sheets like cowards felt bigger, burning up black folks' homes and lynching black men. I never killed white women for dating black men as white men have murdered black men for dating white women. See, Ishmael, our folk were not born with such larceny in their hearts. I was never the one who went into black churches killing black children. I was never the one who experimented on black men with syphilis. I was never the one who dragged a black man behind a truck until his death. I was never the one who wrote into law that if you have a white mama and a black daddy, you cannot come into the white race. Looks like my hands are clean."

"Joey, man, you have to let go of somebody else's hate," Ishmael warned. "It will destroy you. Everyone knows that you have a very high IQ, but you are holding so much hatred for whites." Ishmael placed his hand on Joey's back, as if trying to defuse the situation. "Know who and what you are as a black man, here and now. There is no need for you to carry the torch showcasing the hate of black and white drama in America. Your existence and color can make the rest of us better by you releasing your own creativity, genius and inventions into the world. For your own growth Joey, let the brush paint a canvas of love."

"I am not the one who needs the speech, Ishmael." Joey took his glass and touched his chest with it, saying, "I am not the one carrying the hate. And if I did have hatred in my heart it could never be enough to inflict the hurt and pain legally imposed upon my people by whites. But Ishmael, it is interesting how you give a pass to those who really carry the torch of hatred and me, you make out to be the real bad guy—me you want to call a racist?"

"Joey, for your own sake, man, don't you become the ghost of those white people who were racists. And even if you find those today who are still that way, Joey, don't you be the step for them to continue building on. Don't you be the one to wave their banner of shame. Espouse and advertise those things that God allowed to bring you into health and wealth. Let those who will follow you know your good purpose and the new dawn you are to rally in. Surely, you must be the one deserving of some good news to tell," remarked Ishmael. "African Americans must move on to issues of strength. You cannot talk about racism forever."

Joey was not at all convinced. "Until it is solved, racism is the issue, my brother. There need to be dialogues among all the races and not just black and white folk, either. Sweeping the issue under the rug just makes the pile of mess so big that everybody is sneezing," Joey shot back. He spoke with a sense of resolution; as far as he was concerned, he had spoken the last word.

Not according to Ishmael. "You are fighting the wrong battle; others have priority, Joey," said Ishmael. Ishmael appeared to be a persona of clarity. He stood confidently, his arms folded and his voice calm. "I don't care if white people love me because I hold so much love and respect for myself that theirs just might be an overspill. I don't care if they do not want my black child sitting next to their white child in school because I am capable of teaching my own. I don't care if they do not want me eating in their restaurants because I have a brother who has several restaurants. I do not care if they will not rent to me because I own several places of my own. They cannot trick me using the law because I have a brilliant brother who can stand in my stead. No man determines who I am because Allah has defined me and has placed in me a self-government that overrides the dictates of others. Allah's script and that alone suffices me. Therefore, Joey, I do not look to nurse from white people's limited coffers, for they are not my source. Hating them would mean that I have allowed myself to be the victim, the flame to dim, my eyes to be distracted from the prize. I am sorry, Joey. Allah has freed me from all of that."

Joey and Ishmael held long stares at one another. Joey was the first to look away, then he walked away, and when he did, he sidled up to me. I sensed that the anger had subsided between Joey and Maria, but Joey still seemed tentative about announcing his surprising news to the family. I had already guessed that he and his girlfriend Natasha were going to have a baby. But Joey appeared apprehensive about discussing the bigger picture surrounding Natasha's pregnancy because the pregnancy was without marriage, as commonly defined. I knew that Joey felt that his and Natasha's togetherness was basically Joey's definition of marriage. He did not feel that a written marriage contract solidified a relationship between a man and a woman any more than a woman getting herself pregnant could solidify a relationship. Joey had other concerns about sharing his news: he perhaps knew that some members of the family, including myself, thought that although he was thirty-five, he sometimes acted immaturely for a man that age.

"Zemi." Joey waved both of his hands to me. "Come with me. I personally want to introduce you to my man over here."

"But I already met him during dinner."

Joey grabbed my hand firmly. "C'mon, Sis," he prodded. Together we walked over and sat near Zeth, Joey's friend from North Carolina.

"Zemi" said Joey, "did you know that my friend, Zeth here, breeds horses for a living?"

"No. I didn't know that."

"He owns a ranch on acres and acres of land near Asheville, North Carolina." That Zeth was a businessman evidently was a big thing to Joey.

"Oh, really?" I said. Quite frankly, I had no idea what went into breeding horses, but whatever went into making this black stallion of a man, made me wonder about the ride! Zeth and I spent the rest of the evening talking and getting to know each other. Oooh! Zeth was fine! God had made one so magnificent, but had God saved him just for me? Zeth could be like those Muslims or Mormon folk with a lot of wives and a lot of babies. That's so stupid for me to think! Black men aren't Mormons. Though I don't know what would be the difference between Mormons and black men because black men do have a lot of children, too, from so many different baby mamas, and they have their women on welfare, like the Mormons. I wondered why black men here in America didn't call their own doings a religion.

Zeth seemed to like me. Could it be that he was being nice to me because I am Joey's sister? I am not bad to look at, and my shape is, well, I should work out a little more. I am not married, I don't have any children and I'm very well educated. I have a doctorate, but Joey is always saying that a man can't live by education alone. Joey would know. And it doesn't seem as if much that these things would matter to a man like Zeth, I mean, whether a girl is educated or not. Zeth spoke with a deep Southern and country drawl, still I still gave him my home phone, cell phone number, e-mail address and my Mother's telephone number!

Maria had been spying on me from across the room. After I was alone, she walked over and asked if I was on the desperate side. She scolded, "You should never give a man at the first meeting more than one contact number."

I told her that I was being nice to Zeth because he was Joey's friend.

"Nice and stupid are two different things. Even if you are desperate, have some game about yourself." She then turned and flounced away.

* * * * *

It was now one o'clock in the morning, and Grandma had been taken home. Earlier in the evening, Joey told Grandma and Mother his news, that Natasha was pregnant and that they would not be getting married because he was not ready. Mother was furious and asked Joey if Natasha had gotten pregnant by herself. Joey tried to put a happy spin on the news, but it did not diminish Mother's disappointment. Mother said she just did not feel like giving a grandchild that type of welcome into the world.

Someone else mentioned abortion, and Mother said, "Never my seed!" She said a child was a celebration and would not hear any more measure of the story. That's probably why Joey waited and did not disclose part two of his drama until after Mother had gone to bed: Natasha was twenty-one or more weeks pregnant. Natasha had confided in me earlier that night; she whispered to me that if she and Joey did not get married, she would consider having a late-term abortion.

Mother was excited when she heard that Maria had gotten a role in Hollywood though she made Maria promise that she would never strip before the screen. Maria made that promise, but she was already acting in a role where she was almost stripped naked with a Mexican guy.

My news for Mother was the worst news of her evening. Mother was not at all happy to hear that her baby daughter was turning Republican. I mean, the way the news was received, one would have thought that I was going to have a sex change, meaning that just about anything but becoming a Republican would have been accepted. Mother said out of her own mouth that Republicans don't see blacks as human beings. She said that if I went ahead and became a Republican that would really break her spirit.

But what Mother never learned that evening was what was going on "for real" with E.J. He was perfect in her eyes. She never worried about him and felt he knew how to get himself out of trouble—if ever he got into any....

3

y telephone rang, and I was pleasantly surprised. It was Zeth. I had not spoken with him since we first met at my mother's home more than three months ago. Still, I can visualize his handsome face beautiful physique. There was just something about him there for me to explore. I know that's a strange way to put things, but I have no other description for the way I feel.

"Hello, Zemi, how ya' been doin'?"

"Hi, Zeth, what a nice surprise to hear from you. I am doing fine…and you?"

"I am doin' real well myself." Zeth didn't waste any time getting to the purpose of his call. "I wanted to find out if you were not too busy, and you might want to come down in a couple of weeks to Charlotte. I happened to see some past clippin's of First Lady Laura Bush where she led a U.S. delegation to attend the swearin'-in of Liberia's first female president elect, Ellen Johnson-Sirleaf. They've been showin' it a lot on television here in Charlotte since the Liberian president is goin' to be here in October. And your favorite girl, Secretary of State Condoleezza Rice, was a part of the delegation to Liberia."

I had to listen attentively. Over the telephone, Zeth's southern drawl seemed deeper than when I first met him.

Zeth explained, "I won't have much time to spend with you, but I bought you two tickets to see President Sirleaf. She's gonna be the keynote speaker at a conference down here in Charlotte. And with you bein' an educator, a social scientist and all that kind of stuff—I know that much about you—well, I thought you just might want to come and hear her speak. And, of course, I would pay fer air tickets, too, fer you and your sister Maria—if you think that she might want to come down."

Just then, the thought occurred to me that this country boy might be all right for the pickings, slow speech and all. I was really taken by his generosity.

"Thank you, Zeth, that is so thoughtful and kind of you. I have seen all of the write-ups and everything on that conference. There is another conference being held two days later that I planned on attending but just had not put anything in place to make it happen yet. I mean–I hadn't made any arrangements."

"Well, then I am glad that I could take that worry off of your back, Zemi, and make it happen fer you. Just e-mail me all of the partic'lars, and I'll have everythin' in place when you arrive."

"Okay, I'll do that right away. And thanks so much, again, Zeth."
"All righty and you're quite welcome," said Zeth. "Then I will talk to you later," he signed off, ending the call.

Ah! That's what I am talking about! A real woman knows when she sees a real man! I had proven to myself just how powerful thoughts really were. Zeth had read my thoughts 3,000 miles away and returned them back with my wishes fulfilled. I felt a spiritual surge! I had sent my thoughts out there into the universe, and he was the one chosen to pick them up. I sang a happy tune and skipped around as my world was opening up to all that I desired. I was glad to be attending the North Carolina Conference for Women and to meet Madame President Ellen Johnson-Sirleaf. I was going to get involved big-time now. I had the opportunity already to meet Flight Lt. Jerry Rawlings, former president of Ghana and Yahya Jammeh, president of the Gambia, the youngest president in Africa. When I went to the Caribbean, I even met the prime minister of Turks and Caicos. I attended the inauguration of Prime Minister Sharon Miller, first female prime minister of Jamaica, and there I met a lot of Americans and political folk, too. The photographer, Donna Permell, was there in Jamaica, too. She took a picture of me with Congresswoman Sheila Jackson Lee of Texas and a host of other Democratic politicians from the States who were in attendance. I mean, I'm not trying to remain a Democrat, but I love picture taking with celebrities. Susan Taylor, editor-in-chief of *Essence* magazine, was there as well.

Also while in Jamaica, I met a young African American anchor-woman from Pennsylvania. She and I had a very interesting conversation regarding politics. She was a staunch Democrat. Anyway, she and I talked about the prospect of Hillary Clinton holding the Oval Office. I asked her if she would vote for Hillary if, as the nominee, Hillary selected other than an African American as her running mate. The woman said yes. The woman said that she would have to vote that way because her husband was an African American congressman. I can recall our conversation. We were standing near a bistro table, and the anchor woman laid her purse on it, asking, "What did you say your name was again?"

"Zemi," I answered with a warm smile.

"That's such a distinctive name."

"Thank you."

"I want you to know up front, Zemi, that I am my own woman." The woman scratched one hand with the other. "But politics sometimes makes for strange bed fellas."

"Umm." I tilted my head.

"My husband believes that Hillary understands the workings of the White House, probably more that any other Democrat running. After all, it was her home for eight years. And as a woman, I feel that Hillary is more concerned with women's issues. As a woman, I believe Hillary has shown how to raise a smart kid and still excel in a man's world. Hillary's got guts. She's tough and she has been a great role model for women. In our circle we call her the energizer bunny. You just can't keep a good woman down. And I just love those things about her." The anchorwoman reached inside her purse and handed me a business card.

I read the card, finding the woman to be quite interesting. I love traveling to find out the views and mindsets of people in different places.

With my thoughts back to the present, I got up and sent my sister Maria an e-mail asking her to attend the conference with me. She will probably say my e-mail was a book. I wrote her that it was the mission of the North Carolina Conference to provide an enlightened platform for women of all ages and backgrounds across North Carolina to network with peers and become informed on timely issues that are of concern to today's women; that the conference will attract 1,500 women from across North Carolina, including corporate representatives, community leaders, entrepreneurs, mothers and other interested women. Later on, I called Maria to check if she had read her e-mails yet. She sounded half-asleep when she answered.

I said, "Your voice is throaty. Are you okay?"

"No. No. It's okay. I have a gig to do —some acting in a television sitcom."

"Gee, that's great Maria!"

"Don't go getting all too excited," she said. She sounded exhausted. "The role was small and I do mean small, but anyway my sleeping hours are all helter-skelter. Go ahead, though, it's your call and time, too. Spill the beans."

"Well, did you read the e-mail I sent you?"

"Yeah," said Maria, "if you mean the dissertation, I read it. But tell me, Zemi, aside from it being a free trip and all, why would I want to attend something that's so not me? Am I going to be able to meet anyone there that can help my career? If you told me a man, now maybe that would perk me up to go. But a bunch of women, just talking... Hmmm. I don't know about that, Zemi. I am not getting any good vibes about going."

I could tell that this was going to be a hard sell, but I really needed Maria's support on this one. "Look," I said, "are you kidding? The first female president of an African nation is a black woman. Maybe, she's real kinship to us."

"For God's sake, Zemi, the Liberian president was born in Africa. "Dad's never been to Africa and neither has Mom. Don't go getting Marcus Garvey on me now."

"There were freed slaves from America that returned to Liberia to settle, so some of us might have the same bloodline. And get this, too, Maria, she's not just an economic leader but also Harvard-educated. Now how many black women do you know with such accomplishments?"

"Wow. Harvard, you say? Still, why would the Liberian president attending Harvard have any importance to me?"

"I am not too slow to pick up on your bitter tongue, Maria. But this woman has a difficult task ahead. She has the responsibility to lead a country that lost nearly seven percent of its population to civil war and has an unemployment rate of about 80 percent. The least black women in America could do is to go and support her. Come on, Maria, black women must be about movement so that they will know what is going on and know at what level they need to get involved." With Maria, I had to keep on talking until her defenses were down. I knew that later she would give in.

"Okay. Okay. I'll go," said Maria. "But let me tell you the difference between you and me, so that you will not ask me to do this kind of thing ever again. I am an artist. You know artists are in a different groove and mindset than non-artist people. Sometimes you might rely upon us to think one way and then, boom! Without any signal at all, our vibe might put us in another zone. See, artists are selfish. Life is about ourselves, how we feel at the moment, how we look, and what we want to project. We deal with a lot because sometimes on screen we act as psychologists for people. People get to view an actor playing a certain role and can figure out certain aspects of their own lives. We help people figure out stuff, putting the life in plots that are similar to real situations. We show people how to look, what trend is in, how to wear their hair, what types of children to raise. Hell, sometimes, we even influence their voting patterns. We do a lot for people. But again, we are a selfish set of folk.

I thought Maria had been asleep when I called, but she didn't stop.

"Most times actors make the viewers like them. But when we get off of that stage we really feel like we are better than average people. And you know why, Zemi? Because money, people and fans make us feel that way. So when we get a moment to ourselves, Zemi, we want that time to be spent the way that we want to spend it. We love ourselves, not other people, and you know what else? We want people to love us because we think it is our right for them to love us—we are actors and people watch us. People think that we are really, really smart, but we are not all that smart. We are actors, we read scripts. We read something and say it the way we are told to say it. We are really followers; that's why we have directors to direct us."

I gasped. "Such long windedness for such a small favor."

"See, Zemi, we both have college degrees, but we chose different routes to utilize our degrees. You are the research-type person; you like to predict and quote stats. You, Zemi, you are in a structured career mode, and well, me, I am all over the place trying to see what is going to click for my next gig. You want to change the world, Zemi, and me, I just want to find those fun things to play with and use them to enjoy what's already in the world."

Sometimes Maria forgets to turn off the auditioning button. "Listen, Maria, I should not have to listen to so much Hollywood rhetoric just to get you to improve how you think and what you think about."

I was happy that Maria had agreed to attend the women's conference, but I dared not tell her about the other two-day conference. She would have definitely said no. Sharing the experience, coming to the conference will broaden Maria's horizons, enhance her abilities as an actress. Besides, black Hollywood needs to get more connected to what is going on in the real world. I think when Maria actually arrives at the conference she'll get more into it. It's an exciting time, filled with its own poignancy. Things are happening for women worldwide, but for me it was "the new era of black women demonstrating globally" and from all walks of life. It was even clear to many when Mae Jamison stepped into space as the first black female astronaut. Mae Jamison's soaring high and mighty was yet another sign to me that energies were aligning to fill the voids in both outer space and earth space with black female talent.

* * * * *

Maria and I did attend the conferences. She surprised herself (and me) by her willingness to accompany me to all of the meetings. Returning from our travels on US Airways, I did a lot of reading. I read some great articles from *Social Temperature* magazine on the historic triumph for female political leaders from around the world. They are in front view for 2008. And one such writer, Lisa Cook, wrote: Put them all together, women are getting positioned. I then wondered if maybe female heads of state might become a trend of the future, or is it mostly just Third World countries? Michelle Bachelet was elected in Chile. Bachelet was the first Latin American female president to be elected without the help of a prominent husband. I thought to myself, she would definitely have something on Hillary. The same would be true for Former Jamaica Prime Minister Sharon Miller. Her husband had no influence on her election. Can you imagine little old Jamaica with a female dealing the cards? She must be a tough dealer to win Jamaica; she's got to be one with guts to preside over that country. Angela Merkel was elected chancellor of Germany in 2005, and she, too, is seen as a strong woman. Some have even likened Merkel to Margaret Thatcher.

After reading about these women, I was prompted to think about how America has never had a female commander-in-chief to serve its country. If the women and men, the people of Third World countries could elect female leaders, I thought surely the face of the superpower should be that of a female, come 2012 or 16. Even the face of a black female? With the United States promoting equality and education for females in Iraq and other countries, America's talk should now become her walk for itself. Some say the presence of women in politics is progressing, but there are presently no African American women in the Senate. What would ever be the chances of one holding office as President of the United States?

I continued thumbing through the *Social Temperature* magazine and found more really great articles. These publications showed how in America, women have been shut out, stamped out of the presidential office of the United States. On 60 Minutes former President Bill Clinton was asked about the idea of a female president. His answer: "We already have one—Geena Davis." Geena Davis played on the popular TV show Commander-in-Chief.

On a CNN interview, First Lady Laura Bush predicted recently that the United States soon would have a female president—a Republican, maybe even Secretary of State Condoleezza Rice. "I think it will happen, for sure," Mrs. Bush said about a woman in the Oval Office. She made the comment the day before she left for Liberia's inaugural proceedings. "I think it will happen probably in the next few terms of the presidency in the United States," Mrs. Bush said.

Rice has said she has no desire to be president when President Bush's second term expires. But Mrs. Bush said: "I'd love to see her run. She's terrific." So there. It appears from all indicators that a woman president in the U.S. could just happen as early as 2008 or 2012. In the Republican Party's plan, exactly in which term would the Party be considering placing a female in the Oval Office?

I turned to the end section of *Social Temperature* and found the most amusing survey. The article and survey were two pages long. I skipped down to "the ultimate questionnaire": DOES AMERICA HAVE THE HEART TO CHANGE IN 2008? Maria and I completed the survey together; it was definitely a unique kind of survey that made us both think hard about our responses. Not only was it one hundred questions long, it roused hidden thoughts that made one think before making a mark. Some questions hit on pretty heady subjects; Maria said that some question were just over the top. I agreed, but the questionnaire held both our concentration. It was thought provoking. It was the most unusual survey that I had seen.

Maria commented, "What kind of person would take the time to even think up something like this? Let me tell you something, Zemi, I would not have taken the time to complete this report had I not been sitting in first class."

"Maria, it is a survey, not a report."

"Well," said Maria, folding her arms, "unless there are undisclosed agenda for getting a woman in the Oval Office, I can't see it. I do not see a female President of the United States."

Maria chipped a nail and blamed it on filling out such a long questionnaire. She looked at me with eyes crossed.

I held up Maria's finger. "I'll pay to get this one nail fixed for you."

Maria waved her hand. "Don't bother. I wouldn't want you to make such a big financial move right now in your life."

"Okay," I quickly agreed. No problem.

"I think that you were adopted, Zemi."

"Why would you say such a thing?"

"Because you are so-o-o cheap." Maria made a circle with her thumb and forefinger.

I leaned in closer to Maria. "Yeah, and if I spent my money on all of my desires right now and went broke, not one of my siblings would lend me a penny. But I will change when my ship comes in."

"You know, Zemi," said Maria, wistfully, "it won't matter even if you used both Laura and Oprah to support the same party to get a female in, optimizing female energy will still not be enough influence to make it happen. Hillary can forget it! America just isn't ready to take that leap of faith—we know that a female can perform in that role just as males have performed if not better. Personally, I would like to see it happen—a female. Not necessarily Hillary. I hope it does happen, but do I have enough faith to believe it will happen? Now that would be a whole different subject. I would really like to know how other people marked their answers to this survey."

The airplane took a sudden dip and I rubbed an irritated ear. I told Maria, "I find questions number 16 and 17 rather interesting. Let me read number 16 to you, 'Do you think Barack Obama would help race relations in America if he became president in 2008?' Yes or No." I pulled Maria's arm gently. Number 17 reads, 'Do you think blacks would vote for Barack Obama over Hillary Clinton as the presidential nominee in 2008?'"

Maria toyed with a strand of her hair. "How could a beautiful man like that not have all of the answers to any questions brought forth? He could take my pen himself and mark the answers 'Yes,'" Maria said with a grin.

I laughed. "Maria, Obama wants you to vote for him because of his intellect, for what he knows and for what he can do to make this country better, not for his looks."

Maria snuggled down in her seat. "We all know the man has a great mind. Do you think God would have made somebody that handsome and made him brainless at the same time? God does not have time to waste when dealing with perfection. Just because he didn't give you both angles, Zemi, does not mean that he slighted Barack in any form or fashion. White people love him as well blacks."

I patted Maria's knee and calmly suggested, "Since you think he is all of that, maybe you should go and work for his campaign."

Twice Maria lifted her eyebrows. "Hmmm. Yeah. Good sugges tion. And I just recently heard that Congresswoman Barbara Lee endorsed Senator Barack Obama as presidential candidate for 2008. I share in her strength and wisdom in this opportunity."

"How do you think other people would mark their answers for numbers 18, 19, 20 and 21?" I asked.

"Let me see again." Maria looked more closely at the survey. "Hmm, Number 18. 'If Hillary Clinton won the Democratic presidential nomination for 2008, would she need an African American as her VP in order to reap black votes.' Number 19. 'If Hillary Clinton were selected as the Democratic Party's presidential candidate, would she lose the black and Hispanic votes if she chose a white as her VP?' I definitely need to know how that question was answered," Maria commented. She continued reading the survey. "Number 20. 'If Hillary Clinton were selected as the Democratic Party's presidential candidate, should she choose a female as her vice presidential nominee in 2008?'" Maria rubbed her cheek. "Listen to Number 21. 'If Barack Obama became the Democratic Party's presidential candidate, would he win the votes of whites if he chose a Hispanic as vice presidential nominee?'" Maria pushed her hair away from her face. "I don't think that Barack would accept being Hillary's vice president. At least, I would not want to see him in that role. I think he has more going on than Hillary."

"Are you kidding, Maria?" I raised my voice a bit. "I think Obama had better be happy with a VP post because I don't believe he can make it on his own right now. The man is too tender."

"Yeah, but, Zemi, if you check your memory bank, Barack was the only tender that had the right insights about Iraq, even when Hillary and other senators supported the original decision to go to war in Iraq. Barack has long believed it has also been a failure of conception—that the rationale behind the war itself was misguided."

"The way I see it, the deck is stacked against Hillary just as it relates to her VP. No matter what minority she chooses, another group will abandon her," I stated as a matter of fact.

Maria was still focused on seeing how others answered the survey. "I am going to find a way of getting the results from this survey. I've got to know the findings for number 10," she said. Maria took a long drink from her bottle of water. "'Will African Americans in Hollywood vote the same as white Hollywood if the presidential and vice presidential nominees are Barack Obama and Hillary Clinton in 2008?.'" Maria said, "I have to make sure folk in Hollywood respond to this survey."

A flight attendant passed just then. Maria put up her hand.

"Yes, what can I get for you?"

"Could you answer a question for me?" Maria's asked in an overly nice tone.

"I will certainly try."

"Well, actually, I have a couple of questions," said Maria. "First question, may I take this magazine with me?"

"You certainly may."

"Would you vote for a woman as President of the United States?" asked Maria.

"Whoa!" The flight attendant was taken aback. "I was not expecting that question, but to answer you, in all sincerity, no, I would not vote for a female president to serve over the United States."

"Then you know the next question to follow," said Maria.

The flight attendant bent down and placed her hand on the arm of Maria's chair.

"What would be your reason for not wanting to see a female president in the Oval Office?" Maria asked, her tone direct.

"Well, in my family's religion my husband and I just don't believe a woman should lead. God said that man should be the head of the house, not a woman."

Maria looked as if she was thinking that the woman must be in a cult. "What is your family's religion?"

"My goodness." The flight attendant put her hand up to her chest. "I feel as though I am being cross examined." The flight attendant smiled awkwardly, her growing discomfort obvious. "Why, I am Christian," she answered.

"I am, too," said Maria, perking up in her seat.

The flight attendant appeared more at ease now.

Maria looked the woman in the eye and asked, "Why are you a flight attendant? You are strikingly beautiful."

"Thank you. Everyone tells me that." The flight attendant smiled warmly.

A chime sounded.

"I had better get back to work, but it was interesting talking with you."

"Damn!" said Maria, after the woman left. "I would never have thought that flight attendant and I had the same religion."

"What do you mean?"

"Well, we are both Christians, so we read the same Bible; yet, for me that would not have any bearing upon me voting for a female as President of the United States."

"Then the difference must be that she is a Republican," I said.

Maria's mouth flew open. "I missed that part of the equation. But, you see, Zemi, it is not that easy to get women deprogrammed from accepting their second class citizenship in America."

The flight attendant passed by again.

Maria tapped her arm and said quietly, "You did not give me your name."

The flight attendant straightened her shoulders. "It's Sequana."

"My, that is such a beautiful name. You know, Sequana, I forgot to ask your party affiliation."

"My husband told me not to be so open about that."

"Oh, I am sorry to pry," said Maria.

"That's okay. But I am a Republican. Are you?"

"No, but my sister here is a closet Republican."

"Oh, okay. Can I get either of you something to drink?"

"Thank you, but not right now."

"Well, just let me know when you need something" she said, flashing a smile reserved for first-class passengers, no doubt.

Maria pointed to the questionnaire. "Look at number 5, Zemi. Well, you have to admit that one is kind of weird as well, a nonessential question to ask, 'Would you vote for a qualified homosexual for President of the United States?'"

"No, that one is not just weird; it is more surreal." I huffed. "I am definitely one who would shudder at a gay person in the Oval Office."

"Why, Zemi, you are prejudiced. Why should it matter what a person's sexual orientation might be? I mean, really, in Hollywood some of your greatest creativity comes from gays," Maria said sincerely. "Gay male hairdressers are masters in the beauty and hair industry."

"I don't know if I would clothe myself in garments of prejudice, but you yourself said earlier that Hollywood was strange, and even more bizarre is the stuff that comes out of Hollywood. Everybody knows that the new and the weird happens in Hollywood first. But that's not the real world for most people. Most people do not think like people in Hollywood." I did not want to say too much to the contrary, but I really would be frightened to have a gay person lead America.

Maria shook her head in dismay.

"You are missing the point, Maria."

Maria pointed her finger. "No, you are the one without a point. You would not have to dress up in an anti-gay outfit for one to know that you are homophobic, Zemi." Maria turned and faced me squarely. "Look at you. Your whole demeanor changed the moment we started talking about gays. If you knew all of the people that you interacted with who were gay, you would have to get a thicker black book to take around. Have you forgotten about all of the scandalous stuff that's been going on in the political arena? Need I make it plain by pointing out that that stage was not Hollywood?"

"You have your point," I said, not conceding, merely observing. I moved on to number 15. "What is your take on this one?" I asked.

Maria read the question out loud. "'Would you vote for a female as president if she had sensuous characteristics?'" Yes, I definitely would," Maria answered. "I am a woman, a straight woman, who is very proud of her sensuous gifts. I like exhibiting my feminine charms. Anything that I can use which is a part of my charm to accomplish what I seek in life is just a part of me being a woman, spending out of God's gift." Maria lifted her eyebrows, her face beaming.

I closed the magazine and let it rest on the tray.

"How would you respond to the question, Zemi?"

"That is a bombshell type question. She needs to look feminine. Imagine my amazement, when I heard the story on a news station that Hillary Clinton, the only female presidential candidate, refused to appear on the cover of Vogue Magazine for fear of looking too feminine. I do not want to see a woman as president dressed like a dude," I told her. "She can be feminine and have an executive demeanor at the same time."

"More important, Zemi, no matter the physical look, since that is in the eyes of the beholder, it is always best to make people pay attention to gifts that you possess as did Barbara Jordan and Janet Reno, not so much to a standard of looks. But if I were president, I would have everything done to keep me looking luscious. Nothing would droop. And if it ever became necessary, I would use my womanly charms to challenge some terrorist and probably would never have to fire a gun."

"Maria, you are narcissistic—and nutty. Terrorists have been around beautiful women; they have a different agenda."

"Yeah, narcissistic—that is true about me. I would probably be a female Ronald Reagan president version—into the glamour look."

"Maria, when we get back home, we need to do some research to find the results of the questionnaire."

Since the conference, Maria really seemed more interested in political affairs.

"We," said Maria. "There is no more 'we' after this trip. I am finished trying to know what other women think and what political pundits are trying to say. Okay? So leave me alone." Maria turned her head and pulled her wrap over her face.

"So, Maria, what did you think of the conference and all?" I asked.

"Oh, boy, there is no end to your drive, huh, Zemi? What now, am I supposed to be your critic, too?" she asked.

I shrugged my shoulders. "I just want to know if the perception I am holding is the same as yours."

"Okay, here is my take. I liked meeting the Nigerian President Ellen Johnson-Sirleaf."

"Maria," I said in a distressed tone, "President Sirleaf is the President of Liberia, not Nigeria. Get your facts together, girl!"

Maria played it off as though she were joking. I hoped she was teasing, but I feared she was not.

Predictably, Maria tried to play it off—her faux pas. "You know that I am an actress. Allow me my props. I was paying attention at the conference. I loved the African garb and just the whole persona that President Ellen Johnson-Sirleaf of Liberia exuded," Maria said, affecting a sultry, dramatic voice. "She has a very strong presence of wisdom when she speaks, and she is a person I could listen to. I feel connected to her."

"Me too, Maria. I feel the same way. Maybe it's the serene presence she has about herself… like Mom…," I began to explain before Maria interrupted me.

"Zemi, please let me finish up my critique so that we don't have to hash out this conference all over again. All right?" Maria scolded. She yawned, but she was still on track. "I even liked meeting Senator Dole because usually politicians seem so boring to me, but I just couldn't get over her charming southern drawl." Maria yawned again. "Just the thought of politicians is exhausting," she said, tilting her seat backwards. "I also liked the Cole lady who is president of Spelman College."

I winced. "Maria, I am not even going to trip with you because I know that you know Jonetta Cole is no longer the president of Spelman College. I know that you know she is the president of Benedict College, right there in North Carolina."

"Right, right, right," said Maria.

I just knew she was feigning.

She changed courses, saying, "And another black speaker the judge lady…ah…ah Gwynn Swanson. Now that woman can dress from head to toe in nothing but class. And Lieutenant Governor Beverly Perdue was sharp, too. I remember two other women, but I forgot what I wanted to say about either of them." As the flight attendant passed by, Maria stopped her and asked for more water.

"Okay, Maria, you did well remembering so many names and details. I am impressed. No question—you unmistakably passed the test."

Maria perked up at my compliment. "Of course, I passed. That's what I do for a living. I read scripts and I pay attention to details."

Maria cleared her throat. "When details are not boring and are worth my remembering, like a money incentive, then everything gets crystal clear."

After Maria yawned yet again, I told her, "Maria you can go to sleep now. There is nothing else to talk about."

Maria waggled her finger at me. "No. No. No. You are not getting off that easy, baby girl. Let's talk about your cute country bumpkin, Zethie-baby." Maria loves making men the subject whenever she gets an opportunity.

"There is nothing to talk about," I said.

"Oh, yes, there is, Zemi. I can tell, you like that country man, don't you?"

I could not hold back a smile. "I don't know yet."

"Excuse me, Zemi, but I know that look on your face." Maria and I were very close growing up, so there's not too much that she wouldn't know about me.

"No, you do not," I protested.

"Yes, I do," she insisted.

"Then what do you think about him? Would you date a man like Zeth?" I asked.

"Oh, my Gawd!" Maria's hands flew to her mouth. "I shouldn't have said that."

"Maria, come on, you know that you are going to say whatever is on you mind so you might as well tell me now."

"Frankly, Zemi, with my being an artist-type person and with the field that I represent, why, Sis, he just wouldn't look good on my arm. The man gobbles up every 'g' on the end of his words as if they are going out of style. But that still does not mean he is not right for you, Zemi. You could always dress him up, make him more stylish. That would help a little. Let's see, what else you could do? Yes, you could dye all of his white socks, any color would do. He has nice hair. All you need to do in that area would be to take him to the barbershop and get him an even line at the nape of his neck, and what else can I say? Oh. Oh. His skin is very clear. He must be eating very well. He has beautiful, light brown, romantic eyes, and his teeth are very white and straight. Those traits are his saving grace."

I thought, at least, Maria finds Zeth physically beautiful.

Maria twiddled her fingers. "But, Sis, I have to tell you that the way he chuckles those words out of his mouth…just makes every word sound as if it's rolling out of a pickle jar. Perhaps, you could take him with you to places and be incognito, but he is much too tall to hide." Maria threw her hands apart. "Look, Zemi, I just can't find much to say about him. Either you like him or you don't. He is not the type of man that a woman can easily influence to change. He is who he is. He apparently seems to care about you and for your hopes and dreams, and that's an important measure. Really, he seems like a good catch, and if I were very poor or desperate, I would definitely date a man like Zeth. But if you think you can do better, move with haste."

As we prepared for landing, the flight attendant came over and gave Maria her contact numbers to call later if she needed perhaps to interview her further….

* * * * *

I got back to my house, I had countless voice messages on my telephone and stacks of mail that included two videotapes. Jet lag had taken over my being, and all I wanted to do was to morph back to some state of normalcy. But one message drew my attention immediately. My friend Kaye had e-mailed me about the news that renowned artist and family friend Benny Andrews had passed on. Benny's passing on was an inestimable loss for his wife, Nene Humphrey, and his family. Kaye had known Benny for many years; she had met him through her sister, Sherry Washington, whose fine art gallery in Detroit represents Benny's art work. And Sherry's and Kaye's sister, author Luisa Washington Chapman, has conducted several interviews of Benny Andrews. Members of their family are passionate collectors of the works of Andrews and artist Richard Mayhew. Benny's passing following an illness not long ago made public was a blow to throngs of people who loved and adored him. Benny Andrews was a great American painter. He painted socially-conscious works that addressed many issues, including the Civil Rights movement, the holocaust and the forced relocation of Native Americans. Even in an era dominated by abstract art, he exhibited his work in galleries and won awards and prizes, including a

National Endowment for the Arts Fellowship in 1974. His work is part of the permanent collections of the Museum of Modern Art, the Brooklyn Museum, The High Museum of Art in Atlanta, the Hirshhorn Museum in Washington, D.C., the Detroit Institute of Arts, among others. Kaye knew that I would be concerned about his passing because in our home growing up, my family's art collection included Benny Andrews' works.

Kaye had emailed this poem she had written for all of Benny's loved ones, friends, collectors and fans.

PAINTED TEARS
FOR BENNY ANDREWS ©
By Kaye Washington

The spirit of Benny Andrews rises
Rise Benny! Rise!
The wake of his going upward is flooded with awesome colors, some deep
and definite and others wistful and suffused
Just like in his "Easter Hen."
Wings up! Head toward Heaven.
Legs in aerodynamic position,
Benny flies away
Over clouds and in his freedom
Let loose Benny, your spirit from the
troubles of this world!
Where Benny is going
-there is no war
-no hungry children
-no....
As he lifts, he drifts past
the detritus of life we yet possess
and only the beautiful things he carries along.
In the full palette of his imagination,
Benny travels with a swatch here, a
patch there, a seed for a tree, the flesh tones of all humanity,
and—"Benny, just what is that you have in your hand?"
A backwind guesses, "Inspiration?"
Mid-flight, Benny pauses, and with swirls of ribbon he

146

paints against the ether,
"The backwind is generous if not poetic, but what I have in hand I
now drop to the Earth to leave with you, as I have also left behind
'Inspiration.' You
have use for that now. What I have in hand? It seems I was born with it
now, but I am free to let this go, too. It is simply my brush, a mere tool.
Without any earthly thing, now I can—
as I always have—paint with heart and mind and soul. With an endless
love for my family, my friends, for all that is good."
And so we weep for Benny, for ourselves; this we cannot help.
But you might suspect that, though gone, he is here
When you cry with painted tears.

Sometimes it is very hard to know what things will comfort another in time of loss. I did not know exactly what to say to Kaye though she had comforted me with such a heartfelt piece, but I sat down and wrote her this e-mail:

Dear Kaye,

It's clear to me that Mr. Andrews has passed a baton—one of his brushes left behind—on to you. So with brush in hand you can now experience and know for yourself the confidence of using your brush to paint the world with your words of wisdom, and who would have thunk it? Your words are poignant as well. Thank you for these words.

I look forward to see you.

Loving regards,
Zemi

I really wished then that I could have taken the time right then and there to speak with my friend. But I had accepted an engagement to be a speaker at the Women's Conference on Self-Preservation, and it was everything I could do to prepare, and as a trial lawyer herself I knew Kaye would understand (and later learned that she did, of course). Critic and satirist Billy Charles would be the keynote speaker for the conference. The CEO of JBU Productions had just sent a letter and videotape requesting that I respond with a counteractive critique of what Mr. Charles had said about African American women at a previous conference. The letter stated that JBU was comprised mostly of women who had grave concerns about Mr. Charles' ill-humored shot at black women across the media waves. (Ugh! Smudged ink made the bottom portion of the letter indecipherable, and I was only able to make out the first name of the JBU's CEO: Shelia.) Anyway, the CEO thought it was a godsend that I was given the opportunity to speak on the same podium with Mr. Billy Charles. She thought that I should be the voice in opposition to satire on black women. In that role, I would be positioned to serve the interests of women and my own agenda, in her opinion.

I was thinking about how this speech would help to pay my student loan back to the government although I hadn't really committed my thoughts to an outline yet. The videotape would help me to prepare. I snuggled up on the sofa all comfy, drinking green leaf lemon tea, then used the remote to fast forward the videotape to: Speaker #3: Are Black Women Their Own Worst Enemies? by Billy Charles.

Billy Charles had center stage: Are black women their own worst enemies? Now let me just say this up front, in case I should forget to say it throughout my speech, that when I say black women because I am married to one, I don't mean all black women. Just so you don't come looking for me later or tying up my e-mail with angry messages. Now, 'if the shoe don't fit,' well, you ought to know that I am not talking about you, okay? Okay, now we have that out of the way. As I was saying, black women are their own worst enemies and here is why. I don't believe that black women can resist a welfare mentality to survive. Can they hold weight to today's call for technology, ideologies and innovations to compete on a global stage? How could they know how to compete? Some black women don't even know how to make appropriate decisions for their personal lives. Many black women would be upset about this comment but their priorities are mixed up. They will buy their children expensive sneakers and clothing and the thought never occurred to buy some books once in a while.

A black woman will have five babies from five different men, all born with the assistance of welfare. Then the mother will get pregnant again with a sixth baby. Six babies, all before the woman is the age of 25 and with no husband. This, indeed, seems like a woman in need of psychological assistance; this behavior is not of sound character. Please! Do we need more of a reason to sound the damn alarm! I tell you, no sane woman in today's time would function in this manner. Now this type of behavior is a drain on the progress of African American women.

When I was asked to speak at this conference tonight, I immediately answered Yes. "We Are Our Sister's Keeper—Whether We Want To Be or Not," the theme for this conference, were words piercing my heart. I thought, as a brother, I am dared to ask to know, how do you keep up with a sister who cannot put the reins on her own sexual proclivities and plays hide-and-go- seek with the daddies to get child support? Somebody tell me,—it is not that I want to—but how can you not leave a woman like that behind? Six times and the woman can't make an appropriate decision. The woman has already left herself behind. I don't want to be rude, but enough already!

Sometimes it's just hard to keep making excuses for the course of action of our women. Some will leave this conference saying that Billy Charles is not compassionate enough with our sisters. But I think that I am on the same page as the women who put this conference on. It is understandable why the people of this conference have to ask the question "What's Going On, Black Women?" as the title. Think about that for a minute. What is going on, black women? Do you know why African American people have to keep asking that question? I'll tell you why, because there is no smoke coming out of the chimney when its wintertime in the home. There is no food cooking in the oven because McDonald's or Burger King has become the kitchen. There is no man in the house because he only makes drive-by calls after 2:00 a.m. There are no books in the house because from the mama on down, the television has become the household's primary occupation. There is no nourishment going on in the home because a four-year-old child wakes himself up in the morning and fixes a bowl of 'Captain Candy' cereal, and make no mistake about it, it is candy, and there is no milk in the home.

Then there is the child who cannot work a PC mainly because there is no computer in the home, but can maneuver the complexities of turning on his babysitter (the TV). Do you know how hard it is today to turn on one of those cable boxes or one of those Comcast Systems? But anyway, that's the whole day of the child, sitting from 6:00 am to 6:00 p.m. watching over his baby sister and constantly turning on the babysitter, the Television.

What's going on you've asked of black women? Well, there are some women that you just don't ask that question of because you don't really want to know the answer. They don't read their local newspapers, so don't dare ask them about *USA Today* or *The Wall Street Journal*. And if you ask them if they watched **Hardball,** they would swear you were asking if they saw a hard ball being thrown through a window. They've heard of **FOX, MSNBC** and **CNN,** but they don't watch informational screens. They'll watch entertainment and celebs pouring out. They can tell you all about the relationship of Jay Z and Beyonce and what he gave her for a birthday present. They can spill a whole bio on 50 Cents but these same women would not be able to tell you anything about James Clyburn, Bennie Thompson, John Conyers or Charles Rangel, or who any of these guys were. They can tell you who Britney Spears' baby daddy was as well his other baby mama even before knowing their own baby's daddies. They can tell you about Nicole Richie and her weight as well, but these same women cannot tell you that Nancy Pelosi is the [then] new House Minority Leader. Do they even know what the issues are today other than the war in Iraq? They can tell you that Diddy is worth 346 million dollars, but cannot tell you that African Americans' annual spending power is 845 billion dollars.

And it scares me to think that on election days these are the same ones society wants to go out to the polls and vote because all of a sudden they have become conscientious voters? Some of these black women don't have a clue as to how to define themselves. They don't know where they belong. Their spirits are poisonous. If a man does not call the woman a bitch she thinks that he does not love her. Do black women know the overall image society holds of them? Do they care? Do they think that others hold a positive image of them? They don't have answers because they don't care.

Do I, Billy Charles, have issues with some black women? Yes, I do. And here is why: *Because so many black women are found in their present conditions as they place their value solely on the rotation of their mattresses. These women are big on the Christian scenes, too, and are of the belief system that God will make a way for them and their fatherless children. It is interesting to me that these women have put the responsibility on God thus allowing the 'counterfeit papas' with empty pockets to run out of the back door. Do black women have the will to let go of such beliefs and ways that have staggered their energies and halted their progress? Pardon me, but I am not seeing the light at the end of the tunnel. See, what I can't understand, and I am young myself; thirty-four and a half is young, but why are black women allowing so many elements within American society to use them? And I say allow, because you black women, you are in charge of your own ship, or you should be, and if you are not, then your mamas didn't do their jobs of 'mama-ing' properly.*

Here is what I want to say about that: When these black mamas for generation after generation are having babies at fifteen, well, actually the age has dropped, I think the girls are now starting to have sex at twelve or so. But when these mothers allow their daughters to become pregnant at 13, 14 and 15, anything in the teens, I have a remedy for that nonsense. I say we should take those mothers and…and duct tape their mouths so they can't talk, forcing them to listen, and put them to work somewhere for hard labor, and I mean hard, for neglecting their children. Make it a criminal act when a mother allows her daughter to be the dessert of boys and older men by having sex at the age of twelve. Then when these mamas come off the farm, their names, I mean the names of the mothers should be on a list somewhere letting people know what type of mothers live in their neighborhood. I know some of you want to say that duct tape is mouth-abuse and that I shouldn't joke that way. Okay, you're right. We'll leave the duct tape off, but I am sticking to my guns on everything else. I betcha', that would make some of these mothers obtain some soundness of character.

Now watch. Some people are going to say that I don't like black women because if I did, I wouldn't talk about them that way. But I want to ask you something, women. How can you call it a mother's love when the mother allows her female child to get raped over and over again? Be it by a boy or man, it is called rape. I will let you tell me then mothers. Huh? What do you call it when a girl 12, 13, 14, 15, or 16 has sex and that girl is under age? What authority does that child have to give any male an opportunity to begin the early destruction of her mind and the wearing down of her body? Damn it, somebody should be held accountable! Or, are black women so addicted to suffering and fear that it seems natural that their own children should be left to abuse?

I have something else I must throw in here and I know some of you mothers would rather not hear any more, but not having your school age child learn how to read is abuse, too. That is child neglect. Slavery was abolished in 1865. Though it was not such a long time ago as human history goes, for your generation, 1865 was a long time ago. I say that to say this: *The ex-slave masters can no longer pounce on your daughters' at will anymore because today that would be a crime. Oh my! Why then are you black mothers letting these young black punks and old dirty men diminish your daughter like that, making her self worth nothing? And mothers, another newsflash, also with the abolition of slavery came the freedom for your children to learn how to read today without getting a beating. Now with that bit of news that ought to make all of you mothers be about making sure, if you can't do it, that somebody teaches your child how to read and with comprehension, too.*

Now I want to say this to all black mothers because I am a man and I know. And listen to me carefully on this. It is not, I repeat, it is not a good thing for a man to walk around naked in front of their daughters. I was at a beach in California, and what I saw I just couldn't believe, but it was in San Francisco where anything goes. But here is what I saw with my own eyes. I saw a man who appeared to be my age, naked, holding a young girl dressed in a bikini; she might have been six or seven years. The girl-child had her arms around the man's neck, and her feet were straddling between the man—well, on his private parts because he was holding her low enough that his body parts were touching her. There was this woman about my age with them dressed in a full bathing suit. To this apparent family, this was a natural occurrence because the girl said while laughing, "Mommy, look David is getting bigger again." Well the girl knew what was happening to a degree because she didn't say that David was getting taller. She realized enough, that something that was small was now bigger.

Water can be a sensuous thing. My wife and I would know that because we were in the water at the time in our swimwear, but the thought of what must be happening to that little girl was enough to make us both come out of the water. But here is the thing: a lot of men were walking around that part of the beach naked. Interestingly, not more than one or two women were nude. Honestly, my wife and I did not know it was a nude beach. We really didn't know that at first. We unwittingly happened upon there. But I can't help but wonder why would a parent bring a child to a nude beach? I know this, it is not in the best interest of a young girl to have a male parent, biological or not, walk around a young girl in the nude. And if a mother should allow that to happen to her then she should be sent off to the farm because that is child abuse.

Now what I want to say in closing, I love you black women but you must clean up your acts and clean up yourselves and take care of your children and make sure that they are educated properly. And black women, stop thinking that it is okay for grandmothers to do your job of raising your children! These grandmothers are tired and want to enjoy their own lives. The grandmothers asked me to throw that in for them. Thank you for this evening. I am Billy Charles.

I reached for the remote and hit the button to eject the videotape. I would have to find other means to pay back my student loan.

It was mid-autumn, an early breezy Thursday morning in Charlotte, North Carolina. I lay sprawled on the chaise lounge on the veranda. My soft peach pajamas and a light shawl cloaked my innocence as I enjoyed the taste of a feather smoothie. This was my wake-up surge instead of breakfast. I drink cappuccino when in California, but the South is so easygoing that I don't have a desire for it here. I was indulging in thought about the simple and pastoral ways of the South. I loved the spaciousness of the South, too, the freedom to roam. The freedom to roam—now that conjures up a portrait of sheer irony when the landscape of one's ancestral roots was the very place where the machinations of slavers and slavery occurred. A sense of guilt pierced my spirit. Was I enjoying the forbidden fruit of freedom? Doubt insinuated around my being. Did I deserve to feel so free? Was I entitled to the true education that I had received? Shouldn't my bones ache from exhausting hours of self-employment? Shouldn't I feel a sense of embarrassment when informing my husband-to-be, that I, a great-granddaughter of former slaves, now require a housemaid three times a week to seal any proposal deal? I could have a story to tell of hardships growing up, but such a saga would be the most difficult for me to imagine.

I had found a nice little spot to rent a house in Charlotte, the Canterbury Development off Rea Croft Road. Houses in the South were just so much cheaper than property on the West Coast. Neighbors were different, too. They were warm, hospitable and up front. If I stepped out on the back balcony, they were always looking on from somewhere to greet me. If I stepped out to the front porch, even if I pretended not to see, someone would rush to make his or her presence known. I was building my business on solid ground in the South with a fierce, yet loving passion. It was all here in the South, for even Cupid had shown himself and had shot an arrow intended for romance to come my way.

I especially love quaint, downtown Charlotte. The taste of the South was love and that was okay; my sister Maria had taught me how to use the "control" button. Maybe it was time for me to come out of hiding and be honest with myself. Though born and raised in California, it has become a rather unfamiliar place; it is not a place for my spirit to rest and my soul to evolve. I don't know if it is unethical to say out loud but California's diversity seems to be at best Mexico's intent on returning California to Calidia. It appears obvious that African Americans were not a part of Mexicans' merger combo. It was mainly those from Central and South America who counted as allies. No one is necessarily at fault. Blacks don't speak Spanish, and Mexicans refuse to speak English, so it appears, even though Governor Arnold Schwarzenegger has admonished Mexicans, and rightly so, about assimilating into America by learning the ways and customs, including English.

Maybe I was jealous, envious that Mexicans had learned much of their strategy from the black protests of the '60s and '70s, and blacks today aren't able to share that unity among their own race anymore. My visits to California had become fewer in number though I had not completely migrated to the South. Still, being the youngest in the family made leaving Mother an ordeal. I often vacillated between any possible future plans with Zeth and my desire always to live near Mom. If I had to put it into words, Mom is far more important than any decision I would ever have to make.

Recently, when in Charlotte, I received a rather odd telephone call.

"Dr. Navies, please," a formal and polished voice said when I answered.

"This is she speaking," I said.

"This is Mrs. Tracye Williams, president of the organization called AWALA—Alliance for Women of an African Legacy in

America. We are a relatively new group, so I am not quite sure if you have heard of us yet."

This could have been a prank call, but I remained on the telephone. My thoughts often wander in extraordinary ways, which I think is God's way to guide me. Sometimes I don't like to sleep, preferring to stay awake and meditate, go into God's presence, so my identity and soul can better be molded. So, I listened in case there was a message for me.

I'm back from drifting, but hear nothing now.

"Dr. Navies, are you still there?"

"Yes, I am still on the phone." In a crisply pitched tone, I answered, "But-uh, no, I've never heard of your organization."

"Well, then I certainly need to fill you in on who we are."

It sounded as if Mrs. Williams thought that I should be the one privileged to know, even though I had not expressed any interest. She was still talking. I think I had missed something she said.

"...perhaps tomorrow would be best for you. Say at noontime at Ruffles restaurant. I do apologize for such short notice, but I have to leave town tomorrow night to attend an awards ceremony for World Women of Color Mentors, and since I am a board member, it's imperative that I attend."

I had missed something in conversation. "W-Well," I answered tentatively, expecting more information.

"Dr. Navies, I am positive that you will find this meeting to be very beneficial for future steps. I don't make it a habit of wasting time."

"Then tomorrow it is," I agreed, not really knowing to what.

"That sounds fine. And bring a hearty appetite. Everything on the menu is irresistible."

Even with a thorough search on the Internet, I was not able to pull up very much information on the organization AWALA, except that to learn that it is a non-profit organization. I paid nine dollars to an Internet database company called Just So You Know that provided me with information on Mrs. Tracye Williams. She tops the list as a renowned psychiatrist. She wrote a book called *A Journey Towards Healing and Forgiveness*. I wondered why she did not give me that information up front. While on the Net, I also checked out Ruffles.

The next day I selected my clothing carefully, so that I would be dressed properly no matter the daytime occasion. I wore off-white cashmere pants suit complemented by a pair of black and beige Christian Dior shoes, a black shoulder designer purse and my one pair of pink diamond earrings that E.J. had given to me on my twenty-third birthday. I was dressed to represent my public persona.

Ah! Valet parking for women who walked in shoes not made to take more than seven steps on any given day.

The valet gently took my hand while lifting his eyes. "Enjoy your meal, miss."

I nodded my head in thanks.

The front door to the restaurant was of beveled glass with an artistically etched Egyptian design. My hands were free to wave like a queen if ever the occasion would arise.

Only moments inside and everything was in full operation. A polite voice with an accent said, "And you, Miss, must be Dr. Navies." I nodded with a smile. Was I acting like someone other than myself? Perchance I had taken on the mannerisms of my sister Maria. Her role of who and what she is changes with the colors of a kaleidoscope. Was a black woman in the South included in the grace? I mean, of the Southern belle cliché?

"Ah, yes. Follow me, please."

Following the waiter to the table, I saw unfamiliar faces. This must be a restaurant for the well-to-do. At least, they looked the part, as if they did more than I to earn a living. Nowadays though, appearing with less is a part of the culture of the well to-do. I couldn't help but notice the restaurant's exquisite motif of a deep red hue and glows of green and beige. The napkins were color coordinated.

I couldn't but notice I was on time, but Mrs. Williams was already seated at the table. She stood up and we shook hands.

"My, you look absolutely stunning, Zemi. Do you mind if I call you Zemi? Not only is it a unique name, it has a beautiful ring to it."

"Thank you. You look stunning as well. And it's fine to call me Zemi. I am rather fond of the name myself."

"What is the meaning of your name?"

Mrs. Williams looked different from what I had imagined. She had full lips and her lipstick was expertly applied. She wore diamond hoop earrings and a large ring shone from her finger. Her head was wrapped in a multicolored designer scarf, and she wore a low-cut powder blue cashmere sweater and matching cashmere skirt. Her shoes were sleek, black fox-covered, and she carried a matching purse. Over the phone she sounded older than she looks now. She looks to be about thirty-five to forty years of age, and has a waist small enough to make me envious.

The waiter approached our table. "Mrs. Williams, may I get you and your guest something to drink?"

"Zemi, what would you like?"

I wondered whether I should order wine during a business lunch. Quickly, I searched the file within the archives of my brain on etiquette and decorum. Hmmm. At a lunch or dinner, wine in moderation is acceptable. One cocktail before a business meal is fine. Mrs. Williams was here already and had not ordered anything to drink; this probably meant that she does not drink. The other part to the rule is that you should not feel intimidated and not refrain from ordering liquor for yourself just because someone else is not ordering alcoholic beverages. Perrier with lime always works, and ordering it in a wineglass lessens the pressure as it actually looks like a white wine spritzer. Got it!

"I will have a Perrier with lime, please."

"And for me, the white wine spritzer," said Mrs. Williams, as she handed the wine list back to the waiter. "Thank you."

Then from the attic of my mind played full blast the tune, "Sometimes I Feel Like a Nut."

"Actually, my father chose the name Zemi for me."

The waiter brought the drinks and a basket of rolls and breads.

Mrs. Williams was unfolding her napkin. I waited until she unfolded hers, and then I unfolded mine and placed it on my lap with one-third folded over.

Using my butter knife to butter a bite-sized piece of roll, I added, "My dad said Zemi meant one of a mystical journey."

"I could tell the name had great promise," said Mrs. Williams. "It is good to see a parent giving a child a head start with a purpose already assigned. You know black children need tools early in life just to help them get on a path of duty and responsibility. I am not fond of such names like 'Shaniqua' and regret that some parents don't take more pride and thought in naming their children. But, anyway, let's get to the real purpose of our meeting, shall we?"

"Yes, I am curious about your organization, AWALA." I was thinking that Mrs. Williams might ask me to speak to her organization.

The waiter offered Mrs. Williams another spritzer, but she chose a glass of wine instead. Turning to me, he asked, "Would you like me to bring you a glass of wine, as well, miss?"

"No, thank you." One drink might have allowed me to be at ease and quit some of the pretense, though.

"What grabbed you most, Zemi, when you heard the name AWALA?"

"Well, I am not exactly sure," I said frankly. Again, the nut. Should I have anticipated that question? Which others?

The woman (bless her) saved me; she started talking. "As I am sure you would agree, there is an urgent call for a change in the lives of African American women, and when you make change for the women, the mothers, you make better the whole race. So, our purpose, more accurately, is to change and synergize the thinking of black women from Africa, the Caribbean and wherever else we may come from into a workable and lucrative alliance with African American women. Our agenda is formulation of a platform to address our needs and action on a global stage." Mrs. Williams buttered a small piece of her roll. "Would you agree with that, Zemi?"

"I would agree. And I must say it is an awesome mission, indeed," I remarked, beginning to feel acclimated now.

Mrs. Williams continued. "Our organization wanted to be accountable in a manner that would have long-lasting and positive effects. We have thus far decided upon a summit and a documentary," said Mrs. Williams.

"What outcome are you seeking?"

"Well, we like to think that we perfect the idea each time we are asked that question." Mrs. Williams chuckled. "We are a little uncertain of the anticipated outcome or ramifications. Our primary reference and nucleus, though, are African American women; and to encourage our exchange and collaboration with other women of African descent. Further, our intent is to organize women like you and all of the others who were born here in America of ancestors forced over through the slave trade. We want as thoroughly as possible to solidify our base group, African American women, first to the idea that unity and workable relationships with black women in America, no matter their country of birth, make for a powerful group of women who can influence, mainly, political results. This group meets alone. We feel that we African American women are the beginning of this exchange and connection for anything like this to occur simply, and only because we live in a superpower where everything is available."

I nodded, though I was lost as to how I might fit into the scheme of everything she was talking about.

Mrs. Williams dabbed her lips with her napkin. "Zemi, whenever you have questions, please do not hesitate to ask. As I said before, your questions would help to elucidate the agenda. We still are still in the conceptual stage."

"Well, I do have a question at this point. Since the concept, and agenda focus on black women from the Caribbean as well as Africa, why wouldn't these two groups' presence be required at the beginning of building such a foundation if, indeed, the exchange is to be thoroughly understood and accepted?"

Mrs. Williams continued eating her roll while apparently framing her answer. "Great question, Zemi. African American women already feel undeserving. They are yet to shed their skin of slavery. In America we are a people sold into slavery by our own foreparents. No other race can truly write that into the account of their existence here in America. If our ancestors had given us up to live a better life in America than what existed in Africa at the time, then we would have a different story today to write of African Americans." Mrs. Williams placed her napkin on the table and rested her fork on her plate.

I was slow to eat. Mrs. Williams' ideas on African Americans and slavery had my rapt attention and seemed to awaken some feelings of which I had not been aware.

"Let me give you an example of what I mean, Zemi. A wealthy white woman, Madonna, did a very God-like thing when she went to Africa and brought a child back to America to learn and to be afforded the best education and to live a better life. Madonna did not go there and get that child because she needed him to do things for her but, rather, the reverse; she took great measures to go and get that child to make him a part of her family. I am sure there were other ways for her to get media attention, for certainly she is used to that by now. And even Madonna's act might be beyond her own understanding and might be a grander picture to be understood later. The child's permitted to have contact with his family and country and can return to visit. That same child can go back to Africa and help to create a whole nation free of malaria because someone wanted to show this child a better way to live life." Mrs. Williams' voice trembled with emotion as she spoke. Her wine glass was empty.

I thought, perhaps I could comprehend better if I'd had several glasses by now.

The waiter approached our table. "More wine, Mrs. Williams?"

"Yes, I would, thank you. How about you, Zemi?"

"Yes." Since I was not a wine connoisseur, I simply said, "Bring me a glass of your best red wine."

"Ah, what do you like, Zemi, sweet or dry wines?" Mrs. Williams asked.

"I enjoy both."

"Oh, then, would you please bring a bottle of your Duck Horn Merlot and another wineglass? I think I'll share that bottle with her."

Speaking tentatively, I offered, "You know some people criticized Madonna for not simply adopting a child from right here if she really wanted a black child."

"Well, that is neither here nor there," Mrs. Williams sniffled. "For those who think that Madonna should have adopted a black child here in America, those people are free to act on their own recommendation and advice."

I nodded. I gathered from Mrs. Williams' added remarks that she did not want to address the reasons behind Madonna's actions for adopting an African child any further in our conversation. Instead, she expounded on the post-slavery psychology and what she referred to as "the sleepwalking posture that most African Americans seem unable to shake." She appeared to be a woman on a mission focused on the purpose of our meeting.

"Zemi, have you realized that the masses of African Americans have purposely embraced absent-mindedness to deal with the fact that our forefathers sold us into slavery?"

"To be honest with you, Mrs. Williams, I must say that I have never given the matter any thought." I remained poised as I placed a small amount of salad in my mouth.

"And that is probably because the thought is a very hard pill for the soul to absorb, regardless of whether the thought is conscious or unconscious. It is a tormenting hurt and an open wound that lies there."

I was glad not to know such torment. I felt already under pressure, even if in denial as Mrs. Williams might define it.

"And though it has not been spoken out loud for media to grasp," Mrs. Williams said, "forgiveness for the collaborating role Africa played in elevating slavery to the magnitude to which it grew is almost too much for the heart to fathom. I would say, though it has not been verbalized, that forgiveness has not yet taken place within the souls of African Americans. At best is denial, and it is easier fully and completely to blame white people for having taken us into slavery than to admit the transgressors were also those of our ancestors who participated in the delivery," said Mrs. Williams, taking another roll from the basket.

It was almost too much to have to imagine. I no longer had an appetite. I could only drink wine. "You know, Mrs. Williams, the issue could be raised by the many African Americans who have succeeded although they had to overcome horrendous circumstances. Seemingly, we all began with the same historical reference point here in America. There are the shining examples of Ambassador Andrew Young, Colin Powell, Xernona Clayton, Coach Tony Dungy, Mae Jamison, Cathy Hughes, Susan Taylor,

Condoleezza Rice, Oprah Winfrey, Muhammad Ali, US Congressman James E. Clyburn, Russell Simmons, Sheila Johnson, Diana Ross, US Congresswoman Barbara Lee, Bob Johnson, Denzel Washington, Dr. Harry Edwards, Clarence Thomas and the list goes on."

Mrs. Williams set her glass down and looked at me directly. "Yes, but how often can we find other blacks appearing in those respective fields as a matter of course, as a 'natural progression,' as it were? In America, blacks are still today becoming the first this and the first that as if they just fell from another planet a decade or so ago, and here we are in the twenty-first century. How long did the position as Secretary of State exist in the two parties before Colin Powell and Condoleezza Rice successfully filled those posts? And though the Congressional Black Caucus has been in existence for several years, still the organization is without any viable strategies that could usher in more than one black senator at a time."

This is an awful lot to have to contemplate.

"The organization's output as a machine getting blacks in elected posts is minuscule, so to hold a perception that the organization could carry any real weight for a black presidential candidate is just asinine. No vice president yet, and only one senator. Why, that is shameful! Are we afraid to ask the question why blacks allowed themselves to stay in a stupor and wait for someone else to do roll call? But if one looks a little closer, even those few garbed in some measure of success still bear subtle marks of slavery of which, I might add, even they might be unaware. But, to be fair, the subject on the table is not about the progress of a small number of African Americans. We are talking about a path for healing the lingering and residual after effects of slavery," said Mrs. Williams.

"I am just fascinated by your views," I said.

"Why do we tend to think that only one black person in a field can shine at a time when God has shown that he needs billions of stars to shine at the same time? And thus God allows for so many babies to be born all at the same second. The people you mentioned, Zemi, have done extremely well and their contributions noted, but they are not enough to fill the prescription of what ails the rest of an overly and needlessly docile people," said Mrs. Williams.

For a moment, nothing was said, then after some consideration, I faced Mrs. Williams and said, flatly, "Maybe we need to let go of something that we are holding on to, but we might not have any idea of the garbage that's still in the bag," I said.

This subject matter was unquestionably Mrs. Williams' passion. I was not confident enough to say some things because this healing process was not my field of study. According to Mrs. Williams, this period seemed ripe for African Americans to release a ton of old negative feelings. I had never thought about it, unless subconsciously, but perhaps we do need to release the blockage so that forgiveness can take its course. I do realize the feelings and energies that blacks in America held during and after slavery have not left us, but have merely channeled themselves through negative and pathological expression. Although the main concern is our healing and not so much how we look to others, our people and the whole world witness how the same pathology is made manifest even today.

The waiter removed a plate, then poured more wine into the glasses.

"Thank you," said Mrs. Williams.

Ah, I had partaken of enough food, but even more food for thought.

I noticed that Mrs. Williams was a slow eater, but a fast drinker. Still, she held forth, saying, "Blacks must be able to see the lightness against the dark. Just as we cannot wait for white America to solve the social, political and economic conditions of African Americans, the same can be said for solving the lingering effects of slavery. Though Freud was thought to be the 'the father of psychoanalysis' by some, he cannot be the solution because Freud thought ill of blacks anyway. The priest cannot help the cure because when slavery was in full force, he could not find words to speak out and condemn slavery in God's book."

Mrs. Williams stood up and left the table rather abruptly, saying, "Excuse me, please, Zemi."

Apparently, Mrs. Williams saw someone that she knew. I was glad she had left the table for a moment because I needed time to process. I had questions. Why did she choose the South to initiate her program? And how would the healing take place? So many questions and thoughts to unravel could become overwhelming even for me, and I consider myself well balanced. In fact, I think I am straight-up okay.

Mrs. Williams indicated that the poison of everything that surrounded slavery won't leave our systems, but lies in the pit of our stomachs, and that it is best we take measures to find an anecdote, take steps toward a societal cure that uplifts us in the history of America, and in so doing lift America. I began to analyze the reasons those from the Caribbean and Africa could not yet join the African Americans at the table. I guess we must clear our own debris from our temple first. Probably 1001 different types of psychologists and psychiatrists would be needed on the journey towards forgiveness, a first step in the healing process. Perhaps now the alarm would sound for a "National State of Emergency Summit for Change of Black Women's Status in America." But are our women in denial about their state of affairs? Or are they so implacable, so hard to move that change would be impossible?

Would the healing journey be as necessary or difficult for those who were stolen and taken to the Caribbean during the slave trade but over the years have migrated to the United States and have gone through the process to gain legal citizenship in America? Maybe they do not harbor bad feelings issued about the collaboration of Africans in the slavery business. I do believe, though, that some people from the Caribbean harbor some envy against African Americans. And what would the course of action be for those who are from the Motherland and also have legal status here in America? Why would they need a path for healing? Could it be that they resent African Americans living in a superpower while so many people in African nations struggle beyond belief?

What do we women, African American women, share in common with women from Africa? It is not necessarily the case that we do not like one another, but we do not tend to interact with one another when Africans immigrate to America. When I was in Africa, I was so excited about meeting the women there, while they were as eager to meet me. How would we begin to know their talents so as to begin pooling talent? Did Mrs. Williams consider that maybe the mindset of women from Africa, though they are citizens within

America, may be too different from that of African American women? It might take more time than African American women are willing to give.

What would be the benefit of African American women pooling their talents with women from the Caribbean and Africa? The people from Liberia want dual citizenship in America, but how does that help African Americans that are already here? If I as an African American could have dual citizenship in Liberia, would I take it? The women who have come over from Africa do not seem to assimilate all that much. They want the toys that we African Americans possess but without much understanding of our struggles and history here in America. I can easily tell people who are from Africa even before they open their mouths. Sometimes I guess that people who are from Nigeria will be quick to say that they are from somewhere other than Nigeria. America says that it is very hard to trust the people from Nigeria. Once at the airport in New York, at an international terminal, there was a sign posted that read "If you travel to Nigeria, you do so at your own risk. The United States will not be responsible." What will be the trust level existing among us in order to pool talents? Perhaps women from the Caribbean and Africa would want to join forces with African American women, but the African American women will be more stubborn to gather. Has Mrs. Williams taken these things into consideration?

Mrs. Williams returned to the table with two gentlemen. "Zemi, this is Mr. C. Douglass, who works with the World Bank, and Dr. Lucien from Cote d'Ivoire."

Dr. Lucien smiled broadly, showcasing his perfect white teeth. Seeming a bit embarrassed, Dr. Lucien shook his head and remarked with a French accent, "Mrs. Williams likes all of these fancy titles. I am not bothered by such formalities. So you can just call me Christoph. I like the sound of my first name, Christoph, over Dr. Lucien."

"All right, Christoph," Mrs. Williams said with a smile, "you never gave me that permission before. But, Zemi, I do want you to know that Christoph is doing some extensive land development here in Charlotte. I have explained to both Christoph and Mr.

Douglass the need for our organization to receive funding and aid in hopes that they will be of some financial assistance."

I extended my hand, first to Christoph and then to Mr. Douglass. "It is a pleasure to meet you both."

"Will you two be joining our table?" Mrs. Williams asked, motioning to the two empty chairs.

"I don't think so," said Mr. Douglass, setting his briefcase on one of the chairs. "In fact, we were on our way out of the restaurant when you came and grabbed us. Mr. Douglass pushed his glasses up and then looked down at me. "Mrs. Williams insisted that we come over to meet you and I must say, I am glad that we did."

I tilted my head and smiled.

"Mrs. Williams tells us here that you're very excited about the organization and the potential it has," said Mr. Douglass.

I have been fumbling and asking a thousand questions just to find out about the organization, so I wonder why Mrs. Williams told them about any excitement on my part. Nonetheless, I nodded and smiled to give them the assurance that I was keenly interested.

"Do you mind if I sit?" asked Mr. Douglass, lifting his briefcase out of the chair. He had apparently changed his mind about joining us, to my chagrin. I was not sure I was prepared. Prepared for what?

"Please," Mrs. Williams told him.

I moved my purse from the other chair so that Christoph could be seated there.

As the waiter passed by, Christoph caught his attention and ordered more wine before he sat down.

"Zemi, your name is unique and, moreover, the sound of it is beautiful," said Mr. Douglass.

"Thank you," I answered.

"So, Zemi," said Mr. Douglass, as he leaned his arms on the table, "what is your role with the organization?"

I had no clue as to what Mrs. Williams thought my role to be. I didn't even know if I wanted any role in all of this. I wanted to say out loud that I didn't even understand that much of what Mrs. Williams had been talking about. "Well," I said, clearing my throat, "that was one of the reasons for our meeting today. There are a lot of things on the table, but, in general, the discussion today is about what I might be able to offer to the organization in terms of time and tasks." I shied away from articulating specifics because I really did not think I had very much to offer, and I was still in the process of comprehending.

"What are your thoughts on the idea of African women from the Diaspora uniting efforts with African American women here in the South?" asked Christoph.

It became clear as crystal that Mrs. Williams was allowing me to audition for the role as a one-woman's show, for queen of witticism, or perhaps through Christoph was throwing me enough rope to hang myself? I turned and faced Christoph. "An awesome idea, whose time has come," I said sipping from my glass. I was trying to muster up some calm in the face of these impromptu questions, coming at me like a bat out of hell. I surprised myself when I answered, "In fact, I think we in the South, more specifically in Charlotte, should begin to encourage Liberia to become our sister country for launching such a bold call-out. I think that would work well since Liberia does seek dual citizenship from America."

"I think that you make a great point," said Christoph, adjusting his napkin. "Also, more African countries would see the benefit for women of African ancestry pooling talents in order to make connections for global trade among us. The rules of fair trade would cut down on a lot of the civil war going on in Africa and make for more secure trade between America and Africa. The population of Africa is at 700 million people. It seems to me that the United States should explore and encourage a strong-end, balanced initiative that could greatly urge African Americans to help make Africa the next frontier for real trade."

"Yes," I agreed (and growing more confident, too). "I definitely see your point, Christoph. African American dollars are almost at $845 billion here in the United States. Blacks spend over $2 billon dollars a day while only about 13% of the population. Furthermore, we could be looked upon by the Africans in kinship as opposed to being perceived as some others who are garbed differently," I said.

"Oh, Zemi, I agree. I agree with you so much," said Christoph. "Many see Africa as the continent of depression and gloom, yet it is most rich in oil, gas, diamonds, coal, and copper, as well as platinum and uranium and cocoa, coffee and rubber. We have much land and the list goes on. It is time to deal fairly with Africa. With women making the connection, this could be a great softening situation to create better scenarios for global business exchange among Africans and African Americans. Maybe America could use her blacks to help bring about restoration in so many ways also."

"Yes, perhaps," Mrs. Williams remarked tersely, "but a lot more thought needs to go into the philosophy and theory, trying to weigh full scale."

Was she checking Christoph for some reasons? Christoph seemed confused by her tone. But then I got it. He must not have realized that his stare at me was too intense. But then again, I don't think he cared too much about what the rest of us at the table thought. You would have thought that I was the first African American woman that he had ever seen. I was now intent on showing these men that I was more than just a beautiful, young black face. Most times men could not see the gift for vision skewed by testosterone.

Mr. Douglass poured more wine into Mrs. Williams' glass, then made an effort to pour wine into Christoph's glass, but Christoph put his palm over his glass.

"Perhaps it has become necessary to propose this organization as the pilot initiative, launching it as the explorative committee, indeed, to make such a thing happen for Africans and those from the United States," I said.

"I think that Bill Clinton's organization, The Clinton Foundation, has been working vigorously to help move Africa more towards the front of progress," said Christoph. "He does a lot of great work in Africa. Maybe that would be a good place for your organization to get things moving in the right direction—and swiftly, I might add."

"Yeah, that's a good starting point, but you don't have to get stuck there. There are a lot of windows opened for such a project," replied Mr. Douglass. He seemed by chance to touch my elbow. "Excuse me."

"Watch yourself over there now, Douglass. Don't inconvenience Zemi so much," said Christoph, smiling.

My head was spinning like a yo-yo as I tried to handle the innu-endo. I turned and acknowledged the apology.

"Well, Zemi," said Christoph, standing and reaching into his pocket, "here is my card, please contact me when you have made further steps with the organization, and if you need my help. Oh, yes, I put my cell on the back, and that number rings even if I am in Africa…but of no charge to you."

"Thank you," I said, "for the offer to assist."

"Do you have an e-mail address where I can contact you?" asked Christoph. He pushed his chair up under the table.

"Yes, I do have an e-mail address, but I'm sorry, I changed purses and forgot to put cards in this one." I held up my purse. "But when-ever you talk to Mrs. Williams again, you may get my e-mail address from her. She has it."

"If you don't mind, Zemi, er, would you, er, could you just write it down for me?" Christoph asked.

"Sure." I reached into my purse and took out a piece of paper and a pen. "Here you go." I wrote down my email address and gave the piece of paper to Christoph with my name and e-mail address only. I remembered that my sister Maria said to never give a man more than one contact number.

"Thank you very much. If I don't hear from you very soon, then I will be in contact with you," he said, accepting the piece of paper.

"Well," said Mr. Douglass with a smirk, "Christoph did not leave a door open for anybody else to come through, so I guess it will suf-fice for me to say that it was nice meeting you, Zemi."

I responded, "Likewise, Mr. Douglass," making every attempt to ignore the balance of his comment. When I realized my mouth was hanging wide open, I pressed my lips together. Was the African guy pushy or what? Obviously, he has not been in the states very long. Otherwise, he would have known the difference when approach-ing an African American. He was territorial, too. Maybe that is why African American women do not date men from Africa all that much. Then, too, the men do not have much in the way of finances when they come to America. I heard once that the dating habits of African men lack romance. I think we women have given those men such thumbs down that they don't bother to ask African American women out on dates too often. Maybe it is just too hard to date foreign men, especially if they are as forward as Christoph.

Whatever the reason Mrs. Williams had called this meeting, I was sure that she felt me capable to handle the job. She brought the men to the table for me to sell her program and agenda. Then I began to wonder whether Mrs. Williams knew that Christoph and Mr. Douglass would be having lunch here at Ruffles.

"That was a knockout!" Mrs. Williams spoke, holding both hands under her chin, her eyes glowing with satisfaction. "That was a wonderful pop-up meeting we just had with the gentlemen. Both of them can be of great assistance to the efforts of our programs. I was motivated by their show of interest by asking so many questions."

"Yes. They both showed great interest and enthusiasm in your program," I agreed and disagreed at the same time. I could not believe that Mrs. Williams thought it a small favor that my lunch date with her had just turned into a three-hour promo of explaining her AWALA program to two strangers that she just forced upon me. Mrs. Williams should have known that I was not prepared to speak so much on her program. I wanted to tell her off, but I put off the thought. It then came to me that this was a very well-known, influential woman who had just introduced her contacts to me, even with no guarantee that I would be working with her program.

"Incidentally, Zemi, I found your ability to interact without preparation remarkable and your witticism well received," she said.

Okay, maybe I jumped the gun. She's okay. I smiled. "Then I guess you did a better job of preparing me than anticipated," I said as I pushed my plate away. "But I think it's all due to the idea being such a timely one."

"What do you mean by it being timely?" asked Mrs. Williams as she held her hand up to signal for our waiter.

I could tell that Mrs. Williams was still trying to draw me in for whatever role she had in mind for me. "Well, I think that African Americans would carry more weight in this country as well in parts of Africa, if we could finally come together as one group of people—just as the Hispanics are increasing their numbers with immigrants from Mexico and Central America, making their voting power recognized."

"Uh-huh." Mrs. Williams' response was not easy to interpret at that moment.

I elaborated on my point. "I think that the African Americans should make it a priority to connect themselves to the Africans from the continent, as well to Caribbean Americans, for more political empowerment."

"Not just in the respect on voting alone," said Mrs. Williams. "There is no doubt that Africa is crucial to the whole of American society. She has everything in her womb to help ensure America stays in her superpower status. We need to emphasize the fact that America began her role to superpowerdom with the first "product" from Africa—Africa exported her natives as cargo and trade. America used the trade and willed it a trade of slavery. But now we must take that history and move into the twenty-first century for the well-being of both Africans and African Americans."

"Mrs. Williams, perhaps it is not so plain and simple. Maybe America does need Africa, but African nations cannot afford to continue having civil wars. Many African nations need to be cleaned up, industrialized, perfect the use of technology to radically improve the well-being of their citizens and create growth in the areas of real estate development and tourism," I said.

"I couldn't have said it any better, Zemi."

"I add that whichever country helps African nations to accomplish a task so monumental will be the country in the best position to be the superpower of tomorrow." And I expressed my ambivalence about an issue. "I just don't see America being able to hold on long to her status of superpower without working in co-operation for a more harmonious relationship with African nations and African Americans."

"Why do you say that, Zemi?"

"Africa has been idle far too long in terms of its role in a highly industrialized world. She has been sitting as the world's next expansion for centuries. America holds a key to fixing Africa's broken heart."

"Oh, really, Zemi? What is it then?"

"It is the souls of the African Americans. Why not use the hearts and skills of those who once belonged to Africa to recover sunken treasures and to keep other countries from taking over completely and ravaging the assets of the continent before it is too late?"

Mrs. Williams nodded her head in approval. "I believe that no country has really found a way to bring calm in Africa because she has been raped over time with impunity. Because there have been no repercussions, many countries want to continue to benefit from the status quo instead of dealing fairly with Africa. For example, many still employ unfair trading practices. Different countries bargain so that only a few of Africa's people can profit from God's inheritance bestowed upon Africa's ground for the many. That is why there is civil war," said Mrs. Williams.

I agreed. "It should no longer be business as usual for Africa, for it must help to bring its people closer to world knowledge and understanding," I said.

The waiter Mrs. Williams summoned was finally heading towards our table.

Mrs. Williams told me, "I am glad to see such enthusiasm, but you haven't touched much of your food, my dear."

"I am sorry it took me a moment longer to get over here," the waiter said. "And how may I help you?"

Mrs. Williams gestured towards my plate. "Let's see if we can order her something else since she has not touched much of that food."

"Oh, no!" I protested, not wanting the fuss over me. "The food was good. I just got caught up in the moment, that's all."

"Well, at least have him to take your plate and warm it again. Would you take her plate and heat it, please? I am afraid that I have been talking a little bit too much for her to digest properly."

"No problem, Mrs. Williams, I will be glad to do that for you." He took a napkin off of his arm to cover the plate and took it away. "I'll be back in a few moments."

I was not aware of the full agenda, but felt that I wanted to be a part of something of this magnitude and caliber. "Exactly what is it that you want from me, Mrs. Williams?"

"Well," said Mrs. Williams, "the story of your role has somewhat of a twist to it, but I am going to give you the story straight from the beginning in the event you hear otherwise later. I believe in putting things right out front so that all the cards are on the table."

I felt there was a curve, but did not have a clue as to what it might be.

"Well, Zemi, our organization had already selected a chairperson to try to bring all of what we have been talking about together. Our platform could be presented maybe first, through a summit, then a documentary. The person we had selected was well known and very well respected. Her credentials stood out exceptionally as a board member of the national AKA sorority, a financial planning executive and a former news anchorwoman. So, you see, Zemi, this person has been known on the circuit for implementing programs and plans of this magnitude," said Mrs. Williams.

Though I did not want to suggest that my credentials paled in comparison and still uncertain of Mrs. Williams' request, I said humbly, "That is some résumé to match."

"Well, herein lies the problem, Zemi. The person is a staunch Democrat as are the views of the television station where she was employed, and such ties with us could create a conflict for her she feels. Of course, there is a little bit more to it. Anyway, we made a verbal agreement and set about writing up the contract. Before our organization had a chance to present her with the contract in writing, the person backed out. Some say she backed out because she did not want friction with the issues and direction of her political party as it related to blacks. Others have the story that she has just signed a five-year radio mega-deal."

"That's not too shabby," I commented. "But I don't understand. Why would being Democrat or Republican create a conflict?"

"Because our political affiliation is Independent," said Mrs. Williams.

"Oh. I see."

"Well, that will be more for discussion for another time," said Mrs. Williams. "In any case, Zemi, I hope this was not too much to digest."

The waiter returned with my meal warmed. "Here is your entrée, miss. Is there anything else I can get for you?"

"No. no," said Mrs. Williams. "Thank you."

"I assure you, Mrs. Williams, that I've not missed a beat." I picked up my fork and began eating. Though I had not missed the gist of the conversation, I could not for the life of me figure out why Mrs. Williams kept saying "the person" and would not disclose a name.

Mrs. Williams motioned her head towards the ladies' room.

She got up and placed her napkin in the chair. "Excuse me, please."

While Mrs. Williams was gone, I finished my meal and pushed my plate away.

Mrs. Williams returned, followed by the waiter carrying a tray of desserts.

"Oh, good, you've finished eating. And I am just in time for the dessert tray. Give me the strawberry cheesecake," said Mrs. Williams.

"I'll take that slice," I said.

"Hmmm. This cheesecake is worth the extra pounds," Mrs. Williams remarked.

"With a waist like that, it doesn't look as if you have much to worry about."

"I hope that is the case," said Mrs. Williams, licking some frosting off a finger. In that instant, her persona of class and sophistication had vanished. Boy, sweets can certainly change one's behavior.

"Umm, umm." Mrs. Williams wiped her fingers on her napkin. "To stay above board, Zemi, I just wanted to tell you everything about the summit incident, so nothing comes back to you the wrong way."

If Mrs. Williams really wanted to be so honest, she'd give me a name association. I certainly would be able to follow along better.

"One reason the person gave for not being able to take on such a monumental task was that she has another project scheduled for approximately the same time as our summit date was proposed. And handling both projects would cause too much of a conflict in scheduling. She didn't feel she could give one hundred percent to both. She did, however, apologize for not being able to take on our organization at the time, but wished us success in finding the right person for the job," said Mrs. Williams.

"I see."

"By now, Zemi, you have probably figured out that my organization is on the hunt for someone else who has the wherewithal and everything it takes to make this summit happen—and on a grand scale. Naturally, having to start from scratch again in recruiting has thrown us behind. Zemi, I do not believe in beating around the bush, so right here and now, our organization believes that you are that person. Can you do the job? Or do you perhaps feel that you need more time to think about your answer? And that would be understandable."

I was shocked to traumatized and didn't think I could garner the aplomb to respond in the way that an impeccably-credentialed candidate would.

Mrs. Williams did not remove her stare from me. She was reading my reaction.

"I must be honest with you, Mrs. Williams," I said, trying to speak in a calm voice though my pulse was in overdrive. "I had no idea that was what this meeting was all about. At best, I thought you would ask me to speak on a panel or something. I didn't expect this."

"Hm-m," was Mrs. Williams only response.

Momentarily, neither of us said a thing; she was waiting on me I could tell. I was just shocked that Mrs. Williams thought that I was capable enough to replace the other person chosen! Needless to say, this would be the biggest challenge of my life! But I just don't know if I am the one. I had not totally moved to the South yet and that would probably be a major first step in order to make a project of this magnitude take off.

"Well, Mrs. Williams, the thought of the challenge is overwhelming, and then the act of trying to make it happen the way you want it to happen...I just don't know."

Mrs. Williams smiled, the stare gone. "Ah, but here is the idea of it all. The organization wants you to make things happen or plan things through your vision of what AWALA in the South would be all about. And know that through every step, the organization is here for you in every capacity," said Mrs. Williams.

"But don't you think a Southern woman, a black woman who had real roots in the South would be a better candidate for the job?"

"Why, we were under the impression that you had moved here already."

"Not fully."

"Anyway, Zemi, all of the women involved would not necessarily be from the South but from elsewhere around the country. The point is that the South has the land, lots of it, to create a base of operations for an agenda of this magnitude. This is why Christoph was developing here in Charlotte to house women from his country to learn skills and trades in America for use in their own country. The areas of expertise extend from child care to health care, familyhood to technology—tourism, filming and just about everything you can name. Just think how much faster that could happen if an organization such as ours factored in," said Mrs. Williams. The more excited she grew, the faster she talked.

"I can see that," I said.

"Zemi, you will have pretty much the freedom you need in this project to make things happen. Well, naturally, there will be some specified areas that must be on the agenda, but we don't want to give that bit out until you are ready to sign a contract."

I felt a sudden chill, and my hands felt a little damp. "I haven't entirely moved to the South yet, and I would need the time and opportunity to put personal matters in order, and that must be attended to. I'm not sure how long that will take to get done."

"Do you have any family here in Charlotte, Zemi? What made you come to the South in the first place?" Mrs. Williams pushed her chair back and handed the signed check to the waiter. "Here you go, sir, and thank you."

We stood and moved toward the exit to the restaurant. "I got kind of used to southern life while attending Tuskegee University. But, uh, no. I do not have any family here in Charlotte."

"Hmm. That is something you'll have to get used to, dear. Why, everybody and their mamas will latch on to you, and you'll become someone's cousin, sister or even Auntie Zemi."

We laughed.

Outside, the valet pulled Mrs. Williams' Jaguar up to the curb. "Here are your keys, ma'am." "And your car is gonna be coming up in a minute, miss," the valet said to me.

Mrs. Williams gave me a hug. Everybody seems to want to hug you in the South. They don't do that as often on the West Coast.

"Would you be a dear and get me that binder out of the trunk of my car, young man?" She handed the valet a folded bill.

"Thank you, ma'am."

The valet retrieved the binder and gave it to Mrs. Williams.

"Zemi, here is the contract." Mrs. Williams handed me a folder. "Most of what you need to know about, well, everything is attached to the contract, but if you have any questions please feel free to call me. Please review and sign it and have it in my office no later than next Wednesday, close of business, should you decide to accept the position."

I thanked her, we said our good byes and she drove away.

Alone now in my car, my mind was rushing through new and virgin ground. I was not at all sure how to measure my abilities against the job Mrs. Williams had proposed, had handed to me. Still somehow I felt a thunderous calling, I felt that this was something in which I wanted to be involved. Driving home, questions were popping up left and right. Could this be the opportunity to catapult my career? Was this destiny? Did I have the passion it took to succeed in such an endeavor? Would I be the successful replacement for the other person? Afterwards, would I be able to go shopping without looking for sales racks? That question alone might be the deciding factor.

While I had fast forwarded to wealth, means and non-outlet shopping, something nagged at me. I thought about it, and then I knew. I knew what was bothering me. In all that time and with every opportunity, I had asked Mrs. Williams just about every question except perhaps the most important one: "Why me?"

* * * * *

I called Zeth and talked over the conversation that I had with Mrs. Williams in its entirety.

"...and, Zeth, we are both Ph.D.'s, yet she wanted to call me Zemi, but not once did she say I should call her by her first name. Plus, I don't know. I just don't know how to do all that she wants and everybody else wants done. B-but..." I seemed to have waited far too long to exhale.

Zeth said, "Hold on a moment, Puddin'. You might not want excitement to be your very first step in this thin' if you plan to see it all the way through. Take a deep breath."

I breathed deeply.

"That's good. Now I want you to do that again fer me."

Again, I sighed.

"That's my girl. Now the first thin' you want to do is allow yourself some time to think this situation through. Know fer yourself whether or not you want to do the project and if you have what it's really goin' to take to make it happen. And you need to be fer certain if this is the right time in America fer all of this. You know, Puddin', you can't count on all of those book analyses to do your job; you've got to feel the passion, that's if it's goin' to be your passion. You might need to show it on the outside so people can see it workin'. They need to see it in everythin' that you do." said Zeth.

"For certain, I did not expect this to be the direction while I was in school."

"Puddin', you've got book knowledge, but you need to put those books up on the shelves and start the stirrin' from the middle to create the right mix."

For moments, we both were quiet.

"Zeth, I have some doubts, but overall I think that I can do the job."

"Nah, Puddin', that ain't good enough for a job so big. You are talkin' about plannin' for a hundred thousand people. You know, Zemi, this job ain't like flyin' in somewhere to a hotel, and you get to make your speech and then leave. This is wide-screen, Puddin'. But since you didn't ask me, I'll tell you anyway. I believe in you, girl. May be, this is the right position fer you at this moment in your life. I ain't one into all of that callin' stuff same as preachers, but on this, if you hear the rin', then I will answer it with you. I will face everythin' with you, Zemi. I will never turn my back on you."

"And how will you know if I have your back, Zeth?"

"Could be, it ain't my *back* that you'd be needin'."

Again, silence.

Zeth was the first to speak. "I didn't lose you did I, Puddin'?"

"No, Zeth. My mind was still on whether I could take on such heady matters."

"Then look at the thin' this way, Puddin'. Black folk ain't all the way sleepin'. We know a change has got to come from somewhere fer our folk in order fer us to become connected and more globally related to the rest of the world. America has portrayed her blacks as the most disgraced of blacks around the world, as well, tried to show them as thin-sheeted in morals, too. A change is due."

"Is that white people's fault or black folks' ways and habits?" I asked.

"Well, Puddin', it depends on who black folk see as bein' in charge of them. If black folk feel white folk are in charge of what they do and how they act, if they still see whites as ownin' them, then it would most definitely be the whites' fault. But now, if blacks see themselves in charge of their own destiny, with the freedom God bestowed upon them, well then, guess you would have to say that it was the black folk who made the image that's stickin' around the globe," Zeth answered.

"And what about white people? How do they fit into what is happening to black people?" I asked. "I mean, I know they fit in somewhere with all of what is going on."

"Well, Puddin', white folk are some smart people. They are the social scientists of our folks' ways and habits."

"Then they are the cause," I said.

"Nope, black folk just allow themselves to always be the victims. Our folk have even reached down in their little baloney baggies and labeled themselves as victims of Jews, Arabs and Koreans when it was black people who just allowed them to move in and set up business shops in black neighborhoods."

"So Zeth, you are telling me that you do not feel whites played a role in that situation?"

"Nope, at least they didn't play the biggest role," Zeth said in his slow tongue. "Blacks had the biggest role because they wrote the script fer themselves to play the roles of victims."

"How did blacks play their roles as victims?"

Zeth answered, "By simply sittin' on their asses, watchin' differ-ent groups, immigrants after immigrants, come in and settle in on their turf. Men, blacks took a back seat and acted like guests in their own backyards."

"Then how do you account for the government having made loans more available to Jews, Koreans and immigrants and also given tax cuts as incentives?" I asked.

"Then if the government did thin's fer some groups and not fer blacks, the NAACP should have been brought in fer questionin'," said Zeth.

"It seem as though you have given whites a pass on responsibil-ity."

"Naw, that's just not the case, Puddin'. Whites just know blacks better than them knowin' themselves. Black folk have stayed consis-tently consistent—behind. The only really noticeable change about them since the '60s and '70s is what they call themselves."

"Zeth, you might want to back up just a bit on some of the things you are talking about in your exposé."

"Okay, Puddin', I'll make it simple enough that even a cave man can understand. Our folk have yet to grasp a definition of the term African American and the why and how it all came about. Black folk are confused with the short span from slavery up to the twenty-first century with so many re-brands of the name used to define them —as if they were a soft drink participatin' in a marketin' test."

Zeth was quiet. I realized that I had not made the source of what nagged me part of our conversation, the "Why me?" question.

"You followin' me, Puddin'?" he asked.

"I suppose, just explain your meaning of re-brands."

"Well, here is the story, Puddin'. First we came into this country knowin' ourselves as Africans, quickly we wore the names as slave, Negress, Colored, Negro, black, Afro-American and now African American. To tell the truth, I prefer to just be called an American my-self."

"You must take into account, Zeth, that what has happened to blacks has never come upon any other race in America."

"There is no way that fact can be argued, but the fact existin' does not hold itself a balance against the endless, and I mean endless excuses some of our folk give fer not accomplishin' all we could with our given talents."

"I guess you have a point there."

"But the way I see it, Puddin', white folk are goin' to need our folk to step up to the plate and help hold this country together. This ain't no time fer our folk, black leaders and black wanna-be-Hollywood leaders, to think they need to help other foreign leaders come in and downplay America. Now, we might talk about this country in a bad way as citizens, but nobody else got a right to come in our home and talk ill of our leaders and country as if the citizens themselves can't make a change. That's why they call it a democracy; the people vote the way they want leaders to think and act, and when leaders don't perform the way the citizens expect, the people in turn vote them out—just like what happened in the midterm elections in 2006."

"The people at the polls definitely made a statement," I remarked.

"When you have foreigners who can come into your own country, checkin' to see if you are conductin' votin' fairness, now that is a problem fer me. And when a foreigner can come into New York to talk about your leaders the way Chavez and others did, well, to me they are really downin' the ability of the citizens in this country. Chavez and his folk need to clean up their own country first. His country makes up one of the eleven exportin' countries with OPEC, and their people are poor as hell. Those Hollywood actors that want to stand with those kind of leaders against ours, then I say go and make yourself at home in their country, if you are feelin' like a guest in your own country. But no other leader need to dictate what America should be doin'. If America is a superpower, then it ought to act like one."

"My goodness, Zeth, you sound like the preachers in the pulpits." I'd settled myself against a pile of couch cushions and kicked off my shoes. This was turning into quite a long conversation.

"That's the way I see it, Zemi. I'm a country boy. My name ain't Nat Turner, but I still don't believe in backin' down neither. I also don't believe leaders, black or white, should go and make life so right for a foreign people before they have first settled their affairs properly at home. It ain't right. Republicans and Democrats ought to make those folk who were sittin' on top of the roof durin' Hurricane Katrina have a roof placed over-top of them by now."

"Zeth, you know that I am not a pessimist, and it is shameful to say, but I do not believe the Republicans or Democrats will do any more for the Katrina victims than what has been done already. America is too preoccupied with foreign affairs. And cleaning up Katrina and getting those people to receive psychological repair is a domestic affair and domestic affairs no longer seems to be among our national priorities."

I could tell in Zeth's voice that he felt much compassion for the Katrina victims. He had donated one hundred acres towards rebuilding, using each family's own sweat, taking his first step as part of working with the SHOP, the Self-Help Homeownership Opportunity Program.

Zeth said, "I have to agree with Julian Bond's remark that New Orleans' heavily black Lower Ninth Ward, destroyed by Hurricane Katrina, will probably never be rebuilt because the work of generations was wiped out in a single day and left black landholders homeless."

"In years to come, more likely that will stand as a true statement," I said.

Zeth took a very long pause before he spoke, "A bill ought to be put into law that permits U.S. citizens the right to be placed in jobs first, just like there are bills that guarantee housing for immigrants."

"I feel the same way," I agreed. "In many countries, Americans cannot just go there and work. The companies have to clear it with the government and then run ads in the papers stating their intent to hire a foreigner, and they have to show that the talent sought is not available in their own country."

"I believe former President Gerald Ford summed it up best when he said, 'And I just don't think we should go hellfire damnation around the globe freein' people, unless it is directly related to our own national security.'" Zeth added, "That ain't right, the way government has responded."

"Let me go and find a tape recorder to rewind the moment here," I said. "I am going to need your speech for future reference."

"Ah, girl, don't you ferget I know who you are. You already got this stuff down pat, but that ought to let you know, Puddin', you had me captivated and all caught up with what you delivered, and so will all the rest of the folk. The pains and sufferin's that our great-great grandmas and -grandpas endured were too great, but make no mistake, it was to make sure the situation be settled properly fer their own first. No folk had more of a vested interest in this country the way blacks and whites have had. It just ain't right fer our folk to settle in a low and helpless way, backin' other folks' agendas, before somethin' is in place for their own. I tell ya, I ain't feelin' too good about some of those leaders, black or white."

"I don't know why our folk should have to be and act so helpless, not when they have a Constitution in place, and they have voting powers. Only if they would negotiate as if their votes count, and we know that they do!" I agreed.

"I don't mean to give you a lecture, Puddin', but one thin' this country boy knows about is the South because my folk turned the soil over in the South more times than a tractor will ever be able to take credit. If you look at thin's after Hurricane Katrina, you almost have a *deja vu* of what happened to blacks after the Civil War, beginnin' in 1859 and the Reconstruction era of 1865 to 1877. You know the plot is different, a-and…."

"Sorry to cut you off, Zeth. Actually, the time period of the American Civil War was 1861-65."

"So, I ain't no history buff either, and my dates might be scattered, but I am willin' to make it up to you if ever I cheated you out of any time."

"With that said, you just earned yourself one year, man! But I will let you know when you have earned full count. And it won't be as easy as the one year you just earned either."

"Girl, don't hurt me now. You ain't said nothin' but a word. I want to do whatever is in my power to get your full attention. You, Puddin', you make me want to do that, too."

An awkward energy intruded; it seemed neither of us knew what the next scene would, should or could be.

"The main point is that you could be the one to help jump-start the ball rollin' in the right direction with AWALA to brin' in a new attitude about the South fer African Americans—before they let it totally slip away to foreign groups. All of these foreigners are comin' to the South and takin' the dessert without their labor included in what you see standin' today. My folk worked too hard in the South to just give it up like we have not earned the soil here. That's where black folk went wrong. They had fought fer and won their places in the South, but they ran and gave it all away fer the bright lights in big cities like New York, Chicago and Detroit. My people stayed. That's why my own folks' land is still standin' today with the same last name on the deed as that of my parents and great-grandparents— because I stayed, too, and continued to work the foundation they fought fer and built upon."

"That is truly commendable, Zeth."

"Well, thanks fer the compliment, but I just want you to know that I am not so much into pride and getting puffed up as ownin' where I lay my head and where I work, too."

"Zeth, please accept a compliment from me. I know that you do not have an overly huge head. I must tell you, though, you really make the South sound like fertile ground for blacks."

"Zemi, thank you fer sayin' somethin' so nice to and about me."

"You're welcome."

Zeth added to his point. The man did not waste time; he was a serious individual. "Zemi, when a person is considerin' choices and priorities and life ambition, well if that internal self-government is speakin' to you, then it ain't your choice anyway. You just need to submit and be the willin' vessel. And try to build some fire under your people. And when you do that, Puddin', everythin' else is already on in motion."

"You seem to have an answer for everything," I said.

"Here is your best answer," Zeth advised me. "You need to get on a plane and get into your brother's office right away. Let E.J. go over that contract since he is an attorney and all. Bein' your brother, he ain't goin' to let nobody do you wron'."

"And what about you?" I asked.

"As long as I am around, I won't let anybody do you wron', either. Where you're concerned, Puddin', I want you to always remember that certain thin' about me, that I am the wind beneath your win's, girl."

My eyes welled up and tears streamed down my face. For some reason, I was remembering my father. For me, Zeth had a strong almost paternal side to his love.

"Ah, you are making me cry."

"I reckon that must be someone else who got their telephone wires crossed with yours because my job is to make you smile all the time, Puddin'. But I see my first job is to help you learn how to count Puddin,' because if I don't, I will never collect my points. And I am beginnin' to yearn, Puddin', to feel that I am in desperate need of earnin' those points."

5

W hen I met my brother E.J. in his office, I was surprised to see Joey there. E.J. got up from his desk and gave me a hug. "Hey, Zemi, sit down while I finish up a few more things here for Joey. He's in town to finish up some business concerning his restaurants. It won't take me long." As he turned away, he reared his head and stared. "You're looking kind of tired there, Sis. Hey, are you all right?"

I straightened my jacket and sat down. "Yeah, I'm okay," I said, leaning back in my chair and stretching my legs in front of me. "It seems an extra long flight from Charlotte to San Francisco when you have to sit in coach."

"Are you sure that's all?" E.J. asked, glancing at me from over his reading glasses.

I nodded. "Really, I am okay."

E.J. turned his head, looking down at his paperwork as if trying to keep his mind on work at hand while still trying to make sure I was okay. "Old tall country boy Zeth isn't putting any unwarranted demands on you, is he?"

Joey got up and walked over to me as he answered E.J.'s question.

"Ah, man, don't worry about Zeth. He's not like you or me." Joey bent down, smiling. "Give me a kiss, baby girl."

E.J. shook his head. "Huh! Joey, you are so selfish that you used up the 'O and the G' in the word until nothing's left worthwhile for your two older brothers to play with."

Joey and E.J. were both laughing.

"What's an O G?"

"Oops!" Joey cupped his mouth while grinning.

"Joey, you might be right," said E.J. "We might not have to go and kick that old tall country boy's ass after all."

Still grinning, Joey said, "Zeth's still opening up car doors for women."

"And what's wrong with that?" I asked. "Women like for men to do that kind of thing for them. It is all a part of the romance and love."

Joey bent three of his fingers backwards. "There's nothing wrong with opening a woman's door the first three times out on a date, but after that, I just can't see doing that for the duration of a relation-ship. The rule: three strikes and you ought to know the workings of my car door," said Joey.

E.J. laughed. "Joey, you are crazy, man. There is nothing wrong with getting the door for a lady. But you know, Zemi, Joey doesn't really date ladies. I don't know where he finds half of the kind of women he dates."

"Hey, that's right. I will take all of the women that you fancy guys don't want."

"Zemi," said E.J., "why don't you go ahead and tell me about the meeting you had with Mrs. Williams while I'm on top of this work here? I can take it all in."

I really did not want to discuss my business in front of Joey, but it appeared his business time had overlapped into my time. When I got the opportunity, I told E.J. the story of AWALA and my meeting with Mrs. Williams. Of course, I left out a few details here and there.

Joey gripped the arms of his chair to rise. "AWALA!" he asked with curiosity. "What kind of organization is that?" Getting up, he asked me if I wanted water.

"Yes, I would, thanks, Joey."

Joey opened up the wet bar. "See, Zemi, this is expensive water, expensive juice, expensive liquor. Look, E.J. even has expensive ice. Fuji water, hmm, Voss." Joey snapped his finger and twirled his body around. "Now one can't get any classier than that. E.J. doesn't have to buy cheap water like you and me because he charges his cli-ents so much money that they help him afford the best stock of anything in town." Joey handed me a bottle of water and shook his head. "AWALA and getting women to go back to the South."

"What's wrong with that, Joey?"

With a bottle of water in his hand, Joey hunched his shoulders. "I just want to get an understanding of the idea or theory, Zemi, that's all. Now, you say that the organization wants to pool African American women's talents with other women of African heritage for a New Black South?"

I did not respond.

"Okay, Zemi, don't act as if you didn't hear me. What the hell does that mean?"

There was an awkward pause in the room as E.J. worked tenaciously, finalizing paperwork for Joey's signature. I wished Joey wasn't here while I am trying to take care of my own business. I don't want to confront any battles before I get a clear understanding of the project at hand. I was a bit irritated already, having anticipated Joey's behavior.

"It means just what it says, Joey," I answered sharply.

"My, my, what is my little baby sister turning into?" Joey patted me on the shoulder. "What's up, huh? What? Are you going to have a bunch of husbandless women now running the South—and black at that?"

"Joey, if that was the goal, I would have to do absolutely nothing, you know. They are running their households without men anyway."

"Pulll-lease, Zemi. Women can't do anything without men leading the way," said Joey. "That's why most of the preachers of the churches are men because God knew you women would have your little chips on your shoulders every time your moon rose each month. That's why there will never," he pointed his finger, "and I mean there will never be a female commissioner running the NFL. And I don't care how much Condi wanted to give the impression that she could have succeeded NFL Commissioner Paul Tagliabue had she not been running around the globe, playing threatening tag to North Korea, Syria, Iran and then to the president of Venezuela." Joey took a long swig from his bottle of water. "Donald Trump used to be okay in my book until he said that he liked Condoleezza—but all she does is go flying around the world, never getting anything accomplished. Donald was supposed to say that she was fired! Why would Trump keep Condi on for a job when she is not performing well and in my book not at all? Well, here is my take:

I don't like Condi because she never gets anything accomplished. She has proven that she cannot handle that job better than a man. Colin Powell performed in that position as a gentleman and a statesman."

"Joey," I answered in exasperation, not knowing why I was wasting my breath. "You need to read Dick Morris' book, *Condi vs. Hillary*. Perhaps then you would have a better idea that women are about to run this country," I told him and sank back into my chair.

Joey turned to E.J. and with one of those "man-to-man" looks (like I could not read his drift, like I am not the progeny of black slaves in the U.S. who spoke in and lived by code), and told him, "Man, do you hear her, E.J.? I read that book. Morris was just upset because he was no longer political consultant to Clinton. He wrote that book out of his dislike for the Clintons. There is no possible way either one of those women, Condi or Hillary, will become president. And Morris can throw that Condi scenario of her candidacy out the window. Condi Club or no Condi Club, women don't like Condi at all, and they really aren't that fond of Hillary either."

Joey had addressed E.J., but I answered him first.

"I like Condi a lot. Truly, I just adore her. As a matter of fact, if I would model myself after any woman, it would definitely be Condoleezza Rice," I said proudly.

"I could see that would be you, Zemi. Your style and characteristics remind me of her," said E.J.

"Thank you very much," I said, tugging my shirt collar and leaning forward.

"Zemi, if you knew the rest of what I was thinking about Condoleezza, you wouldn't thank me so fast," said E.J., showing his legendary dimples. "Personally, I think Oprah would be a better fit to emulate."

"E.J., you are just saying that because she has more money," I said.

"Maybe I am saying that because of Oprah's wealth, but even so, knowing your limited bank account, if not her, then find her twin. You need to study someone like that fast, quick and in a hurry."

Joey chimed in. "Now, if Hillary were to run in order to place Bill behind the helm for a third time, then I would consider voting for Hillary. But she would have to guarantee me that Bill was going to be steering the ship. Women don't know how to take care of business. Men are not going to take to a female as a serious candidate. And that's why there'll never be a female president running this country."

"You know, Joey, you just might have to eat those words someday," I told him.

Joey wiped the edge of his mouth. "Well, one thing for sure, I won't have to eat them, come 2008, and you can take that one to the bank. No matter how many Geena Davises play the role on television, and each may look the spitting image of Hillary, it won't help. I will tell you this much, in the end, if the Democrats put a woman in as their presidential candidate, I would never be loyal to the Democrats again—even as much as I hate the Republicans." Joey slammed his bottle of water on E.J.'s desk to emphasis his point (I guess).

"Be careful you don't get water on any of these papers," said E.J.

"Sorry about that, man." Joey pivoted around and addressed me. "I would cast a vote for Rudy Giuliani or write in New York's Mayor Michael Bloomberg before I cast my vote for a woman. I would vote for Al Sharpton, and you know he can't win. Or I would write in Bill Maher because I won't have to worry about him saying God told him to do anything, and I know the bill that he won't veto. But any one of these would get my vote before Hillary. I would vote in a black Santa Claus first, and you know off the bat he would have as much of a chance as a real life black man." Joey was in his element (which to date I have not quite been able to fathom).

E.J. took off his glasses and laid them on top of the paperwork. "Hold on now, Joey, before you go casting your vote for unreal people. Now, you know Barack Obama is a probable and very serious presidential candidate for the Democratic Party. So you might want to hold off on that black Santa vote."

Joey slanted his hand. "Man, that is exactly why I didn't mention Barack. He just does not stand a chance."

"Don't be too quick to shave him off of your ballot," said E.J. "Barack is a great Democratic candidate to consider. He is of black and white parentage, a scholar from an Ivy League university, and he has been a great Senator for the state of Illinois. Hillary has done no more for this country than Barack in terms of their political service and duty as senators."

Joey twitched his nose. "I know you've read the Constitution, E.J., and unless something has been amended, a person owning one-fourth drop of black blood in this country was not accounted for as a whole man. Now, that is the truer color of democracy at work here in this country," said Joey. "I mean, now that is some insane thinking. What part did they not count as human, or for that matter, what part did they count?"

"Come on, Joey, that is just too asinine to address," I remarked with disgust.

"You see, Zemi, how messed up your mind is," Joey shot back. "I am not the one who wrote that rule into law, but I am the one crazy because I want to know what kind of sick thinking was at play that made others go along."

E.J. put his glasses back on. "You are right, Joey. It was a law that was enforced, too. Blacks were the only people in America that by law were deemed three-fifths of a person."

"There it is. White America does not care about Barack coming from a white mother and black father." Joey threw his empty water bottle in the trash can. "To them he is all black, and he has no choice in the way America perceives him although he has the choice himself to say whether he is black or white. But how could you have a black daddy and say you are a white man anyway? The point is, don't try to make it seem like Barack can calm the waters because he is mixed. If so, Halle Berry could have done a little bit more to bring blacks and whites together in segregated Hollywood." Joey spoke as if things were some how E.J.'s fault.

Joey argued further, saying "Don't forget, E.J., now you do know that mixed babies were slaves, too, and all of them were not your house servants either. No way, big brother. Can't let you run away with that one. It ain't holding water." Joey walked over to the bar and opened a can of cashew nuts.

I unbuttoned my jacket, and just had to say, "I have to agree with Joey. I think it will be very difficult for white America to vote for a black man. No matter how much Barack is for change, America is not about to change that much! It is a sad thing to say that in this day and time in America the country has not really progressed enough, but the only way Barack can win anything close to the presidency is to be Hillary Clinton's vice presidential running mate," I said.

"Ah, naw. Hell, naw!" E.J. erupted. He threw down his pen so hard it rolled off his desk onto the floor. "It is not going down like that! Now, black folk have been voting for the Democrats like loyal puppies. We voted for white folk in the Democratic Party since they have been running. Now they are going to have to show some love. It is time for that party to prove love for black folk," said E.J. angrily.

"Oops!" I tried to hide a grin of satisfaction. "Maybe, E.J., you just might have to call in Kanye West to recant his verbiage about President Bush not liking black people and to rap about the Democratic Party not liking black people either. After all, Howard Dean has informed the country that the Democratic Party has taken black people for granted. The truth comes out of the mouth of a white politician. I keep telling you guys, the Democratic Party's routine is to screw the blacks in their party. That is all they have been used to doing. Or can I just say that the ass has just shown us its ass and not much more? Maybe now you will listen to your wise baby sister," I said, my grin betraying my glee in having to school my brothers.

E.J. was in no mood to make light of the discussion. "It is pay-off time. Now that's the mood for African Americans." E.J. picked up his pen. Democrats did not win because they were so great in deeds in the 2006 mid-term election. You could have given a saddle to Al Sharpton, and he probably could have ridden that old donkey, that ass, as you say, to the finish line. As a matter of fact, more blacks should have run for office in 2006 because it was supposed to be an easy win for the Democrats," said E.J. He was pacing around his desk. "I just don't understand it. What the hell is the Congressional Black Caucus doing? If they're about anything, now should be the time to show something. If African Americans aren't elected as senators and governors—then—how in the world do they make steps to head the Oval Office? One black senator," E.J. shook his head, "only one. That picture should be an outrage to the Black Caucus, they should be up in arms that the Democratic Party has helped to put only one of its kind in as senator. What is the Black Caucus doing—sleeping on the job?"

"What job?" Joey put his hands together to the side of his face to imitate sleeping.

"The Black Caucus is doing like everyone else in Washington—taking a vacation," E.J. answered.

"Now, E.J., I know that you do not want to hear this from your young and gifted baby sister, but Al has become much too heavy for that old donkey to carry anymore. He needs to give that a rest. He has shown too many times that he just cannot win, riding that donkey. I don't care how desperate America is for a change. Big Al is not the answer."

Joey nodded his head emphatically. "I have to agree with you, Sis," said Joey, "The people won't call Al Sharpton in, even as a substitute. He has run for mayor of New York City and lost that one, president of the Oval Office and lost, and I believe he ran for the Senate. If Al runs again, I will be wondering just what agenda is he pursuing, and I happen to like the man."

I sensed E.J.'s disgust with the Democratic Party, but I knew he would stick with that party no matter what it did. How could one as intelligent as he stick with something knowing it was not working for him? Why do so many blacks do that? I am having an epiphany right now! I suddenly realize that it is not the poor blacks who keep voting Democrat; it is the black middle class, people who were supposed to be a little bit more informed and a little more proactive.

"Ahem—hem," Joey cleared his throat, mocking one upsmanship. "So, E.J., how do you account for Harold Ford's loss in 2006?" asked Joey. "Ahem. I believe he was unable to get those white folk to see differently than that ad placed by the Republicans. And some of those blacks in Tennessee had a change in heart, too, and kept him from being the first black senator from their state."

"It was a foul and a nasty trick played by the Republicans, using that commercial of the white girl. Everybody knows that white southerners still hold fearfully to the old thinking that the black man wants their women. And voters fell for the dupery even though they know Harold Ford to be a decent, reputable, stand up guy. Republicans are known for being underhanded. They will do anything to win," E.J. explained, putting the rim of his glasses to the edge of his mouth.

Joey countered, "But it is not just that old white men think that way, E.J. It is that it is the truth." He opened a bag of veggie chips from the bar, and went on, "You do have to admit that some of these black men do prefer to have the white man's daughter over that of their own kind. And nowadays they almost have to be blonde in order for some black men to feel that they really have the pure white."

"That may hold a certain amount of truth," said E.J. "But that does not mean the scenario held any truth in weight with Harold Ford. I certainly believe that he would not have picked a white woman who looked as classless as they made that one appear in the ad. In fact, the news media has been sporting a picture of his fiancée and though white, she is a beautiful classy-looking blonde. Anyway the point to be made is that no black person should have fallen for that ad either. Harold should be senator right today. The Democratic Party didn't work hard enough to ensure that to be the case. In 2008 they want to use that as their excuse to say, 'See, blacks cannot win elections. America just is not ready.'"

I added my fifty cents. "Some high-profile white women of the feminist movement have said that it is more realistic for a woman to become president than an African American. Obviously, the white feminists didn't think that way in July of 1971 when Shirley Chisholm, Member of Congress from New York's Twelfth District, began to explore the possibility of running for President. When she formally announced her candidacy the following January, she became the first woman and the first African American to seek the nomination of the Democratic Party for the nation's highest office. But Chisholm's candidacy was a double first for the Democrats. I wonder if Hillary ever acknowledged the pioneer who came before her? That, of course, would have been a black woman. It seems as though race might be the issue for the Democratic Party. Blacks might get a real dose of the Democratic Party's prejudice," I said. "But then again our folk might stay in denial—or they could come out of denial." I threw up my hands. "I just do not know."

"I am surprised to hear that from you, Zemi. For a moment you scared me because I thought you were completely lost," said Joey.

"I am still on the planet with you, Joey." I smiled at my brother.

Joey scratched his forehead and asked, "E.J., I want to make sure that I understand you." He began rubbing his chin as he spoke. "Are you saying that it is okay for whites to be offended that their daughters should date black men, but that blacks should be okay with their sons dating white women—and especially the kind that most black men pull in?"

E.J. didn't look up and continued writing. "Come on, Joey. You can do better than that for an argument."

"E.J.," Joey said. "Black men who have money love to go after the poorest white women who are out there on the prowl." Joey adjusted himself in his chair to find a comfortable position, then folded his hands behind his head. "For the life of me, I cannot understand why a poor white man would mind his poor daughter marrying into black wealth. I think the black mamas have more cause to be upset when their wealthy sons marry poor white women. It is not like these wealthy black men are going out and getting somebody well-groomed and educated like a Chelsea. These black men are picking women who have no more to offer than a second-time-around foam implant as their best bait," said Joey. He eyed me knowingly. "I know you would agree with me, Zemi."

E.J. answered before I could.

"I don't believe parents of either race, black or white, necessarily want to see their children marry outside of their race," he began. "That's a normal psychology. But while I say that, I also think each race holds a different reason for not being desirous of interracial dating and marriage in their families. White folk most of the times just plain outright don't like black people, whereas black people fear more for the consequences of beatings and murders that interracial marriages have brought upon the race. That psychology still prevails among many African Americans. But no doubt about it, blacks have embraced mixed children—of black and white parents, really black mixed with anything else—who come into the African

American race. Blacks along with whites will treat mulatto children like the cream of the crop. So from one point of view, I am not saying that black parents should not be upset. You know me better than that, Joey."

"Yeah, I know, but uh…"

"Let me finish," said E.J.. He leaned against the wall, both hands in his pockets. "When children are mixed with black blood, black folk are the first to take in those types of children in their race and call them their own. But do you know how many white grandparents refuse to acknowledge their black- and white-mixed grandchildren? Frankly, entering the twenty-first century, the issue is not who marries blacks or who marries whites, but rather, unfortunately whether the darkest of our race can handle themselves with as much confidence as those in our race who are of the lightest complexion. There are just far too many grave issues that blacks and whites need to be concerned about in this country other than color, but "color" is still an issue, whether it should be or not. And I have to point out from a legal standpoint, the law does not only forbid racial, ethnicity and national origin prejudice, but prejudice on account of color, too, and that includes color discrimination going on within a race, including African Americans."

"Wow," I said. I did not realize the things E.J. was talking about. I could tell from Joey's expression that Joey was getting an education as well.

E.J. was still talking. He had moved to other problems in America. "…we have a serious war going on though no one has really declared war. We have babies being aborted near term, millions of folk without health care, the middle class slipping, folks losing their homes, our children being under-educated in schools, losing our teenagers to the war on drugs, small business loans going to more immigrants (and some illegal at that) than African Americans, loss of jobs to foreign countries, and lack of control of our borders. So what I am saying about Harold Ford is that he should have won his seat. He would have been a fine senator. Harold Ford might be where Nancy Pelosi is today had the Democrats not been so afraid early on. But nobody wants to talk about that, not even the Congressional Black Caucus, and I don't either right now."

"Like I said, E.J., you just keep proving my point. America is not ready for a black president," said Joey.

"Like I said, Joey, the mood is different. Barack needs to be the Democratic presidential nominee and that ought to be the voice of all Americans alike," said E.J. "America has its first black governor of the twenty-first century, Deval L. Patrick of Massachusetts, the second in the nation since Reconstruction. And, Joey, I am not saying that is any indication of how far we have come, far from that. I am admonishing America to accept the need and time for change. So if ever a black is to become president, now is the time," said E.J. "Hell, let Hillary be Barack's running mate."

Joey held his position. "I hate to blow you away like this, E.J., but they will change the Constitution and allow Arnold Schwarzenegger to be president before an African American. An immigrant was governor of California before a black man. I don't like wasting my vote for a black president because I'd just feel like I did not really vote. Black presidential nominees don't run to win. Jesse didn't run to win, Carol Moseley Braun didn't, and you surely know that Al Sharpton didn't run to win," said Joey as he turned and looked at me. "But don't misunderstand me here, Zemi, I will vote a black man as president before I vote for a white female president."

Reluctantly, I smiled at Joey. I suppose it was like the kind of smile you might give someone to express sympathy. "Joey, you had better get ready to cast your vote for a Republican candidate because Hillary is going to be the presidential candidate for the Democratic Party," I told him.

"Hmmmph!" he grumbled. "I don't want to send a woman out there to fight a man's battle. Ain't no female presidential candidate a match for those Iranians or Iraqi guys. You put a woman in that Oval Office, and I promise you those boys will have no fear. They will gush up like a tsunami and try to rip this country to shreds." Joey lifted his arms up over his head. "This is no time for feminist chanting. Maybe if you had the hippie era going again, but please, God, not now," he said, joining his hands together as though in prayer. "Women are just not built to run any country today. A woman in office is an invitation for every terrorist in the world to strike America. With a woman, America will exist, but it will not be able to wear the crown as superpower."

I smiled again. The same smile.

"Oh, yeah, believe me, Zemi, the power in America will be gone with a woman in office."

I thought to myself, why couldn't God have made me clairvoyant and given me a warning that Joey was going to be in the office today.

"Joey, are you even up to date on what's going on in the world today? There is a female president running Liberia and a female prime minister recently ran Jamaica. Thank you very much."

Joey shook his head. "Baby Sis, I said a female president would never run a country. I didn't say anything about a female running some Rasta men or a female running some people with sticks on some peninsula type area. And give me a break. That piece that you call Liberia belongs to the United States and Firestone anyway. That is why those people today from Liberia are asking for dual citizenship here in America because America is a country. Liberia is more like a 'wanna-be.'"

"Joey, you know up until now I did not know that you were such a negative person. Women would be smart to stay shy of you and your kind," I said.

"Why would you say such a thing, Sis? Is it because I tell the truth?" Joey jingled the keys in his pocket. "African men don't even run their own countries, and you think just because this Liberian woman was educated at Harvard that she's really running something. Get real! Nigeria is what, the fifth or sixth largest oil-producing country in the world, and the black men there aren't in charge. They don't know how to control their own natural resources, and you think a woman does? South Africa's natural resource is diamonds, and they don't control their natural resources. If a woman knows what to do, why isn't she doing something for a wealth-poor country? A woman, please. Do you know what they do with their women over there? They keep their women pregnant, poor and in the fields. Ghana has gold, and they don't even have the wherewithal to have public toilets. Yet they want tourists to come over there as they sport big bold signs 'Please don't urinate on the location.' And that's real. Once the men over there learn how to rule, then you can tell me that you have a female president. Please. And upon whose wall should your Ph.D. be hanging?" Joey jested to my irritation, thumping his finger into his chest repeatedly.

Joey was pushing my mad buttons all at the same time. "Well, at least they have a country to claim as their own."

Joey blurted out, "Claim what? Dirt to make mud pies?"

"No matter what, it is still their country to claim," I said.

"How are they going to claim it, and they're killing each other, and none of them—and I mean none of them—has even a pot to piss in? I am so sorry, Zemi, it may be troublesome for you to be objective, but Africa needs to come out of its nonsense. You heard how Barack Obama had to criticize South African leaders for their slow response to the AIDS epidemic, saying they were wrong to contrast 'African science and Western science.' Even some AIDS activists say the health minister over there is creating deadly confusion by pushing traditional medicines with an old-timey recipe of garlic, beetroot, lemon and African potatoes to combat AIDS while underplaying the role of real and proven medicines. Baby girl, Africa needs answers, not more excuses," Joey declared.

"And what is your answer?" I snapped back.

Joey stood and squared his shoulders as if he were getting ready for a public oration. "It's pathetic the way Africa is today in the twenty first century. Japan got up on her feet after World War II; China is out and about trying to run neck-and-neck with a superpower; starving India is now becoming the thriving India, and what they call Bollywood, Hollywood for East Indians, is doing an awesome job of portraying that image. Even North Korea and Iran are making their presence known. Tell me something, Zemi, what is wrong with your sisters and brothers over there on the Dark Continent? And they've had an African man born in Ghana who was the UN Secretary-General. How could he have a solution for other countries when he can't help what languishes in Africa?" Joey twined his two fingers together. "Shame, shame, and more shame. What kind of leadership was he about?"

E.J. injected his view. "Joey, no one man can fix what ails Africa today. I think Kofi Annan was a great UN secretary general for two terms, so others must have thought the same of him. He is gracious, and he good-naturedly brought together humanitarianism with realism. He generally was an effective consensus-builder. Annan has particularly emphasized the UN's traditional obligations in the area of human rights and the newer challenges of the HIV/AIDS pandemic and international terrorism. The man took responsibility on his shoulders as much as anyone in that position could have done."

"Joey, you are the diary of a mad black man," I charged. Shaking my head, I put my palms up to my cheeks. "Somebody got it all wrong."

"Yeah, I know poor, rich Africa. Here is something else to make you eat you heart out. I would rather have a white man in the position over the UN than a black. Do you want to know why that is, Zemi and E.J.?"

I shook my head. "No. I don't know, but I have a feeling you won't spare us the absurd." I yawned. Maybe the plane ride had tired me out more than I realized.

Joey was still at it. "...because it is easier for blacks and the world to cry out when inequity was poured out over poor and black folk by whites, but then when some heavy immoral iniquities are perpetrated by blacks against blacks, then blacks are slow to criticize, if they so do at all. And it is a habit thing, too. No matter what, blacks want to believe that blacks are working in their best interests."

Although on this point Joey had made some sense, he had worked me hard, and all I could do was to shake my head. I could not give any more thought to Joey's theory of socio-politico-eco-nomic-racial-ethno-military-strong/male and weaker/female relativity. Intelligent he was, but my brother Joey, was no Einstein; he was a hodgepodge of thought dwarfed by sundry and scattered biases.

"Joey, I am going to do you a favor and get you some help by shouting, SOS, man overboard." I shook out my hands, as if ridding something undesirable from them.

"Sis, really, it's true. You are not going to get much accomplished with black political leaders worldwide. They do the bidding for white folk, and I definitely include black political leaders from the United States as the ones to follow on such a beckoning trend. These black politicians don't have any power. Black leaders will work their asses off for white folk and throw black folk a bone or two while in office. That's just the way it is."

I held up one hand to Joey in the "stop" also known as "talk to the hand" position. "Look, Joey," I attempted to reason, "the United States gave Japan money to get up on her feet, and now our own country is taking jobs and giving them to people in China and India. Why won't they give Africa some of those jobs and businesses?"

Joey yelled, "For Christ's sake, wake up, Zemi." He had started sweating now and looked like he was getting ready to go ballistic. "The growing demand for oil is evident in China, India and the United States. If there were no Africa supplying these countries, there wouldn't be jobs going from the U.S. over to some of those countries. Have I reached your brain yet, Zemi?"

I stayed quiet; I was somewhere between fed up and tired. All the esoterica behind my Ph.D. was no help to me now.

"You are missing the whole point, Zemi," said Joey. "Why would they have to give jobs to rich oil-producing Africa or rich diamond-studded Africa when Africa holds the key? Africa not only holds the key, damn it, Africa is the key. You're talking about taking jobs over there."

"Give Africa more time," I pleaded.

Joey laughed. "Time? You want us to give Africa more time? Zemi, do you remember when you were in Africa, in the midst of showering with soap all over your body, and the water just shut off? And you couldn't wash the soap off but could only rub down with lotion and your skin began to itch and you broke out in a rash. Do you remember telling the stories of all your experiences in Africa, Zemi?"

"Of course, I remember. How could I forget?"

"Most of the people, unless they have cable, only have one channel to watch television that only comes on half a day. Remember, Zemi, you said you couldn't do much studying during the nights, to speak of, because there was no real electricity. Finally, you had to leave from among the indigenous people because there were certain times when you needed to be able to count on water flowing. Then you stayed at two plush hotels in Africa where folk with money visited, one called the Golden Tulip and the other Novatel. Remember that story, Zemi? You also said that you could not understand how such opulence existed at those hotels, when no more than a half-block outside of those two compounds was the worst poverty you had ever seen. Who'd in their right mind want to take business to Africa? The idea is to take business out of Africa."

Joey was whining so much that I was certain something was wrong, maybe something in his business was off. Why else the ranting and raving?

"Okay, you two, hurry into round nine because I am about to wrap up my portion. Excuse me for a minute," E.J. said.

I guess for a while, I forgot he was there. He stepped out of the office, telling us he would return shortly.

"Okay," I said, "now that your big old audience has gone, can you bring your whining down a notch?"

"Hey, you can make light of this all you want to, but the fact remains: Africa has no infrastructure in place to accommodate businesses. That is why people go in and just take what they want from Africa. Her inside is messed up because it accepted rape as the order of doing business; therefore, it is not set up to accommodate the twenty-first century."

With my hand up to my mouth, I nodded. "Uh-huh. I see what the problem is. You are all confused, and you don't know doodley squat about the true Africa, Joey. Everybody and their mamas go to Africa to do business."

"Zemi, interacting in this conversation with you is like playing dirty pool." Joey held his hands to imitate shooting pool. "It is not fair to talk with you this way because you don't have the same tool to play with—logic. Now when I talk business in Africa, I am not talking mom and pop business, you know—braids, Kente cloth, Dashikis, drums or even your ebony art. We are talking about a continent here, so I am talking businesses that use oil, real estate development, tourism, or open up a Disneyland. It is one thing to go over there and visit The Slave Castle in Ghana and see buzzards still flying high but after something so mentally depressing, can you please take me to an amusement park or something to bring my spirits up? And another thing, how in the world does Ghana call a place—that held the most gruesome, ghastly and harrowing atrocities ever committed upon man—a castle? Do you see where Africa's thinking is? It's crazy." Joey's words were venomous.

"Okay, I agree with you on that one, Joey." I said sheepishly. I could not disagree in any form or fashion, but I had given Joey a bigger stage from which to gloat. "But I was told that Dionne Warwick and Isaac Hayes had something to do with the name being changed to The Slave Dungeon."

Joey grinned scornfully. "That was big of you, Zemi, because I am not the only one who sees the foolishness going on. If I see things and Dionne and Isaac see things, then surely your black leaders must see things. But your black leaders worldwide are scared. Just like they saw us being taken from Africa for centuries, decades after decades, and they did nothing but let that evil persist upon us. Just like black leaders saw Katrina victims and pretended their hands were tied while they played partisan in order for a particular party to win in upcoming elections."

I agreed that's what really made the Democrats win in the 2006 election. Katrina was the Party's lottery ticket, but that was not the debate I wanted to engage in with Joey.

"Joey, I am not so sure that everything is tied to color or racism, not always black and white," I said.

Joey came back with sarcasm. "You are right, Zemi, not everything is tied to racism. You know a place like Angola was constantly in civil war when wealth, their oil, was all around Africa, yet there is not much electricity flowing in Africa's neighborhood to make hot water. Hell, solar energy is even theirs without asking. And since Angola's admission as the twelfth member of OPEC, it has surpassed Saudi Arabia in production, yet the people are still poor. I wonder if the world will treat Angolans the way they treated and respected the Saudis. Oh, my bad. Angola is part of the Dark Continent."

"If people of Angola are treated differently from the Saudis, then perhaps it is not about oil, you think, Joey?"

"You poor thing, Sis," Joey took my hand and patted it. "Oil today, Zemi, is what makes the world go 'round, and yet Africa exists as a poor, humiliated continent. The question you should be asking yourself is if the people of Africa are still poor, then who benefits from OPEC's expansion? Might just a little bit be wrong with the answer to that picture? Might Kofi Annan have wondered about Africa's backwardness just a little bit more? Even persons like you, with the least of their faculties operating, would be able to reason that Africa is being tricked."

I snatched my hand from Joey's. "You obviously don't understand the magnitude of apartheid, Joey."

"Maybe I don't understand apartheid, but I do remember Stevie Wonder saying it was wrong. But I'll tell you this much, in the twenty first century Africa is sitting on just about every natural resource that can be found in the world. Why hasn't God allowed Africa to come out of the wilderness? Africa has been wandering in it for just a little bit too long for me. I won't tell you why that is, Zemi, not right now, because I seriously don't think you would be able to handle the inferences."

"You sound just like the black people who lack the heart to feel passionate about their roots, Joey."

"Awwww. Whoo! Whoo! Africa is the motherland, a wealthy nation, and it is time that Africa stands up and answers the roll call. God appears to have tired himself of Africa acting always the beggar. And He is going to soon tire of those little black islanders over there in the Caribbean if they don't start handling their business, and leading the list is Trinidad's blacks. Trinidad and Tobago, an important oil and natural gas producing country, is fast moving forward towards the status of an industrialized country and one where blacks make up forty percent of its population. I just don't understand why the blacks are not doing anything to help themselves out because in T & T, East Indians are the prominent ones in business and the professions," said Joey.

"Joey, just because there is oil in a country does not mean that the black people there should automatically be rich," I remarked bitterly.

"Hmm. So, to you it means that the people who are not indigenous to that country should be the ones automatically rich?" Joey sighed heavily. "Right kind of thinking, Zemi. I am sure the blacks there would not want you negotiating for their side."

"Dear brother, that is not what I mean, but I just wonder why are you so hung up on blacks in countries with oil? That seems to be your first thought for improving the status of blacks, no matter where in the world you find them and oil."

Joey pointed his finger at me. "Zemi, turn off the light switch above your head for me," he ordered.

"Why?" I thought it was an odd demand. "It would become too dark in here, and, worse, it might turn off all of the computers. Are you crazy, Joey?"

"If you don't get the point, then you might as well be as much in the dark as the people in those countries. I feel guilty having you as a baby sister because I did not teach you well. It's not that I didn't try but, rather, the problem is faulty wiring," said Joey.

My eyes darted to the window. Joey's words hit a raw nerve; I did not want him to see the pain he had caused me. I felt he was attacking me, and I could not cry because Joey is the kind who would pour salt on a wound.

"Zemi, when Natasha and I went to Trinidad last year, we thought we could hang out with the brothers and sisters over there. Nada! It was unreal. At first I thought it was a holiday or something because the black folk were sitting on their butts taking a siesta all day long and saying 'No problem' while their children begged. The only folk I saw tending to business were the Indians. Even Syrians were doing business over there. The crime was so bad that my girl and I left and went to stay the rest of our vacation in beautiful Tobago. Naw, Zemi, you can't help a man if he won't tire of being down on the ground," said Joey. He folded his arms across his chest as if to say he knew he was right.

I was cloaked in shame and stupidity. I wished for the first time that I had not received a Ph.D. I was expected to know too much. Everyone expected me to analyze what I did not see in the picture frame. That is what Dad taught the older siblings to study most. My inner self had surrendered. At that moment Joey knew that he had won the fight. I was silent. The engine had no fuel left to go any further, but Joey wanted me back in the ring.

"I can sense your chagrin, Zemi." Joey licked his lips. "You are faint-hearted in thought, yet alarmed by my sagacity of mind. I am a god because of how I think. And you, Zemi, are a kitten, mesmerized by the power of others that have made you docile. You and others like you cannot figure your way out beyond the two- and three-letter bars—as in caged or prison—as it were, that follow your last names. Those fancy letters first define your existence, but then go on to thwart growth, thinking, analysis and discernment, too. You think you care about others because you accept excuses, but you don't truly know how to care. I don't care about your type of author who writes a book for every season, nor do I care what anyone says about not being embarrassed for black folk and that we shouldn't air our dirty laundry out in public. I, Joey Navies, am very much embarrassed to say that those men and women over there are kin to me."

Still hurting, I managed, "Joey, I think that you are making yourself agitated by taking in so much applesauce."

Joey laughed. "Okay, so I am the one eating applesauce. If I had a stage I would say to Michael Dyson, 'Tell your African brothers and sisters over there to stop some of that damn dancing and tell them that they are not scaring anybody throwing those sticks and rocks either. Zemi, they are beating and killing their own sisters and brothers while others are allowed to just prance into their countries and rob, rape and ravage. Still, God still leaves them with more natural resources in the earth than just about any other peoples. That, Bro' Dyson is the real subject matter for the stage-of-forever-holding-forth.'"

My brother's arguments about the Motherland held sway, I knew, but he had been gratuitously nasty and had hurt me, and there was just no way I would concede an iota of a point to him. Even though something he said rang so true: It was like God was just letting our African kin to continue sitting on a pot of gold that was replenished even as they were robbed, and maybe God was just waiting for Africans to wake up, take up and claim what was theirs. And so many others, like yours truly, were waiting right along with God. Pride hurt and my hard-earned doctorate belittled, I went where Joey had been with me—I went personal, evading the substance of the discussion, if one might call a diatribe that. So, here I go: "Joey, my self-described learned and erudite one, do you envy Dyson's superior intellect and mass appeal?"

"Tsk," Joey tutted through his teeth. "Pull-ease. You can stack your deck full of so-called intellectuals, and it won't make a difference. Call out your brother Cornel West, your Michael Dyson and tell them both to give some pertinent print on the pages. Tell Tavis Smiley, along with his two sidekicks, to make a covenant with our African brothers and sisters for our share of the wealth in the ground of Africa. African Americans want reparations from America. Why on earth would they leave out Africa? Her hand was dirty first. Tell those philosophers to put the story together to seal the real covenant."

"Joey, maybe you should not have opted out of college. I have never seen one so upset over the hard-earned degrees of other people." I suddenly became very hot; heat seemed to have come from nowhere. I took off my jacket.

"I might not have those three letters behind my last name, nor do I wear the two letters behind my name. America knew slavery was wrong and made a broken promise of forty acres, but Africa has yet to offer openly and fully an apology for her role in what is known as one of the most inhumane acts ever perpetrated throughout human history. Africa, too, needs to tally up that inheritance with African Americans and the Caribbean, those who came through the Atlantic slave trade. Africa is wrong. Some of the oil, gold and diamonds should be for settling with the descendants of those who were sold away from our lands and inheritance—us, for example, meaning, you, too. When Africa does right about the children she threw into slavery, then maybe God will lend a listening ear and heart to Africa. That's when Africa can call me her brother and sister, when Africans themselves have dealt fairly with us. Now, how will your social scientists deal with that?" Joey took off his jacket and threw it on his chair.

"Joey, you ascribe blame to a whole continent of people for what some West African tribal collaborators did centuries ago," I answered, shaking my head. I thought for a second. Was this the type of anger that Mrs. Williams had spoken of earlier? Why couldn't leaders of Africa provide for its citizens? Where is Africa headed with its goals? I wanted to ask the questions out loud, but I just couldn't do that. I just did not think it was fair to Africa. But why was the God in black people still operating on such a small level all around the globe? How long will they use as reasoning "It is written" to continue being slow in step? Will black folk stay on the page that says, "The race is not given to the swift but to those who endure?" What about being stewards over time and energies and speeding up some? Why don't some black men care enough about their children and women to think that now is the time for all good men to stand and lead their kind to winning heights? Why would the black people's God tell them to wait while others advanced? What is this God made out of that black people serve?

E.J. had not returned to his office, and Joey sat on the edge of his desk and continued talking.

"Maybe now would be the time for Africa to ask God, 'Why hast thou forsaken me?' The African leaders over there need to step up to the plate. They, too, are a part of this dramatically changing world, and time is out for them acting as if they still can't mend the fabric of the grand and majestic quilt called Africa. We especially need Nigeria and Angola to get it together. What is taking you guys so long, Africa, to be business people? So I think that it's a fair and balanced question, Zemi. Don't you and your two- and three-lettered colleagues?"

I felt as if a large elephant had crushed by chest. I needed to release, but I couldn't let Joey have the satisfaction. "Joey, I think some of what you have been talking about is just so insane. That's all I have to say."

"Yeah, just crazy enough to be sane. Zemi, do you mean like the pundits kept saying of the late, great attorney Johnny Cochran: 'crazy like a fox?'"

"Joey," I said, trying to think of the latest hip comeback—okay, I got it. "Don't get it skewed...."

"Twisted," he said, interrupting me.

"Twisted?"

"That's right, 'Don't get it twisted,' is how it goes, baby girl. You could have gotten some life smarts along with book knowledge up in those ivory towers, my lovely," he chided.

Attorney E.J. Navies saved me; he returned to his office, and Joey scooted his backside off of E.J.'s desk. Would my witness to Joey's "getting into his place," that is, the seat his behind had warmed, have to suffice for the satisfaction of my brother getting brought down a notch? And why would I want to have that happen to Joey? To any black man? Was anything easy?

E.J. sat down, leaned back in his chair and began looking over the contract Mrs. Williams had offered me.

Silence. Joey and I let E.J. do his work. Silence. A respite from banter's battlefield for me.

"Well, isn't somebody going to say something?" asked E.J.

Joey looked confused. "Say something about what?"

"I want to know who won the *Word* War I."

"Ah, man, need you ask such a question?" Joey remarked, poking out his chest to acknowledge triumph.

"I have been looking over this contract, Zemi. Are you sure you want to handle this… uh…AWALA, this back-to-the-South sort of thing?"

Joey laughed. "Yeah, Zemi, you were kind of light on the whole African scene, and I didn't even have to use my stingray stuff on you. Though you have degrees and you do have the book smarts, but –er well…." Joey clasped his hands and propelled his arms in a practiced golf swing. "…you were missing the oomph in your swing, baby girl. Your presentation stinks. Knowing what you know is one thing, but if you are trying to sell what you know, and you're unable to deliver, then you might as well hang your wares on the markdown rack. An audience would walk out on you. If I were not your brother, I would have walked out on you already. You had better get more prepared than you are, Sis. The wolves would not even take the time to eat you because you have no flavor for them. I mean, this is your field; this is the kind of work you do. Maybe you should run that business which women run best—a household," said Joey, grinning cruelly.

I knew that I had gotten beaten up in that round by Joey or maybe even sustained a TKO; he didn't have to tell me that. But I wasn't sure how to come back or even if I could. Though E.J. hadn't said anything, I could tell that he was expecting me to come back with some venom of my own. Just then I was overtaken by a surge of confidence.

"Joey, could be that your level of comprehension could not rise to the occasion. You are such a misogynist that you and men like you can't move further because you have blockage. You want to hold women back, but this is not Iraq. From my view of what really stinks, if black men were running businesses and taking care of things the way they should have been, black neighborhoods would not have been inundated with drugs and crime; instead, they were left defenseless by black men. Hopefully, that won't mess with your ego, Joey, but from the front view, some black men don't seem to be holding up their end of the bargain as heads of anything."

"Now that was hardihood," said E.J. as he thumped his pen up and down on the contract.

E.J.'s comment spurred me on. "I did not want to take it there, Joey, but since you are not among the associates of the lettered, then I have to bring the mountain to you. Which, by the way, is not a problem to do," I said. A shock wave ripped through my insides. I do not know where such talk came from. This is not my style, and I don't remember ever having done it before. But I could not stop; the quake was *on-n-n-n-n!* Tsunami or earth, I did not care; I was on shake, rattle and roll.

E.J. sat up in his chair, his eyebrows raised.

"You know, a black man loves to say that he is the 'man of the house.' Well, what house is that, Joey? He let a matriarch, Nancy Pelosi, become Speaker of the House, and it appears the females are setting the stage. Well, let's suffice it to say, it does not appear that the country will see the black patriarch in the White House before seeing the white matriarch." I was indifferent to how my words might strike. Could the cause be my time of the month? "Tell me something, Joey, how are we supposed to tally up the nature of you guys' manhood? You say African leaders don't know how to run and lead their own countries, but by the same token, I don't see the likes of your kind ever running the White House, but maybe you guys are thinking this is not your country. I was just wondering, Joey, after black men support the white matriarch as President of the United States, then will the black men have the courage to stand, perhaps, to be next in line for that spot? Joey, where is the dignity in that, huh?" I couldn't help giving Joey a miniscule, and sympathetic smile.

Joey jerked his head. "Wow! You've got a sharp tongue now, huh, Zemi?"

"Perchance this would be a better discussion for your social scientists, such as Cornel West, Michael Dyson and Tavis Smiley or better yet, Juan Williams," I said.

E.J. swivelled his chair. "Joey, you are about to set yourself up for a knockout, brother man."

I clasped my hands together. "I am not saying that black men in America are not up to par with white men—we know that's fiction. But are we now to accept a judgment that they are not even up to par with white women???!!! Now that is fantasy!!! *But that is the channel somebody is trying to turn to.* Would this make some black women wonder whether black men should lead them anymore? Take note of the gender thing, Joey. Maybe God could have a modern prophet write a clearer message on a notepad. Perhaps that would even be the more appropriate question to ask your spiritual and religious gurus. Why weren't black men, leaders, preachers, black organizations and the Democratic Party participating in succession planning to make sure that a black man was one of the aces in either political party's deck come 2008? We have seen it happen to a black man in South Africa." I started lifting my feet in high steps. "You know, the man who had to take a 'Long Walk to Freedom.' But maybe the black man in America is still trying to find which place to call home."

"Yeah, Zemi, and do you know how long that walk was for Mandela? Twenty-seven years and more," declared Joey.

"What?" I put my hand up to my cheek. "First, he is the *Honorable* Nelson Mandela. And, second, have not African American men meandered for that long and more? Has God not told the African American man of 'his time,' or is he just not listening? Have black men in America been the ones wandering around in the wilderness far longer than need be, perhaps, because they are disobedient to the will of God? You are always saying that slavery is over and America is your country."

I pointed to Joey. "When are you, Joey, going to do anything to prove that American slavery is over? Your women can't depend on you, your children can't depend on you, society can't depend on you, you won't lead and you won't follow. In fact, you don't even know what it is like to run a house."

Joey said, "be serious."

"Tell me something, Joey, since the struggles of the Civil Rights, what has your generation of men done to uphold the legacy? It looks as though a lot of black men are getting a free ride off of their granddaddies' and grandmamas' toil. Harriet Tubman, Sojourner Truth, Booker T. Washington, W.E.B. DuBois, Marcus Garvey, Martin Luther King, Jr., Malcolm X, Mary McLeod Bethune and Rosa Parks—all have led in the struggles. Shouldn't black men by now have filled all positions of political leadership, I mean, run the spectrum of leadership by now? Joey, you say that Africa has stagnated the position of blacks in America. Well, should the script be flexible to offer as cause African American women's stagnation, suspended in mid-air waiting for black men to move?"

"Ooooh! Can I get somebody something to drink?" E.J. interrupted. "Maybe water or juice, perhaps?"

I noticed the blood coming to Joey's face, reddening his brown complexion. And I could actually feel a rage swell up inside of me. Had I discredited myself by stooping to Joey's level, and displaying deep hostility?

"Damn, baby girl," said Joey. "You know I love you, but I think you are too much in the deep for any more of my help."

E.J. picked up the contract from his desk. "Well, well, just look at Zemi all grown up now, huh, Brother Joey. She's got herself a little movement going here. Zemi, that was quite a rallying speech you made; it took my breath away." E.J. held his chest.

"Exhale, then. You, too, Joey." I was upset, but did not quite understand why.

"Why, I don't know now whether to call you preacher Zemi, ambassador Zemi, politician Zemi, spiritual guru Zemi or humanitarian Zemi," E.J. added.

Joey said, "Whichever. She's got me going over here, too. I don't know if I feel ten feet taller after that speech or ten feet shorter or if I am yet to exhale."

Both E.J. and Joey seemed to want to make light of my position, but I could tell they both felt the sting.

E.J. told Joey, "You asked for it. You ought to know better, man. Now you know when your sister gets fired up in speech like that, not caring about what she is saying, she could even tell off the president when she is like this. Man, you are supposed to be courteous and just go along with the program. I am embarrassed, Joey. What else did you not pick up from me as your older brother? You should have been able to tell that your baby sister was irritated, carrying a few extra pounds here and there. What's wrong with you anyway, man? Don't you know how to pay attention? That's why your baby sister is acting this way. Man, how else could one explain her inflammable remarks?" E.J. tilted his chair back on its two hind legs.

"I am glad you enlightened me, Big Bro. I knew something awful was wrong with her," said Joey.

"Anyway, it's time for Zemi and me to get down to our business now. You two can debate the problems of black folk another time. Maybe by then the world will be able to pronounce you as world 'solutionaries.'"

Joey got up to leave. He had a plane to catch in a couple of hours.

"Don't forget your jacket," I reminded him. I was glad Joey was leaving.

As Joey reached for his jacket, E.J. grabbed his arm. "Oh, Joey," said E.J., "hang on a minute. Please, hand these papers to my secretary on your way out. Wait. Wait. One more thing I forgot to mention. Be sure and call up your brother Ishmael and properly thank him for helping you acquire this business loan. And Joey, you know you would not have been able to pull this transaction off without the banking acumen and signature of your brother Ishmael. Needless to say, of course, the whole transaction required my ingenuity from beginning to end. Yes. Yes. Yes," E.J. declared, his ego ballooning. Ballooned.

"I get what you are saying," said Joey.

"Ah, how sweet it is." E.J. stacked copies of Joey's papers in a pile and set them aside. "Life can be what you make it, but you've got to have the masters in place. Well, now, Mr. Provocateur, I believe you and I have successfully completed our business here."

"I believe so," Joey seconded.

"And, Ambassador Zemi, compliment your brother before he leaves. You are looking at the new owner of the Vegan 12 restaurant chain. Your brother's got twelve of them going now. Joey, I must say the timing of your vegan restaurants is perfect. With the Food and Drug Administration indicating that it would approve cloned livestock and the U.S. government deciding that food from cloned animals is safe to eat and does not require special labeling, I would say that you hit an entrepreneurial jackpot."

"I know, man, I definitely read the signs."

"I don't believe the FDA. Who wants to eat cloned meats? And the nerve of them not wanting to label it also," I said. "We shouldn't let the government get away with that."

"Hey, that is why Russell Simmons and Hollywood were so strongly against killing animals. They saw the handwriting on the wall years ago," Joey said. "And Whole Foods has committed to making sure that its meats, fish and poultry do not come from cloned animals. They came out with a statement saying so."

I realized that I was very proud of and happy for Joey. "Since you are doing so well with your Vegan 12 restaurants in the powerful city of Atlanta, which, by the way, is under the guardianship of female mayor, Shirley Franklin, I guess you might have to plan on opening up a Vegan 12 in Charlotte," I told him.

"I caught your drift, your ploy to entrap me, Zemi, but, for your information, Ambassador Andrew Young brought the real light to shine upon the great city of Atlanta. The Olympics and all, that's where the real credit goes. Former Mayor Maynard Jackson left a blueprint for the city of Atlanta that will carry it throughout the next millennium, making it easier for a female like Franklin to handle things. She is just following the plan. Like a woman is supposed to do…she is just following."

"Yeah r-i-g-h-t," I retorted. I nodded my head slowly. "Anyway, your restaurant would probably do well in Charlotte, so make that a plan."

"That would be ideal and, hopefully, soon." Joey bent over and kissed me goodbye. Leaving, he opened the door and called back, "Okay, later. E.J. I'll call you. And I hope to see you soon, Zemi."

"That's Dr. Navies to you," I managed to get out right before he shut the door. That felt good. Joey heard me, but attempted no comeback. I got in the last word after all; both my ego and my hard-earned piece of paper in tact.

E.J. chuckled and picked up the contract. He came and sat on the couch next to me. "Okay, Dr. Navies, let's you and I get down, dig down deep, to see if this venture is worth our time and effort." While reading the contract, E.J. grumbled, "AWALA, Inc. A New Black South. This is all very fascinating. I mean you tend to get yourself involved with some of the most peculiar and whimsical ventures. A New Black South," E.J. shook his head as if in disbelief. He repeated 'A New Black South,' at least four times. "Zemi, in as few words as possible, tell me why a 'New Black South?'"

"Well, Mrs. Williams said the purpose is to concentrate the talent pool of women of an African legacy here in America for political empowerment. I believe that Mrs. Williams wants to garner the voting power of African Americans along with others from the Caribbean and Africans who have obtained citizenship here in America. I think she wants to be able to position her organization of women to negotiate with tremendous leverage come election time."

"So, you say you think, but Mrs. Williams didn't articulate that?" E.J. pushed his pencil behind his ear. "Well, what makes you think so then, Zemi?"

"Because on certain things, she was unclear unlike her detailed discussion on other matters."

"Okay, all right. I got you."

I did not want to tell E.J. certain things because Mrs. Williams did not give me the name of the woman who was a first choice; I knew E.J. would caution me about not having that bit of information. Still, although Mrs. Williams espoused her organization as being community based and altruistic, the smell of politics was all around it. It appeared that Mrs. Williams wanted to do what Jesse and Al have done in past elections, to build a large membership for its organization and hold it up for the highest bidding candidate. Mrs. Williams believed that black women have been the segment most taken for granted, and with her pedigree and skills, she could pull women in around a more beneficial and inclusive cause, as opposed to their votes being hijacked all of the time. I believe that Mrs. Williams' intentions to empower black women are genuine.

"You know, E.J., Mrs. Williams is very passionate about what she's doing and truly wants to see black women get the large piece of the pie we have earned since way back when."

"Zemi. That could happen if circumstances surrounding the movement are in step with the vibes of the country. So far, it seems as though your role to play and your challenge will be in the art of persuasion. I just hope all of these efforts benefit the right party." E.J. removed his glasses and stared keenly at me. "Do you know if this organization has a red or blue party lean?"

I squared my shoulders. "I don't believe that Mrs. Williams knows that right now. The answer will depend mostly upon the organization's agenda, probably whichever party wants to do more to help support the organization's program. As I said, she believes in what she is doing, so it is not so much for money as it is to get the organization off its feet."

E.J. raised his brow. "Don't you be so naïve, Zemi. Mrs. Williams already knows which party she supports. Usually, one does not start an organization of this nature and then decide who will be their main support base. She is just not letting you in on who her money base is. For all we know, the organization might have already received its first huge donation or grant, especially if monies are donated over a period of four years from a main entity; so her organization AWALA already belongs to the highest bidder."

I thought to myself I have more than a lot to learn.

"It's that simple. All politicians are not just your faces elected to serve in Washington, Zemi. Hollywood's got its politicians, like outspoken pundit Bill Maher, and you have closet politicians like talk show hosts, Leno and Letterman. Everybody who plays gets paid. Jesse has never been elected to an office, but he is a politician and a brilliant one at that. Jesse is supporting Barack Obama as the Democratic presidential candidate same as his son, Representative Jesse Jackson Jr. But the senior Jackson's wife Jacqueline and their other son Yusef, are supporting Hillary Clinton. You've got to give it to Jesse. One couldn't have created a better political landscape for a family to play in. Isn't there a term for that? Win-win? Another thing—as quiet as it's kept, Danny Glover is politicking for somebody's cause, too. Whoever you see as the power out front, always look for what's behind that person or organization. And don't you ever forget that, Zemi. Even your journalists are politicians; that's exactly why President Bush had journalist Tony Snow serving as his press secretary."

"I did not know this project was going to have that much of a political agenda." I admitted sheepishly. Naïve, he had said. The word stung. I have been stung so often and so badly today I need an antihistamine.

E.J. was still talking. "...and now you know, Zemi, now you know. Anything that makes money has to have politics tied to it, politics is either steering or in the wake, in fact everything had politics in its wake when you think about it—in any case, the flow is, the waters are still political. You do not want to get caught up in the undertow, or in the rip current—that is lethal—trying to swim to shore as hard as you can, but getting forced out farther and farther to sea."

"Umm, Hmmm," I said, nodding my head.

"Sis, I will give you one example that should bring you to the front of the class, which qualifies you to at least sit as a student," E.J. said unmannerly.

His talking down to me was not right. I was not a student; I am a professor, if anything, in a classroom—just like our Daddy. Could it be my own brothers could not give me my propers? The self-proclaimed teacher was still schooling me.

"Now take a look at the priests in the Catholic Church. Scrutinize closely what has been going on. The Catholic churches have been hurting in turns of receiving donations because of the outbreak of sex and sexual abuse scandals involving priests and parishes. You cannot begin to count the dollars and real estate that this base had accumulated," said E.J.

"Really," I answered, just like a student.

E.J.'s face grew stern. "Yes, really. The Catholic Church is one of the largest owners of real estate worldwide. Now you are beginning to see the real estate owned by this group sold off. The Catholic Church has had to pay out over a billion dollars in lawsuits. Just recently, Cardinal Roger Mahony, leader of the nation's largest Roman Catholic archdiocese, apologized to thousands of people who will get a share of a $666 million settlement over allegations of clerical sexual abuse. The Catholic Church is one of the biggest proponents for an open border and illegal immigrants. You see how they harbor illegal immigrants."

My eyes widened. "Wow. Anything can happen like that in the name of religion?"

E.J. leaned forward, his dark eyes flashing. "The Catholic Church wants you to think its stance for breaking America's laws is all about Jesus and how we are to treat folk. But the Catholic Church's breaking of America's law has nothing to do with the teaching of Jesus as much as it has to do with politics. While most of your Mexicans are Catholic, the Catholic churches cannot exist on the Mexican peso to maintain their style of distinction, so the Catholic Church has to ensure that illegal Mexicans cross the border in order to give the church those American dollars. The Catholic Church receives its fair amount from Mexicans for being the symbolic lobbyists for illegal immigrants. So the real question would be 'Are Americans Breaking Jesus' Law'? or "Is the Catholic Church Breaking America's law?'"

I had never given much thought to the Catholic Church and illegal immigrants being so interwoven that way—in politics.

E.J. studied my face to see how I was taking his spiel.

"What stands out in my mind then," I said, "is if the illegal Mexicans don't cross the border, what would happen to the status of the Catholic Church? Are the American citizens, in a way, footing the bills for all of those lawsuits and allegations brought upon the Catholic Church by hiring and paying wages to those who are illegal? And if so, then the Catholic Church also plays a tremendous role in devaluing the wages of the American citizens. Am I right?"

E.J. smiled and slapped his hands on his knees. E.J. got up from the couch and walked over to his desk. "That is exactly what I wanted to hear, your becoming more inquisitive, but internalizing information. Because, Zemi, you are not going to get that tidbit from a politician, especially not one who is running."

I sighed. I did not want E.J. thinking I was simpleminded.

"Don't presume that you know a thing. Investigate to learn what you do not know, and then analyze what you learn." E.J. got up and went to his desk to look for something. Apparently not finding whatever it was, he threw up his hands and said, "Do me a favor, Zemi, for yourself. Go to Barnes & Noble or somewhere and pick up two books. One is called, *State of Emergency: The Third World Invasion and Conquest of America* by Patrick J. Buchanan and...uhh..." E.J. reached in a drawer. "Umm. I thought I had the other book in here somewhere. Anyway, the title of the other book is *In Mortal Danger: The Battle for America's Border and Security,* and that one is by Tom Tancredo. Since you are out of school, you need to start reading other kinds of books to gain different people's perspectives to give you a more balanced view of this country and the world so that your perspectives are broader."

At least he acknowledged that I was out of school, I thought, feeling a bit less knee-jerked. Somewhat mollified, I told him, "I saw that book by Buchanan when I first came in your main office. May I have it?"

"Did you see one or two *State of Emergency* books out there?"

"One."

"Was it a part of my library or just sitting on the table?"

"Okay, I suspect where you are going with this, E.J."

"Nah. Let me complete where I was going so that neither of us has to be repetitive—you in asking and me in answering questions out of order." E.J. walked over to his bar and tossed a couple of nuts in his mouth. Chewing, he asked, "Are you unable to get the book on your own? Now, if I only have one copy of that book and it is a significant part of my library, why should I inconvenience myself by giving you my one and only copy?"

"Because you love me and I am the baby of the family," I teased.

"Uh-huh. And that last reasoning is the very reason I am not giving you my book. I want you to grow up and do things that we grownups do—buy your own book. And you had better stop being so cheap. Learn to invest in those things in life that will make you better at what you want to do."

"Okay. But I am grownup."

"Good, because you must always practice what you want to project. Role play the role before you have to play it for real. Stay on guard."

"Right," I said sharply. The advice was good, but again I felt like the tutee.

"Now another question for you: Do you know the name of the other person that Mrs. Williams spoke of who was to head AWALA before you came into the picture?"

"Nope."

"Well, we need to know that. Who was that other person, and why did she back out of the chairperson role?"

"Why is that important?"

"Well, we need to find that out," E.J. advised me, "because the information will give us better leverage."

"Leverage for what?" I asked, throwing up my hands. I didn't understand why we would need any leverage; the amount and everything is spelled out in the contract even down to what I am to accomplish.

E.J. was very intense. "Leverage so that when this summit and documentary are over, no one will have a hold on you, your image or reputation for the rest of your life. How do you know what you should be getting paid for doing this project? Just because they have a price written down doesn't mean that it is a fair price for you. We don't even know if this is enough money for you to pull off a project of this nature and style. You don't know where you are going to hold the conference and what you might have to give or gain, for that matter, to even get the conference held where you want it, Zemi; you don't know what people are going to charge you for anything yet." E.J. looked down at the contract again. "The contract provides for a working budget and capital, but who has done any pricing? For things like speakers, and so forth. And you know that you have to pay speakers big-time to sanction what it is that you want to expound upon in the documentary or on stage. You are essentially buying people who have followers already and that helps to boost your attendance numbers, the 100,000 people you have to pull to the summit."

"Some speakers will probably participate for free since the organization is non-profit," I said.

"Zemi, these people will not be your philanthropic speakers, whether they believe in your cause or not. The bottom line is the entire success of this summit and documentary depends on acquiring beforehand the actual dollars needed to pull it off. You will have to hire tons of people to make this happen, and right now you don't know such costs. I don't think you realize the magnitude in cost, do you?"

Reluctantly, I agreed. "No. I can't say that I know anything about costs."

"Hell, you don't even know what my cost is going to amount to, now do you? That's why you need to know everything up front because you surely can't pull this thing off without an attorney in your corner," E.J. said.

My stomach was knotting up. I got up and paced around E.J.'s office as it were my own. Was I getting cold feet? Joey's words resonated through my being: *"Women don't really know how to do business or how to run things."* I began wondering if I could actually pull off the summit and documentary.

E.J. read my thoughts. I had to admit. My brother was good at what he did.

"Now, I know what you are thinking, Zemi. You are wondering if you are capable enough to pull this summit off. You want to know if you have bitten off more than you can chew. Well, we can answer these questions once we are better informed," he said. He got up and to get more nuts.

I stopped pacing and sat in E.J.'s chair behind the desk.

E.J. looked at me sternly.

"What's wrong?" I asked.

"Zemi, you have not paid me not one solitary penny, so that means that you have not earned any right to sit yourself in my chair. Get up and go sit in one of those other chairs until you have paid the cost to be the boss, and it is not likely that you will be boss here," he said, waving his hands across the breath of his office.

I got up and sat in another chair.

Looking back at the contract, E.J. said, "Zemi, they put down here in the contract that the whole process is to be filmed. We need to find out if you are marketing this organization as much as they want the summit and documentary to be marketed. The organization will be able to use the piece for the rest of its existence to obtain funds. We have to find out for sure, but it appears that you will be doing two jobs for the price of one salary. Who gets the credit for filming? The organization or you? Are you the producer? Who will have rights to the film? That's why we have to find out who and what they were going to pay the other person. Don't you want to know what they were going to pay her?"

"I guess I do."

"Of course you do. See, Zemi these people, whoever they are, sought you out. Am I right?"

I nodded my head.

"They are an organization that obviously has money backing them. Somebody or someone feels that you are capable enough to gather and concentrate women in the South for a certain reason. Who or what wants that to happen? Who is sponsoring this organization? That is what we want to know. Who are they covertly lobbying for and why did that other person not want to chair this thing? See, they are not telling you everything. Nevertheless, it is your responsibility to always search for the esoteric because that's where most of your important answers will lie. Are you following me, Zemi?"

I rose from my chair.

"Where are you going, girl?"

"To the ladies' room."

"Okay, but let me make this point before you go." E.J. got up to open the door for me. "This woman or this organization that sought you out knows that you are brilliant, a dedicated person, and that you are anxious and hungry to make a name for yourself. Yeah. Yes, yes."

He, trying to process, began popping his knuckles, a habit he's had since childhood. I tried to duck out the door, but E.J. blocked my passage.

"They've figured you out down to your goals and even the substance you're made out of, Zemi. When a young person is hungry, they will do a task and perform it well, for just about peanuts. These people are no dummies. And you can't posture yourself as being a dummy either."

I frowned. "E.J., what makes you think that Mrs. Williams and her organization would even want to hire someone they felt was a dummy?"

"Zemi, my excellent training and substantial experience tell me that's a plausible angle. I am paid to ask the hard questions, to suspect, to be skeptical. Doing the same won't hurt anybody, no matter what they do in life. So don't go getting an attitude here. You have to grow up and start analyzing so that others will not be able to readily distinguish between your youth and your comprehension. Zemi, though you may have mastered the critical study of a specific science, you must still observe matters from all possible angles covered because everything is interdependent."

I nodded my head in agreement. "I know that you're right, E.J."

E.J. pulled my chin upwards. "See, what you need is to add on, pile on to your education you received in those universities. Grab hold to some of that knowledge that mogul-rappers possess and control. They make people play into their field as if they are the gurus. I will tell you something else, too. Many rappers are smarter than most people want to give them credit for. Politicians would do well to use them more to espouse their issues for the 2008 election. They are the ones who have the non-voters' attention already. Rappers have a law-of-science kind of schooling where they harness their wealth of experience and channel it in a masterful way. They will do this and deal their own marketing arena. Whereas you, Zemi, have a social, analytical but manageable kind of schooling, which society sees as a mainstream brand, no doubt, but one to control and define and pay peanuts for," he coached.

"Do you mean to tell me that instead of all of the money and time that I've spent sitting in those schools that I could have taken a shortcut to all of this?" I asked.

"No, I am not saying that at all. Anyway, shortcuts at the end of the day will only deliver you cold cuts. Eliminate every unnecessary step, Zemi. I'm saying that people have to be capable to learn in the environment that they're placed, but no matter where the education takes place, an education can never serve best if it is taught one-sidedly."

"Yes." I agreed.

E. J. was teaching as my daddy had taught. "Utilize the examples of the masters who walked there before you, making the blunders that you don't have to make because you get to bypass the boo-boos, and the delays that are caused by such miscalculations. Start with the examples of those who know it better. You can add your personal idea, impressions, and imaginative innovations after you get it right."

"Keep holding that thought. I'll be right back."

But E.J. tugged at the sleeve of my sweater. "I want you to be clear of what my job would entail, should we decide to take on this project. It would be to provide you with information in order for you to create a format of interest that will lend itself to flexibility and cover a broad spectrum of topics. I am trying to make you, meaning Zemi, prepared to accomplish that task. I am saying it is just as important for you to learn about the worldly matters as it was for you to learn book knowledge, and to be a lettered woman."

"I am not following you," I said, becoming impatient. I really wished E.J. would let me through the door to go to the ladies' room.

"You need to upgrade your business acumen to brand yourself. And that can be done in many ways, but for right now it needs to be readied, garbed in business game. You have to know who you are first. Define yourself to others, but never let others define you. Whether you like how you define yourself or not, you are the only one who can work the magic of being you. See, you've got to know how to understand the business game when it's being played, especially if someone is trying to play it on you. You've got to know how to play it. Different scenarios and circumstances call for certain types and levels of finesse. It means that you take all of the factors, you know, ingredients, those that are shown to you and the ones you have to discover by your own wits." E.J. took his pen and tapped his palm. "For instance, why is this other person's name being withheld from you?"

I was about to try to answer the question, but E.J. was moving fast in thought and just as fast in speech. I didn't get a chance to say anything.

"How much time did they give you to return this contract, Zemi?"

"She gave me until Wednesday evening to have it on her desk."

E.J., releasing tension, loosened the neck of his tie. "Um. That's a rush. See, you need to know why they are rushing you, giving you such short notice to sign a long contract before being able to do some background checking. They probably didn't know you had a gifted brother and attorney backing you. I will never allow anyone to cheapen your value. While defining yourself, it won't hurt to add high-dollar values to your worth, either. Set some monetary standards for the types of work you will or will not accept. Don't forget how much you are always moaning about your student loans."

"Now I am getting the hang of your talk, brother man." I ducked under his arm and headed for the ladies' room. During the time I was gone, I realized how fortunate I was to have E.J. and wondered what others did without any legal representation whatsoever. Now that was another matter. I knew by this morning's events that I had some fast learning and deep internalizing to do. I realized I had to be in a position to deal with the Joeys and the Mrs. Williamses who entered my world. The restroom break gave me an opportunity to understand that I needed to be more open to what E. J. was trying to tell me.

When I returned, E.J. picked up where he'd left off, not missing a beat.

"And you must set standards for a man, too. What I'm saying, you can apply all this to your personal life, too." E.J., the attorney, had segued into his big-brother role. "Place high value on yourself so that whenever you do get a man, Zemi, you'll know, not just feel, that he's truly worthy of you, and appreciates that you are rarer and more precious than the most prized jewel. A man must be patient with you, Zemi. You'll definitely need that ingredient from him. But now don't get it twisted. You must never pity a man, for when you do that, you will spend most of the time making excuses for him and the rest of the time getting spent yourself. Spent carrying the weight of responsibility, spent—just like money—gone, used up. Being the kind of woman you are, Zemi, you'll need a very strong man. But then another thing—choose a man who loves you more than you love him."

"Why must he love me more?" I asked, almost oblivious to my succumbing to E.J.'s newly presumed role as advisor in what I considered my intimate affairs.

"It is artful of a woman to attract a man who loves her more. She is more alluring in that way. A man will do so very much for a woman he loves more. The challenge for him is always present."

"Do I have what it takes to make a man love me more?"

E.J. answered slowly, "You do, b-but, you must step up your game for a man to do that."

"How can I step up my game?" Now I knew I had succumbed, but felt I could use tips from a man I could trust.

"First, don't be too eager for a man. Be slow to his charm but quick fast with your playful witticism. Never let a man think he is an expert in your modus operandi."

"What's that?" I asked, remembering the answer to my own question just when E.J. explained.

"Your ways, style, etc. Your mode of operation. He must not ever be so confident that he knows you inside and out. Maintain your mystery; keep it so he always has something about you to discover. But always study the man you want; know more about him than he knows about you. Take what you know to maneuver, take the time to acclimate him and his habits to your desires. That way you are asserting, but he mustn't have a clue. He must think that pleasing you is all his idea."

"How in the world is that done?"

"Practice asking, instead of telling."

"What do you mean?"

"Well Dr. Navies, our father—that Dr. Navies—was a strong man, but he was Mama's man at the end of the day."

"…..and? Did I miss something, E.J.?"

"I don't know, let's see."

I couldn't believe he was going Socratic method on me; that was how he learned in law school. This was too much like work.

"What did Mama say when she wanted her way, Zemi?"

I paused, and thought about my parents. I got it. "She would ask him something like whether he considered doing something a certain way." *Honey, have you thought about getting the house painted for Easter?* I could hear Mother in my head right now. I told E.J., "She never preached to Daddy."

"You got it!" he said, congratulating me. "And, Sis, Daddy always thought he was ruling, but I saw things differently. He did rule, but so did Mother. Our Mother is a strong woman and our father was a strong man."

"How will I be able to tell a strong man?"

"If he can help you obtain your dreams. And I don't mean with just words of encouragement, either. You do not need a man who blows hot air. You have mastered the art of gab and glib well enough yourself."

"Then should I look for a man who has money?"

E.J. sighed as he rubbed his bald head. "Zemi, that is like asking if you should look for a man who has sun when you know that you can't live without it. Don't try and do too much separating; things go hand in hand. You have taken some steps in life to better yourself and your condition. Why wouldn't you want a man who has done the same, if not more? And that means being able to take care of you and any babies financially. If you had all of the money you wanted, I could see you asking that question, but, Zemi, on that one, you know yourself all too well. You are the one who does not give her money to anyone because you'll take money from a beggar. You asked me that question, and here you didn't want to buy your own book." E.J. shook his head.

"E.J., why I don't know if I have just spent the last couple of hours with a therapist or an attorney," I said with mock Southern charm.

"You'll best know that answer when you've received my bill. Anyway, we might have to call Mrs. Williams because we've got to research this thing. We need more time to give an answer that is right for you, whether it's yes or no. At least, you need to know everything up front if you are to be successful in this venture. Frankly, Zemi, twelve months to complete a job on the scale requested is not enough time. This is not something you can just do right away. You need planning time, and without it you could be setting yourself up for failure."

"If we get a budget that will cover the necessary staffing, the work and dedication then can it be done in twelve months?" I asked.

"Maybe, but now you're talking about doing a job where the other person was given one year just to do planning, but you have been afforded only half a year. Whatever amount of money she was going to get for her year's work, then you must get double that because now you have to work twice as hard—and me, too. And that is presuming that the amount was a fair price to begin with."

"I want to do it."

"I can see that."

"Then get me the amount I need to hire the experts, E.J."

"Okay. But here is the deal. If I cannot get you the amount of money required, then I cannot represent you on this contract, and you will not do the summit. Deal or no deal?" asked E.J.

"Deal." I shook my brother's outstretched hand, thinking everyone should be so lucky to have a good attorney in the family.

* * * * *

I left E.J.'s office feeling confident; I knew that he would leave no stone unturned. He would take great care in taking all of the necessary steps to safeguard me from any snares that I might have fallen into while trying to take on a project and summit of this magnitude. E.J. was determined because he wanted to make me a stronger match-up for Mrs. Williams and any challenges I would face to complete the work with her. I knew that for certain. E.J. never wanted any Navies to ever fall prey to anyone's plotting—and plotting is what she was up to. Truly. After my session with E.J., my persona had taken on a more sophisticated aura; I could tell it in how I walked and the new height self-esteem I felt. Plus, E.J. took great patience to help me understand men a bit more. I guess it's kind of nice to have an older brother like him, even if he was borderline into my business—my personal business.

* * * * *

A couple of days later I received a telephone called from E.J.

"Here's the deal, Zemi." E.J.'s voice was energetic and surprisingly excited. "My office located the woman who was initially sought after for the summit AWALA," he was eager to report.

I felt anxious. I asked E.J. hurriedly, "What's her name?" Anxious at hearing this news, I assaulted E.J. with a barrage of questions: "When will you get a chance to meet with her personally? Do you think that she will disclose any information on the summit or Mrs. Williams? Maybe I should speak with her myself. Sometimes it is easier for women to talk to women to get the scoop on certain things."

"Hold on now, Zemi. Understand who it is that you have at the other end of the phone line," E.J. answered firmly.

By his tone, I knew right away that I had crossed over into E.J.'s sphere of control.

"Don't ever tell me how to do my job."

I retreated into my role as the baby girl. "I am sorry, E.J. I didn't mean to suggest that you didn't know how to do your job."

"Then be quiet and listen to the rest of what I have to tell you." E.J. took a deep breath. "The last name of the lady that Mrs. Williams had asked to do the summit is Swopes. —S-W-O-P-E-S, but its pronounced 'Swoops.' I spoke with her over the telephone, but I did not feel the need to get too personal. So I did not inquire if she was a Miss or Mrs., nor did I ask her for a first name. She sounds like a very charming lady. I have made arrangements to fly out to Charlotte and meet with her. But to answer one of your questions, Ms. Swopes did give me a whole lot of information about the summit and Mrs. Williams."

My excitement and anxiety rose. Knowing E.J., he probably cross-examined the poor lady so intensely that she felt compelled to give up the goods on everything involving the summit. I would not want to be in her position, I thought, and then realized that I was already.

"Now do you have any questions, Zemi?"

"You know that I have questions, E.J. and you know exactly what they are."

E.J. said playfully, "Speak up girl. I can't hear you."

My voice was tentative. "Does it sound as though the summit, I mean, the whole project, is it something that you feel I can be successful at doing?"

E.J. did not answer.

"E.J., come on now," I implored.

After a long (and for me, uncomfortable) pause, all I got from him was, "Hmmm."

"E.J., don't do me like that. Am I capable of doing the job or not?"

"Okay, Zemi. I've held you in suspense long enough. You will not only be able to do the job successfully, but you will get a fair amount of money for doing the summit. With the massive publicity and PR arranged, you not only will be able to get the best speakers around as presenters, but my office has done enough negotiating with Mrs. Williams to guarantee that the entire project will be produced by your very own company. The filming, however, will remain the property and copyright of AWALA. Now how does that sound to you, Zemi?"

"Oh, my God! E.J. Oh, my God! Are you being real with me? Come on, E.J., my heart cannot take any joking around about this."

"I am serious, Zemi. I will make everything happen for you. And you deserve everything to happen this way, too."

The excitement was overwhelming. Loudly enough for him to hear through natural airwaves, I asked, "But E.J, what did you do to make all of this happen? Oh, my God, this is big!"

"I know people and I have my connections," E.J. answered smoothly.

"But, Zemi, be a lady and stop being so loud over the telephone. You'll make people want to hang up on you. Okay, girl?"

"Okay. But, E.J., there is just one thing."

"What might that be?" he asked calmly.

I took a deep breath. "You said that the entire project and filming will be produced by my very own company."

"That's right. And?" asked E.J.

"I don't have a company."

"Oh I forgot to tell you that part. My office took the liberty and started the paperwork for you to do this project under an already existing parent company. So, Zemi, your entire project will take off just as you wanted. You'll become known as a social scientist, for I knew that was important to you, too. I promise you that this summit will be one of your biggest and best projects ever. After you've completed this one, you'll be ready for anything."

My heart became heavy with the exciting news and the appreciation of how much my brother had done, and my eyes welled up. I started crying. Sniffling, I said, "Oh, E.J., I will forever be grateful to you."

"Well that's about it, and I will talk to you, Miss Entrepreneur, a little bit later."

"E.J., wait before you hang up. What is the name of the parent company?" I asked.

"My Private Stock Enterprise."

"Oh E.J., I love that name."

E.J. said confidently, "I knew you would. And you can relax and let My Private Stock Enterprise do all the prep work for you."

* * * * *

Mom wanted to throw a birthday party for me in California, but I wanted to be with Zeth on that day. He had planned something very special, and the surprise had to be given to me in person. So I spent the next several days in Asheville, North Carolina. It made Zeth happy to know that I had chosen to spend time with him over my family. Zeth did not have a lot of friends his own age and he'd spent most of his childhood around older aunts and uncles. He was an only child, born to his parents quite late in their lives. Both of his parents, who have now passed on, were from very large families. With Zeth being the youngest of the relatives, he was pretty much the only one left to take care of the elderly ones. He was the executor over their estates. Most of the land he looked after was all over the South and spread over even more acres than the land Zeth owned. Zeth's ranch was a wide open space where my mind could roam free for days.

If Zeth was ever going to bring me closer into his world, I thought now would be the time. He was trying hard to get the message across to me that I was more than he had dreamed. During my stay, Zeth seemed to do all he could to make each day and evening special. He told me that tomorrow would be a very extraordinary day, but offered—both quite out of context and unromantically—that he did not wear diamonds given their conflicted status because of the killings and intolerable labor conditions associated with the diamond industry. I was not quite sure what that had to do with anything. Surely, they sold non-conflicted diamonds? Didn't they? For sure, I know that I am a woman who loves diamonds, even if the extent of my grand collection is one pair of diamond earrings. What better way could a man prove his love for a woman than with diamonds? Just like the TV commercials! But I was wearing them right now! Maybe he didn't notice them. Why he did not think it was okay to tell me that he didn't wear diamonds? Well, that was fine. I mean—the part about Zeth not wearing diamonds. That did not bother me. These earrings were a gift from E.J. on my twenty-third birthday… I love them.

We relaxed in the great room of Zeth's home by the hearth that stood six feet tall. Everything in Zeth's home seemed tall. The candles were tall and extravagant, and evoked sentiments of home, comfort, warmth and coziness. The rug was beautiful, a huge Parisian. It looked most expensive. It was wool of excellent strength, luster, resilience, and had a softness that complemented my own softness.

Zeth rubbed my face. I smiled and rubbed his hand; it was warm. "I love your face, Zemi," he said, "and I love the way you smile at me. You are my open door that lets the sunshine in. It lights my world, my day begins. I love your face, Puddin'. I love the look that's in your eyes." Zeth kissed me, and whispered, "You see right through the deepest part of me. Right down into the heart of me. I wouldn't want you to ever change on me, Puddin'. You're just right fer me. I love all of you. And especially, I love your face. I love the message there fer me. You and me are the greatest love story I ever heard of." His eyes shone. "I want you to know that, Zemi."

I had never seen Zeth look at me this way. What words God had given him—just to say to me! That must have been the love E.J. spoke of, a man loving a woman more. I returned Zeth's kissed passionately, but at the same time I was trying to control a flame that just seemed like it was being stoked, and stoked and….Well, how else could one show gratitude for such emotions expressed from a heart so open?

"Zeth your words, so poetic, they took me into a space that I have never experienced before. I don't know…for a moment I lost myself."

Zeth pressed a finger to my lips, "Shh! Maybe in that space you found yourself—. Let me take up that space forever, Puddin'. Let me. Let me relax that part of who you really are." He rested his face on my chest.

And the part of me that was my essence relaxed. I felt safe, I felt home?

Zeth had mentioned earlier that he had a surprise for me that evening, and now he told me what it was: *Smokey Robinson in Concert*! I was thrilled; I love "The Poet," the handle earned by the native Detroiter and smooth, velvet-voiced crooner. One of Motown's and America's greatest performers ever. I mean, Smokey is still "Cruisin" and he is still huge. I remember when mom told me of when my dad had bought front-row seats for them to see Smokey perform at a dinner show in Lake Tahoe. In the audience were mostly white fans of Smokey, as was typical for Tahoe then. My mom said that during the show, Smokey pointed to my mother and called her up to the stage. Smokey told the audience that he was happy to see some of his people in the audience. He was proud that some black people had spent big money to see him perform in such a fine place. Smokey kissed Mother on her cheek! After all these years, I think she is yet to wash that side of her face!

We finished dinner in time to make the eleven o'clock show. As if on a cue sent from Zeth, Smokey sang a special song, and Zeth and I slow-danced to it: Smokey's "I Love Your Face." Zeth stroked my face and we smiled—at each other.

The following day Zeth continued to impress me in every way to show me that he wanted me to be a part of his life. He was talking to me about opening a business right here in Asheville. Asheville has been his home for all of his life, although he has been every place in the South you could name. Asheville's population is not that big, and is showcased as a quaint town. It is chock full of old-fashioned charm. Zeth said that North Carolina is a big state, but he really sees

Asheville as the place for my mission in life. He says the city has a black mayor named Terry Bellamy, and that she's a pretty, young and fiery woman, the same way he sees me—a mover and shaker. (Zeth says the mayor has a son with a name close to his except her son's name is spelled Seth.) Zeth thinks Asheville could benefit from my starting a business here.

My, he thinks a lot of me! My benefiting a city? Asheville is looking for what I could bring, he says, and that I, in turn, could benefit from the city's capacity for growth. But I told him it was going to take me a few more years to save up money before actually opening up my own business.

When Zeth and I strolled around his property that afternoon, I was tempted to think about this as home because in California you just don't see yards so huge.

"If you like," Zeth offered carefully, "I could show you how to get a business up and runnin' in no time. Later, I could show you some programs out there that could help you out and get you goin' in the right direction. Zemi, I would do anythin' to have you make this your home."

I didn't mention it to Zeth, but while in Charlotte several months ago, I had already looked into the possibility of working at Johnson C. Smith University. Maria claimed that the reason for my keen interest was the pedigree of the school's president, Dr. Dorothy Cowser Yancy. Anyway, the job I wanted had already been taken, but it is true that I do admire Dr. Yancy. Plus, Johnson C. Smith is a highly respected university. But now, I mostly see myself as self-employed, owning by own company.

Spending quality time with Zeth made me look at him in a different light. I didn't know he was involved in so much and in so many ways with the South. He made plans for us to attend the Charlotte Mecklenburg African American Town Hall Meeting, featuring Dr. Julianne Malveaux and Tavis Smiley. Zeth owns a lot of property in Mecklenburg County, and he runs all sorts of businesses there situated on land he owns.

"You make everything sound just so easy—too easy," I told him.

He took my hand, "Come, I want to show you my flower nursery. But you bein' a city girl and all, I don't know if you can cut the mustard to walk, or if I should drive you there."

"How far is it?"

"Oh, it's up the road a little ways. But you know 'up the road' in the South can be from a half-mile to ten miles. It just depends on who's doin' the talkin'. But I wouldn't do that to you, girl. I'll take you there in my pickup, just in case you might need that energy a little bit later."

We climbed into his Nissan pickup truck and he drove to the nursery. "Puddin', why don't you move on down here right now and begin your business plannin' in North Carolina? I am here fer you, I mean, if you ever needed my assistance. I betcha doors would open up fer you a lot faster here than in California as far as the business that you want to make happen." Zeth turned his head and surveyed the nursery with a once over.

Was it Zeth's romantic heart speaking, or did he really believe business was here for me? Both?

"You know, Zemi, I can't pinpoint too much what it is that you really want to do in life even though you might still be searchin'. Just know that you are not too young to begin operatin' your own business. You are through with that hard studyin' phase of your life now, though people must always keep their ears and hearts open to the ground and sky to keep learnin'. But the next level is better because it is on-the-job, real-life trainin'. You can find out whether or not that schoolin' was worth that big old student loan you have to pay back to Uncle Sam."

"You are right about that. I owe a lot of money to Uncle Sam," I conceded reluctantly.

"Boy," Zeth shook his head. "They like to sweeten it by callin' him Uncle Sam, but I call him Uncle Smooth. We need to examine the kind of love America is showin' her own young citizens. Exactly what does she mean when she tells her young to stay in school and earn a high school diploma so that they will be able to compete? These young kids soon come out to experience what kind of competition Uncle Sam was really talkin' about. In essence, some of America's best are teachin' at a Third World level—obviously passin' is equivalent to competin' with illegal immigrants, some who might be low in studyin' or schoolin'."

"Zeth, just how long can America stay a superpower when those from other countries can compete better than her citizens? I think that is the question the public should be most concerned with." I got so excited as I spoke and accidentally knocked a plant over. "I am so sorry."

"Ain't nothin' to be concerned about." Zeth picked up the plant and wiped the dirt from his hands onto his jeans. "Students with a high school diploma and legitimate Social Security numbers have to compete with illegal immigrants fer minimum wage jobs even though those illegal immigrants never attended a high school here or anywhere. They also get Social Security numbers. Why should persons who speak English and hand their diplomas and Social Security numbers over to a Wal-Mart, Target or Sears enter the work force on the same payin' scale as illegal immigrants with no such credentials?"

"I wonder what special programs are afforded illegal aliens under the veil."

"Ain't nobody said so, but we all know. Sometimes our young are told that they are overqualified with just a high school education, and that is why they didn't get certain jobs. Every poor U.S. citizen ought to be outraged and should come together in the name of makin' this country more accountable to its own children and grandchildren before they make it a heaven on earth fer foreigners," said Zeth.

Zeth and I walked back to the pickup, and he drove us to the other side of the nursery. He was very compassionate about what he felt was an intentional disregard for the loyalty blacks have shown to the country. He felt illegal immigrants' issues had somehow advanced to the front ahead of African Americans, and that so many assumed that both blacks and browns have the same concerns. The media is all over the question, "Should illegals be given drivers' licenses?" They got blacks discussin' that when it ain't a black issue.

Still inside the truck, Zeth caressed my shoulders. "I wondered if grace will ever kick in fer our people? Come on, let's get out of this truck so I can show you the reason I brought you over to this side."

Zeth had brought to light for me a new reality. I was able to call to mind the things E.J. had told me about, not about the broad subject called men, but what kind of man I should attract. Also, through E.J.'s representation of me in his role as lawyer, I gained a greater understanding of how to process information. In my case, E.J. used politics to show me how to examine what's shown and to look for what is not shown. He also cautioned me to look for and determine motive, intent, and agenda. If I had gotten an appointment with E.J. before my meeting with Mrs. Williams, I definitely would have asked more questions, including the questions that would have added up to "Why me?" It took a session with E.J. to speculate about where Mrs. Williams was coming from and why she picked me. Aaaah! Another epiphany. The meeting had to take place so soon after Mrs. Williams contacted me so that I did not have either the time or the opportunity to ask or tell anyone about her call. I vow never again to be played for the chump!

Anyhow, no matter what, I am beginning to see more and more things in the pictures others frame for me, and I see more in general, too. For example, black folk seemed to be slighted in more serious ways than the tawdry attention afforded by black leaders. Our citizens and our children fight wars for America, and are among those who return home impaired physically and mentally. Is America's programs for veterans equal to the entitlements provided by our government to illegal immigrants? I just wonder. Shouldn't programs and benefits for veterans be greater than what illegal immigrants get, no matter where they came from? Exactly how much money is spent to accommodate the illegal immigrants in this country compared with the dollars spent on veterans' programs? Why should blacks and whites go and fight for this country while illegal immigrants can waltz in and get free medical care and education while we send our own citizens away to be maimed in war? Is it not the case that some soldiers who just came back from Iraq are complaining that they cannot get full benefits? That they cannot do anything, but that the military has claimed that they were less than a hundred percent disabled?

Zeth broke into my thoughts, and thank goodness for that! "I call this section of my nursery my second heaven next to you, Puddin'."

Zeth picked up an orchid and placed it in my palm. "I have just about any kind of plant you can think of in this nursery, and I ship them all over the country."

"The United States must have a heck of a guest worker program going on. It looks like you have every Mexican on this side of the border working here," I said.

"Don't gauge what you see here as misleadin' to what I said in the truck, which is my true belief. There are times when one has to consider some commonalties in comin' to a workable thought, and on some occasions you have to do so accordin' to the present circumstances."

"Now, really?" I teased. "A different tune when it comes to expediency?" I gave Zeth a poke in the ribs. "Just kidding with you. I understand the usefulness of laborers to successful businesses. We need them."

"See, Puddin', my runoff was that illegal immigrants have displaced a lot of poor black and white Americans, at least they are poor now if they were not before. When I see blacks and whites who are in the streets homeless and holdin' up signs that they are hungry and will work for food, then I say make guest workers' programs second to the needs of your own citizens who are beggin' in the street. Foreigners who want to come to America and work should be allowed to do that through some agreeable guest worker program voted on by the citizens. Place guest worker programs as propositions on ballots and let the people vote accordin' to the local people's need in a city or state. If the citizens voted for them to be in America, then that's the end of the story, but be decent and let the citizens' voices be heard first above illegal immigrants. I believe that is a fair way to look at the situation and the mess America finds herself in."

Zeth would have made a good politician. I guess at the end of the day one survives by any means necessary.

"Oh!" I cried, surprised by a spray of water. Zeth grabbed me by the waist, and we made a quick dash away from the automatic sprinklers. I grabbed my head, trying to hold my scarf on, but I got misted all over.

"Ain't nothin' wrong with bein' all wetted up. The water brin's out your fragrance the way it does the smell of fresh flowers in the nursery."

Zeth picked me up and set me down on a tall work table nearby. He was strong and tall with the physique of a football player who worked out all day long. I had never gone out with a man as strong as Zeth and as kind in so many ways. Still, I held back. I did not want to take the time to understand why I was not letting go of my feelings. Whatever, I held it all inside. I gave Zeth not a clue as to how he should proceed with me; he didn't know if he should go left or right, up or down. But he was not doing too badly without a compass.

"So, Zemi, what do you think of my nursery business?"

"It looks to be a wonderful business."

Zeth smiled. "Aw shucks. I do all right. It's a business that helps to pay the bills."

"And I am sure that it pays a lot of employees, too," I said.

"Let's go." Zeth lifted me from the work table so that I could stand. "I've got somethin' else I want to show you," he said. Zeth opened my side of the door to the pickup truck. "Watch your scarf," he was careful to say.

All the roads on Zeth's scenic acres were smooth. Before coming to visit Zeth, I just had no idea of the concept of land value and how land tied into so much of the history of black people and the South. A couple of months ago Zeth had taken me to see some land he owned some eighty miles from his ranch. On that land stood his father's old church, two handsomely appointed homes, a couple of red barns and about thirty to forty headstones. The large family tree seemed to cover everything in the family graveyard, including the front headstones for Zeth's parents, then one for a sister who died at birth. The remaining headstones were for the resting places of uncles, aunts and other kinfolk. There could exist no confusion within Zeth's family or the city hall that the Higgenbottom, his family surname, owned the land. Because of this experience with Zeth, I was rid of the naiveté I had held about owning land as opposed to just owning a house. And to think—my family still thinks that people in the South are slow of speech and pace.

The pickup braked suddenly and Zeth sounded the horn at a rambling goat. "How in the world did that goat get on this side?" he asked himself.

Just then, a worker came by and prodded the goat along.

"Gee, Zeth! You have goats, too?"

"Yeah, we've got a couple." Zeth drove across an overpass. When we stopped and got out, he nudged me to walk forward.

"Oh, my goodness! You have an actual assembly line operating," I said.

"On this right side of the plant is our milkin' parlor where we ultrapasteurize goat's milk," Zeth explained proudly. "And ultra-pasteurization just refers to the process of heatin' our goat's milk at ultra-high temperatures for a brief time. And this here method kills all viruses and microorganisms that could harm the milk. Plus, it helps the milk to last longer. When the milk reaches 282 degrees Fahrenheit, it's held at that temperature for three seconds. Then the milk is flash cooled and packaged in steam-sterilized cartons. And just in case you want to know, pasteurization and ultrapasteurize do not affect the nutritional value of the milk."

"I'm overwhelmed, Zeth! I'm just speechless."

"That's all right. It makes you a unique kind of woman. Not too many women have experienced times as a speechless bein'," said Zeth.

Teasing, I pinched Zeth on the elbow.

"Just goes to show you, Zemi, I can stand a little physical pain from you but can't take any hurt to the heart." Zeth took my hand and pointed to the left, saying, "Let's walk through here. In this portion of the plant is the goat cheese room."

"Hmmm," I thought aloud, "I can't recall ever tasting either goat cheese or goat's milk."

"It's good. More people around the world drink goat's milk over cow's milk. Well really, I am just gettin' my feet wet in this area, experimentin' with different types of cheeses. Right now, we are only packagin' Swiss and a first-place cheddar and marketin' them on my own," said Zeth. "There are not a lot of licensed goat dairies around these parts, but my company is growin' and, hopefully, in a couple of years we will see some headway in milk and cheese productivity. We try to supply milk all year round, and we are slowly gettin' the hang of thin's—like learnin' how to trick our goats with special lightin' so they'll breed not only in the fall—their normal breedin' time—but also in the sprin' to ensure milk production come fall."

Zeth seemed to have employed an equal number of blacks and Mexicans to work in the plant. When we passed the office at the plant where Zeth told me that accounting and other business was handled, I glanced in to see mostly black and Filipino employees, and a few white workers, too.

"Is your milk organic?" I asked.

"Well, we are not authorized yet to put that label on our products, but we are organic with all of our products being free of pesticides, antibiotics and preservatives. It takes time and patience to develop all of our strategies."

"If you don't mind my asking, does it take a lot of capital to operate a business of this nature?"

"I love so much the sound of your voice, Puddin', that you can ask me any question you want to, and I will try my absolute best to answer."

Zeth was looking down, eying me with that special look I am beginning to cherish.

"With all the major technological advances and trends in cheese, if I were larger, overhead would be much more. Goats do not like bein' wet and don't have the wool to keep them warm, so shelter for goats costs more. Goat farmers are subject to more imported feed cost fluctuations, and the labor is intense. You know, you always want and strive to make the most money in your businesses but more than money, my concern is the rewards I receive from bein' able to employ people, givin' them jobs so that they can put food on the table and take care of their families. I would like to see more middle-class African Americans take on the challenge of entrepreneurship and help employ some of our own people. No longer are black people able to count on government programs like affirmative action."

"Truly, Zeth, this is so much to comprehend that my questions seem a little silly. Being from a California city, the opportunity to visit a ranch or learn about these kinds of businesses on large acres of land is very special. This had never occurred to me. I mean that this is such a grand opportunity to earn a living."

I was in awe to shock over all the activity going on around me. I realized that some people in California, including many of our people, had no idea about what to do with a lot of land beyond creating places like Neverland. I just never thought about the concept of utilizing land the way Zeth had done.

"Are you learnin' anythin', Puddin'?"

"Beyond measure. But what I want to know, Zeth, is what made you go into the goat business?"

"First off, I was raised in the country, and ever since I was weaned from breast milk, I could not take cow milk. Lactose intolerant. My parents had to give me goat's milk, so we always had goats around. My parents made their own cheeses, too, but not for sellin', just for family and kinfolk. It wasn't like I had a passion to do this or anythin' like that. Like it is sometimes said in these parts, 'Nobody ever intends to go into the goat business.' But since I still drink goat's milk as an adult, I figure why not make it fer myself? Bein' that I had the basics to go further, I then thought why not start up a business? But a lot of thanks goes to North Carolina's Department of Agriculture fer guidin' me in the right direction."

Gently, Zeth nudged me. "Here, let's walk this way to get out of here. I want to show you somethin' else." Once we were outside, I stumbled when the heel of my boot got caught in some rocks. Zeth grabbed me by my waist, "Puddin', you all right?"

"I'm okay. I just lost my balance for a moment." Again? Was I always looking for a reason for him to catch me? I was not clumsy!

Zeth bent down to check on my boots. "Lesson number one, whenever you are trippin' around the land with me, you don't need to wear high-heeled boots. You will still stand tall in my world."

I was embarrassed that I had nearly fallen down. "When you saw me leaving the ranch with these boots on, Zeth, why didn't you say something? I am not familiar with this country lifestyle yet," I said.

Zeth seemed a little amused by the comment. "I don't know what country has to do with anythin', but unless it was somethin' that was goin' to kill you, I always thought experience was the best teacher."

"I am sorry, but 'country' wasn't meant to be anything negative. I just meant had I known more of what to expect on our outing today, I would not have worn high-heeled boots. That was more of what I intended to say."

Zeth tickled the palm of my hand. "Puddin', you are so beautiful and so innocent. You are just a rare find. Umm! Umm!" Zeth elevator-eyed me— (conveyor belt-eyed me? —I will stick with elevator-eyed me!) —from head to toe and shook his head. "Now I understand why Adam and Eve had to sin."

"Why did they?"

"Because it was worth it."

"Then why aren't you sinning?"

"Because you won't let me."

"If I let you, would you sin?"

"A little sinnin' won't hurt you."

"It might not hurt you, but how do you know it won't hurt a woman like me?"

"Because if you only knew, I have already sinned with you—deep down in my heart."

"And did God smile?" I teased.

Zeth smiled and tugged at the neck of his shirt, "I ain't heard Him complain none."

We laughed.

"Come on, girl," Zeth grabbed my hand, "let me show you more."

"I haven't seen all of your business ventures yet, but what I have seen is intriguing. That was a real treat, Zeth. Thank you so much for taking the time."

"Well, one thing I know that is true about you and me, Zemi, is that opposites attract."

"How is that?"

"Because you feel like you have already received the treat, and I feel like I am still holdin' the treat."

"Hmm."

Zeth cleared his throat. "Okay, and movin' right along to my next business venture and challenge. In here is the assembly line for the honey and molasses products that we sell. The companies are called Taste of Honey and Taste of Molasses. I'm not a man who likes to brag, but as Muhammad Ali would put it, I am not conceited. I am just convinced that this is just about the best honey that you will taste in your lifetime, Zemi."

I saw where Zeth also grows tons and tons of sweet potatoes, tomatoes, onions and other kinds of produce. A huge, huge garden! Eden? Sin? A little bit of sin? Shame on me! And on him, too, for broaching such a hot topic!

When we left the fields, Zeth took me to see his vintage car collection, then to the gated community he developed for senior citizens. Some of the homes are condos and the others are one-story single family homes. He has so much going on without the benefit of a college degree. I just had to know if he went to some type of trade school after high school. How could he have amassed so much learning without higher education? I wanted to ask, but it seemed too bold to do so, especially since Zeth seemed to think that I saw him as "country". So I kept quiet.

"Are you hungry yet, Puddin'? The cook ought to have lunch ready by now. I know you folk like to skip meals in California, but down here we like to catch at least two squares with a piece of fruit in between." Zeth pulled out two red apples from a bag in the back seat and handed me one.

Adam handed Eve an apple in one version of the Eden saga, although the Book of Genesis says nothing about an apple. Still….

"Here, Zemi. They've been washed already. When you are with me, I am goin' to make sure that you eat properly so that you can have healthy babies."

"Babies!" I almost choked on the first (*proverbial?*) bite! "I never thought about having babies."

"I meant when the time came, when everythin' was right." Zeth's eyes widened. "You do want to have babies, don't you, Zemi?"

"Zeth, I don't think about babies and changing diapers at all. I just completed my studying, and now I want to think about owning my own business."

"Would you breastfeed?"

Zeth and I got out of the truck and began walking. I think about his question. "To answer your question honestly, I don't know," is what I told Zeth, while at the same time I am thinking about whether I would like the idea of something constantly nibbling on me all day long—about being a virtual nursing bottle.

We were near a rustic bench. "Let's sit here for a moment," I said.

"You ever had an abortion, Zemi?" Zeth looked at me curiously.

I was uneasy and suspicious of the question but I answered, "No."

Zeth waited for elaboration. We both got very, very quiet.

"Do you believe in abortion?"

"Not for myself because I would not get pregnant unless I wanted a child, but I would not want to make that decision for other women."

"Interestin' answer."

"Let's walk more, Zeth." Annoyed about getting put on the hot seat, I decided to do some of my own interrogating. "Do you believe in abortion, Zeth?"

"Nope. I think that too many women use abortions as a form of birth control. And it would just tear my flesh to know that a woman would destroy somethin' so precious," said Zeth. He pulled me to him. "Besides that, I think the laws should state that a woman should not be able to have an abortion without the consent of the father of that child."

I pulled away, and looked up so that I could watch his expression. "Well, good luck with that law. Haven't you seen Judge Hatchett and all of the paternity test results revealed on her show? It does not appear that daddies are rushing to claim their little ones these days. So, if they make the law about a woman and her body, then that same court should make a ruling that it will stand in as the caretaker of that child for eighteen years. Perhaps that would make men a little more responsible and perhaps the government might just back off. Anyway, I could be sympathetic towards a pregnant woman who did not want to have a child if the situation was not good for her at that time of her life."

"What would have to be in place for you to have a child, Zemi?" Zeth was really pushing me farther than where I wanted to go, but I was happy to answer this particular one. "Without a doubt, I would have to be married, would not want to have a child before the age of thirty, would not want to work once pregnant and would need to stay at home with my child, at least until my child was ten years old. I also would need a nanny and a cook."

Zeth was taking everything in, his mind seemed to be processing my every word. "Interestin'," he answered, as if to himself.

Maybe I was sounding too immature for Zeth. Good. Because if ever I should swell for a man, things would have to be my way. I could not be pregnant, a superwoman and throw up all at the same time. Now that sounds like slavery to me. I don't take Zeth to be the type of man who would allow a nanny to come in and take care of his children. I think black men have problems with black women having help with household duties. They are so used to seeing white women having everything done for them, and perhaps have become too accustomed to seeing black women in work uniforms, and have not seen us enough in negligees and finery.

The way black women work too hard, run households by themselves without help and endure stress day in and day out has to account for some of the statistics showing that black women do not live as long as white women. I am sure. That is one of the most valuable things that I have learned from white women: they do know how to spoil themselves. White women have the guts to demand what they want out of life because, if not, they will start a movement. If they do not have the paradigm within which they choose to live, they will create a new one. A new paradigm, a new model for life and living, is what black women need. And it is up to black women to create this paradigm for ourselves!

Again, no one is saying a thing. A pregnant pause? Hmmph, it was so easy for men to say women should have babies, even if women have been raped and abused, or are underage girls or "over-age" women or poorer than dirt that won't grow weeds.

"No comment, Zeth?"

"Uh-uh." He shook his head. "Nope."

"Could you see yourself providing that for a woman in order for her to have your child?"

"I admire that you would want to stay at home for a while and raise your own child, Zemi. I would want more than one child, though. I didn't know fer sure if you were the type of woman who would want to stay at home, bein' that would be a sacrifice for a career-oriented woman like you. And if havin' someone to do the housecleanin' and cookin' will make you a better homemaker and a more readied wife fer me, then I am all fer that. I mean, I did not grow up that way. My mama did everythin' even though my dad had the means to make happen all the things you're askin' about. I never thought about it, but folk say my mama always been a hard worker and liked to do thin's fer herself."

I wondered if the reason Zeth's mother lost her other child was from working too hard.

"I am of a different mindset in that respect, Zemi. I like to cook sometimes, whenever I am in the mood. I have a cook in twice a week, but I love to contribute to lowerin' the employment rate by hirin' housecleanin' folk all the time." Zeth smiled broadly.

I smiled, too, to let him know that I respected his thoughts, his lifestyle, too.

"And I am not the kind of man who would put somethin' on you what you didn't want to do and especially if I don't want to do it neither. But I would not want you to wait until you were thirty to start bein' fruitful. That would be too long fer me to wait fer a woman."

I thought finally, there was something about me that he would not accept, and there were some things about me that I would not budge on. Anyway, I do not know if Zeth would be the man that I would want to have children with. They would be pretty children, for sure, but how intelligent would they come out? He did not go past high school himself.

"Zemi, I think I pretty much know the kind of woman that you are, and all that I don't know is because you don't want me to know. But by the same token, when you consider me, know what it is that you are examinin'. I want you bad, girl, and there ain't nothin' in this world that I wouldn't make happen fer you."

"I don't understand. How do you want me?"

"I want you, Puddin', in every way that a man can have a woman and in every way a man dreams of havin' a woman. Now ain't much to understandin' that, unless you just don't want to understand," he answered.

"A tall order there."

"Wasn't put out there to be an order."

Across the road from Zeth's truck was a huge rock. Zeth motioned toward it. "Let's sit here for a spell." After I had sat, Zeth removed my boots and rubbed my feet.

Thank you, God! My silent prayer was answered. Those tall high-heeled boots were doing a number on my feet!

"I know you want to get your own business goin'. And I know enough about you to know that you have to do thin's your own way. But I am here fer you if you let me. I also know that you are caught between if you should work on a job for someone else in order to pay your student loan debt or take a chance makin' your own business work now." Zeth took my feet and placed them across his lap.

"Oh, my! That student loan seems to be forever lurking."

"Sometimes it seems horseplay to me that a person spends so much money to sit in a learnin' institution designed by the government, and the education is supposed to guide people into more creative and productive paths in society." Zeth grunted. "What's funny to me is that the government leaves out how so many people who attend higher institutions of learnin' are not able to match the amount of money made by people who did not attend college. Some people who have never seen the inside of a lecture hall make quadruple what some college-educated folk their same age make. Goin' to college is like openin' up a business because you have to borrow the money from Uncle Sam, same as a business owner would, but college can put you four, five or even six years behind someone who does not go to college and starts a business right away," he reasoned.

And I am worried about this man's ability to sire intelligent babies?

"Please elaborate on that for me."

Zeth licked his lips. "I guess I ought to stop lookin' at you this way."

"Why?"

"Because you make me want you more, Zemi. And God knows, I didn't know that it was possible to want you more than I already do."

"You haven't answered my question about Uncle Sam and school and owning one's own business."

"Well, look at it this way. You owe a debt to Uncle Sam for what you have learned. Now you come out an eager beaver, but your next step is shaken because you have a debt that is already owed to the government. If you should try to apply fer another government loan, they will tell you first, you already have a debt outstandin' and secondly, you don't have enough experience to run a business. So they make you stay in the workforce longer than those who never went to college, never got a student loan, but might have gotten a business loan and started in business not long after high school. A student loan puts you in a box that is very hard to crawl out of. And that is why I think you should move permanently and right away to North Carolina." Zeth kissed me sweetly. "That was a sweet hint just in case you needed the simplification."

"Oh, I don't know if this city girl can give up the Golden Gate Bridge, fanfare of San Francisco and the sands of China Beach. I really do like being by the water in California. The water seems to cleanse my spirit and balance me." I could not ignore that Zeth was the main reason for my being in South Carolina, but my family and California were reasons from another standpoint.

Zeth said, "I guess you don't mind those earthquakes there either, huh? And we got different kinds of water right close to us here." He caressed my cheek and then my neck. "And where would that water be in South Carolina—Myrtle Beach?" I asked.

We moved from the rock to the pickup. Zeth walked to my side and opened the door for me.

Zeth climbed in the truck and starting the engine, and answered, "Naw, girl, I got you some fine water right there in Turks and Caicos where I own a villa, and as often as you like you could wake up every mornin' to glistenin' pink sand. Well, it ain't really pink, but

Astronaut John Glenn said from space the island's sand looked all pink.

Glenn circled the island on his map, and when he reached back to earth, he had to visit a place that expressed itself in such a way to be noticed from the heavens. When I read that such a place existed, I had to see fer myself to believe. And I believed it enough to buy a small piece of that pink sand. If you get bored with that body of water, well, we can always lay you out on the island of St. Kitts. It's beautiful there, too. But whenever you allow me to, I want to take you to my favorite spot, the big daddy of them all, Peter Island in the British Virgin Islands. I want you to see the brand new 10,000-square-foot spa with its own pool. If you were livin' here permanently, shucks, I could take you over there whenever you liked."

"Do you own land in the British Virgin Islands, too?"

"No, just my villa in Turks and Caicos."

"You know, Zeth, you don't have to wait until I have moved here permanently before you take me to your 'big daddy spot.' See Zeth, my family is there in Northern California, all except for Joey, and I just don't know if I am strong enough to be somewhere else permanently, living in another state, without them."

Zeth reached over and lifted my chin to his. "You are all grown up now in your own season to soon start a family of your own." He traced my eyebrows with his fingers. "When I was little, a lot of my older kinfolk used to say that I had eyes to start and put out a fire both at the same time. Let me in, Puddin'. Let me ignite your flame so that the woman I see in you becomes the woman that you want to be seen."

My heart fluttered at these words, but they were words to which I was forced to have a deaf ear without commitment. Forced to think about it now, I don't even know for certain if I wanted to have babies. None of my siblings have children. Condoleezza and Oprah don't have children, and look how successful they are and how far they have gotten without men as big financial supporters? I wanted first to stand strong on my own. My dad said that if I received an education, I would never have to bow down. I felt something, but it would not open up to let Zeth in. It was not so easy to describe because it was a new and extraordinary feeling. I had no words to give back to Zeth, and I could not even utter the words to reassure him. Yet inside, all the way through, his message resonated with me. Some deaf ears.

Did I not want to let Zeth in? Did I love Zeth? How does one begin to measure love? Mother gave much and taught her children a lot but did not share the teaching of how to give a lot to another. Mother had done as Grandma did after the physical loss of her husband and immersed herself in the gratification of love for her children. After Dad, I never saw Mother embrace the thought of love or affection with another man. Plus the church had always scared me away from giving into emotions that had anything to do with carnal love. The way the Mary and Joseph story went wasn't really a turn-on to a love story for me. The school only referenced love when teaching sex education as if in actuality they went hand in hand. What is love? And what's it got to do with it? Most women my age probably think that they know already. Hey! Should I even be asking this question now? I am just twenty-four! Well, actually my birthday is tomorrow, but once I near the next age, I start thinking of myself as that age. I even tell others I am the age I have yet to turn. Maybe I want to feel older like my siblings. If my father were still alive, would I know more about these things? My reluctance to requite Zeth's feelings by expressing my own emotions seemed unfair to Zeth.

"Zeth, if you don't mind, I would like to leave now."

"Okay." Zeth locked his arm in mine. "We'll go back to the ranch so you can rest up for tonight. I want to show you my observatory. We'll do a little stargazin'. I built my own telescope. You didn't know that I was an amateur astronomer, did you? I picked that talent up from my Uncle Clifton. He photographed Haley's Comet. I'll show you those pictures when we get back to the house. They did big write-ups on my Uncle Clifton in several newspapers. It wasn't so much that he photographed a comet; hell, a lot of people did that. It was that an African American today was interested in astronomy."

Zeth was talking so fast. He must have known already that I meant leaving Asheville to go to my own home.

"Zeth, I am leaving to go back to Charlotte this evening."

It took him a moment to answer. "Okay."

Driving back, Zeth reached over to the glove compartment. He removed a pair of sunglasses and put them on. But there was no sun.

"If you don't mind, Zemi, since you won't be here tomorrow fer your birthday I'd like to give you your present before leavin'."

"Zeth, you don't have to do that. I mean if I w-were…"

"Your leavin' doesn't change the fact that I bought a present for you." Zeth pulled up to his stable.

We walked into the stable, and Zeth took my hand, as I realized he liked to do, and led me to a beautiful creature. "Come closer to this beautiful horse. Don't be afraid. He won't bite you. Here, rub him like this. That feels good to him right there, in that spot. When I saw him, I loved him right away. It's like when I first saw you at your mom's house. Well, anyway, happy birthday. He is all yours, Zemi."

I was nearly breathless. "Oh, my God, Zeth, it's a horse! I don't even know how to ride a horse, let alone own one. It is so big! I know that much! Once I rode a mare when I was in Jamaica." I was so excited. Then thought: did seeing this horse remind him of me? He said that? Silly girl! That is what he said, but you know full well what this man meant. I was overcome and my eyes filled with tears. "Oh, Zeth!"

Zeth smiled. "Zemi, this here is a stallion, not a mare. He is big but he'll be just fine for you because I trained him fer you. A stallion can have an unfavorable temperament, but I know horses. Remember, I am a horse breeder. So he will be just fine fer you. Do you like him, Zemi?"

"How could I not? No one has ever thought to do anything like this for me. I mean, I don't know anyone who owns a horse, and you are the first person I even know to own a ranch. I mean a real ranch with all of the trimmings, too. Oh, my God, this horse is so big! Where will I keep my horse? Oh my God, a horse for my birthday! Wait until I tell Maria and Mama and my grandma. They won't believe me. And when I tell Joey, he'll make it a political horse, no doubt about that, and E.J. will just love it. And I don't quite know what Ishmael will think. Oh my, Zeth, I forgot to ask you his name. I am so excited that I forgot." I was still rubbing the horse, and I also forgot to be afraid anymore. "What is my horse's name, Zeth?"

"I gave you the gift. Now you can give him a name yourself."

"I don't want to give him a silly name. I mean he is such a beautiful horse."

"Feel him, Zemi, rub him all over and pat him." Zeth took my hand and showed me how. "Here, rub him like you want to rub him. He can sense that. Touch him like only you can touch him. Make the touch so special that he won't allow anyone else to touch him that way. Touch him so that he can sense your smell, too, and know to expect your touch every time your scent is around. Stroke him so he knows you know what to do with him. Make him desire your presence even when you are not around. Love him so he can love you back, and that way you can master his temperament. But you have to be around him often to do so."

"Oh, Zeth, his coat is so shiny. He looks and feels so strong. He is my first horse and I do love him and he seems to have loved me right off too. I am going to call him Power of Love."

Power of Love bowed his head down and grunted three times.

"You see that, Zeth. Power of Love likes his name. Is that what you think, too?"

Zeth laughed. "That is exactly what it means. He was showin' you that he approves of his name. Just remember he is naturally sensitive, so do not rush him or force him. Be patient with him, and that way you keep him calm and keep stress off of him. Shucks, by the time you get ready fer trainin', you will have him eatin' out of your hands." Zeth took an envelope out of his pocket and handed it to me. "Here."

"What's inside?"

"It is the other part to your birthday present. I wanted to present it to you another way, but with you leavin', this way will just have to do."

"Zeth, what is this?"

"It's a deed."

"I know that, but who is it for?"

"You are not sufferin' amnesia on me, are you? Can't you still remember how your name is written? Whose name do you see at the top?"

"My name. I see my name on this deed, Zemi Navies. You are giving me land?"

"Past tense. I gave you five hundred acres of land right outside of Charlotte. That way when you are ready to figure what your business will be, you won't have to search for that special piece of property. And when you are ready to move your mama and your grandma out here near you, the land is already there to take care of where they will live."

I was so excited that I nearly tackled Zeth with a hug. I tried to kiss him, but he removed my arms.

"Ah, Zemi, all of that ain't necessary fer you to do. I just gave you that land because I got more acres of land than I can count, so I ain't goin' to miss those little pieces. Plus I know how much you love your mama and all, so it was my duty to help make that happen in order that you can settle your life here in the South. I know how much you want to live in the South. A friend would do that fer a friend."

"Zeth, I don't know what to say. I mean a person doesn't just give somebody five hundred acres of land. At least, I don't know anyone who would do that, and for sure no one in California."

"Yes Zemi, a true friend who loves someone would want to see that person happy if it's in that person's power to do so and with no strin's attached. But as far as California goes, nobody does what you folk do out there. San Francisco is a planet unto itself."

"I don't know what to say, and I don't know what to do. The gift is like a dream. I mean, who does this kind of thing for a woman and n-not...."

"Like I said earlier, a friend with no strin's attached. Hey, let's get on back to the house. You can gather your thin's, and I'll get a driver to take you back to Charlotte."

"But aren't you going to show me the land in Charlotte that you just gave to me?"

"Oh yeah, whenever you are ready to go and see it, just let me know. I'll have the caretaker come and show it to you. Won't be a problem. I'll help you so that you can learn about land development. There is no reason why you should not have a stable on your own property to keep Power of Love closer to you. I fergot about that part of the present. I'll have a stable and everythin' built up fer you so you can enjoy Power of Love on your own land."

6

I had taken the ultimate step to become a registered Republican only to be tagged with the pejorative label—*Oreo*. As in the cookie. I was born a free black woman in American society but not free enough to forego the onslaught of name calling that followed my decision to change to the political party of the president who had lent a hand in freeing my ancestors from slavery. My friends thought that I had crossed over, no longer embracing the soul of blackness. One friend said that I was the real definition of an Oreo, white on the inside and black only on the outside, and that I had no choice in the matter: I was of that uncelebrated category of blacks called, yes, OR-EE-OH. Needless to say, my actions and thoughts were not sanctioned by my family. Suddenly guilty was I. For everything abominable the Republicans did and had done, and stood for, too. Did they hate me, Baby Girl, too? I love my family for so many reasons, but cannot understand their unconditional (*conditioned?*) loyalty to the Democratic Party. That party does not regard black people worthy enough to place them in positions of political power.

It hurts me to my core that the rest of the family considers me an outcast, like someone with a dread disease, and are not eager to see me in California. I enjoyed enormous success, if not critical acclaim, with the AWALA project, and was hoping to be congratulated by a family proud of me. The snub from my family devastated me. All the good I had done with AWALA was overshadowed by what my family saw as betrayal if not treachery.

Because I miss Grandma so much, she and Maria came down to Charlotte for a week. The house I'd rented has plenty of room. Though Grandma is kind, she is still not your typical grandmother. Her wisdom always touches me deeply; it is steadfast and a twin to her fiery passion. So different from Mom and Mom's philosophy. Maybe Grandma is that way because she still considers herself the reigning matriarch of the Navies family. This is beautiful because Mom finds it comforting to have Grandma by her side as it relates to her children—they do agree on most things, anyway. Grandma's grandchildren are her pride and joy, and Mom uses the same words when she speaks of her children.

Grandma must have smelled the pot of coffee brewing. She tip-toed into the kitchen as Maria slept. "Hmmm. That smells good. Since when did you start drinking coffee, Zemi?" Grandma asked, pulling on her flannel robe.

I turned the coffee pot on low. "Well, I don't really, but whenever I am around Maria, I tend to do what she does. But for you I made a chilled feather smoothie, one of my favorite morning drinks." Retrieving Grandma's treat from the refrigerator, I explained, "It has all kinds of flavorful juices, and I added wheat grass to yours."

Grandma sipped cold feather smoothie. "Hmm. This is good. Thank you, sweetie. Could you go and get my beige shawl lying across my bed and bring those thermal socks. The batteries are on the nightstand."

As I headed to Grandma's bedroom, I caught the beginning of her grumbling.

"Young people today just don't think sometimes. Now that girl knows it is fifty degrees in here, and Lord knows what the temperature is outside. And she has the nerve to give me a chilled morning drink. Thank God, she doesn't have any children yet because they would freeze to death. They just would....."

I went on and did as I was told. "Here, Grandma, is your shawl," I said when I returned.

She flung the shawl over her shoulders.

"And I'll put your socks on for you."

"Yes, thank you, sweetie." Grandma bent forward with one hand on her knee. "Now, if you can, sweetie, take this one foot out of the slipper and put a sock on it first. You know, the doctor has put me on a strict morning routine for breakfast, so could you fix me some oatmeal with a banana cut in half and put it on the side of my plate for me, please? You better add a slice of toast. Make sure it's wheat, and I'd like a cup of hot tea. Do you have any of that angel tea? You know, that is sweet enough without putting sugar in it. Since I have diabetes, I eat specific foods to help control it better. I am very careful of what I eat nowadays. Yeah, I follow the doctor's orders and I don't deviate a bit. And you can put that feather drink back in the 'fridge, and I'll drink it with my dinner today or maybe tomorrow evening. But sometime today if we get a chance, we need to go to the store and pick up some Boost glucose control nutritional drinks."

Affectionately, I said, "Here you go, Grandma." I placed a bowl of oatmeal on the table in front of Grandma.

Grandma looked down at the bowl of oatmeal, "Gee, sweetie, you sure are a fast cook." Grandma tasted the oatmeal. "You better give me a glass of orange juice."

I then cut a banana in half and placed it on the side of Grandma's plate and walked back over to the counter for the toast. "Here's your toast, Grandma."

Grandma gently pulled on my arm. "Baby, you are going to walk yourself to death. Take a break and rest a while."

"Oooh," I sighed. "Now we can finally talk." I sat down at the table with Grandma.

"Don't work yourself too hard, sweetie. Save some of that energy for cooking dinner now."

"Grandma, I am so glad that you came all the way down here to see me. It makes me feel special. I really needed to talk with you because no one else seems to understand me. Now, I don't think Zeth even understands me. Everyone seems so disconnected from me. I am a grown woman, and yet nobody will let me make my own decisions." My heart truly ached and I started crying. "I miss my family. The way we joked and clowned around whenever one of us lost at pool, meeting once a month for dinner, knowing what the others were doing with their lives and having a family member's back when needed. They must not care about me at all. They won't even call anymore. And I had to beg Maria to come down."

Grandma rubbed my hands. "Whenever you need reassurance, I'll always be around. Even if you don't see me, you will feel me." Grandma raised her hand and touched my face. "Sweetie, save those tears for something else."

It is so nice to have Grandma here. She never placed any demands on me. She gave me unconditional love even when I was a bit naughty as a little girl. But I was never unruly or hardheaded.

Grandma got up to get a paper towel. There was only one sheet left on the roll. Wiping my eyes, she said, "Why, next year, this whole situation won't even matter to you as much. Your priority right now is not to defend your right and choice. Now the part that people should pay attention to is the reason you came to your decision. Everybody reaches a point in life when they feel they are not accountable to anyone else for their independent actions. Sometimes rather than explain, you might want to just withdraw from those who may disagree with your choice and bother you because you made it."

"Yes." I answered.

"I'm a Democrat myself, and I will probably die a Democrat, but you can care enough about your family, to explain, and help them understand what you perceived to be a rational decision for becoming a Republican. Though the family mantra had been Democrat over the years, I really cannot be sure now about how your brothers might vote. E.J. seems to want Obama in. I'm old now, and all that change that Obama fellow speaks of is probably good, but Hillary Clinton is my presidential choice. Even President Bush and Karl Rove have said she would make the better Democratic candidate. Course I don't know if President Bush's endorsement helps or harm her chances with some folks."

Grandma exhaled, breathed deeply and went on. "Sweetie, think about and remember what your brother E.J. said when everyone was against Rodney for becoming Muslim and changing his name to Ishmael Muhammad. It made me do some reflecting myself because you know old folks just aren't too receptive to change. You know that to be the case about your grandma. I don't want to be the kind of grandmother imposing my will on my grandchildren just because of age, and at the same time I do not want to take advantage of the respect that my grandchildren have for me and my role as a grandparent."

"You are precious, Grandma, and all of your grandchildren think that of you," I said, my eyes filling again.

Grandma smiled. "I know that now, sweetie. Your brother E.J. made me feel so proud, speaking of how I had raised your father. That let me know that I had done a good job when my grandchildren can talk that way about their father. E.J. put a real fine interpretation to what your father was and what he meant to all of you. It was for your benefit especially Zemi because you were too young to know for yourself. Zemi, I would keep those words close to my heart, sweetie. That's the real inheritance that your father left for you besides the Social Security check until age twenty one."

I wiped tears from my face. I don't remember receiving any Social Security checks, but I did not want to ask Grandma anything right at that moment because she might lose her train of thought. Did those checks come in my name, I wondered?

Grandma told me, repeating words she had often imparted over the years, "Remember those words, each and every one of them, when you need something to hold on to from your daddy. He taught his children about wanting to learn…getting an education and gaining knowledge. And when you do that, it sometimes puts you on different journeys and different paths from things that might not be so familiar to others. Some of the journeys we take are temporary and some permanent. But the one thing when you gain an understanding of something for yourself, it makes you look at situations and people maybe differently, but always, the perception should be through your our own eyes. Think on things with your own mind and just don't go willy nilly accepting somebody else's truth. You have your own truth; just find what it is. The same with another's perceived fears. You were taught not to be frightful, but if you do fear, your fears should be your own, too. Not what you hear on the news everyday. Now'days, they want you to be afraid of everything! Diseases, viruses, foreigners, the water, the soil, the air, violence, terrorists, music, teens, everything."

Grandma's shawl fell to the floor. I reached down and picked it up. As I wrapped the shawl around her shoulders, Grandma told me, "Zemi, it's hard for a child when a parent ascends from this physical plane, but when I see the type of children your father produced, it just makes me real proud. And you should be proud, too, because your daddy left his children with a blueprint for living after he was gone." Grandma looked around for more paper towels. "Go in the bathroom and clean your face."

As I studied my face in the bathroom mirror, I removed my scarf from my head. I had lost a few strands of hair here and there. It might've been from a bad perm or perhaps because of anxiety. Anxiety. I know I have had that. I tied up my head again, feeling better because of Grandma's words.

Walking back into the kitchen, I found Maria in front of me. Script in hand, she was wearing a short-sleeved pajama top with a low-cut V neckline and matching shorties. She sported a flawless designer pedicure, and her long, soft hair was combed back off her face. She took her hair after Dad's side of the family; his grandfather was half-white.

Maria's mouth dropped open after she saw me. She bent down and kissed Grandma. "Good morning, Grandma." Then she looked at me funny again.

"What? Good grief, Maria, why are you staring at me?"

Maria put her hands on her hips and shook her head, "Jesus Christ! Is this what the South has reduced you to, Zemi? What on God's earth are you wearing on your head?" she shrieked. "An Aint Jemima designer scarf?"

I patted the top of my head. "It's a T.A.G. designer scarf, and my friend Amy gave it to me."

"Frankly, I don't care if it is a Queen Nefertiti scarf," said Maria, folding her arms. "And I don't care if Janet Jackson delivered it in person. The look makes you look poor. There are two looks to always avoid as a black woman. Never look poor when you don't have to. Because when you cannot even 'fake it until you make it', then you know you have seriously hit rock bottom! And the other rule is Don't try to wear that ghetto fabulous look. There is nothing fabulous about the ghetto unless you are lucky enough to get a role playing it on TV, and not reality TV either."

Breaking her bread, Grandma said, "My goodness, Maria, you are being so mean-spirited until I can't help but wonder who'd you wake up as this morning? You just don't seem like the same person that you were last night."

"I am just saying that you don't see Hollywood actors living ghetto or wearing ghetto after hours when they are not on the screen. See, that is the exact point—the page where blacks in the ghettoes are left behind. As actors and actresses, we mirror the ghettoes on television, adding more drama on top of the real-life drama found there. But actors, when 'keeping it real' are not trying to be like folk in the ghettoes. In fact, no one with a sane mind wants to be like people in the ghettoes because if ever a hell existed, it is ghetto hell. Even rappers who make their money rapping about the life of the ghettoes and those things that go on there in the ghettoes don't come back to the ghettoes," said Maria.

"I'll remember that," I said, and poured a cup of coffee.

"Zemi, if you weren't my sister, I would really talk about you. And the sad part about it is you are wearing that scarf as if you are so comfortable dressing like that. Zemi, please, take that rag off of your head. That is just not you." Maria reached out to snatch the scarf off my head.

"Stop, Maria." I used both of my hands to try to keep the scarf on.

Maria covered her mouth with both hands. "Oh, no!" she cried when she saw. "Zemi, I don't know what to say. I am so sorry. What happened? Your hair looks worse than the scarf." Maria backed up against the cabinet.

Grandma got up and put her hand on Maria's shoulder. In a matter of fact tone, she said, "Sit down, Maria. Why are you troubling your baby sister so? Whatever is going on with Zemi, you are not helping by your reaction."

Maria sat down. "Wow," said Maria, "the South has got you looking so drab."

Grandma is here with me, so I refused to let Maria dampen that joy. "Maria, I fixed your favorite blend," I told her. I got up to pour her a cup of coffee.

Just then the doorbell rang.

"No. No. I'll pour it, Zemi. You go on and get the door. Just let me know if it's a man. I am a little bit overexposed here."

I rewrapped the scarf around my head and headed to the door when I noticed Grandma give Maria a prickly stare.

"I'm just kidding, Grandma," Maria said as she pulled her chair up closer to the kitchen table. "Zemi," Maria called out, "where did you get these chairs from? My goodness, the cushions feel like stones. They are too hard for my back, and I am pretty firm at my back. Now, there is no reason for anyone to have cheap furniture in North Carolina when this is, like, the furniture capital of America."

I opened the front door and yelled back, "Don't worry. It's only Shauna."

"Well, gee, thanks. I flew almost three thousand miles to visit you, and you have the audacity to say 'It is only Shauna.' Maybe I should just take my pretty little self and go back home." Shauna put her luggage down. "And give me a hug, girl."

I sniffled. "I smell something." I told Shauna. "Do you smell anything, Shauna?"

Shauna took in a deep breath. "I don't know. What does it smell like to you?"

"It smells like some stuff to me," I said, narrowing my eyes at Shauna. "You know that you should not come into my household with that stuff I know that you were already in town putting on one of your events."

"Oh, yeah, I forgot I gave you all the details." Shauna rushed over to hug Grandma. "Hey, Miss Lady. This is my favorite person in the whole wide world. And look at you," Shauna said, rubbing Grandma's back. "Looking as if you are not a day over twenty-one. You know, I would have put you younger, but I had to keep you at legal age just in case your granddaughters started talking in the rated S-zone." Shauna walked towards her luggage. "Listen, you guys, I'm going upstairs to change into something more comfortable but on the sexy side of lounging—like Miss Maria over there. She has it going on like she is ready to entertain company, if you know what I mean." Shauna put her hand on her luggage. "Zemi, do you have anyone who can take my bags upstairs?"

"Yeah, Maria, you are being paged," I answered.

"Shauna," Maria said, "I think you must have left the bellhop at the hotel where you were staying. What hotel hosted your event?" Maria asked, picking up her script off of the kitchen table.

Grandma hunched her shoulders and pulled her robe tighter around her.

"There were two parts to the event with the first part held at the Westin Hotel and the second part at the Hilton," Shauna answered, heading for the stairs.

Maria piped in. "Hey, I heard that Bob Johnson of the Charlotte Bobcats bought up a bunch of those Hilton Hotels." Maria had a curious look on her face. She asked, "Did that particular Hilton belong to Bob's hotel conglomerate?"

"I don't know," Shauna answered.

"Hmmmm, I might have to give Charlotte another looking-over since Bob Johnson's planting some of his financial roots here. I wonder if Bobbie is going to open up one of his Urban Trust Banks here in Charlotte, too."

"I hope so," I said twisting my scarf to the other side. "It is hard to know that bit of info with Bank of America being the banking center of Charlotte. But he did just open the first branch in handsome, downtown Washington in September."

"Sweetie, turn on your fireplace for me, please," said Grandma.

I walked over and lit the fireplace.

"I will race you over to the big couch, Grandma," said Maria. Maria moved lazily toward the couch and laid down her script on the sofa table.

"Maria," I shouted. "Get yourself off of the big couch and let Grandma rest there."

"Oh, you scared me, girl. I thought something was the matter." Maria went over and playfully ran her hand through Grandma's hair.

"My bad, Grandma, my bad. Hey, Zemi, I betcha can't run your hands through your hair like this."

Grandma shook her head. "Sometimes you are so impish, Maria, until I just don't know what I am going to do with you."

Shauna strolled into the family room wearing a sleek, black silk jumpsuit that tied at the neck with a peek-a-boo slit in the back and classy gold pumps. She had a cream-colored shawl thrown over her arm and carried a Judith Leiber purse. "Would anyone like any Godiva?" she asked, passing the candy box to Grandma. "Compliments from my company. We served this at the event."

All eyes were on Shauna. Maria stared at her from head to toe.

"What kind of chocolate is it?" Grandma reached for the box.

Maria took her eyes off Shauna and focused on Grandma.

She told Grandma, speaking in no uncertain tone, "Now, Grandma, do not act as if you have forgotten the rules about sweets. They haven't changed just because you are not in Caly where Mother can keep an eye on you. Zemi and I are Mother's watchful eyes."

"I just wanted to find out what kind. That's all," Grandma said innocently.

Maria bounced up from the couch, laid down her script and eyed the different candies. "Okay, Shauna, let me have the box please, so Grandma can get her mind off of this candy. Let's see," Maria said pointing at each piece, "there's chocolate with nuts, chocolate with cream, chocolate with cherry, chocolate without nuts, yummy vanilla chocolate with pecans." Maria put a piece in her mouth and said in a sultry voice, "Now that is some very good candy. Okay, Grandma, now you know what kind of candy is in the box."

Grandma gave Maria a not so friendly look. Frowning, she lay her head back on the couch and closed her eyes.

Maria put her hands to her lips. "Ouuwa! And I love you, too, Grandma," Maria teased.

"My God," Shauna said, her hair flouncing as she sat down, "it feels so good to be able to relax this way when you know you've got your sh—, I meant stuff togeth—. Oops! I'm sorry, Grandma," she said.

"Oh, don't worry. Grandma has fallen asleep," said Maria. "She took her diabetes medication a little while ago, so I don't know, maybe it made her sleepy. She stayed up very late with us last night."

"I'll just place this throw over her to make sure she stays warm," I said.

It was time for Maria to meddle again. "What is country Zeth doing with himself nowadays, Zemi? I don't hear you mentioning his name much anymore," she asked.

"We don't really see each other anymore," I answered flatly. "Ah! That's too bad," said Shauna. "I don't know whether I should say anything or not, but I saw Zeth at the Black Media Expo yesterday. And he was not looking all that country with the keynote speaker, a beautiful slender woman, I might add, hanging onto his arm." Shauna leaned forward and whispered, "The woman appeared to be older than Zeth, or maybe she just acted overly confident and gave that impression."

Maria sat up on the couch, wide-eyed. "How old did she look and what did she look like?"

"Hum, she looked to be a sophisticated forty-year-old." Shauna turned and looked at me. "Zemi, didn't you say Zeth would be thirty-four on his next birthday?"

I nodded. Shauna was trying to bait me, giving out too many details on this woman. Why was she doing this?

"In fact, Zeth came up and hugged me and introduced her. I was surprised that he remembered me. I mean, we only saw each other that one time at your mom's house," said Shauna.

In the event I had any question about being on the spot, a shaft of light from the window streamed down upon me. And just me. "How did he introduce the woman to you?" I asked and got up from my chair to lower the shades.

Shauna shifted her eyes towards Maria and took a deep breath as if uncertain how to answer. "Well, ah, Zeth said, 'This is Miss Vickie.'" Shauna struggled to remember, "ah, ah dang, I can't remember her last name. Anyway, I tried to shake her hand, but the sister had her back to me; everybody was trying to get introduced to her. So I got a look at her, but did not get a chance to meet her actually. But Zeth placed a whole lot of emphasis on the 'Miss' part. I noticed, too, that he had his arm slightly around her waist. The woman had a beautiful set of Hollywood teeth. Too, she was not afraid to exude her sex appeal in her smile, walk, talk and looks. She was quite gregarious." Shauna straightened the tie at the back of her neck. "She had a smooth, mahogany and silky complexion. Zeth seems to like the 'darker-the-flesh and deeper-the-root girls.' He might be the kind who'll dig deep in the Neapolitan just to come up with the last scoop of chocolate."

Maria smiled, moving around anxiously on the couch. "Hey, now, Zethie baby must have something going on that we don't know about. Maybe Zethie has a trail of money or something stashed. Maybe that is why the woman seemed to pamper him."

"I don't know about that. She looked to have been holding her own." Shauna crossed her legs and turned sideways. "Let me tell you—this woman smells like money, in the way people who have money just smell that way. And she was very polished."

"I want to know more about her show," said Maria, as she ran her fingers through her hair.

Shauna reached down for her tote bag. "I thought I might have her card here. I guess not. Anyway, she's in media and has a show programming people in the community and popular personalities, but here's the catch: in actuality she is sporting her forum for the Democratic Party. The sister got hers up front, so she is not a dumb woman. Whether the Democratic Party wins or loses the election in 2008, the sister will already be wearing her green."

I cut in. "Tell me, Shauna, exactly what is this woman getting paid to do?"

"I hear you, Zemi," Shauna said, laughing as she leaned back into her chair. "You want to know what type of work a woman has to produce in order to get paid mega-sums of money, huh? Well, one thing we can take off of the table about her is that she did not sleep at the bottom to get to the top. She just has a persona that has been unmatched and unchallenged—so far."

"You still didn't answer my question, Shauna," I said, trying to scratch my head through my scarf. "What does she do or what did she have to do to make that amount of money?"

Shauna widened her eyes and held her hands out. "What else but to serve as a conduit to garner more votes for the Democratic Party? I suspect she has the trump power to put fire under the 'ordinary' voters, black and white, particularly those whose loyalty could shift with the wind."

Shauna had a whimsical look on her face as if she was studying me. I hope my suspicions and emotions are not so transparent. I did not want to appear resentful. But I wanted to understand the kinds of skills a woman needed in order to make those very large dollars. Maybe in some ways Zeth was responsible. But Shauna read me well. She gave up the 411 on this woman.

"Some people say that with all of the glitzy and glamorous panache she has in her other roles she might not have any grassroots appeal any more," said Shauna.

Maria expressed her opinion with a mouth full of candy. "I still do not see how Zeth plays any role of significance. I mean with the woman having so much going on, according to you. Unless Zeth is a front for some private agenda. You know the public is always the last to know. Maybe she is just using Zeth. He is such an unexciting type. She seemed like a woman who looked for a certain kind of man."

Shauna let her shawl slip from around her back as she fanned her hand. She offered, "From where I sit, Zeth does not appear to be the one being used. Duh! He is on the arms of a woman who might be very wealthy. Don't get it twisted. And, besides, Maria, have you taken any time to get to know Zeth?"

I was still curious. "I wish you would help me to figure something else out, Shauna. What was Zeth's value to this woman? How has she reaped benefits?"

"I like the way you cross-examine, Zemi," Shauna said, smiling. "See, Maria wants to engage in conversation with a mouth full of candy, but you, Zemi, you know how to pull answers out of a person."

Maria put another piece of candy in her mouth.

"Girl, you are going to mess up that pretty acting face eating so much chocolate," said Shauna.

Maria licked her fingers. "I know, but I can't stop."

Shauna got up and took the box of candy away from Maria. Placing it on a high shelf, she said, "At face value, Zeth is a black man—a black man who not only lives in the South but a man who also knows black people all over the South and a man whose family owns thousands of acres of land all over the South. I made some inquiries about Zeth, talking to some of the North Carolina movers and shakers I met at the event. Now, these folk in the South know that Zeth is a genuine man who cares about African American people. I mean, he loves them from his heart; the betterment of black people is his purpose in life, and that kind of love makes him a compassionate man. People can feel Zeth when he is in their presence. And he is an humble man. To put it in plain and simple terms, Zeth is a very simple man on the outside and complex on the inside."

"Oh, really," Maria said, her tone incredulous.

Shauna fixed her eyes on me. "This woman needs for people to see Zeth as someone important to her, a man without the hoopla, a portrait of stability. Shucks, I wouldn't be surprised if we heard of Zeth being a guest on her radio show every now and then. But that might be hard to speculate on because you don't know what Zeth might say—or how." Shauna threw her shawl around her back as she continued the 411 on Zeth's new friend. "Does he speak his mind, can he be controlled? Make no mistake about it; this woman is about taking charge through any means available. She wants to be seen as the queen who can pull and persuade the black female votary."

Pointedly, I remarked, "Maybe the woman is stepping into the spaces of Jesse and Al, sporting as the new lead." My face felt a little damp, and a bit warm. I asked Maria, closest to the fireplace, to turn the fireplace switch down to low. "I think it's getting rather warm in here for Grandma."

Stretching her arms, Maria answered, "Yeah, in a minute."

Grandma did not go to bed until two o'clock this morning. "Are you okay, Grandma?" I asked.

Grandma nodded and got up from the couch. Quietly, she padded to the bedroom on the main level.

I followed closely behind her to make sure she was okay. Seeing that she was, I went to the kitchen and brought the rest of the feather smoothie along with some grapes and cheese into the family room. I went back for more snacks, paper plates and plastic cutlery, and situated everything on the table in the family room.

"Oh, Zemi, are we going on a picnic today?" Shauna asked excitedly.

I thought it rather an odd question. "I don't believe so," I answered slowly. "What makes you ask?"

"Well, I saw all of those paper plates, tall red plastic cups, long plastic forks and paper napkins...it just made me wonder, that's all."

Shauna could not hold back rolling in laughter.

Maria was a part of the gibe. Jive.

With a smirk on her face, Maria said, "In Shauna's *beau monde* society she orchestrates affairs for the 'best of the best,' and well, to interpret what she is saying, she is expressing concern about lowering her standards, even as a guest in your home, with some homey-style hosting."

Shauna was still snickering. "Maria, why would you say such a thing to Zemi?"

"Okay, you two. I get it. After I have used up all of the plastic in my pantry, it will be the end of the plastic world in my life." My face tightened. "Now, Shauna, you are back on the mike. Where does this woman fit into the scheme of garnering black votes for the Democratic Party? Where does that leave Jesse and Al?"

"You know, comedians have given Al a new first name, 'Jumping Al.' That's because he will jump on just about any 'drive-by' band wagon playing a noisy tune. Remember him trotting around the country with talk of suing Cracker Barrel restaurants in South Carolina on behalf of a celebrity's mother. They alleged that the mother and daughter were racially discriminated against at a Cracker Barrel restaurant," said Shauna.

Maria looked up, now totally distracted from her script. "Ah, fuddyduddy, not again. Wasn't Al just addressing some issue about whites' ill treatment of folk in some part of Louisiana several months ago? Remember the incident of nine black children and the white female school bus driver who told the kids to sit in the back of her bus and designated the seats up front for white students. The woman was fired from the school district but was able to receive benefits of full retirement."

"Yeah, I remember that incident," said Shauna.

Maria pulled at the side of her shortles. "See, I think the parents down there should have been able to handle that pathetic situation themselves. They paid taxes for that school. What the hell are those parents doing, allowing such a thing to happen in this day and age?" Maria's voice rose at least half an octave. "See, that is why I don't like the 'New' Black South. Black folk down here haven't changed, and they never will because they cannot accept nor believe that God has freed them. And they call much of the South the Bible Belt. I wonder what part of the Bible they do not understand."

Shauna toyed with an ankle bracelet, and chirped, "Could be those down here are still waiting on the promise of that second back-up coming before acting with any real purpose," she said. "You know, sort of saving that big old incident for the Big Guy. And you know how slow black folk are about recognizing a promise."

"Well, I don't know what damages are being sought in the Cracker Barrel lawsuit, but with 'Jumping Al' representing the plaintiff, the most she will receive is an 'I'm sorry'," Maria declared.

"You know," said Shauna, "I don't think Al is seeking money on this one. I think what Al wants is for the company to show how it will enforce the agreed upon policies of fairness, how it will make sure their employees do not engage in discrimination, and examine whether they have abided by the agreement they made just two years ago with the Justice Department. I think Cracker Barrel admittedly was the repeat offender."

"Rewind," said Maria, circling her arms around. "If these are repeat actions for this company, then why keep patronizing them? It is not like blacks don't have other options of where to eat, like opening up their own restaurants. That is one solution. Frankly, I am tired of the whining about somebody won't let you play in their sandbox. For Christ's sake, go and build your own!" Maria was in high gear. "If this is the full measure of Civil Rights groups today, then I find it rather embarrassing. What is Al? A new rendition of the NAACP? Such small undertakings, huh?"

"Maria, I think that you should show compassion for the black folk down here in the South," I said. "Some of them are not as fortunate as you are."

"Why aren't they? My ancestors started coming over here in 1619, the same time as theirs. I don't believe my folk had a head start over theirs, unless you are counting the house Negroes," said Maria.

I was done with her. "All I am saying, Maria, is show a little more understanding for your brothers and sisters. They don't need any more rock throwing."

"Awwwww. You want me to show some P – M- S, some Pity Me Suffering, huh, Zemi? I am sorry, Zemi, but even a fool would know to get out of the way of thrown rocks. And another thing, Bush says he was called to be the compassionate one, not me. I was called to be an actress, and that is my role. So don't expect me to be something that I am not. Putting that aside, our folk twiddle their thumbs too much. They need to be about greater things, making business or something happen on a grander scale."

"You are right to a degree," I conceded, "but Maria, the African American middle class failed black Americans. Let's not forget that African Americans were hired and promoted into higher ranks of employment through the momentum of affirmative action as executives, VPs, CEO's of major corporations, coaches of NFL/NBA teams, and deans and professors of Ivy League universities. These positions that seem more common today were the result of laws, lawsuits, plaintiff awards, and platforms discouraging unlawful hiring practices. Such laws, events and measures by far were no panacea, but the result a few decades ago was a burgeoning black middle class. Parenthetically, the dwindling of this class is counted among today's losses from yesterday's from the Civil Rights gains," I said evenly.

"Humph," was Maria's answer. Typically, Maria eschewed anything analytical.

I elaborated on what I meant. "After gaining such opportunities and experiences under their belts, did those same people who benefitted from marches and beatings of others come out and open up savvy businesses and entrepreneurial programs to hire other minorities? Is this supposed to be the picture-theory that W.E.B. DuBois was intending? The black middle class wants to pretend as if it is helping the unfortunate of the race, but it is not. And as for the blacks that own lucrative businesses, pretty soon you'll need affirmative action to make them hire their own kind. Sad, but true," I told them.

Shauna sat up, poised in her chair. "Well, now hold on a minute, Zemi," Shauna said, the aggravation heard in her tone, "yours might be a point without much merit. You have some very lucrative businesses owned by African Americans that do employ a large percentage of blacks. Cathy Hughes of Radio One owns or operates seventy-one radio stations located in twenty-two urban markets in the United States that reach approximately fourteen million listeners every week. Bob Johnson just hired an African American female to head his new filming business called Our Stories, and you know his Urban Trust Bank has a black CEO, and his list goes on and on. Quincy Jones has done an awful lot to bring African Americans into the Hollywood music and entertainment arena, including in his *Vibe Magazine*. You've got to give credit where credit is due, Zemi."

Maria had shifted her interest. In fact, sleepiness was all over her. She put her elbow on the arm of the couch and cradled.

I wanted to keep Maria talking so that she could become more socially conscious and a little less dispassionate to the plight of many blacks in this country. I told anyone there to hear me that, "I still believe that the middle class has done the least and brought the most to shame our race. They placated the opposition by acting more Uncle Tommish. They didn't make upward moves. And for all the education that the middle class obtained, it undoubtedly just made the people more selfish—even after benefiting the most from the Civil Rights Movement. I think this class forgot about reaching back."

Maria sunk down farther into the couch if to say, That's all, folks.

And Shauna yawned. "I think I am beginning to feel just like Grandma. California time zone and jetlag seem to have caught up with me. Hey, Zemi, since you are already standing, put some music on. What kind of sounds do you have over there to liven things up a bit?"

I played an album that was already on the turntable. The music began with Paul Robeson's "I Dreamed I Saw Joe Hill." It was a part of my father's collection of jazz albums. Most young people in my age group loved hip-hop, but I was more of a jazz lover like my mom and dad. I loved the sounds from the era of Bessie Smith, Ella

Fitzgerald, Dinah Washington and Billie Holiday. I just adore Billy Eckstine and his "Everything I Have Is Yours," and another song that will remain in my heart forever is Nat "King" Cole's "Unforgettable." I was thinking about how I wish I could have been born in that era to experience that music and see those artists live, when both my thoughts and the music were violated by noise.

"No, she didn't!" Shauna whined. She turned to Maria and said in a whisper loud enough for me to hear, "Maria, we need to bring Zemi into the here and now world because she is really tripping, playing Paul Robeson for women of our age. I don't know if there is any hope left for the girl. I asked her to put on some music. I am already kind of sleepy, and she plays Paul Robeson. It is so unreal that it has just got to be funny."

I was not amused.

"Zemi, take that dull music off the wave," Maria shouted from across the room.

Not in a warring mood, I played "Love Is All" by Yanni.

Then Maria clowned me with a seizure of loud, fake coughing. "What's with that song? Are you in love with someone? I know it is not Zeth. Nada! I know you don't like rap, Zemi, but please...."

"What type of young black person would not like rap?" asked Shauna.

I held up the CD "Isley Meets Bacharach."

Shauna shook her head and waved a finger back and forth, and muttered, "Umph, umph, umph."

I offered a different song. "Ah. How about 'One Tear' by Eddie Kendricks. Oh, here is a great one." I held up "Intimacy Calling" by Wynton Marsalis.

Shauna said, "Now I liked that piece, but, Zemi, it is two o'clock in the afternoon, and you have three women and a grandmamma here. So keep it real."

"Zemi, please go and look in my suitcase and bring out my CD case," Maria told me.

Maria had all types of music. A lot of her CDs I hadn't heard before. I did as she asked, came back and handed her the CD case.

Maria picked out a CD. "Here, Zemi, play any song on this CD." Maria's CD's had her favorite songs on them.

"Which one should I play first?"

"I don't care. Play 'Unconditional Love' by 2 Pac," said Maria.

"No. No!" Shauna disagreed. "Play my favorite one, 'California Love,' with 2 Pac and his boys."

I put on 2 Pac's CD. "Are you girls finally happy?" I asked.

Shauna got up and started dancing. "H-e-y now," she whooped. "I'm a woman from Caly and I know how to party. Come on, Maria, we're going to show Zemi how to party."

Maria got up, shaking her bottom and snapping her fingers. She is really a great dancer.

I let Maria pull me up. "Come on, Zemi, get on the floor and keep it rockin', girl," she coaxed.

Shauna sang her own words to the music. "Zemi, let's go out tonight and show how the women from the West Coast shake it, that we know how to party in the city of Charlotte." Facing me now, Shauna clasped my shoulders. "Now move that left shoulder forward and then slide it low now. Let's do that with the other shoulder, too. Yeah! Now move both shoulders at the same time. Stick out that chest some, then drop back and shake it, shake it." Next, I was Maria's dance student. She placed her hands on my hips and motioned them in a circle, making them gyrate. She told me "Okay, Zemi, that's it, girl. Shake it as if you just got freed."

"Freed from what?" I asked. I was just kidding, but Shauna and Maria took me seriously.

Maria looked at me and held up her hands up in the air. "Ump—pretend that you are on a plantation in Texas and you have been working for no pay for over two hundred years. At last and finally, the Thirteenth Amendment to the Constitution abolishes slavery. Everyone who was able to read was alerted to the message, 'Slavery was over!' All plantation owners had informed their slaves of the good news—all plantation owners except for the plantation that you were on, Zemi. Your master did not let you and the rest of his slaves know until nine months later of the words that 'all of you have been freed from slavery.' So when you found out that you had done nine extra months of excruciating, free labor when you didn't have to, well, that ought to make you throw your hands up in the air to keep it rockin' into Juneteenth," Maria said excitedly.

"Jesus!" Sweating on her forehead now, Shauna rocked all the way to the refrigerator.

"What a frightening and scary thing to know—," Maria continued, "that because blacks could not read, they stayed in bondage longer. Girl, that should cause every black mother from the moment she knows she is pregnant to start reading to her child in the womb! If the child is growing and is nourished and affected by everything else that the mother eats and does, then it stands to reason the child should be able to get hooked on phonics in the womb, too."

"More disturbing," I added, "is how a mother has a child in her care for six years and gets upset because the teacher cannot get her child to read in the first year of school when the mother had six years and nine months to prepare the child. That is child abuse. It all points to the mother when a child is allowed to grow up in this society not knowing how to read. That should be made criminal."

"It is a good thing that you are not a politician, Zemi, or else everybody would be locked up for something they did not do right," Maria said, frowning.

The CD had stopped, but Maria kept on dancing.

Shauna returned to the couch with her hands full of snacks. "I never really thought about Juneteenth in that sense until today," Shauna volunteered. She went on to say, "While dancing, something spiritual came over me. In today's time of celebrating the holiday, the dedication has always edified those slaves who worked nine extra months for free because no one had informed those slaves of their legal freedom. But even more significant is that God left a group in Texas to work those extra nine months for free, as a reminder to the rest of us of the gift. The gift was a light, a path to show the rest of us blacks the importance of studying for self, learning to read and to interpret what's on the printed page."

I agree with Shauna—the blessing is in the lesson.

"Self-knowledge was the way out of a bad situation. The message was very clear: no one else is more responsible for our knowing than we are. If blacks don't know first for themselves, what makes them so self-righteous that they can point the finger of blame? We cannot blame white people for our own children not learning—not today—maybe yesterday but not today in the twenty-first century. I think the culture should express more what lessons we can take from the historical events that led to the commemoration of June-teenth," Shauna said.

"Now, I've got it!" I shouted. Even though there was no music I, too, rocked over to the couch. Nothing else needed to be said following the point Shauna made.

"Now, my sister, you got it rockin'," said Maria.

Each of us was able to turn the page to the next lesson, a new reminder of the reason for observing Juneteenth.

Maria fanned her shirt. "Zemi, turn off the fireplace," she told me. Did she ever ask?

"Maria, you are one lazy child," I chided.

Slightly out of breath, Maria answered, with all her nerve, "And why are you acting shocked? You know that I am on vacation. Anyway, I only came down because I wanted Zeth to teach me how to ride your stallion, Power of Love." Maria lifted a leg and rested it on the arm of the couch. "Zemi, the horse that Zeth gave you, who named it? That is an amazing name. I like it a lot."

"Actually, I did, but Zeth told me to touch and feel the horse and the name would come to me. That experience inspired the name. Of course, he was right," I said, re-tying my scarf.

"Zemi, why don't you call Zeth so Grandma can see his ranch, and we can go horseback riding?" asked Maria.

"No way!" I told her. "I am not calling Zeth any more. He blew it with me. Besides, last time I went over to his ranch to ride Power of Love, he left the ranch before I even got there and had someone else there to train me. Plus, I have keys to the stable, so he does not have to be there. Zeth said whenever I wanted to ride Power of Love, I could until my own stable is completed."

Shauna pushed her hair away from her face. "Zemi, I know you've heard the song 'Too Many Fish in the Sea,' but I think Zeth is a good catch, not the kind of fish that you throw back into the sea. Girl, something I could see about Zeth right away was his genuineness, and that's a quality you don't find too easily. And if he was unhappy with sophisticated Miss Vicki, then he's a great actor. I think you and your family might have misread Zeth." By her tone, I gathered that Shauna was both serious, and her sympathy for Zeth?

Well, she made that pretty plain. Shauna picked up the emptied cups and headed for the kitchen. "Refills anyone?" she called out.

I heard Maria answer, "Thank you" and that had to work for me, too. My thoughts were elsewhere. I really did not want to listen to where this conversation was going, but I couldn't escape either. I was in my home.

"Oh, please," said Maria, making a face, "don't let the dress-up fool you. The man dresses up wearing white socks, for God's sakes!"

"Maybe so Maria," Shauna answered, her hands full as she returned, "but I think Zeth really loved Zemi. Your 'family-power' did so much ridiculing about his 'countrified-ness' until Zemi became accustomed to that shaded canvas her family painted for her. She couldn't be used to that portrait and grow to love Zeth at the same time. Zemi couldn't or was unable to embrace and understand the Zeth who professed his love for her. I mean, really, what kind of guy gives a woman a horse and five hundred acres if he's not married to her?"

"A fool!" Maria answered right away.

"Maria," Shauna told her, "you are so stuck on yourself that you don't take the time to really see what someone else is all about. You obviously do not know how to go deep enough because if ever there was a Prince Charming..." I could imagine Shauna rolling her eyes. "Zeth was it or the closest we'll ever see to one," she added.

"Why are you sweating me, Shauna?" asked Maria. She stood up. "It's not like I am the one who doesn't know how to hold on to a man. And I still say it's not like Zeth is worth being broken up over just because he gave Zemi a horse and some country acres out in the boondocks."

"Country acres or not, five hundred acres is no small piece of change," Shauna shot back.

Then Maria turned to me and said quietly, "Maybe it is true what Joey said. Zeth mentioned several reasons you and he broke up. Joey didn't want to tell you those things, Zemi, because he didn't believe the story. But after listening to you talk just now, w-well, maybe Zeth's side is the truer version." Maria got up to go into the kitchen.

I could feel my cheeks warming. Where was this going? I wondered.

There was a very long silence.

When Maria came back into the room, she held out a bag of chips, but got no takers.

"Come on out with it, Maria," I said, bitterly. "I am just dying to hear the drama, what Joey said Zeth said."

Maria positioned herself on the floor. She dipped chips into a bowl of salsa. "Are you sure you want to hear this?"

"Nah. But I know you can't hold water," I said.

"Okay, but don't get mad with me now." Maria looked into my face and said, "Zeth told Joey that you were not woman enough for him, and that you needed to do a lot more growing up because it was taking you too long to learn how to please him. He needs a woman who can satisfy his needs better than what you have been doing."

"Wait a minute," I said in a huff. "It is not all about his needs. I have needs, too. Apparently, he was not doing all that he needed to do to keep me. Besides, he was not educated enough for me."

Maria licked salsa off her fingers. "Zemi," she said, "do you really know what your needs are? Would a man who had a lot of degrees be what you need? Would you know how to please him? Is that what you are saying? When there is a man that you want, you have to learn the rules of pleasing, and obviously you haven't learned those too well."

"What makes you think that I ever tried to please Zeth?"

Stunned, Shauna held up two fingers, "Wait. Zemi, look me straight in the eyes and tell me the truth now. Are you saying that you never had sex with Zeth? Nah. That's not what you are saying to us, is it? You just mean that you didn't try hard enough to please him, you know, in certain ways. Tell us the truth now, Zemi," Shauna insisted. She twirled her straw around her mouth.

"W-well. First, why do you guys want to pry into my sex life so much? Don't ask and I won't have to tell. Why is that so important for you two to know?"

Shauna said, moving her shoes, "I don't know about Maria's reason, but I'll give you my reason for wanting to know. I need to be more relaxed just to express myself on this one. Here I am a woman more than ten years older than you, Zemi, and I have given a man everything down to the kitchen sink; but I have yet to have any man be the way about me the way Zeth has been with you. Now, I cannot speak for Maria, but not too many women have experienced what you had going on with Zeth. It is difficult to admit to myself that I love E.J. more than he loves me. I've waited for a wedding date for better than a decade and have delayed having babies until he is ready. I was even willing to sell my home, just so we could move in together and pay one house note, but E.J. refused my offer. I have done everything to pin E.J. into settling down, to no avail." Shauna frowned and shook her head. "Zeth has given you more than any other man you've dated, which has not been that many, and you did not indulge Zeth? I don't get it. You know you might be delusional from staying in those books too long, girl. No wonder he went to Vickie. The man needed sexual healing from somewhere or somebody."

"Shauna, I am not like you and Maria. I don't indulge in casual sex. I never have."

"Excuse me, I don't have casual sex," said Shauna. "I stayed a virgin until almost twenty and was in college then. I have been dating your brother for a decade, and in all of that time I have not had sex with anyone else. E.J. happens to be the man I am committed to. I don't call that casual sex, do you, Maria?"

"Nope," Maria, told her. "I call that 'foolish sex' to even date a man past a year and not have a ring by the second year and married by the third. Hell, unless you and E.J. are both retards, you two should be able to recognize if you are for each other, at least enough to get married even if it ends up in divorce down the road later. I know E.J. is my brother, but you have been dating him since you've been in your twenties, Shauna. Are you two trying to get in the *Guinness World Book of Records* for the longest pre-marriage relationship ever?"

"I agree with Maria on pros to marriage, Shauna," I said. Maria jumped up from the floor, "Uh-huh, Zemi. I know you. You are trying to get the attention off of your butt, but I know about you now."

"What?" She caught me off balance.

"My God!" Maria threw her bag of chips to the side. "Zemi! You're a virgin!"

"Arrest me. I'm guilty," I said, extended my arms and holding my wrists together. At that moment I no longer felt ashamed. No one knew that about me. No one. I knew what people would think about a woman, age twenty four and still a virgin. I could not disclose that to Zeth. Maybe that is why I never did anything. Young girls getting pregnant at the age of twelve and thirteen is not my way of proving love, not even at twenty four. I thought if a girl started having sex at twelve and got pregnant young, then somebody should be arrested, even if it meant the parent. Black women having three and four children by three different daddies were not the portraits I wanted to hang on my wall. I was naïve about a lot of things, especially so-called street life, but I had control of my mind and body because I promised to make that control count for complete fulfillment.

"What are you practicing to become? A nun? Or are you practicing abstinence until marriage?" Shauna, asked, drilling me.

"That's just the way it is, Shauna," I said. "Once I have sex, things will never be the same with me, my mind, body and soul. My womb is not to be bequeathed as if it is up for sampling like wine at a tasting. I am the gatekeeper to all of me, and I take that to be a very serious onus. I cherish my body too much to be with a guy just for him to take advantage of heaven. I don't need to prove to him what heaven is like; rather, he needs to prove to me that he should be bless enough to enter heaven."

Shauna looked at Maria and grinned. "Damn! Maria, how did she get away with being around that man? He gave up five hundred acres and a horse and then some while Zemi gave up nothing? Damn, I feel so abused, don't you, Maria?"

"Again from what I heard," said Maria, "Zeth was giving those five hundred acres as an engagement present instead of an engagement ring."

"Oh, that's right," said Shauna, "he doesn't buy diamonds because of the value placed on them over the value of human lives killed everyday in Africa. But, see, I didn't even know that the man was setting the stage to ask this woman to join him in matrimony. Did you know that, Zemi?" asked Shauna.

"I would rather have diamonds myself because diamonds are a girl's best friend—and they can't tell your business," said Maria.

"Yeah, diamonds might be a best friend, but those five hundred acres, if sold, would take care of Zemi for life, and then she could buy her own diamonds," said Shauna.

"Okay, you two act as if it is a bad thing being a virgin at my age, but I'll tell you this much. It was easier for me to let Zeth go because it was his loss more than mine."

"How do you figure?" asked Maria.

"Because Zeth wanted me that way. I'd never decided upon him that way—yet. So I don't miss what I never sought to have."

"Zemi," said Shauna, pressing clasped hands close to her chest, "Zeth is a man. I mean a real man. He wanted you, but you can't expect a man to wait like that forever until you start to percolate. That's not the way it is."

"Listen," I told them. "I was not expecting him to wait forever but at least until we got to know each other's habits, and at the appropriate time, it definitely would have happened. But you two act as if a woman must let a man have his way when he's ready and on his terms—even if the woman is not ready. Why would a man even want a woman who is not ready for him?" I said.

"Well, that explains why you are here and Zeth is elsewhere," Shauna answered. "Gee, you really are slow about men," she said, "and that is scary to a man—a woman your age never having sex. You have to keep it real, Zemi, at least where men are concerned."

I shook my head. "Shauna, it is scarier to me as an African American woman that we lead the country with the highest number of new AIDS cases." I put my hands on my hips. "My mother didn't raise me to fall as a casualty for the sexual desires of men." Shauna and Maria might be older than I am, but their sexual consciousness was at the level of immature teenagers, as I saw things. "I just won't play Russian roulette with my life," I told them finally.

Shauna rubbed her hands together. "Zemi, it's not as if I've had sex with a drug addict or a gay or bi-sexual guy." Shauna smiled, "I know my man, and he is all the way heterosexual. So I'm okay, girl."

"Shauna, do you use protection?" I asked.

Shauna shrugged her shoulders, then shook her head, "Well, um, no. But when you are a woman my age and you have been going with the same man for as long as I have, and he doesn't fool around, there doesn't seem to be a need to use protection. At least I don't think so for myself. Besides E.J. doesn't like using condoms, and he knows that I haven't been with another man since we first started dating."

"Maybe you could use a bit of 'enlightenment' on your dimly lit parlor of pleasure that you say is for just the two of you," I said wryly, and cruelly perhaps. But I would not stop. The Bible said we are not to call people fools, but right here in front of me is at least one woman wearing blinders and no condoms, and the other one had not yet said. "Listen," I told them both, the condomless one and the one who had not yet said, "The Kaiser Family Foundation, a non-profit health organization, has found that in 2001 roughly 67 percent of black women with AIDS had contracted the virus through heterosexual sex, up from 58 percent four years earlier." I was going for the brain, but hit a nerve.

"Zemi," Shauna began.

I could hear hurt in her voice. What was she more concerned about? The prospect of E.J. cheating on her? Or contracting an STD? I only hoped that Shauna was not so shallow as to ignore the latter.

"Do you walk around with a little black book with statistics in it to try and scare normal women like me and Maria who actually enjoy what God has bestowed? Sometimes I don't believe you, Zemi. When you get on to something, you just run it until no more wind is left," she said, her voice and mood subdued.

"Shauna, Maria," I told them, "it's just that these kinds of numbers are real, and when I see that my own age group is the hardest hit, well, common sense tells me that we women have to start making changes and set standards of how we treat and care for our bodies. And that change begins with me, and the two of you," I said, pointing at them. I knew that they were not pleased about how I had interacted with men (or not), but I was up in arms over their nonchalance and ignorance about AIDS and STDs. I had read that government studies in 29 states found that black women comprised roughly half of all HIV infections acquired through heterosexual sex from 1999 to 2002. Medical experts put the sharp increase down to a combination of segregation, social exclusion and social and sexual habits.

Maria said, "Well, Zemi, since you've moved to the South and are trying to get other black women to move to the South, don't you forget to make note that most AIDS cases of blacks are found in the South—and I am a West Coast girl."

"Dang, Maria, I can't believe your stubbornness. Did you know that researchers say in many ways the epidemic in the South more closely resembles the situation of the developing world?" Now that's bad. This is America, and AIDS cases are appearing for black American women as if they lived in what we unPC'edly used to refer to as The Third World??????????????? I understood what actress Sheryl Lee Ralph meant about her purpose in Sometimes I Cry. She says it's about real stories from real God-fearing women who are living with AIDS. Ms. Ralph, who also is a black woman, says that she has two children, and when her children come into their sexual well-being, she does not want it to kill them. She says redemption for us begins with a conversation—conversations with ourselves, our children and conversations with God. She also said that we shouldn't shy away from the conversations and the actions—prophylactic actions—that can save our lives." Talking to Maria and Shauna, I felt the need to meet with Ms. Ralph. I wanted to do whatever I could do to help her organization because I would be helping my family.

Shauna broke a momentary, but uncomfortable silence. "After thinking for a minute, I have to admit it is a little scary to find out that AIDS is now the leading cause of death for African American women, ages twenty-five to thirty-four," she conceded earnestly. Then she asked me—*baby girl*—"Zemi, for people like me and Maria who want to continue having sex, what should we do?"

"You and E.J. should both be tested for HIV—together. Barack and his wife both tested for AIDS in Kenya, and they have been married for years."

Shauna confided that there would be a problem. "Girl, if I ask your brother to take an AIDS test, I know him. The first thing he will ask me is if I have been cheating on him, and secondly, he would probably want to break up with me. I don't want to chance that in our relationship. I am not ready for him to have a reason for leaving me. But in the meantime, if you can come up with something else, I will consider doing something perhaps not so drastic."

Maria said pointedly, "Now I understand why Zeth left you, Zemi. No man wants to be asked to take an AIDS test. Do you think these girls who have an opportunity to date football players and rappers ask those guys to take an AIDS test?"

"They should ask them to take the test, but women today don't think much of themselves," an angry voice said.

The three of us looked at one another, our face all saying, Who? Unbeknownst to us, Grandma had been standing in the hallway listening. I don't know for how long.

In a very stern, "no-uncertain-terms" voice, Grandma continued, "They are so busy letting the man define them until so many of the women come out looking—what's that they call it? Androgynous. Yes. Why, I just don't know how any woman could let a man tell her what she should do with her own body, and at the same time, I don't know why these same men wouldn't ask the women to take a test. You know the women could have it, too, the way some of these women let men run through them like they are number runners. And sometimes those boys can be real unsafe that way. The man will have one girl early in the night, and later that same night he does a drive-by—I know the guys all call it something else, and do not think I do not know—at another girl's home. That is not the proper way to treat a fine woman."

I am taken aback! We all wore shock on our faces. Grandma knows what? Booty call? I, for one, never, not evvv-er liked the phrase. "Booty call" topped my "where you at?" list. It took effort to re-set the vibe in the room to normal, but I was trying. Grandma helped. Her fine fragrance wafted through the air as she neared us. She had changed into expensive apparel. "Uh-uhum," I said, clearing my throat, and perhaps some discomfort, too? "Grandma, do you want to sit down?" I asked.

"No. I have to let these old bones wrinkle out some." Grandma glanced at her watch. "It's almost time for me to take my medication, but before I fix myself something to eat, here's what I want to say to you girls. Now, Zemi, you are young, but don't let those two over there make you have a lack of sophistication about yourself. If you want that man back in your life, there is nothing wrong in making that known to him. And there is a way to do it without putting the body out there as bait." She held up three bony fingers. "There are three things that a woman must remember when using her essence to get the man of her choice—when to bait him, when to go fish and when to catch him. Now your Zethie…is that what you call him, Zemi?" asked Grandma.

We all laughed.

"No. I call him Zeth, Grandma."

"I like that name. So Zeth showed you he cherished that innocence about yourself. A real man could see that about you. What Maria and Shauna don't understand about your high class and quality is that you were the one being choosy about who deserved you, not the other way around. It wasn't all about what he could give you because you are just as much equipped to get finances as a man. What Maria and Shauna need to understand is that men don't always like driving a shiny car with used tires. That young man expressly desired a woman of your character because he knew for sure that you could soothe his nature. But you obviously were not too sure about him," she told me. "At that time," Grandma added, regarding me with a knowing smile.

"Grandma," said Maria, "men are not the same as they were in your day."

"What about them has changed so much, Maria, that today women are left holding empty bags?"

No one answered.

Grandma stood straight, her youthfulness brought joy to my heart.

"Are you saying the nature of a man is different today than yesterday, Maria? Tell me what the difference is. When a woman sacrifices herself on his altar and donates herself to a man without his contribution first and, when she allows a man to take possession of her mind and body without commitment, she opens a door and leaves it wide open for other women to make claim on him."

Shauna's focus on Grandma was intense, her eyes penetrating. "Grandma, why do you use the word 'donate'?"

Grandma grew sad and shook her head. "You sweeties are so tender. Today, most men will take it from anybody making the contribution. Most men today don't court those girls out there," said Grandma. "First off, they don't know what courtship is all about, and secondly, the women have made it too easy. All men have to say today is 'Come here, girl, and show me what you've got,' and that's pretty much all the effort behind the conquest. Easy, wouldn't you say?"

"Go on, Grandma, we know that you know what's going on," Shauna urged.

"Honey child, a man does not know everything that he needs from a woman. He wants to tell her what to do and how to do it, so he never gets to experience any true rapture; suspense and savoring mystery take time, and a one night stand or a first night feast cannot delivery suspense. Plus, he doesn't allow the time for the woman to be creative. Today, the mystique of a woman is gone. Uniqueness and individuality have just vanished. The women all dress and look alike. They all wear the same type perfumes, same hair dos, and the make-up is the same, too. Looking at these women today is like looking at a Barbie doll, just with real legs that can walk."

"Okay, Grandma, I have one more question to ask you," said Shauna.

"Ooh, baby doll, I have to go into the kitchen and eat something so I can take my medication," Grandma answered.

Shauna whispered to Maria, "I think Grandma just called me a Barbie doll on the sly." Grandma started to walk out of the room. I was getting ready to follow her.

"Zemi, keep your seat, I'll be all right. But what you can do for me is figure out what to do with the five hundred acres of land. You don't want to just sit on it. Show Zeth you know how to handle business despite your youth. That will bring that man back to you in no time. The other woman is just for baiting. But let your youth move you quickly. He gave you that land for something bigger than what you can think of right now. And if it happens that you have to ask him to come back to you, don't you be too proud. After all, he did not ask you to return the deed after you two went your separate ways, or saw less of each other—whatever you two did. And don't mess yourself up and stay out there too long now. Men have pride, too, and theirs is more steadfast." Grandma turned as she was leaving the room. "Don't you girls eat too much of the food here in Charlotte."

"Why not?" asked Maria.

"Well," said Grandma, "I just don't know what they feed these women down here, but it seems one out of every two women I see is obese. I mean, they really have a lot of overly big women down here. Just whatever you girls do, watch what you eat. You don't want a man to have to work so hard that he wears down over exerting."

On that note, Grandma had the last word. But my last thoughts before I turned in that night were not about politics per se, or love, lust, stooping to conquer, or standing up for my rights. Not exactly. Not that night. This thing about AIDS grabbed a hold of me and would not let go. What could I do?

7

I am not prepared to give more to live life and receive less. That includes a romantic relationship, too, although at this point, I don't have much of a relationship to speak of. Day by day my relationship with Zeth became more of a question. In spite of that, he remained cautious and placed no demands upon me to rush into a committed courtship. Yet, through it all, my happiness was Zeth's greatest concern. When we began to spend time together again (he called me), he tried relentlessly to make bliss a part of our together-ness, but I made closeness a tug of war. He was the giver and I the taker. This scenario presented no difficulties because it was not as though we were on task toward any articulated goal—say marriage, for example. All that could change with a turn at the next corner. But for this moment, today, no goal was declared, so no added stress; there was no measuring stick against which our (my) actions would be rated.

But an undercurrent was there even so. I imagined Zeth's desire for me, and he also knew what I needed, though, not necessarily from him. That gave me leverage, if not one-ups(woman)ship!!! I could go through life acquiring what I especially liked, and Zeth would not have to be the reason I got what I wanted. In keeping it real, I knew, too, that if love were ever present, I would not hesitate to yield in a relationship.

My brothers, Joey and E.J., said I had overpriced myself in life, that I had become too spoiled because I was the baby in the family. I disagreed, but remained driven to sustain my independence like Condoleezza and Oprah. Yes, ma'am. I am so proud to use their accolades as markers in my pages of progress. And I am just as happy to take a page from the biographical summary of Oregon State Senator Margaret Carter and emulate her, too. She is the first African American woman to serve as Senate President Pro Tempore. I have so many more to look up to, even Rosemary Cloud, the first African American woman ever to become fire chief of a career level fire department. It was a necessity for me to know that I had the confidence and that I was capable of standing on my own first. Surely, a woman has a natural need to feel self-assured and to know power? (I love Patti LaBelle's and Michael McDonald's "On My Own.")

My father said a female should get an education as the first back up. Men are taught how to obtain power as well as what to do with that power. It is too often the case that women are never taught to recognize, let alone, use their power unless it has something to do with snaring a man. But women blindly sacrificed themselves only to open their eyes later and recognize the enormity of what they just freely gave; well, if it had no value to them, then, hey, why not give it away? And I do not just mean their bodies, but a woman will give all that is essential within herself without any understanding of "what's in it for me?" This has zip to do with selfishness, and everything to do with recognition of one's own value.

I guess women must have wondered sometimes why others should have harvested so much more from their output than they themselves have reaped. But sex and intimacy (not the same things) do factor big time; there is no fooling there. And, speaking of which, while I continue to explore my life purpose, Zeth contemplates the ways and means of capturing the rapture from my essence. No doubt the progress of my moving to the South raised Zeth's level of confidence and hope for a sound and meaningful relationship.

We had our times, our moments when we did fun things together, though our playtime would probably be considered odd by others. We even took The Culture Warrior Test together. We talked of a show and tell, the traditional man and wife in a marriage as our way of answering question number two on the test. We marked the same answers to all the questions that show that we both "lean heavily towards being a traditional warrior."

Zeth appeared to be more of a Republican than he did a Democrat. But I did not know for sure because I won't ask and he won't tell. He also could be neither; in some respects I could peg him for an Independent at heart, meaning irrespective of how he actually marked a ballot. Right now it does not seem to matter. But if we decided to turn a corner in our relationship, and became engaged to be married, then it would be more of a concern. I bet on his being a Democrat and leaning.

I am not one for unnecessary problems in a relationship. Why walk into a marriage when some of the problems are already written upon the wall? My mother thinks that those with significant cultural differences would have more problems in a marriage than those in the same or similar culture. Anyway, say in my case, Zeth's the Democrat and I'm the Republican; I certainly would not conform to his political party, and with his strong will he would not be the one to switch. So where would that leave the two of us in agreeing on family and other issues? And the children, towards whose politics would they lean? Would different voting habits foment discord among siblings? Again, I don't have to be much concerned about that subject now because I don't have a bridal magazine countdown-to-wedding-day worksheet (do they publish those things in men's magazines? Is there a magazine called "Modern Groom?"). Anyway, the subject matter (and the corner) remain remote at this juncture.

I find it quite interesting that when people get together as a couple, one will most commonly change and conform to the other one's religion, but not so when the consciousness is centered around political parties. That's hardly an issue for an African American couple. Usually, for black couples a Democrat will marry a Democrat. Well, that's just sheer genius at stating the obvious.

Republican Governor Arnold Schwarzenegger and his Democratic wife Maria Shriver (somewhere in there is the name Kennedy) most famously epitomize the paradigm for "mixed politics couples." For those who might have a need to understand how this arrangement works (or not), the models are out there. How does one from the Kennedy's Democratic dynasty—with a legacy that includes a President of the United States of America, senators, a U.S. Attorney

General, and many runs for all sorts of political offices—part ways and vote on everything that is Republican? Could it mean that the Kennedys represent a dynasty headed for extinction? Why didn't Arnold try to flex his mighty muscles to uphold the Kennedy legacy—Camelot and all of that? Why didn't he to try to keep that hope alive?

Even the matriarch of the Kennedys, Eunice Kennedy Shriver, supported Arnold Schwarzenegger for governor. Did she pass her baton on already to Maria Shriver to join the race and perhaps one day become the Kennedy matriarch in the Republican Party? If Maria Shriver should run for a political office, would it be under the Republican banner or Democratic? She could probably run faster and more victoriously, too, as a Republican. Maybe the 2008 GOP presidential nominee would have a better chance with women if he or she would choose Shriver as a running mate. For example, Mayor Michael Bloomberg of New York and Shriver might be a viable pair for the 2008 presidential ticket. And if she did not run, (the likely scenario), would Shriver vote for Obama or Hillary, come 2008?

Another thing—the plantation mentality thing revisited—if one from the Kennedy dynasty has left the Democratic Party—(and the Kennedys got a lot out of being Democrats, a President, U.S. Attorney, Senator, a second presidential nominee), why couldn't blacks, for whom the Democrats have done so little lately, board that same train? Or a different train? Could blacks harness the power to make that train a sort of freedom train? Could people really get ready for a train a comin'? A train whose destination is determined by black people versus our voting like there is some electoral GPS satellite that zooms in on blacks and tells blacks where to take our support and for whom to vote???

If ever the Constitution should be amended and Arnold could run for president, the Clinton era would not stand a chance of continuing. How will the children of the famous and noble Schwarzenegger's vote? Perhaps they will begin the new Schwarzenegger dynasty in politics. Could it be that the Democratic Party is no longer the traditional party for a whole lot of folk. I mean the Dems can count on black people just like a turkey can count on being Thanksgiving dinner. Thank you for nothing. Perhaps the fabric of what that Party stands for now has been shredded and re-stitched to make a quilt that is majestic on its high end, but as one nears the bottom, the quilt becomes, I mean, way raggedy. And what's that dangling from loose threads half way down the quilt? Could that really be the middle class? Yep, what's left of it. What's that saying? What's wrong with that…? Yes, you got it. A pretty shoddy tapestry? But no shaded canvas there—not if it's that clear!!! What don't black people get? Blacks continue to look out into La-La Land, looking for bailouts like affirmative action.

A thought crosses my mind. Why are some folk bent on labeling Secretary of State Condoleezza Rice, former Secretary of State Colin Powell and former Maryland Lieutenant-Governor Michael Steele Oreos? Well, assuming for the sake of argument that they are Oreos, what do you call voting the same way over and over again to get crumbs? If doing the same thing over and over again and expecting different results is today's cute definition of insanity, then the blacks who do that might not be Oreos, but could you call them—er, Twinkies? I think black people keep thinking that the Dems will do it for them one fine day. Well one fine day when the Dems will is as real as once upon a time when the Dems did (and we know there was no "did").

Whatever other people did, I knew that I, Zemi Navies, Ph.D., U.S. citizen, free, black and of voting age, could no longer hold any more loyalty to the Democratic Party. I wondered, too, if Republican blacks in the South went public with their affiliation. When I've reached the South with my consummated affiliation, would I disclose it?

It's weird, but I was unable to acknowledge, even to myself, that my move to the South was official. There was not much left to do, yet the thought lingered: Would leaving California and my family feel like I was breaking up with them? The move had already begun to change my life, making visits to California less frequent. Even the family passion that I could count on like my next breath seemed harder to conjure up. Would memories of love, warmth and safety begin to fade over time? Was I protecting myself from hurt? Did I wish that the memories would fade? When I thought further, I realized my fear and that chances are my family misses me as I do them when we are apart. I was longing to have my family together in the way we were. But was destiny—the greater call?

Our siblings used to joke around with each other, we clowned whomever lost at pool, we debated one another, trying to prove who was the most persuasive speaker. Thinking again, I realize now that the family I once knew was no more and not because we were miles apart. There was not the love from a distance because up close the love was not as strong. The bond was no longer felt. Trampled upon. We had all taken on different belief systems, philosophies, and no longer were in the same political party—yes, that one. The bond my family once shared was no more. But how could siblings who shared the same DNA, who grew up reading from the same Bible, praying the same prayer, learning from the same books, obeying the same rules, eating the same food and living in the same household now exist with mindsets so different from one another? Share so little in common? Hardly any of us has the same belief systems, the same thought patterns. If we were a country, we would all be nomads, and there would be no neighborhoods. Biologically speaking, we were like free radicals. But were we each toxic to the family corporate being?

Everyone in the family is up in arms, beyond speech; we all have taken our sister Maria's decision to marry a Mexican a slap in the face, and a compromise to the family's integrity. She is an ingrate, a near no count, for taking all the raising our parents gave her to do what? Maria took that and her God-given beauty and talents to go out and find that kind of person to marry and mix our blood with.

My politics aside, I am the most liberal in regards to accepting my siblings lifestyles, but see nothing good to come of such a hopeless mix for my sister. Maria had to have known the family would be outraged by her capricious and detestable action. We all felt such a marriage would be a fraud and a travesty: for the man Maria was to marry was an illegal alien. Only one person in the family knew the true reason behind what once would have been thought of as an implausible coupling, but the plot of Maria's secret was never to be revealed.

Maria broke the news of her engagement at what used to be the family's monthly dinner and gathering, but what has now lapsed to the every-now-and-then family get together. Hmmph. Some together. Today's dinner was hosted at E.J.'s home. As usual, the food was deliciously prepared and beautifully served, but joy just was not present—not like before. Maria's news left the family in the dark as to the identity of this mysterious Mexican who might soon be labeled our brother-in-law and therefore associated with the cherished pedigree of the Navies family name. Yes. Maria had always declared she would hyphenate her family name with her husband's name whenever she married. Joey was two seconds from being wrought-up. He swore that he was compelled by the wrath of Dad manifest through the blood in his veins to insure the family name should not be tarnished.

"Maria, are you using drugs?"

Maria pulled up her sleeve to show no that she had no tracks. "Do I look like I am using drugs?" Maria widened her eyes and looked with hurt and anger straight into Joey's face. Louder, she said, "Do I act like I am on drugs, Joey?"

Joey pulled his chair away from Maria and answered, "Yes. As a matter of fact, you do act as if you are using." Joey knew that all of the siblings had said no to drugs a long time ago, but his gratuitous torment of Maria was a work in progress.

Now Ishmael butts in. "Joey, there is no need to inject nonsense into the discussion. There is just no need to go into that territory."

"Why is that such nonsense?" Joey challenged. "Perhaps Maria is following the trend of the naughtiness set by Hollywood lifestyle." Joey turned toward Maria. "Otherwise, Maria, give me a damn good reason to accept or just an argument for why a young and beautiful black woman with a dream career could stoop so low to give her father's name away like its homeless. Hell, you don't even see Mexicans on the streets as homeless." Joey pleaded with Maria, his voice breaking and his hands outstretched. "Please, help the family understand, Maria. Is that too much to ask? Don't you think the family deserves at least an explanation from you? Because something is missing here and, because something's missing, the family cannot see the whole picture. What's behind the picture in this frame? What don't we see? Please, help us to comprehend."

Joey's assault put Maria not just on the defensive but in attack mode. But she asked for this. She knew us all too well, and had to appreciate beforehand that the family would cross-examine her.

"Just because you guys don't understand the why and how I happen to be in love with José does not mean that it isn't right," Maria shot back angrily.

"Well," said Joey just as angrily as he placed a roll on his plate, "no wonder José wants to marry you and hyphenate our family surname with his last name. It doesn't seem as though his daddy gave him a last name of his own or, at least, not a last name that would elevate him to the next level here in America." Joey put his finger to his chin. "Does José think that by acquiring the Navies family last name he can hide his ethnicity? Is José trying to mask his Mexican identity by marrying into the African American race? Or is he trying to make it more difficult to track his wrongdoings?" Joey's stare at Maria is lethal. He yells at her: "No matter, that guy will never assume my father's name along with his Mexican surname as long as I live. And I mean never!" Bitterly, Joey charges, "So, Maria, you can take that tip back to José, and the two of you guys can look up a plan B because plan A will not fly. Not using the Navies family name."

Maria grabbed the bread basket and started for the kitchen.

Mother said sharply, "Maria, where are you going? Please let Rosalita serve the bread. She's been doing it for nine years now. Nothing's changed just because we're having dinner here at E.J.'s home."

Slowly, Maria took her seat.

"Does this José fellow have a last name?" asked Joey.

"His name is José Gonzales," an exasperated Maria revealed.

"Wow! Now that's a unique name. Is he an illegal alien?" Joey goaded.

Rosalita walked into the room and placed the bread on the table and said, in an accent that now seemed heavier, "Here we go." She walked out of the dining room, shaking her head.

"They like to be called immigrants," said Maria.

"Okay Maria," said Joey, "illegal immigrants. The question is not whether they are illegal aliens or illegal immigrants because I don't care about semantics here. The question is did José enter here into our country, America, illegally? Any way you say or write it, those who do have broken the law."

When the subject of Maria intended nuptials was broached, the rest of us at the dinner table, Grandma, Mother, E.J., Shauna and I, tried to remain far from the fray. This was a very serious time for our family. In the truest sense of the words, I felt as though this was our "Last Supper."

E.J. and Shauna had gone out of their way to make the dinner a superb occasion. Shauna prepared everything exquisitely as if to demonstrate that she was a gracious hostess and wanted everyone to feel comfortable with the warm accommodations of E.J.'s home. Shauna, who enjoyed pouring the wine for the family members, filled everyone's glass except Ishmael's. Since his conversion to the Muslim faith, Ishmael had not taken a drink. But this evening, Ishmael's request drew everyone's attention. (Even, momentarily Joey's from Maria.)

He said, "Shauna, would you please pour some wine in my glass? I uh, think that it will make this dinner more digestible."

Shauna placed a hand to her ear, "Eh? Wine did you ask for, sir?" In spite of all the talk, Shauna's mood was jolly. "I am so sorry, Ishmael. I thought that you had just said no to alcohol."

"Shauna," said E.J., lifting his glass, "would you stop playing around and pour Ishmael some wine?"

Shauna answered softly, "I will, E.J. I am just having some fun with Ishmael if you don't mind."

"It's okay. I knew that Shauna was just joking," said Ishmael with a smile.

Joey went back to it. "Now the question still remains on the table: Maria, Is José Gonzales in this country illegally?" he asked.

Maria rolled her eyes and sighed heavily. "For your information, Joey, he has been here in this country for six years."

"So he's illegal," remarked Joey.

Maria's tone was venomous. "Did anyone in the family ask if Rosalita was illegal when the family decided to hire her?" she charged.

Grandma and Mother are usually quiet and try to stay out of matters of the heart. This evening, neither of them has seemed this emotional for quite some time.

Mother's fork clattered to her plate. "Maria, try to keep things in perspective here. Rosalita works for the family. She is not trying to become a part of the family. If so, that would have constituted another type of background check on our part. Our family is not tangled up in Rosalita's affairs, nor is she tied up into ours."

Grandma chimed in as a second matriarch. "Maria, when you speak about giving another man my husband's name and my son's name, well, sweetie, it makes me have to question you on exactly what it is that this young man has done to deserve our family's name—and so quickly, too?" Grandma put her hand to her chest. The lines in her furrowed brow seemed deeper than ever before. "Why does our family surname have to be tied to his last name? Maria, why isn't his surname alone good enough for you?" asked Grandma pointedly. "If there exists love between a couple and they become one, what is the sense in two names?"

"Please, Grandma," said Maria, "there are more important things to be concerned with than who I want to marry."

Grandma reached under her glasses, wiped her eyes, then said, "I know I am not of your generation and your Hollywood crowd. Maybe it is something common with your period of time where a woman joins her maiden name to a man's last name in a hyphenated manner."

"Grandma, I am not a follower. This has nothing to do with Hollywood's drama," Maria said back.

"But what has this José done for you that affords him to be able to just waltz in and get so much with little or no down payment to you or earn credit for a name that belongs to us all? Why, honey," Grandma said, "you don't even have a ring on your finger, and you're going around saying that you are engaged. How do you know that you are engaged when you have no proof of any such thing? Are you affording him or can he afford you? Not once have we heard you say that this fella loves you. Sweetie, you just dishonor yourself this way, and you make me feel sad for you." Grandma had tears in her eyes.

Maria got up and sat by Grandma, and tried to console her. "Grandma, you don't have to worry about me." She took Grandma's hands in her own. "I am all grown up, a woman now, and I know how to take care of myself. Please trust me on this."

Mother cut in, and said, "The issue here is not about trust; it's the lack of confidence you seem to have in yourself and your abilities. You cannot be so afraid of challenge that you forget in what you are rooted." Mother cleared her throat, then drank from her water glass. "You have to draw the line somewhere. I do not know why you want to do such a thing, Maria. I just have to figure that something unfavorable is going on in your life for you to give up your last name to that man, a foreigner, someone that the family does not know if he belongs in this country or not."

"Mother, I am not naïve to life." Maria was struggling to remain calm.

"Well, I hope you heed my words," said Mother. "You cannot fall an easy prey to men. And to say that your situation is based on love is like a woman in denial, headed for a train wreck."

"The whole thing sounds as if someone is being misused by another to gain an easy passport into the United States," stated Grandma.

"Grandma, José has lived in Texas for two of the six years he's been in the United States, so what you're thinking doesn't necessarily make it so."

"Oh, so that's it." Joey slapped his forehead, and said "I got it now. The Mexicans have just about taken over and reclaimed Texas. They are remembering the Alamo for sho'! So I guess now José wants you to become some kind of activist with him to take back California, too. That's it, isn't it, Maria?"

"Joey, I will not dignify your absurdity. I will only tell you that if you were more than half an idiot, you would be dangerous," Maria told him.

"Yeah, Maria," said Joey. "This family is not sympathizing with their chant, 'We didn't cross the border, the borders crossed us.' I believe America won the Mexican War. America did not use Mexicans to build the railroad empire; she used the Chinese. She did not use the Mexicans to pick cotton; she used blacks. America used more of her black and white citizens than her Mexican citizens to fight in the Vietnam War, too, I believe." Joey straightened out his wristband. "Did you forget, Maria, that we had five, not one, but five black uncles that died in the Vietnam War? And today, Maria, we only have one living uncle, and he came back from the war half-crazy. Take a look at the black, polished granite face of the Vietnam Veterans Memorial in Washington and see how many Mexican names can be counted out of the 58,000 servicemen and women listed."

"Nay, nay, Joey. Show more fairness and some justice. The Mexicans served America well during the Vietnam War. They were many in numbers," said Ishmael.

Joey dropped crumbs from his napkin onto the tablecloth. "We are not just talking about their numbers. We are talking about the comparisons of how African Americans have overly served America considering our percentage of people. So, I don't like it when Mexicans try and compare their backbreaking to that of black people. I don't take much to them making minor the free toil that built this country into a superior empire. They crossed over as some Johnny-come-latelys only to weigh claim to this country. How did they help to build this country? Because they picked some broccoli and spinach, oh, and some strawberries?" asked Joey.

"There is no need for that, Joey," Ishmael said evenly. Ishmael took a sip from his wineglass and calmly continued. "That's exactly what many folk in this country want, the blacks and browns to become and stay upset with each other. Neither group can rise above their present conditions without the two uniting as one powerful and meaningful force."

"Yeah, well, you keep thinking that, that's really going to happen, Ishmael, while you continue to see the numbers of blacks in the military count rise higher than that of Mexicans, and that is real, with or without a draft," Joey countered.

"Well, you know," said Shauna, wiping her mouth with her napkin, "now that the Democrats have control of the House and Senate, the rumor is that some of the Democrats want to bring back a draft."

Mother disagreed. She folded her hands beneath her chin and, reasoned, "I do not think that is going to happen. Any bills having to do with the draft quickly disappeared. I do think that Democratic

Congressman Charles Rangel introduced a bill after the Iraq War started, but it went nowhere. When he reintroduced a modified version, it had the same result."

"Huh," Joey smirked, "if Charles Rangel ever has his way, we'd see how many Mexicans make claim to America's citizenship then. I bet you those Gonzaleses would jump back over that border quicker than a bird flying because they know who would be the first ones sent to war. America has a tradition of sending her darkest citizens first," he said, his disgust palpable.

Maria braved, "Joey, you just have such a negative view of Mexicans, but I am curious, though, would you have been this hawkish if I was going to marry an Italian?" Maria recognized that the family all knew that Ishmael's wife, Nadir, was Iranian. Yet no one had ever brought up his marriage as a problem for the family, at least, not at the dinner table. I guessed that Maria was hesitant to bring Nadir in the picture because Ishmael had come to her rescue tonight and so many times before.

Grandma placed her fork on her plate. "This is no time to deal in a hypothetical screenplay. You are not acting in Hollywood right this moment, Maria. This is your family that you owe some reasoning to. The conversation on the table is your Mexican partner," said Grandma in a no-nonsense tone.

Mother asked, no one in particular, "Why is it that blacks are so easy to just go and mix their blood with anything other than their own? What makes blacks think so little of their own bloodline?"

Ishmael knew that Mother was also low-profiling him in her talk about mixed relationships. He spared Nadir family members' indignant voices by not bringing her to family dinners.

"Mom," said Maria, "José has a bloodline and heritage too, you know." I had never seen Maria use that tone with Mother. She was direct and bold.

"I am sure of that," said Mother, with no hint that she paid any mind to Maria's forgetfulness, "so with him having such a heritage, why does he want your family's last name attached to his surname, Maria? Don't you see the game in that? He can maneuver and do all kinds of things in your name—establish credit using your last name and get a passport, too."

"Congress passed a bill that the Homeland Security Department requires virtually all air travelers entering the United States to show passports, even U.S. citizens," I pointed out.

"Yeah, like Homeland Security is really doing its job when folk like José Gonzales are already here illegally, trying to marry my sister," Joey said venomously. "Folks who want to do harm don't always pass through the ports where passports are required. If I know that tidbit, then surely Mr. Brilliant Homeland Security Secretary Michael Chertoff should know enough to secure our borders. And an unsecured fence at the border is not security. That's exactly why the Republicans are going to lose the 2008 election. By errors of omission. Don't those people in Washington get it? Or are they just not concerned about real security since Bush cannot run again as president?"

"Joey," said Ishmael, "Man, you are espousing such terrible views that I am becoming a bit concerned about you. You are not reasoning and are overlooking a lot that tears your views to shreds." Ishmael's face was a mix of dread and pity. "Mexicans are not your terrorists. They are hardworking people who are trying to make a decent living to take care of their families. That's all to it, man."

"I am so tired of people saying that they are just here to take care of their families," said Joey, slamming his hand on the table. "Well, what about the poor blacks and poor white people here who need to take care of their families? Is anybody giving a damn about the poor citizens of this country? And what about the Katrina victims getting some of that taking care of? Huh? Huh?"

"I share your sentiments, Joey," said Shauna, "not all Mexicans are here to take care of their families. Some Mexicans are so aggressive that they even have our border patrol and national guards backing down and running away from protecting the border. Now that is the most embarrassing thing to ever have occurred."

E.J. uttered a word for the first time in over 45 minutes. "I would run away, too, from organized, armed Mexican drug dealers and criminals," said E.J. "Matter of fact, there is another incident that I find more embarrassing than those incidents." E.J. waited for Shauna to wipe his mouth with her napkin before going on. "Thank you, babe," said E.J. Shauna rested her elbow on E.J.'s chair and stroked his cheek. "It is just so unfathomable, the criminal prosecutions and convictions of two former El Paso border agents, Jose Compean and Ignacio Ramos. The two agents were convicted of shooting and wounding an unarmed illegal immigrant near Fabens, Texas. That illegal immigrant was suspected of drug smuggling and was granted immunity by federal authorities in exchange for his testimony against the agents. Those two men were just doing their jobs. Now they should be the ones pardoned by Bush." E.J. frowned. "And the public should be more outspoken on the matter."

Grandma shook her head. "The worst thing I have heard yet is that now the illegal aliens want to collect Social Security. Now if that happens, the U.S. government is most definitely broken."

"I am telling you," said Joey, "illegal aliens pose more problems than good to America. Illegal aliens are able to take billions of dollars out of America's economy. They wire the money they make on jobs that others are not working to their own country, supporting a foreign economy. They even have frequent user cards for wiring money! They have overloaded our hospitals and emergency rooms and have overburdened taxpayers. And because of the Mexicans, blacks are getting paid less in salaries today than what Grandma received when she worked over thirty-five years ago."

"You have a lot to say, Joey, without facts, without statistics to back up your talk," Ishmael said. That Ishmael was not pleased with his brother's comments was all over his face.

"Oh, didn't you know?" Maria said. "Joey is really good at making false accusations," she added, bobbing her head.

Joey, true to his nature, did not back down. "I have my own stats. Yeah, buddy, and I will say my piece because I know my history." With his hand, Joey swept the air around him as he went on. "I am not letting anyone come into this country to downplay the significant role African Americans have made in building this country since 1619. Vicente Fox said the Mexicans will do work that blacks don't want to do." Joey lifted his head. "Well, blacks have been in America for over six hundred years now and have done their work. Where were your Mexicans then, Vicente? Just because African Americans don't want to continue being babysitters for Miss Ann's little spoiled brats does not mean that blacks do not want to work. I am not trying to be the sacrificial lamb for Mexicans. As quiet as it is kept, they seem to be making their gains more off of the backs of African Americans and poor whites. Were Mexicans anywhere around helping blacks chant for their sole right to their forty acres and a mule? Hell, all the freebies America has given Mexicans in the last few decades would have tallied up to make a big dent in the debt of reparations."

"Joey," Maria charged back, "You sound like other blacks who want to blame the rest of minorities for their present situation in America. And you know what else I think is crazy? The ways different races fight for the status of which group of people was treated the worst throughout history, who suffered the biggest or worst holocaust? How many Jews died at the hands of Hitler versus the number of Africans murdered during the Euro-American slave trade. Why are we all vying for recognition of who was done the worst like it's a trophy or anything else to be held on to? I know atrocities should not be forgotten; but neither should they be celebrated. And truth to be told, these competitions have gotten folk nowhere. When will you and other blacks like you, Joey, become accountable and make what you need in your life to happen without blaming others?" Maria fidgeted with her napkin. "Our race should have been so much further ahead in this country; we should really be at a point in this society where we can welcome Mexicans employees without feeling the competition."

"What is going on, Maria?" Joey snorted. Again, Joey banged his hand on the table in disgust, and handpicked which of Maria's points he would address. "Are you now Ishmael's sound bite for regurgitating his philosophy? Your talk is about as messed up as the talk from black so-called leaders, encouraging my folk to set aside their needs and fight for Mexicans' causes. We do not have the same causes as Mexicans in America. I tell you what, when Mexicans help blacks obtain their forty acres and a mule, then we owe them. Until then, I am not trying to hear about what I should do to help our brown brothers if we do not benefit. Word."

"But, Joey," Shauna said, holding out her hands, "now, now. Maria does make a good point. Blacks should be further along in this country in owning businesses so that we can hire more Mexicans ourselves. How can black people fault others for our not having done more to be more to have more and to be further along as a people? So now, when others, and not just Mexicans, come into this country, we are fighting over the same crumbs! And we blame them?" Shauna lowered her voice to a barely audible whisper. "Because if it was not for Rosalita being in this country, I would have to be in that kitchen right now, and I might add, along with your two sisters, preparing dinner."

"Uh-uh." I shook my head. "I am not for that," I said. "I know I did not get a Ph.D. just to cook and serve my brothers dinner." Grinning, I added, "Shauna, don't count me in on stuff like that, ever!" I was hoping to lighten up the tone of the conversation.

Joey held a hand to his chest. "Maria, if I might digress for a moment, I want to raise the level of your understanding as it relates to blacks blaming other minorities for our condition here in America. First off, I don't hear any leaders disagreeing with that position. Maybe it is not a politically correct thing to say, but it is in no way a trivial matter. Further, our real leaders know exactly what the deal is because you cannot fool wisdom. History dictates what must be said for a better future for blacks. And leaders who speak out will always be right in my book. That's why I respect Al Sharpton so much. He has no fear."

At last, Maria's face relaxed and she managed a faint smile; she had managed to deflect the attention away from herself just by pushing another of Joey's race buttons. She stayed this safe course: "I don't hear any black leaders speaking out loud enough on what should be done to rectify the problem."

"Ah, you know black leaders," Joey told her, "they haven't changed just because it is the twenty-first century. They only speak out when they've been given the OK to do so." Joey leaned back in his chair. He was confident holding forth on his own truth. "Everybody knows the deal, but they don't have the guts to say what is truth."

Everybody? Hmmm. Well, Joey can humor himself by thinking that what crosses his mind might be universal. Not!

Shauna leaned forward and addressed the man she wished to be her brother-in-law. "Joey, I think you are right about that. Our leaders would rather play low ball and deal with that Duke case in North Carolina than deal with pertinent issues already on the table."

Mother rubbed her palms together. "You are so right, Shauna. I am very disappointed in our leaders today. There seems to be very little expectation of them accomplishing anything of significance. For the past few decades there is very little they have accomplished by talk, talk, and more talk. They are not at the table dealing and they are absent from or have little presence at places where power is wielded."

Ishmael tilted his head back and sighed heavily, saying, "Seriously, it is possible that the time has come and gone for African Americans to use color as a first factor when seeking out leaders. Rather, we should place leaders in positions who are skilled and resourceful enough to force the government to live up to the words of the Constitution and do what is supposed to be done for its own American citizens, first and foremost."

Joey jumped up, and celebrated. "Yes! Finally, you said something that makes sense, Ishmael, I have been waiting for this moment all evening, when someone would get it! And you rose to the occasion." Joey walked over to Ishmael and rewarded him with a brotherly slap on the back.

"I am glad, Joey, that you felt what I was trying to say," Ishmael answered, his tone sarcastic. "But it was inevitable that I might say something you would agree with, Brother."

It is rare to see Ishmael indulge in satire. He placed a hand to his chin, and coaxed, "Please continue. Teach, my brother."

I could not tell whether Ishmael was clowning Joey or just playing to Joey's grandiose ego. But I could tell that Joey didn't think a thing was amiss. Is all truly vanity? Blindness, too?

Obligingly, Joey went on. "You know that's what I have been trying to get across all afternoon—that the Constitution was established for its own citizens. But America and some officials seemed to have forgotten its intent." Joey wiped his brow. "Whew! For a moment there, Ishmael, I thought that you might have forgotten."

Shauna was up next. "That's really what real school should be about today, teaching to make sure our children understand the

Constitution," she said. "No child should graduate from high school unless he or she comprehends the Constitution of their own country. Students would come out of high school eagle-eyed, and become informed and smart voters. And needless to say, government would perform better—it would be accountable to the people because the people would be astute enough to enforce their own check and balance system."

"That is supposed to be the job of our elected officials," said Grandma.

"Of course it is, Grandma," said E.J. assuredly "but when your elected officials have forgotten that the oath they took was to serve their country and not private mega-corporations, then you have no choice but to look out for self."

My napkin slipped from my lap and I scooted back in my chair to pick it up. "Yeah," I piped in as I sat up again, "and while learning their rights given by Constitution and the amendments, our folk had better put into place their real back-up, which is doing for self. I have a Ph.D. and have been out there in the job market and have not found the pay commensurate to my education and talent." I looked at E.J., and added, "Not to mention what I think I am worth." E.J. gave me an approving look and smiled.

Grandma pushed her glasses up on her face and encouraged, "Just keep searching, sweetie. You owe that to yourself."

"More importantly, Grandma, I owe something back," I said. I honestly thought everyone at the table had overlooked our need to commit to giving back. "Therefore, before I leave the proletariat class, I have one big contribution to make to my people out there in society."

"Oh!" Grandma's eyes brightened with anticipation. "Ahh, and what is that, sweetie?"

"A big, illuminated sign in bold letters that reads, 'America can no longer provide jobs for her own citizens—self-employment by any means necessary!'"

"Look Zemi," said Joey, "just because you had a whiff of success with that AWALA project, don't go and fool yourself into thinking you're the chosen one to speak for self-employment and entrepreneurship on behalf of those African women. Now don't let your ego get bigger than the skills you possess."

Hmmph, I thought to myself, he would know about that!

With outstretched arms, Grandma looked over her glasses and around the table, "E.J. told us all just how you did real well with the AWALA project and its chairman, Mrs. Williams. He said you made out with more dollars in your pocket than what you started out with. Everyone is so proud of you, Zemi, for stepping out there and showing real strength, for doing something on your own and where you were in charge. You put your thinking cap on and with your vision made something big happen for women who share an African legacy."

Maria applauded, "Yes Zemi, congratulations. Who would have thought that one could gather a talent pool of women for a platform of self-empowerment for women of African descent? The whole thing was really exciting—Alliance for Women of an African Legacy in America. I understand that most of your women from South Africa came to get heads-up on entrepreneurial strategies that our women could combine with theirs for import/export businesses."

I smiled; it warmed my heart to know that my family acknowledged my hard work. "You know—I was really happy to gain the experience from AWALA along with the money I made from my first real entrepreneurial project," I said.

The doorbell rang. A moment later, Rosalita ushered Zeth into the dining room. I didn't know he was coming. Who extended an invitation to him?

"Hey, Zeth, my main man, how's it going?" Joey got up from the table and gave Zeth the "brother man" hug and handshake. "What's going on, man?" Joey asked. "I tried contacting you to let you know that I was on an earlier flight, but, man, my cell phone could not get a signal in the airport."

"It's all good," Zeth told him. He walked around to where I was sitting and gave me a hug. Then he went over to Mother and Grandma. He handed Mother a box of chocolates and presented a bouquet of flowers to Grandma. From a flight bag he pulled out two bottles of Dom Perignon and gave the champagne to E.J.

"Man, I am really glad you could make it out here. I heard the weather was a little foggy out of Charlotte," Joey said.

I then realized that Joey had invited Zeth as if he were already a part of the family. Still, I was glad he came.

"Here, take my seat, Zeth," Ishmael said standing. "Come sit next to Zemi. I'll sit over there next to Maria."

Zeth waved his hand. "No. No need for that," he said. "Everybody stay put, please. I will sit anywhere to taste some of this good old, home-cooked food." Zeth pulled out the chair next to Maria, and Rosalita came in and prepared a place setting for him.

Shauna held up a bottle of wine. "Would you like wine, Zeth?" she asked.

"Naw. I think I better put somethin' solid in my belly first off."

Zeth stacked his plate with food from every platter passed around. Was he feeding six stomachs?

Joey pointed to Zeth's plate. "Man, I know that you are tall like a giant, but you don't have to eat like one," said Joey. "This is a land of plenty. There is enough food here. You don't have to put everything on your plate at once."

"Man, don't waste your words of wisdom on me," said Zeth, while he was eating as if he were starving, "because when it comes to eatin', you can't school me, and you won't be able to muster up a debate tryin' to bait me, either. As we used to say way back when, 'I ain't stuttin' you.'"

I was amused. Zeth's comeback reminded me that it was years before I realized that the idiom in more understandable English was actually, 'I ain't studying you,' meaning not paying attention to someone.

Joey chuckled. He got a kick out of what Zeth had to say, too. "Zeth," Joey said, "you should have been here earlier, man. I have had to re-educate the whole family on matters, and I do not think all of them are taking the teaching to heart. Some of the teachings are just, you know, plain old common sense but some…uh…uh." Joey paused for dramatic effect before finishing up with, "…are having a hard time merging reality with twenty-first century matters."

Shauna wiped her mouth and carefully replaced her napkin on her lap, saying, "When I listened to you, Joey, I was able to appreciate some salient points."

"Salient points," E.J. jibed. E.J. tweaked the back of Shauna's neck. "Baby," he told her, "there is nothing Joey can do for you, so why are you trying to give him undeserved accolades?"

"Seriously, if you listened carefully, Joey does offer some points on what African Americans need to do, indeed. And I share many of his viewpoints, especially concerning immigrants," Shauna answered. She leaned forward, and said, "We might not like the bold and frank way Joey puts things, but I think that a lot of blacks share his viewpoints. Those who do just don't have the platform to be heard like some of our Civil Rights leaders." Shauna's voice rose. "There are blacks who have made verbal attacks against Al Sharpton and Jesse Jackson because of their support for illegal immigrants."

"Wait a minute!" said Joey, sitting erect in his chair. "That's because they need to pay more attention to our own flock. We don't see many black businesses opening, not the way the Mexicans are opening up new shops." Joey rubbed the side of his chin and tilted his head. He continued, saying, "And another thing, too, I see Mexicans speaking at gatherings of other ethnic groups about the rights of illegal aliens. I see Mexican churches and schools all over the place, but—and you can call me misguided—I don't see either Mexicans or the Catholic churches giving up their platforms so that other ethnic groups can speak to their own issues and concerns. I don't understand that one. I really don't. And I wish the Vatican wouldn't have stayed as silent as a lamb when slavery was going on for over four hundred years."

"Oh, yeah, there are also a lot of black churches in support of Mexican immigrants," said Shauna. "Sometimes the illegal aliens would…"

"Would you please stop calling them illegal aliens, Shauna!!??" Maria yelled. "You know, I have been thinking about this conversation. Does anyone here care about whether or not we love each other? What we are sitting here saying about Mexicans is the same trash some whites still say about black people. It is not right. Who here cares about how I feel? I am marrying one man, and the fact that he is Mexican should not taint my marriage with all the political mess that is going on. Another thing. A lot of this is so sexist. I am being attacked because I am a female. Black men can marry anything other than one of their own and they do not get this type of harassment. At least not to their faces. So you can talk behind my back, too! If one of my brothers had chosen a Chicana bride, I do not believe we would be having this conversation. I am marrying someone whom I love and care for; he can be accepted or not. But show some respect; I am not marrying ET; I am not marrying an alien. I cannot understand why you all are so hard on Mexicans who are here illegally. So what? As far as the law is concerned, running away from a slave plantation used to be illegal, didn't it?"

Another show?—Maria is always on stage. She's good though, I thought to myself.

Maria continued, "Not one of you has said a word about the Native Americans who kicked out the Indians with black blood in them when the reservations got casino paid. Why don't you spend the energy getting reparations instead of hatin' on other people as bad or worse off than some black folk? Why are you even competing with the have nots and the have lesses? I think it's the same crab barrel mentality stuff; it's just that some of the crabs are from other waters. Why are not black people saying that they should be getting what the Daddy and Mama Warbucks are getting paid? Why do you have your sights set on what's worth little instead of looking to wealth? You really have got it twisted!"

No one said a thing, so Maria did. "And as far as the family name is concerned, the name 'Navies' is my birthright, and cannot be taken from me." Maria faced Shauna, and pleaded. "Please."

Shauna was hurt. Quietly, she apologized. "I am sorry. I will just call them immigrants from now on."

E.J. stopped eating. He wiped his mouth with his napkin, and went lightening quick to Shauna's defense. "Catch yourself, Maria. Now, Shauna expressed herself according to her own theory and belief. Just because you have a Mexican fiancé and feel a need to defend Mexicans does not mean that Shauna has to agree. In this household we are allowed to express our feelings without another flying off into a rage. And Maria, just so you know, your point about

Native Americans made our point; do you know how many black people joined the struggle for Native Americans to gain rights? And then for some of them to turn around and kick out the blacks in their tribes! Wow! Long ago, marrying blacks was how a lot of them got off reservations. This is not about hatred or hating. I guess the sentiment is that black people are so quick to take up the cause of other people who are treated badly, and that black people need to focus on the needs of black people as we cannot count on others to do that for us. I mean, look at our neighborhoods. Traditionally, we take in anybody who moves in, but, still, we cannot move any and everywhere without catching hell." E.J., at Shauna's side now, rubbed her back. "You, okay, baby?" he asked.

Shauna smiley coyly at her man, her face relaxed. She seemed satisfied that her man came to her rescue. But Maria and I both knew all too well that Shauna could handle just about any situation with aplomb. But she often likes to play coy and vulnerable when E.J. is around.

"And Shauna," said E.J., "stop backing down on your beliefs just because this is my family. I am an attorney, and I cannot have my woman vacillating on issues depending on who she's talking to. Stick to your principles."

"Okay, I will E.J. Thank you," Shauna answered, gleaming at her knight (in tarnishable armor, as she would learn).

Maria expressed her regrets. "I am sorry. I really do apologize, Shauna. I didn't mean to yell at you, but you all have hurt me and should know it."

Shauna smiled at her. "I accept your apology. But America had better soon solve the Iraq War and deal with what's happening inside these borders. If blacks and browns have not worked this thing out by 2008, either blacks might walk to another party or the Mexicans, the ones who can vote, will. But the two are surely moving away from the aisle. The Democrats might not be out of the woods for 2008 unless they come out with the right spin for the two groups. Blacks know that they can show their power at the polls because they are all legal voters. Blacks are upset and that is the bottom line," said Shauna. "Hillary might not want to act like she has the corner on the black vote, come 2008. I hope she knows that she has work to do. In the village, I mean."

E.J. looked pleased. "Cold, but true, Shauna. That was good," He said proudly. "But I have to share a point of distinction. It is naïve to lump all brown people together. Brown people come here not only from Mexico, but from South America, too. Point one. Point two is that not all brown people who are citizens or have proper papers empathize with illegal immigrants. Some of them say that illegal immigrants make it harder for them. Sorry, Maria, sometimes there is no other way to say 'illegal,' but 'illegal.' I needed to make this point, because just like black people are all lumped together and it is presumed we all look, act, want, need and whatever the same, we know that is not true. Nor is it true of the people lumped together as brown."

"Yes," I agreed. "Try asking someone with an Hispanic surname about Mexico for him to look at you crazy and let you know he is Spanish, as in Spain. Nonetheless, whatever might be said about brown people, it is black individuals who need to deal with whom or what party has earned his or her vote," I added.

Zeth took a pause from eating. "Yes. Folk better listen to Howard Dean. He said it plainly enough that the Democratic Party had taken the black voters for granted. Folks who voted fer the Democrats in the election of 2006 might not want to get happy too fast and start runnin' buck wild just 'cause of a midterm tsunami. If blacks are not able to ride some of those waves, somebody might fall off."

My spirits lifted. I knew I was blushing, and I did not mind if it showed. "You said that all too well, Zeth. I could not have said it any better."

"Ah, thank you, Zemi, but anythin' you say would turn out right," Zeth said. "Folk, you know Wolf Blitzer highlighted a segment on his CNN show on the question, Are African Americans too loyal to the Democratic Party? Neither Dean nor Wolf has to repeat the question in order fer me to take the matter into account," said Zeth.

I felt compelled to speak right after Zeth. Right now, to be politically noticed, correctly or incorrectly was of little concern. I just wanted to make sure that Zeth could realize that I heard and regarded his opinion. So, I expressed another point. "Today some blacks are carrying on about how unfortunate the situation of illegal immigrants. When I was working at some of the schools here in California, teachers were furious over extra pay given to teachers who spoke Spanish over teachers who taught English well. Some teachers even cried out reverse discrimination. The teachers saw where most of the new programs in schools were for the benefit of Hispanics."

Shauna looked at E.J. while addressing everyone. I guess she was on a roll to make him proud. "I tend to believe that God is calling out the African American. It is something that we are not doing. But we are the ones who are supposed to be doing it. Does that make sense to anyone?" Shauna then looked around the table for support. Why didn't she look for support in her man—her eyes were right there on him? Shauna speaks: "I believe that we are the ones who can make America a better country. America needs to heal itself and find a way to have peace among the different races and with other countries. I don't believe America can continue ignoring the pus building up in a sore that needs to be lanced."

I do not know what I felt about that analogy; we were having dinner!

The pus comment gave Joey no cause for pause. He twirled his finger, and chided, "Maybe, Shauna, when God stops giving you the spin and offers you a clue, then you can interrupt us and put it on the table."

"Be quiet, brother-in-law." Shauna flicked her hand at Joey. Shauna and Joey have a good relationship with each other and act like sister and brother even though she and E.J. are not married.

"See, Shauna, that's what I am telling you. Joey has no loyalty. Don't let him just cut you up like that," said E.J., smirking.

"It's okay, baby, every now and then the brother says something that suggests he has potential," Shauna assured E.J.

"You know folks," said Ishmael, as he sipped his third glass of wine, "I think there is just possibly another way to assess these malcontents about Mexicans. First off, let us understand that there are those who would love to see blacks against Mexicans and vice versa. Regardless, legally or illegally, Mexicans are in America to stay. If the government and big businesses did not want Mexicans in American, trust me, they would not be here. They were wanted here to plant and harvest for mega-farmers decades ago, and so they were here. For big farming interests, they are no longer seen as indispensable, but they are here. Still. So, Joey, you might be upset with the wrong group of people. And another thing. All these folk who have come, from Asia, Africa, Latin America, South America and the Caribbean, have come after America and its cohorts in the so-called developed world, including the World Bank and the IMF have done their do, if not their do-do, excuse me Mother and Grandma, all throughout all of the developing world. But Americans who have benefitted from imperialistic-manifesting- the-pitiful-destinies-of-other-people policies, do not want them here, let alone as neighbors."

"I guess that is another way to look at this," I said.

"Sure it is," said Ishmael. "Sometimes to see the painting, you've got to take a few steps back. Go too close to the canvas and you get damn near cross-eyed, just like some of the views expressed here tonight about Mexicans, including some of my own, I admit. Look. When we were young, we were told that the U.S.S.R. was evil on earth. But let that republic fall and the doors to this country are just thrown open for Russians and Eastern Europeans! Why? Because they are white? Perhaps due to their isolation over decades the purest whites on the earth? Beats the hell oughta me, but we were brainwashed to hate the Russians, and now they are on the welfare rolls of the U.S. government? No wonder young girls in this country had to be kicked off the welfare rolls and made to go miles and miles to work for not much more than bus fare even if their children had to be left in the care of no counts—the government had to make room for Russian indigents! And you never know how the hand of God will move. As a Christian, I learned that the earth is the Lord's, right there in Psalm 24. We must know that we do not know all. Not about illegals, Mexicans or anything else. They are God's children, too. Just like the Boat People, Russians and the European girls who come as nannies and overstay their visas."

Wow! That was more than the mouthfuls of food Zeth had just ingested. Ishmael? He had a lot to say. Well, Mother and Grandma seemed happy that Ishmael remembered his Christian roots. But did they hear the rest?

No one said a word. Not until Zeth laid down his fork and knife on his empty plate, and addressed a matter Ishmael spoke on at least five of Zeth's mouthfuls before. "I think you might have a consensus around the table on your explanation." He winked at me on the sly. "But somethin' in partic'lar I want to address. Big Brother's government is always watchin'. And now Congress wants to enact the 'shock and awe.' Leaders don't just look up one day and notice that the country has an influx of thirteen to fifteen million illegals of a specific group within its borders when those people are receivin' aid and shelter from government and big businesses. If the illegals are wron' and should be punished, then so should the government and corporations."

In the room, I sensed a shift.

"Exactly," said Ishmael as he reached for another whole wheat roll. "Had not incentives of entitlement been made available from the government and by corporations to entice the Mexicans, then they would not be in America in mega-numbers. At this point, there is very little that can be done about it. The Republican politicians turned their heads to the issue of immigrants because those politicians thought they could continue to be of support in supplying big businesses with cheap labor. So they talk one talk and walk another. The Democrats are just as much the culprits because they wanted to count the votes of Mexicans for their party. Besides all of that, Joey, you are naïve to think that if it were not for the Mexicans here in this country, minimum wages would be higher for blacks."

"Now, Rodney," Joey said, refusing to call Ishmael by his Muslim name, "given your critique, let us see if you can speak out earnestly about the next question on the table." Joey tilted his chair and steadied himself with his hand holding onto the edge of the table. "Would you say that the Mexicans were the minority group that pretty much helped to seal the deal of Bush and the Republicans getting into office the last two presidential elections?"

"Well-uh..." began Ishmael, "a lot of the Cubans in Florida are big time GOP supporters 'cause some of them are waiting for the

Republicans to free their homeland. But Fidel says he is not dead yet, you know, but aside from that I, well-uh...I...."

Joey faced Ishmael. "Let me put it this way then, Rodney, to help you deal with your sudden, not heretofore observed, speech impediment, the Republicans had taken on what is typically noted as the fastest-growing group of voters, which means the Hispanics. Some statistics show that the voting distribution of the Hispanics is now about 80-20 in favor of the Democrats, instead of 60-40 as it was two years ago for the Republicans. Keep in mind, Rodney, these stats are not convoluted by either my politics or opportunity, that is, your inability to check up at this instance. These numbers come from erudite, reputable social scientists. So, now may I ask you, Rodney, again, did the Hispanic community give Bush the edge in the past elections, and then did Bush win and got in a position to wreak havoc upon minorities?"

Ishmael said nothing—at that moment.

"No need for you to wonder why the Hispanics jumped over to the Democratic Party, while African Americans have been consistent with the Democratic Party, come hell or high water. Ow, ow, uh, uh," growled Joey. "Is it too hard of a question for you to answer, huh, Rodney?"

"No, it is not a difficult question to answer," said Ishmael sharply.

"Well, do you need for me to paint a clearer picture? Do you need me to put it in high-def? Rodney?" asked Joey. "I mean, we know that the Republicans had to have one of the minority groups vote their way in order for them to get in office, and it surely was not the blacks who voted for them like they were the Second Coming!"

Ishmael brought clasp hands to his face. "I can answer if you will just be patient enough to let me do so. I was slow in answering because I wanted to make sure that I could put my answer in simplistic enough terms for your mind to comprehend," said Ishmael.

"Ouch!" E.J. exclaimed, cupping his hands to his mouth. "That was below the belt, Joey, or did you call fair catch?"

Joey shook his head. "Don't beat around the bush on the question, Rodney. Since you want to deal in simplistic terms, then the answer would merely be a yes or no," said Joey.

Ishmael leaned on the table. "This will probably not be rudimen-tary enough, Joey, but if I made it any simpler, I would be address-ing a lower species."

Everyone hoo-rahhed, just like Joey had just gotten hoo-rahhed, and leading the cheer was E.J. "Hey, Joey, is this another fair catch?" he jeered.

Even Grandma added fuel to the fire. She shook her head and looked away from Joey, a smirk pasted on her face. "Get back up in the saddle now, Joey," she encouraged. "I know you have more to say."

But Ishmael was not finished yet. He got wicked and became wickeder if that's a word. Ishmael had more words for Joey.

"Let's see if I can connect the dots for you this time, Joey. The Monica Lewinski scandal and other playful dalliances that sur-rounded President Clinton at the time, and along with the media witch-hunt on alleged perjury, is what pretty much sealed the fate of the Dems and deal for the Republicans," said Ishmael. "The Re-publicans did not earn the office through effort as much as the peo-ple wanted change—that is the curse of being the last party in—I mean people often want you to be the first party out! With nothing left as a choice other than the Republican Party and the behavior of persons who represented the Dems, well the voting public at the time was too through. They wanted the Democrats to repent or at best atone for their disloyalty to the constituency."

Zeth looked around and stopped when he got to me. "Well," said Zeth, grinning. "I do have a Charlotte newspaper that first called Gore out as the winner. But seriously, now would be the time fer the Independent Party to become stronger so that the American public's choices and ideas can be better represented."

I thought more than ever before that Zeth really could be an In-dependent.

"Something else to consider, too: Clinton had been in office two terms already," said Ishmael. "Conventional wisdom reminds us that when a party stays in office too long, it begins to take the people for granted. Some presidents become less like leaders of a republic and more like emperors, with cultlike followers. The party in office, at the very least, becomes the old guard, the establishment, stale—certainly, no longer dynamic. Dynamic people and agenda are needed for the change people seek. Let's just call it 'incumbentitis,' being in office or not out long enough." To that Ishmael got some nods, one from me too.

I bet Zeth is an independent voter. I turned sideways in my chair, and offered an observation. "What I find most interesting is that Bill Clinton attributed the Democrats' loss to the Republicans in obtaining control of Congress in 1994 as due in part to their inability or reluctance to stand up and be heard on concerns that were of interest to the people. Hmmm. Like—when he stood up—when his concerns and interests were around Monica Lewinski."

Joey, a die-hard Bill Clinton fan, narrowed his eyes and said, "don't mess with Bill. Leave him alone."

"I did already," I sliced back.

"Really, Rodney, you and everyone have proved my point," said Joey.

"And what might that minor footnote be?" asked Ishmael sardonically.

Joey was quick to answer. "That African Americans and Mexicans don't share the same agenda. African Americans would never have voted for Republicans no matter what. Face it, the Mexicans put Bush in office the last two times, and now they want to jump to the front of the line for relief from the Democratic Party because Bush and the Republican Party turned their backs on them and did not keep a promise. Did the Mexicans vote for a Democratic governor in California? No! Instead, they voted in Republican Arnold Schwarzenegger. Man, the Democrats can't trust Mexicans. Blacks are the only minority group that the Democrats can truly depend on to be loyal to them," Joey postured.

"Geez, Joey!" I looked at him in disbelief. "You talk as if you are a house servant speaking from days of old. Really, Joey, do you know how pathetic you sound?" I pushed my plate away, and told him, "Such talk appeals to the blind, meaning that no matter where the Democratic Party leads, African Americans will follow because of a void in leadership. You make the Democratic Party of today sound like the Plantation Party that it has always been. If indeed, the Mexicans did vote differently the other two elections, then they are smarter than blacks because they deal and negotiate their votes as though they have choices and their votes have value."

"Whee, whee, whee, Joey," said Shauna. "Such a foolish notion. You took me by surprise, too, with that immature remark: 'loyal,' as though blacks were owned by the Democratic Party."

Gesturing to Joey, E.J. said, "I, too, have to join the consensus on your remarks, Joey. That 'loyal' spiel was a bit over the top."

Ishmael got up from the table and went over and put an arm across Joey's shoulders. "Joey, man, you've got to pull yourself through this. Now, I know that it hurts, but you are just not the darling minority of the Democratic Party any more. But if it's any consolation, what 'minority' means shifts with the birth of every new baby; in the year 2050 over half of America's population will be made up of people of color."

"Yeah, Joey," I said, "please get it together. Maybe that's why the Democratic Party was taking your kind for granted the way Dean frankly admitted is the case; the man just states a fact, like saying a donkey brays."

Joey got up to help Grandma to an oversized chair. "Grandma, your grandchildren can't accept the truth. They are in denial."

Shauna said, "Oh yeah, I think that Dean only made that statement so blacks would feel as though it was an apology from the Party for their wrongdoings; our folk felt amends were made and so the votes just came pouring in."

I pointed to Shauna. "Go ahead, Shauna, and tell them of how it goes. That if anybody wants to get over on blacks, all that need be done is to throw out some feely-feely sentiments because blacks are just a ball of feely-emotions. All they have to say is that they feel our pain."

"Well now, y'all," said Zeth, "maybe we should look first to examine and see if there is any such truth to what Joey mentioned about this here 'loyal' picture. If we question this any further, might be that the truth may hurt those who vote Democrat." Zeth's eyes widened.

"Man, Zeth! You of all people should know not to agree with Joey," said E.J.

"Naw. Naw, naw. Rig your horses in for a breeder, my man. Now, I know that you are an attorney, E.J., but let us not be so quick to rebuke Brother Joey." Zeth's face was flushed as he could see all eyes were on him. "Joey is not the type of man who talks out of both sides of his neck."

"Man, how do you think Joey has been talking all day?" E.J. pointed at one side of his neck. "I, at least, know the talk that has been coming from one side of his neck."

Joey raised his head and hand in an attempt to speak.

Zeth held his hand higher. "Please, let me handle this one, Brother Joey."

Joey folded his hands. "Hey, be my guest."

Zeth squared his shoulders and faced E.J. "The truer truth is that blacks are more drawn to the Democratic Party because the Party speaks to promises that one day black people hope they will reap. Admittedly, the Democratic Party does have the loyalty of African Americans because the Party keeps hope alive fer blacks, especially when always throwin' up affirmative action programs as still the best thin' fer us."

I tried to make it plain. "The Democrats can do whatever they want with and to African Americans," I said evenly and with no apology.

"True, Zemi," said E.J., "and that's because the Democratic Party knows blacks are still tied to the bosom of their Party even though the milk is all dried up. And on the other side, the Republicans painted even a bleaker picture for blacks. Check out what's in the picture frame. So I guess what Joey just said does hurt, but the truth of what he said speaks for itself and for me, too."

My Dad came to mind when E.J. spoke of seeing what's in the picture frame; Dad often used analogies to pictures in his lessons to his children. "I wish they would take that affirmative action thing and bury it," I said. "It appears to have served its usefulness as far as I am concerned. In recent years that has been the tallest of the Democratic Party's deeds for blacks, and all they have done, in essence, was to keep hope on life support, dangling affirmative action."

"Umm, Zemi," said Ishmael, looking skeptical. "I would not want to go and bury affirmative action so soon. There's a lot more that can be accomplished through such a measure. The momentum that stood for the Civil Rights of the 1960s remains unmatched by the combined efforts of all African Americans ever since. Therefore, both pressure and concerted strategies must still be applied to enforce justice. It is not time to take the guardsmen off duty yet. White privilege is alive and kicking and whites don't see racism until racism thought has metastasized into vile deed. Even if affirmative action is never resurrected, proactive measures must be put in place to ensure rights and progress, especially as long as white privilege is still breathing."

"But, Ishmael, out of the five of us siblings, none of us was able to make use of affirmative action. Mom and Dad did, back some years ago. Now, when I go and apply for a job, and I'm told that I am overqualified. Folk in the ghettoes are not able to make use of affirmative action; they are hanging on fighting today to get federal minimum wage raised even. So who and what class of people are still riding on affirmative action?" I asked.

"I could see keepin' affirmative action if it still carried its initial weight and sincerity fer African Americans. But we are the back burners to the bill. Let's examine to see who's profited most from affirmative action," remarked Zeth bluntly.

"Frankly speaking," said Joey, patting the table with his knife, "I think that the Mexicans employed all the strategies employed by blacks of that era. Blacks showed the Mexicans how you do it in America."

"I could not agree with you more on that score, Joey," said Ishmael. "But, in addition, blacks showed all minority groups, including women's rights organizations, how to stand up for themselves in America. Let's not sell ourselves short in history once again, Brother Joey."

My focus was on Zeth. "I still say that blacks can do better for themselves without affirmative action, especially since that is the main and only carrot used by the Democratic Party to keep folk salivating every time they hear those words. And who would have thought that Pavlov's theory would have worked so well on humans? As quiet as it's kept, the Republican stance opposing racial quotas, racial preferences and welfare reform was not all that different from the 'New Democrat' platform. Just look at some of documents bearing Bill Clinton's signature," I pointed out.

Zeth seconded, "Zemi, it would take forever and a day to get blacks to scrutinize Bill Clinton—he really failed to address a whole lot of quality-of-life issues as promised when runnin'—anyway, it would take even longer for African Americans to analyze the common denominators between the two parties. If they did, they could see that there are few differences between the Republican and Democratic Parties. And so makin' one party your one and only makes little sense, no politics to speak of."

I was happy to see Zeth agreeing with me. For a minute, it appeared I was the only person at the table leaning in favor of giving another party a chance. What was there to lose? I am touched that Zeth came to the dinner. I am looking at his honey brown eyes as I put my two cents in. "See, blacks need to analyze situations for themselves and not always have others interpreting for them," I said.

"Especially the folk waiting for black leaders to inform them," said Joey.

Zeth zoomed in on me as he steadily earned points. "You are right, Zemi. Blacks will even listen to Hollywood. Don't folks know that some of the folk they send out to tell our people how to vote don't even vote themselves? They will put in our faces folk who have not studied politics one bit or anythin' else for the matter and some who don't even graduate from high school, but our folk are expected to take their advice."

"That's why Bill Maher doesn't have them much on his show because, on political situations, black Hollywood's lips are glued and can only become unglued when given a one-line script to read," said Joey.

"Uh-uh." Shauna put her hand over her mouth. "Maria is not going to like you talking about Hollywood that way."

"Well," Zeth chipped in, "I ain't tryin' to make Maria feel bad none." Zeth surveyed his audience. "But any of you ever notice durin' election time, political organizers will send celebrity folk to speak out with a passion about votin' when those same folk have often been seen high off of drugs and alcohol, and others have exhibited lewd behavior. But they act like folk don' remember, and show up like they just got an A in citizenship. And blacks are expected to vote in the way that these folk tell them?" Zeth ended that spiel with a heavy sigh.

"Yeah, and next time that happens, we need to round up blacks in Hollywood and give them a quiz in political science and see how their political IQ registers," said Joey.

"You might be surprised, Joey. It is conceivable that the results could be higher than your own," Maria snorted. "Just because we are in Hollywood doesn't mean we are not abreast of today's events."

"Well, I hope you guys aren't using Kanye West as an indication of celebrity political savvy," I said flippantly. "To have blurted out that President Bush did not like black people during the catastrophes caused by Hurricane Katrina did not do anything to help the victims. It was not savvy to have expressed that sentiment on a public stage. Furthermore, government leaders before Bush allowed bad conditions to persist in Louisiana and just wait on something like a Katrina to happen. Katrina. I know people are not naming their babies that these days," I finished offhandedly.

Zeth says, "Last time I looked, the Democratic Party was not able to wear the heavyweight championship belt of tender lovin' care fer blacks, either. Maybe the Democratic Party deliberately held back on playin' a more successful role to achieve results themselves fer the Katrina victims. Then blacks and Mexicans would become more disillusioned with Bush in an effort to get Democratic candidates to win elections."

"What are you saying, Zeth?" Shauna demanded.

"Well, now, I ain't sayin' that President Bush didn't fail the Katrina victims himself because he did, but the Democrats just might have underhandedly used the tragedy to their own political advantage."

"Well, I known one thing, West is my guy and he will always be right in my book. The brother is very intelligent. He just spoke what was on his mind, and his sentiments were shared by a whole bunch of folk. He was right and said the right thing," said Shauna pointedly.

Joey massaged his glass. "Right on, West."

"Folk from Hollywood are not equipped to speak to folk on voting or political issues, but they just had to seem like they had something to say, so they just said something, helpful or otherwise," I replied.

"Yeah, I bet if you quizzed our folk in Hollywood on who were the top rankin' black Democrats controllin' Congress, few if any could answer correctly," said Zeth. "Shucks, those folk wouldn't even know that Carolyn Cheeks Kilpatrick was the new chair of the Congressional Black Caucus."

"Oh, please, Zeth," said Maria, "I am in Hollywood, and I can tell you that nobody even knows what the Black Caucus does anymore."

Mother remarked sadly, "After Shirley Chisholm, Ron Dellums and others were no longer there, I think the Caucus sort of lost its way."

"Hold up," Zeth said as he pushed himself away from the table. "Now I heard Chair of the Black Caucus Mrs. Kilpatrick's speech at her swearin'-in ceremony, and I think she's got a lot of fire in her. Since her son Kwame is now the young mayor of Detroit, she's connected with the young at heart, and I think she is goin' to put fire back into that organization. The Congressional Black Caucus has a lot of clout in Democratic circles. Now they may not have Chisholm and Dellums anymore, but don't underestimate the organization. It still has some fire. Influence, too."

Ishmael nodded his head eagerly. "I know that fire is still in Ron Dellums. The man is now Mayor of Oakland. He is in his seventies, and you know he has his work cut out for himself. Yes, the old guard is still trying to hold up its end."

"I hope you are right about the Black Caucus group, Zeth," Mother said. "Maybe Chairlady Kilpatrick will be innovative enough for us to see black women keeping pace with white women in politics. Because it is shameful that there is no African American female coming in to be a senator or governor in the Democratic Party after our loyalty has been demonstrated. If the NAACP cannot get African Americans ready to serve and lead in high offices, then hopefully the Congressional Black Caucus can do something."

Shauna added, "I just hope Mrs. Kilpatrick will make a difference in the perception most of us hold of that group. But again, that just might be the way things change sometimes."

Joey held up a tablespoon. "Here, Shauna, you had better go and get some medication," said Joey.

"For what?" Shauna sounded puzzled.

"To keep your hope alive because black leaders are already lacking in leadership with that organization—Nancy Pelosi has the National Black Caucus on lockdown. They stood silently while Pelosi requested the immediate resignation of Democratic Congressman William Jefferson from the Ways and Means Committee. Yet she allowed Democratic Congressman Alan Mollohan to remain as ranking member on the House Ethics Committee," said Joey.

"Zemi, why is your jaw puffed out?" Shauna asked.

I exhaled heavily. "I was holding my breath waiting for Joey to play the race card with the Democratic Party."

"No need to. Pelosi already did her thing," said Joey. "Mollohan remains with the deck stacked huge against him, and Jefferson was tossed for his alleged naughtiness."

"Jefferson should have known better," I said.

"Why, because he's black?" asked Joey.

"Why, yes. Because blacks cannot do what they want and get away with it the same as whites, and if I know that, then Jefferson should have known," I answered.

Zeth expressed his gratitude. "Joey, I am glad you brought that one up because I didn't know the situation had that kinda spin on it. The Democratic Party was able to slide that by the African Americans fer the mid-term election, but come 2008, it's gonna burn 'em unless they deflect attention or make big amends," said Zeth.

Shauna shook her head. "I don't know about that, Zeth. Do you really think that will matter to the Democratic voters in 2008?"

"Of course it will," said Zeth, turning in his seat to stretch his leg. "The Democrats are in office because of the scandals and deception of the Republican Party. And before the Democrats can get people to keep their attention focused on GOP mess, the people are distracted by the stench from the deeds of the Dems."

"Though artfully, a 'culture of corruption' could be wrapped around the hem of a lot of pants in politics," I offered. "Skirts have hems, too," I added. "And to think that Hillary should be the one to describe the Republican House of Representatives as a 'plantation.' With Pelosi's loyalty to Mollohan and her disloyalty to Jefferson, hmm, maybe Pelosi is showing everybody how a party has to be undercover with 'plantation' management so their stuff is not detected by Hillary's radar."

"You might be on to somethin' there, girl," said Zeth, smiling.

Everyone grew quiet.

Grandma said, "I am full now, but I saved enough room for dessert."

Mother touched Maria's arm and whispered, "Go and let Rosalita know that she may come and clear the table for dessert."

Zeth observed everyone around the table. "I don't know, but Mrs. Kilpatrick seems promisin' for her new post, and I hope she does well."

"I just want to know which of the black organizations is doing succession planning? Who is getting black women prepared to step into leadership roles in politics? One black senator," I shook my head. "No black female senator and one black male senator? What century is this? The Democratic Party needs to be exposed."

"Now, Zemi, don't go gettin' yourself too upset. Most black women voted for the Democratic Party because when it comes to the reds, black folk just go on automatic and then end up with *the blues* for real. The Democrats own black people. They own them. No party owns me for life and that's a fact," said Zeth.

"Need I repeat myself?" asked Joey. "The Democrats are the Mafia that owns black folk, and that ain't likely to change ever. And you guys don't want it said that way, but why else would blacks stay with a party unless it was a matter of loyalty, even if the blind kind? It was not as if the Democrats were giving up anything that significant, like Mardi Gras treats. There is just no better way to describe blacks' loyalty to the Democratic Party."

"I think there is a better way to describe blacks' loyalty to the Democratic Party: obscene. It is sickening and pathetic the way black leaders have blacks sucking up to the tail of that party," I said.

"Well, since everybody is standing up for somebody and repeating themselves, I am going to say something good about Kanye West, in spite of what he said about George Bush," said Maria. "At least as a celebrity, he spoke up about an important issue of concern to blacks, so he is all right in my book. Kanye and Spike Lee are real celebrities. While others stayed quiet, they spoke up for those who could not speak for themselves."

Shauna looked pleased. "Thank you, Maria, for seeing the real side of Kanye. Like I said earlier, it's not as if Kanye needed to hog the cameras like Al or Jesse."

"Can't let you slide on that one, Shauna," said Ishmael, balling up his fist. "I think the media and blacks speak unfairly of Al and Jesse, but especially Al. Still, the two have done more than they have been given credit for. That's a fact."

"Come on, Ishmael, you have to admit that Brother Al is overexposed on the tube. If it wasn't for white folk hating him so much, Al would be out of a tube job," said Shauna mockingly.

"That's just the point, Shauna," said Ishmael. "Al is out there on the tube as the lone ranger, fighting the cancer of hatred. It's the same way Oprah might catch the brunt of something because she is the only African American mega talk show host, and the same could be said of Tiger Woods or Michael Jordan—as far as the catching the brunt of things goes. Society has set it up so only one black in a field can pass through the gates of superstardom at a time."

"Well, I guess you might have something there on the last part," Shauna conceded.

Kidding around, Ishmael still had his fist balled. "Hey, Shauna, I am going to have to stay in sparring position just in case you disrespect Al again. But check out how things played out again with Al at the forefront with Michael Richards. You know, the white guy who played Kramer on the Seinfield sitcom. He went into a racial tirade at a comedy club. He called an audience of mostly black and Mexican folk such blatantly racist names on a public stage until I must admit," said Ishmael, "it was the worst hatred I have seen displayed in any public forum."

"Well, you know that boy, why, he apologized on the Letterman show," said Grandma, "but Al said that Michael Richards should have made the apology in a black forum because Letterman was not a sufficient enough stage for an apology to be heard or accepted."

I held my peace, but thought that in today's time blacks should be further along with an agenda that elevated them. I wished they would not be so ready to take steps backward every time idiots with a public stage espoused hatred or unveiled their own insecurities. I take heed to the real response of Professor Deborah McFadden's write-up in an Oakland editorial: *Enough of the "N" word, including, especially talking about it. If we discuss the word, it should be to educate people of the younger generation. "N" word flare ups sometimes serve as a distraction from more important issues such as the war in Iraq and sending more young people to fight for justice in a country that has no connection to them whatsoever. As well, it may be a distraction from studying the best person to serve as the next President of this country. I believe people in my generation over fifty can intellectualize about why they should not use the "N" word, but the key is to help the younger generation understand "No" on "N" and "Yes" on moving forward. Deflection of the bigger issues is not just the American way, it is, for many, the African American way, too.*

Though the "N" word may be addressed and possibly the use of the word may be discouraged through meaningful dialogue and education, these efforts are most effective in group settings. Even learning ways on how to handle the discussions can help this society to move towards the next level. As a political and educational activist, I would much rather aspire to effect a change that can help to place an African American President in the Oval Office. Let us not stay so focused on the "N" word that we pay no attention to what needs to be done in this country right now."

I realize that the "N" word issue is so inflammatory that it can be a no-win situation to talk about it: if you say there has been enough talk, it's like you're saying you do not care or think the word is okay to use, and if you say it must be discussed, then you're inflicted with a bad case of tunnel vision.

"…earth to Zemi," I hear Joey saying, so I look to see Joey reaching for the bowl of string beans. The bowl is being passed around and he wants to know if anyone else wants any. "Okay, this is the last of the green beans, so does anyone want to share this small portion? If not, I will clean the bowl so that Rosalita won't have to throw them away."

"Go ahead and knock yourself out, Joey," said E.J., rubbing his stomach. "I think most of us have had our fill."

"Listen up," said Zeth, "I think we should place Al Sharpton in our hearts because he is man enough to take a stance on the ugly heart of America. He's got backbone while most of Hollywood blacks and whites have sat back on their butts and said nothin' on the really important issues that our folk must deal with," said Zeth.

"Don't count on Hollywood to comment on too many matters of real concern to the masses, and I don't count too much on them changing either," said Maria, passing an empty platter to Rosalita. "Hollywood talks a picture of diversity better than they are able to walk it," said Maria. "I should have been the one to play the role Halle played; I would have gotten the Oscar Halle took home."

"Oh, Maria!" screeched Grandma. "You wouldn't have displayed your godly body to a public would you, granddaughter? Because there is no way I could ever be proud of you if you did something that God has forbidden."

"No, Grandma, I would never get nude in public. I just meant that I should have been the first African American woman to receive an Oscar because I am a great actress too. I just wish Hollywood would do the right thing when it comes to African American women. Maybe Halle and I will be co-stars in a movie together. That's what I meant, Grandma."

Grandma removed her hand from her chest. "Thank you, Jesus! Thank you, Jesus."

I thought to myself about how much nerve Maria had thinking she could just sashay pass Dorothy Dandridge, Diana Ross, Angela Bassett, Pam Grier, and others who had earned, but were not awarded, Best Actress Awards. I will not ever forget Diana Ross's portrayal of Billie Holiday in "Lady Sings the Blues." Then on the nudity issue, I thought about how God must have forgiven Eve, and Grandma must have forgotten what Eve did. Anyway, I wanted to discourage any further questions from Grandma's lips on the subject of Maria and nudity. "We have all known that about white Hollywood, but how is it that blacks in Hollywood will not stand up for anything social or political? They always want to play safe on issues such as global warming or save some baby mama whales, but if it is something that relates to African American issues specifically, they are afraid to have a voice," I said.

"Wait a moment, Zemi, because I, too, am a big supporter of global warming awareness. Al Gore has made a believer out of me," said Maria.

"Black Hollywood punk'd out a long time ago," said Joey, wiping his mouth. "Blacks in Hollywood do not think they're African Americans when things go wrong or happen upon our race. They want to pretend that they live in a different world than the rest of African Americans, while they appear to benefit from the work of blacks who have gone before them. Bob Marley told them, 'You can't run away from yourselves.'"

Maria gnawed on her lower lip. "Being an actress myself, I do know that blacks more often than not like to pretend everything is okey dokey in the name of artistic freedom."

I was surprised to hear Maria say this about black Hollywood. But it is sad to admit what Chris Rock emphasized and summed up in a discussion with Spike Lee—that blacks are not producing good acting and movies anymore.

Zeth made his suggestion on addressing the matter. "I say until Hollywood shows more care and support of the African American race on the public stage, then black reviewers need to see no evil and no TV or movies either until it is made all good, or at least some better."

Mother said, "All of Hollywood needs to clean up its act, black and white. We need to see more than drug rehab story, drunk driving celebrities and who is breaking up or cheating. Seems to me Hollywood is trying to put reality shows out of business."

Grandma patted her lips with her napkin. "I don't think many in Hollywood have much in the way of lofty purposes. That's why so many of the little things get themselves into so much trouble. If they are not in rehab, then they are in and out of jail or doing something immoral. They are just not the ones to hold up as role models today for our young ones."

"I think what Zeth said earlier should be heard by sponsors," I added. Right now, my thoughts are all the way on Zeth. He looks more appealing and seems more exciting to me now.

Mother said, "Blacks in Hollywood have gotten too much of a free ride—as if they are some of the special ones to be granted the most from the civil rights movement. The black community needs to see them be more accountable." Mother turned to Maria. "What do you think, Maria? I mean, does black Hollywood know what the black public feels about them, that our folk feel a sense of betrayal from black Hollywood?"

"To be honest with you, Mom, I don't really think that they have taken much social consciousness into consideration that way. Their motto is that they cannot live their lives the way others might want them to live," said Maria. "They are actors, not leaders or politicians."

"Yep. That sounds like those athletes who say that they are not role models and mentors. Those words have come back to haunt some of them. Few are placed in coaching positions. Things find a way to come back and haunt you," said Joey.

I am thinking that at least they admit that they are not role models. People need to raise their own kids; we know Hollywood and TV cannot. And we cannot have it both ways: say who should not lead when they are put out there, but then turn around and say other celebrities should be role modeling, another form of leading I would say. This is Joey talking and I think I will pass on this one.

Shauna placed the last of the veggie patties on Ishmael's plate.

"Thank you, Shauna, but I am stuffed already," Ishmael told her, and then honed in on Joey. "Say, Joey do you know whether you are having a girl or a boy?"

"No. Not yet. At least Natasha hasn't told me," Joey answered.

That got Mother's attention. "How can you say you don't know about the child that you helped to create? That is shameful son," Mother scolded.

"What can I do, Mama? Natasha and I are not getting along. What am I supposed to do? It is her call, her fault. I can't go licking her up, Mama," said Joey.

"Now is not the time, Joey, for you to think that this situation is all about what is convenient and beneficial for you," said Mother, wiping her eyes. "How could you pass that responsibility on to Natasha, to raise your child alone?"

"If she has the baby, her mother said that she would help to raise the child, and I could pay for the child's needs."

"The child needs a father, too," Grandma piped in. "Will the baby carry your last name?" Grandma asked him. I could see that Grandma did not like Joey's answer. She frowned on her way to the bathroom as she heard him say, "I don't know, Grandma. Natasha has not said if she will do that or not. I don't have the say-so on the subject. I don't even know if she is going to have the baby...."

Before Joey could finish, everyone charged him at once. And anyone who said anything to him seemed to want to shame him into either being more informed about the baby situation or taking a lead in the welfare of this child. Joey's head hung in cradled hands.

A disgusted Ishmael remonstrated, "At twenty-four weeks, you both had better know that baby must be born. It's the law!"

"Son, your way of thinking about this baby is intolerable!" Mother shook her head emphatically. "I understand that Natasha has been pregnant for more than twenty weeks already. But if you two should come to an unfavorable decision, then you must know that I will bring criminal charges against the doctor if an abortion is performed." Mother's eyes got teary again.

Joey looked at his mother's face. "That is not what I was saying. That's not what I meant at all. Of course, we are going to have that baby! I am just uncertain about if Natasha will have the baby carry my last name."

Mother sighed heavily.

Ishmael dropped his arm to the table, and faced Joey. "If you do not have a say-so over your own child, then who will, Joey?"

"E.J., you know the law. Tell them for me, please," Joey answered. I heard a tremble in his voice. "E.J.," he said, "tell them that if a man is not married to the woman, in most states he does not have rights to what goes on with that child except for paying child support."

"Joey is right," said E.J. "If he and Natasha don't get married, then Joey does not have any rights over many of her decisions about the child. And he has no say so on whether or not she decides to have an abortion. Until the child reaches majority, you will have financial responsibility for your child born outside of marriage, as decided by law."

"Are there things that Joey can do to gain more rights over the life of the child?" asked Mother, twisting her napkin. "Lordy," she sighed.

"Yes," said E.J. "As the father, Joey can establish rights and responsibilities for the child by applying to the court for a Parental Responsibility Order or by making a Parental Responsibility Agreement with the mother."

Rosalita quietly cleared the table.

E.J. put both hands on the table and leaned forward. "There are a lot of things that the father can do, even if the mother of the child is unwilling to sign a Parental Responsibility Agreement. But those are questions Joey should be asking. He has to want these types of responsibilities for his child, and well, he seems a bit too unperturbed about the whole matter. So unless Joey is more interested, it makes no sense for me to sit here and quote the laws for sheer knowing."

I broached a touchy subject. "Joey, do you have any doubts about your being the father of this child?" I asked. No one had asked Joey before if the baby Natasha was carrying was his baby, and I am not sure why I just did.

Joey rolled his eyes.

Ishmael whispered in my ear, "Zemi, that is not a question you should ask a man out loud and in front of everyone."

"Oh."

"Joey, I cannot pretend here today," said Mother, sobbing. "As it is, I am just so disappointed in you and Maria." Mother lifted her glasses and used her napkin to wipe her eyes. "Maria wants to marry a man who, I'm told, has three babies, who perhaps may be illegal, and you do not want to marry the woman who is giving you your own child. And on top of all of that, Natasha seems to be so nonchalant about giving it a good future. A child's future hangs in the balance when these type of problems arise even before the child takes his first breath." Mother sighed deeply. "Joey and Maria, how can either of you explain the terrible situation that you two have gotten yourselves into? That's not the way I wanted to have grandchildren. And Maria, if that Mexican is here illegally, you need to know this: I will report him to the authorities."

Maria's fury was so intense I could swear I could feel heat from her body and could see steam coming from her head. Could she restrain herself? No one ever talks back to Mother. No one uses a foul tongue or act in a disrespectful manner, no matter what.

Shocked, Maria said, "Mother I am a grown woman. This is my business and you have no right to interfere that way." Maria's chest began to swell and her voice cracked. "And I don't think God feels that I am being a bad woman because I want to marry a man and help give his three children a better life. And as for the children, they have already felt great pain through the loss of their mom." Tears rolled down Maria's face.

Ishmael picked up a napkin and wiped Maria's cheeks. Maria's invoking God's Name to buttress her argument was Maria the actress, but I am not sure bringing God into the picture like that would sit well with Mother and Grandma. I think I am the only one present who knows this is like rehearsal for Maria. But, I do know Maria pretty well.

Maria's outburst handed Joey an opportunity to steer the conversation away from himself and his sins of omission.

He told his sister, "Maria, I can see Madonna going over to Africa and adopting a child and being humane and idealistic. She has situated herself and life financially. And hers was a gracious and noble act. I am sure that child will grow up appreciating the comforts Madonna brings to his life compared to the hell he was living in Africa. But Maria, what do you have to offer three Mexican children and an illegal daddy, who, at best, will make minimum wages? Why, the best you can offer them would be English, a language they might not want to learn. But your three stepchildren will learn quickly how to say, 'Mommy I don't have anything because right now, Mommy, you only have enough to take care of yourself with your part-time acting job.'"

I looked over to see that Shauna placed the desserts on the table. Mother had made a persimmon cake and Grandma made home-made ice cream.

The tracks of Maria's tears must have been very short because they had passed on, leaving her face both dry and straightened out. Recomposed, Maria took the first serving of ice cream and cake. Loaded for bear, she aimed right at Joey. Again, backed by the Good Book, she yelled, "Joey," she told him, "brother, your issues are ten times greater than mine, so you do not have a thing to say to me. You cannot remove a splinter from my eye when you got a log in your own."

I had no idea Maria had paid so much attention in Sunday School.

"Ah, I don't know about all of that," said Joey. "You got some log heavy stuff to deal with yourself."

Maria looked at Joey and said something to him in Spanish that no one knew, and since Mother didn't know either, the deed was done with impunity. She smiled and said "Gracias," when Shauna handed her a slice of cake. Still smiling, she said, "M-mum, yummy. This is mouth-watering, Mom." Maria was mixing her cake into her ice cream bowl. "This cake is dangerously good. You haven't made a persimmon cake since my college days."

"That's because I have to look so hard to find the right type of persimmon for my recipe," said Mother.

Maria is really a great actor. She eased Mother into a comfort zone with little or no effort, even after she had the nerve to speak some Spanish.

Chagrinned, clowned, too, Joey went for help. Or sympathy? He cried out, "E.J.? Big Brother, you have been totally quiet over there. What gives? Don't you have something to say about your sister making such a stupid, very stupid move? I mean, say something, Big Brother."

E.J. threw his napkin on the table as he relaxed in his chair. "Well, her name is Maria." He rolled the 'r' in Maria and threw up his hands. "I don't know, maybe she feels some kind of kinship. You know, maybe she thinks she's Mexican."

Neither Mother nor Joey saw the humor in E.J.'s remark. Mother was saying something about how her family, because of the children she had made with our late father, "was looking like the UN." She also said that if Maria and her Mexican fiancé should have a child together, that child would look mixed, but no doubt the "one-drop of blood rule" would have settled the child in America's society as black, and, forcing the child into the African American race.

I wondered why Mother used the word "forced." Ishmael, while changing his religion to Islam, has married an Iranian woman. Should they have children, the children would look mixed, but they, too, would be tossed into the African American race. As Mother said, no wonder the African American race was so confused and could never get its bearings.

The African American race has been mixed with so many other races that a proper definition of the black race needs now to be determined. Mother thought that psychiatrists or even perhaps social scientists could settle on a definition of African American that would be motivating and uplifting, and for the psychological well-being of the children. For the good of children born into the race from two black parents as well as for those born of one black parent and one of another race. Mother says that a more respectful image of the black race would help our darker-hued brothers and sisters; so that darker-skinned African Americans would not continue to be the least preferred (whenever that is the case); would no longer be viewed by the ignorant and the stupid as somehow not as good as the lighter-hued of the black race.

She said that a definition of African American that makes people proud would help those who are mixed not to fall prey to thinking that they are either better than or not as good as those with two black parents. She says that when people carry stigmas about skin color and other things, these stigmas stand in the way of spiritual healing and wholeness. Wow! Mother is trying to dismantle the pathology of pigmentocracy among black people? Power to her—I am done with that ignorance, and bored, to wit. I have moved a bit higher; I have left crab barrel mentality and all such other ails to the crabs, et alia.

Moving on. Zeth says America needs to clean the awful dirty stains off her sheets for they have been soiled far too long. He wonders why other minorities that complain of racism turn around and try to walk in the same kind of boots that, even in this day and age, try to bear down on the souls of black folk. He said the Jews experienced the holocaust and knew prejudice all too well, and the Japanese knew of being held in concentration camps, as did the Chinese. All minority groups have felt the deepest wounds of America's prejudice. Yet Zeth, says that when closely examined, even such groups who have been hurt by prejudice find that their scarred hearts cannot find enough room for the offspring that have their blood and black blood, too. He could not understand why Koreans and Filipinos did not accept children born with black blood and labeled them outcasts. Shame, he thought, so many of those children were so pleasing to the eye.

Usually, Joey stays with Mom when he is in town, but he spent the next day with Grandma. He knew Mother was too upset to have Joey around the house. Grandma and Joey were on the same page concerning Maria and Ishmael.

Thinking about Grandma's and Joey's quality time together, I had some time to myself to imagine myself as the proverbial fly on the walls of Grandma's home. Alas, I had to settle for getting it second- and third-hand. And do you know? What I had imagined was not too far from what I pieced together from family gossip—er, from Joey, Grandma and different versions of Joey's visit!

Well, Grandma kept saying her son, our dad, was turning over in his grave. "I can only call your brother Rodney by the name that your daddy gave him," she told Joey as she rocked back and forth in her cane rocker. "I am never going to get used to any Ishmael Muhammad. I guess that's how he says it. To tell you the truth, I don't even want to know how he spells his name. Rodney can be a banker and make all the money he wants to make in life, but God just is not going to bless him. He will not go to heaven for that!"

"Ah, Grandma," said Joey, "I know that you want God to bless all of your son's children. You know Dad depends on your prayers as the matriarch to keep the family steering in the right direction." Grandma had her music playing and a cup of tea beside her on the table. E.J. had made Grandma a CD of all her favorite oldies. The song "Jimmy Lee" by Aretha Franklin was playing. Perhaps the beat sounded like a spiritual to her. But Grandma knows spiritual beats all too well; she has been listening to Bobby Jones Gospel Hour for over twenty-eight years.

"I guess you are right about that, Joey, but how could Rodney turn his back on God like that and turn to such a frightful religion? I am too old to try and relearn my family all over again. And then he goes and gets an Iranian girl! Is your brother missing his mind?" Grandma asked frantically. "Maybe that ganja from Jamaica did it. You know Rodney says his Iranian wife works at the hospital drawing blood, and should I ever need blood drawn that she'd gladly draw it for me. Is your brother crazy?"

"Rodney just wants you to know that he is there for you in case you need his help that way," said Joey, bobbing his head to Grandma's CD tunes. "He just wants you to know that everyone is here for you, Grandma."

"Well, I don't need that kind of help. Does he really think that I would let somebody like an Iranian touch my blood? I don't know what she might do with my blood. Anyway, those sorts of people don't know how to find black people's veins. They have to keep poking, puncturing you here and there, while always telling you that your veins are too small. I don't know if those folk have degrees anyway. They go and get those online degrees and stick them on their walls in double size as if they are real."

"Grandma," said Joey smiling, "Rodney loves you too much to bring anyone around you to cause you any harm. Always remember that about him."

"But, it's just not right for Rodney to embarrass his family like that. Why bring that mid-Eastern blood, that kind of mix home? It's not right, I tell you."

"Grandma, you probably have a better answer to that question."

"Hmmm. Nowadays, whenever I go over to Rodney's house," said Grandma as she buttoned up her sweater, "he and the Iranian girl have a ritual going on. First thing they do is to take off their shoes when they walk into the house. Shortly after that, they stand up with both their hands held out like cult people do. He speaks in some kind of tongue, chanting sounds like 'Laa ilaaha illallaah.' I tell you that they are both strange when he and that Iranian girl start talking together, whispering in tongues, I don't really know why they whisper, as if I could understand what they were saying anyhow. I don't like saying things about your brother, but he just confounds me!"

"Grandma, did you know that Rodney's wife is expecting?"

"I know that bit of information already, and he's male and she's female, I would be half an idiot not to expect that kind of news. But I just don't feel right having my blood put into that kind of mix. That mid-Eastern blood is a peculiar type. I don't know anything about those folk, their thinking and all, because I've never lived around them. I don't feel as if I would be able to own up to their child as my grandchild. Well, it would be a great-grandchild; that's if I would accept it, and I don't know if I could do that. I just wish they would not have gone as far as to have a child together. Those kinds of kids will come off thinking like Zemi's mixed friend Amy, not wanting to acknowledge the black blood flowing through their veins. That mid-Eastern blood, it just 'don't mix well.'"

"I can't say too much on that subject. I am in such hot water with the family myself," said Joey.

"And another thing, I forgot to mention," Grandma went on, like Joey had not said a word, "when you go over to their house, they play all of that funny kind of music. It sounds a lot to be Indian music to my ears—I guess because I have never heard Arab music before, or I just never paid any attention to it. And, you know Joey, Rodney's wife does belly dancing, offering to teach your sisters, Zemi and Maria, how to do those moves. And when I walk into their home, I just feel like calling the fire department with so much incense clouding up the house." Grandma coughed. "How could someone, a black man who had so much going on, just flip to another culture like that? Please explain that to me."

"I don't have an explanation to offer, Grandma."

"What was in your brother's mind that made him flip out that way? Why did he have to get so engrossed in her culture? Oh, my Father, why is it so easy for a black boy to give up himself so easily?

Why has your brother abandoned all of his father's ways? Joey, where did your mother and I go wrong?"

Joey shook his head. "I don't know, Grandma. Rodney has definitely changed. He and I don't even hang out together anymore. I mean, we used to be so close. Now whenever I see him, which isn't often, we just sort of give a 'Hey, what's going on' to each other. He's changed. I really feel like we've lost him, Grandma."

Grandma bellowed from the deep within her being. When she recovered, Joey took her hand and lifted her from the rocker. He led her out to the rear deck. "Grandma, sit down for a moment, please. I want to talk to you. But first, how are you really doing? Are you still keeping yourself healthy while watching your grownup grandchildren make all of these crazy and drastic shifts in their lives?"

Grandma rubbed her hands together, then placed them in her lap, and said, "You know Joey, at my age, I live for my grandchildren. That's my life. But with everybody being different now, it looks like I have to learn life all over again, and it's just not so easy for me to make the adjustment. I am probably too contrary now to even want to change."

Joey stroked her hands. "Everything is going to be all right, Grandma, but sometimes you have to change to keep up with life," he said.

Grandma placed one arm around Joey's waist. "Go on now and explain yourself, Joey. What's troubling you so much? You know ever since you've been a baby, I used to just gaze into those wide eyes of yours, and I could always tell when something was wrong with you. You've always been my favorite, you know that, but I try not to let the other grandchildren know."

Joey reached over and gave his grandma a kiss. "I know, Grandma, and I've always felt like your favorite, too," said Joey.

Grandma patted Joey's knee.

"I feel bad about Mom," said Joey. "She is not talking to me right now. She's upset with me about wanting Natasha to have an abortion. How do you think Mom's handling things?"

Grandma faced Joey. "Your mom is doing the best she can, one day at a time. You and I have always been able to say to each other whatever was on our minds, right Joey?"

"Right, right, Grandma."

"But your mama has a right to be upset with you, Joey. First, you tell her that she is going to be a grandmother, making her all proud, and then in the same breath you tell her that you are not going to have the baby. Joey, you allowed your mother to rub on Natasha's stomach for four and a half months, and now you tell the grandmother that her grandchild is going to be aborted. Well, Joey, that is a hard pill to swallow. Your mother told everybody that she was going to be a grandmother, and she even started buying baby stuff. This was going to be her very first grandchild," said Grandma.

"But Grandma, you must know that I would never hurt Mama intentionally."

"Grandson, try and understand what you did to your mother. You gave your mother a nicely wrapped gift box, only to snatch the box away. Your mother even offered to take care of the baby. If you kill that baby, your mother's heart might not be able to handle that. You would be killing something that is a part of her, too. That's just how your mother is, Joey. After taking care of your father through his illness, why, it is just not that easy for her to let someone with your father's blood coursing through his veins to be put away while she sits back and does nothing. And she is going to fight you on that, Joey, all the way through the courts if she has to. You know she's been talking with your brother E.J. to find out if there is any legal action she can take," said Grandma.

"I thought she dropped that idea at dinner the other day," Joey said.

"She had dropped the idea, but she kept probing and feeling out E.J. There is nothing your mother cannot get out of E.J. You know how that boy loves his mama."

"I just don't love Natasha enough to marry her, Grandma. I would still have the baby, but Natasha said that if I was not going to marry her, then she did not want to have the baby. So it's really Natasha's fault," said Joey.

"Faulting Natasha for something you helped to make is unbecoming of you, Joey. From what Natasha says, you two were planning on getting married a couple of months before the baby was to be born. You two even went looking at wedding rings. Now is that true, Joey?"

"At first, it was true," said Joey.

"Oh, Joey, you are such a boy sometimes. There's no such thing as 'it was true.' You just cannot do that to a woman, Joey, and go around changing your mind like that, not when that woman is carrying your child. It is not God-like. It is not proper," Grandma pronounced.

"Okay," Joey sat on the deck railing and dragged one along the redwood floor. "I hear what you are saying, Grandma. But try to see it from this angle, too. I told Natasha I did not want to have any children right now because I knew I just didn't love Natasha enough to want a child with her. I had that conversation with her before she became pregnant. I told her that I was married to my restaurants. She was okay with that for a while."

"Are you that naïve to think that a young woman wants to keep giving herself with no future in sight?" Grandma moaned. "Did the woman appear that desperate, Joey, until you thought she would continue in that spirit? And now to wait to have a late-term abortion?"

"But Grandma, when Natasha first told me she was pregnant, I asked her then if she wanted to have an abortion before we told anybody. She said no because she no longer believed in abortions. Later in the pregnancy, she decides that she cannot bring this child into the world without us being married. I told her that I would try to marry her two months before the baby is due. I meant it at the time. But Grandma, I have tried, but she and I just aren't meant for each other. I am not going to let her force me into marriage by using the baby," said Joey.

"It's getting a little chilly out here," said Grandma.

Joey went inside and retrieved Grandma's light throw. Grandma leaned forward so that Joey could drape the throw around her shoulders.

"Grandma," said Joey, "tell me, how do you feel about all of this?"

"Well, Joey, I don't like any of this at all, but it is not my place to fight you, and I certainly wouldn't fight to take you to court over the matter. But E.J. keeps your mother informed of what is legal and what is not as it relates to the pregnancy. Too much involvement by too many people over these legal things will only make bad blood."

"Those are my sentiments exactly. Mom has no right to get involved to the point of wanting to make something legal out of this."

"Who then should speak up for this child who has a heartbeat but no voice?" remarked Grandma.

With a firm resolve, Joey told his grandmother, "I am a grown man and if I don't want to get married and have the baby, then that should settle the case. I love Mom, but I think she is overstepping her boundaries. This is between Natasha and me to work out, not Mom." Joey gave his Grandma a kiss goodbye.

* * * * *

My portrayal of Joey's visit with Grandma is as near fact as I could determine through due diligence. Bad blood. Sad. A metaphor for the state of our family?

Anyhow (but not really *anyhow* like I do not care as I do), this next scenario hails from the same "resources" with as much care for accuracy:

After Joey reached E.J.'s law offices, he walked straight into E.J.'s private office without stopping to speak with the secretary. "So what are you trying to do? Get Mom to force me into some legal drama?" he asked E.J.

E.J. looked up from his desk, and took stock of his younger brother. "Nah, Lil' Joe," E.J. said with a wry smile.

"Since when did you start calling me Lil' Joe? My name is Joey, a grown man's name."

"Mea maxima culpa, my worst kinda bad," said E.J. "I must have been getting the wrong information on you. Because the information I received was about someone who has not been acting so manly lately. I mean, this is your girl's second time getting pregnant from you."

Joey, crestfallen, looked worried, but he was angry, too. 'Who knew?' and 'How did they?' were all over his face.

Fingering his mustache, E.J., who could read people the way people read the time of day, told his brother, "Thought nobody else knew that other than you and Natasha, huh?"

"How did you find that out?"

"I am a lawyer. I can find out whatever it is that I need or want to know."

"How do you figure you need to know my business?"

"Because Mother made it her business," said E.J., getting up from his desk. "What are you and Natasha doing, using abortion as some form of birth control, Joey?"

Joey shrugged his shoulders. "It was a mistake, man. It just kind of happened."

E.J. smiled.

"Why are you smiling, man?"

"You are so on target in developing your Vegan 12 restaurant chains and you think through every business move. I just wonder how you can be so on in business and so off in your personal affairs?"

"How do you stop when a woman is all over you, almost begging?"

"As a man, Joey, you take control of your life and the situation. You can allow yourself to indulge, but men have reproductive responsibility, too."

Joey sighs and looks wide-eyed at E.J., wondering what's coming next.

Hitting below the proverbial belt, E.J. tells his younger brother: "Why are men so surprised about what happens or what can happen after sex without a brain? Maybe men cannot relate to the term 'birth control' 'cause they do not give the birthing, so what about 'conception' control for the tool that you use. Joey, where do you get off letting a woman take control if a baby was not something you wanted to have happen? And twice?"

"Are you telling me, E.J., that you never got a girl pregnant?"

"Since becoming a man, I stopped messing with girls. A woman would be the way for me to go."

"You are an attorney. You know how to cover things up. But I betcha you have gotten a woman pregnant before."

"Joey, stop trying to detract from your problems. You carried on that way with Maria at the family dinner, but all your talk about her issues did not make yours disappear. Besides, trying to avoid your own stuff makes you look weak, man."

Joey just looked at E.J. and said nothing, perhaps as close as he could come right now to conceding that he needed to handle his business. If he opened his mouth now, no way could he slam Maria. Joey had to talk Joey. Today, Joey was the man. In the mirror.

"So, Joey, what are you going to do? I mean, this is Natasha's second time getting pregnant. What are her ambitions in life? You know, this is a classic: mostly poor, uneducated women, which includes poor whites and poor blacks, have these abortions—two, three and four times. When two or more of those abortions are after pregnancies from the same guy, then you have to admit that the guy's faculties and sense need to be examined. His level of education? In most cases, he hasn't had a lot of it. The first time, a man will say that he did not want or plan the baby. Okay, well, how does the second pregnancy happen? Dude's not wearing his galoshes, and he's out there just splashing away like there is no tomorrow! Why is it like that, man?" E.J. motioned for Joey to sit down. "Joey, man, today, is your yesterday's tomorrow."

"My education level has nothing to do with this," said Joey. "And you may be older than me, E.J., and a lawyer, too, but whatever I do is still none of your business."

E.J. positioned himself on the edge of his desk. "Normally, I would say that you are correct, but no one but you told Mother that you were giving her a grandchild in nine months. So you see, Joey, this is my business now; it's my mother who is hurting, whose heart is broken because, in her mind, she is trying to save a life from being murdered by her son's decision. She is fighting for her own bloodline. It wouldn't be my business, except you hurt my mother, and it's my business because I will always protect my Mother. That's something you and everybody else needs to remember."

"Hurting Mom was the furthermost thing from my mind. You know that, E.J."

E.J.'s next words did not acknowledge Joey's plea for understanding. "But you can know this one thing for sure, Joey, if

Mother's heart was not involved, you would not be sitting in that chair at no cost. This is not a free legal aid center. That means that I don't have all day. So since you didn't have an appointment and you are here, you must have something you want to say about resolving the situation."

"Well, Mom won't talk to me, so I need to know what it is that she is trying to stir up. Natasha said Mom called her house and said she was too far gone in her pregnancy to have an abortion. She said there were legal ramifications for partial or late-term abortions. Natasha believes that Mom is trying to frighten her into not going ahead with the procedure. She said Mother is trying to turn back the clock to ban Roe v. Wade, which guarantees the right of an abortion," said Joey.

"And who told you that Mother was trying to take some legal action against you and Natasha?" asked E.J.

"Naw, naw, naw." Joey pointed his fingers. "I came here to get some answers."

"Okay. That's fair enough, Bro Joe. You are all right with me calling you that? And then again, you might as well be, anyway, because that's all I am giving up on the name thing. First off, Joey, Mother has no intentions of taking legal actions against you. But she does warn that any doctor who would perform a partial abortion on Natasha at twenty-four weeks would be endangering her life and could face criminal charges. Now exactly what your mother's declaring, should a doctor perform a partial abortion on Natasha, and it was found to be an illegal one, is that she will make sure that doctor is punished for that crime," said E.J.

Joey was dripping with sweat. "Is it a crime?"

"Well, Joey, I've just begun trying to find out what all is included in the Partial Abortion Ban Act that was signed by the President in 2003. Now I have to keep researching and studying to know exactly what is punishable because there is some ambiguity about the repercussions for a doctor who performs such a procedure."

Joey grew real nervous. "What do you think?" he asked. "Do you think I will be able to find a doctor who will perform an abortion at this late date?"

"I cannot say for sure but I believe that there is no way in hell a doctor would want to risk his license for some poor pregnant folk. It just isn't likely to happen because of how the law is so ambiguous on the subject." To try to answer Joey's questions, E.J. read from his notes: "Partial-birth abortion also confuses the medical, legal, and ethical duties of physicians to preserve and promote life, as the physician acts directly against the physical life of a child, whom he or she had just delivered, all but the head, out of the womb, in order to end that life. Partial-birth abortion thus appropriates the terminology and techniques used by obstetricians in the delivery of living children—obstetricians who preserve and protect the life of the mother and the child—and instead uses those techniques to end the life of the partially born child."

"If doctors and all of those legal folk are confused, there is no way Natasha and I would understand."

"How many weeks is Natasha?"

Joey tapped his palm with his index finger, as if trying to figure and answered, "I think about nineteen, twenty, twenty-one or twenty-something weeks."

E.J. shook his head. "Well, one thing we know for sure about you, Joey, is that you can count. But here is some information that you need to read through a little bit yourself. Now, I don't know how much of that you are going to understand because I don't know yet what all I can understand. The reading in some areas is a bit vague. But I highlighted a few paragraphs in yellow that sort of stood out and made a little sense, to make it a bit easier for you to understand." E.J. handed the document to Joey. Joey looked at the papers.

"How can they expect for you to obey and follow a law when they write it in terms only judges can understand and then interpret as they please to pass sentence?" Joey sat down again. "If, as you say, E.J., that mostly poor and uneducated people make use of abortions, and if they are the ones who will be most concerned by the new law, perhaps someone should have done a brochure, you know, making it easier for everyday, lay people to understand."

"Joey, come election time, this is how the politicians do it; they make bills and initiatives so ambiguous that it is difficult to judge however a politician voted. This way what was written was not necessarily what was meant, or can be interpreted broadly to suit different philosophies. But for right now, Joey, just read what I gave you so you can consider your next move," E.J. advised.

Joey sat up straight in his chair. Crossing his leg over his knee, he read out loud: The Congress finds and declares: (1) A moral, medical, and ethical consensus exists that the practice of performing a partial-birth abortion an abortion in which a physician deliberately and intentionally vaginally delivers a living, unborn child's body until either the entire baby's head is outside the body of the mother, or any part of the baby's trunk past the navel is outside the body of the mother and only the head remains inside the womb, for the purpose of performing an overt act (usually the puncturing of the back of the child's skull and removing the baby's brains) that the person knows will kill the partially delivered infant, performs this act, and then completes delivery of the dead infant is a gruesome and inhumane procedure that is never medically necessary and should be prohibited. (2) Rather than being an abortion procedure that is embraced by the medical community, particularly among physicians who routinely perform other abortion procedures, partial-birth abortion remains a disfavored procedure that is not only unnecessary to preserve the health of the mother, but in fact poses serious risks to the long-term health of women and in some circumstances, their lives. As a result, at least 27 States banned the procedure as did the United States Congress which voted to ban the procedure during the 104th, 105th, and 106th Congresses.

Joey rubbed his head. "But isn't this the 110th Congress?"

"Just keep reading, Joey."

Joey kept reading, and he got further into the material, shouted, "Jesus! Is this what happens when a woman has an abortion? Man, I did not know America would ever have allowed such a procedure, something so awful and barbaric, to be legal. And they have the nerve to say suicide bombing is savage and tasteless. I can hardly stand to read this stuff, it is just so inhumane," said Joey.

"Try not to think about yourself right now, Joey. In Congressional testimony, medical experts testified that by the late second trimester, the unborn child is very responsive to painful stimuli, and that this is not much affected by any anesthesia administered. Read to get an understanding so that you will know what to do to solve your problems."

"Okay. Okay, I'm reading. You would have thought the writers would have known a thing or two about brevity for clarity," said Joey as he flipped through pages. Partial-birth abortions prohibited (a) Any physician who, in or affecting interstate or foreign commerce, knowingly performs a partial-birth abortion and thereby kills a human fetus shall be fined under this title or imprisoned not more than 2 years, or both. This subsection does not apply to a partial-birth abortion that is necessary to save the life of a mother whose life is endangered by a physical disorder, physical illness, or physical injury, including a life-endangering physical condition caused by or arising from the pregnancy itself. This subsection takes effect 1 day after the date of enactment of this chapter.

Joey kept reading while E.J. pretended to be engrossed in other paperwork.

Joey read for another half hour and stopped when he came to another highlighted paragraph but in a different color.

"E.J., man, why is this paragraph highlighted in a different color?"

"Read it to me so I know which paragraph you're referring to," said E.J., looking up from his desk.

Joey held the paper up close to his face but was silent.

"Joey, do you expect for me to read through the paper you are holding, or do you want to read out loud?" E.J. asked.

"Oh, wow." Joey took a deep breath. "I'm sorry, man, but listen to this." Joey leaned forward in his chair holding the papers down. (c)(1) The father, if married to the mother at the time she receives a partial-birth abortion procedure, and if the mother has not attained the age of 18 years at the time of the abortion, the maternal grandparents of the fetus, may in a civil action obtain appropriate relief, unless the pregnancy resulted from the plaintiff's criminal conduct or the plaintiff consented to the abortion.

"Everything all clear now, Joey?"

"Man, are you kidding? But Natasha is over eighteen, so this part does not apply to me, so maybe everything will be all right." Joey kept scratching his head.

"Man, don't do your droppings here in my office," said E.J.

"What do you mean 'droppings'?"

"You are scratching your head like it is full of lice."

"Ah, man, get out of here. This is serious stuff here, E.J." Joey stared scared at the paperwork.

"Don't I know it, brother man?" E.J. answered sternly.

"Does Mother know the details of the procedure involved?" asked Joey.

"Man, your mother is a college graduate, so she is no dummy. Why the heck do you think she was so concerned?" E.J. could not tell Joey that those were the only pages on the subject that Mother wanted Joey to read. Mother and E.J. both knew that though the medical procedure was the same, there were revised rulings of the terms. E.J. had also read: Because of the lawsuits, the Partial-Birth Abortion Ban Act of 2003 cannot be enforced, though it could be years before the abortion debate winds its way through the system and heads back to the Supreme Court.

E.J. said, "Now I have been pulling data from several different sources, and I'll be damned, if I'm not coming up with several different interpretations. But, you know, Joey, I've got to tell you, man, that I agree with Mother. She says that it is beyond her grasp how any man who created his likeness could destroy something so valuable. When two people with children split up, they should not make the child suffer because of the parents' problems. At least, they shouldn't."

Joey's eyes began to water, and tears streamed down his face. Weeping, Joey placed the papers on E.J.'s desk, and said, "Man, I just never took the time to think things through. I need to talk to Natasha and Mom."

"Yeah, you should do that. Mother has been very disturbed about the act of murder, period. But, my God, Joey, can you really comprehend the technique being used to destroy your baby—puncturing the back of the child's skull and removing the baby's brains? Come on, Joey. Man, you are better than that. You can't hate this woman that much that you would want to see this done to your baby, your child." E.J. took out a handkerchief and wiped his fore-head. He handed another hanky to his brother and said, "Man, here, wipe your face. I have to tell you that I am very worried about you."

Joey wiped his face, then placed the papers on E.J.'s desk. "Should I marry Natasha?" he asked his older brother.

"I cannot answer that for you, Joey. Time on the marriage thing might prove the best solution. Somewhere down the line if you and Natasha should go through with the abortion, man, moments that should be gratifying will be zapped away from you two because you will remember the agony caused to your child with your permis-sion." E.J. picked up the paper and handed it back to Joey as he pointed with his pen. "Here, read again the middle section of this page."

"Which paragraph?"

E.J. put his finger on the paper and circled the paragraph. Joey read slowly each word: *(A) Partial-birth abortion poses serious risks to the health of a woman undergoing the procedure. Those risks include, among other things: An increase in a woman's risk of suffering from cervical incompetence, a result of cervical dilation making it difficult or impossible for a woman to successfully carry a subsequent pregnancy to term; an in-creased risk of uterine rupture, abruption, amniotic fluid embolus, and trauma to the uterus as a result of converting the child to a footling breech position, a procedure which, according to a leading obstetrics textbook, `there are very few, if any, indications for * * * other than for delivery of a second twin; and a risk of lacerations and secondary hemorrhaging due to the doctor blindly forcing a sharp instrument into the base of the unborn child's skull while he or she is lodged in the birth canal, an act which could result in severe bleeding, brings with it the threat of shock, and could ulti-mately result in maternal death.*

When Joey finished reading, his pained face looked askance at E.J.

E.J. read his brother and answered, "Right now I just don't know what else to tell you, Joey. I might not have given you a lot of infor-mation, but you have enough to act responsibly and in the best in-terest of all concerned."

* * * * *

Everyone was worried about Mother. E.J. was the most worried. He called Shauna while she was at a restaurant with friends and told her how badly he felt about Mother, Joey, Natasha and the baby. This was yet another situation that further strained once blessed ties that did bind his family not so long ago. Shauna, however, could not quite understand why Mother was the one so upset. My resources for this tidbit? Right. Ditto! News travels, bad news travels well, and the raunchy, salacious, lewd, lascivious or scandalous? First class!

Shauna was having lunch with seven of her girlfriends at Rusty Scuppers, a waterfront restaurant on the Oakland estuary. They were meeting to discuss plans for a bachelorette party for two other girlfriends who were getting married at the same time. The girlfriends at the meeting were closer to Shauna than they were to anyone in the Navies family, but they all knew the family, mostly through a word here or there from Shauna. Shauna explained to the girls around the table why she had to take the call from E.J. and told them of her future in-laws' dilemma and all the drama surrounding the possible abortion. Ordinarily, Shauna was not so dangerously indiscreet, but lately she grabbed almost every opportunity to remind herself (and others) of her intended lifelong assignation with E.J. A pitiable situation and perhaps a pathetic woman in the making.

"Late term or not, I do not think E.J.'s mother should be that upset. I have twelve girlfriends, and every month one of them has had an abortion," said Shauna.

"Oooh! You are so wrong, Shauna, to talk about your girlfriends that way," said Eva, one of the eight women at the table.

"No, no, no, I am just kidding," said Shauna laughing, "I do not have those types of friends."

"Then apologize to us all," said girlfriend Pat.

"Girl, if E.J. heard me say that, he'd be so upset, especially with his mother feeling the way she does about abortions. E.J. thinks that ghetto folk use abortion as a method of birth control."

Eva said, "I hope by ghetto, E.J. is talking about people other than black people; that word and 'urban' have become synonymous in the media with black and poor."

A chorus of affirmations followed. "True." "You got that right." "I know that's right."

Eva continued, "But, for some reason 'urban' is on the fast track to regain respectability, and of course that could have no correlation with the repopulation of the cities with people from suburban communities." Eva's tone was laced with sarcasm, her eyes rolled in disgust. "Anyhow," Eva tells them, "I am a 35-year-old exec making six figures and it's not the $100,000 bracket, either. I have a college degree, a post-graduate degree, two kids and no more husband. I own my own home and a big nice one too, five thousand square feet in a wonderful, gated community, although I do rent out two Section Eight houses in West Oakland, and I am leasing a 2008 Lexus. I am just joking about the leasing part of the story. Oooh! But did you guys see how girlfriend's face frowned up over there when I said I was leasing? On the real side though, guys, see that pretty black bad boy parked outside of the window? Well, that's me. What you see is what I own, and I am beautiful in it."

"Did you come here to brag about what you own or what?" asked Shauna.

Eva picked up her menu. "I said all of that to say I have had an abortion, so if a ghetto woman's got it going on like that, well, maybe it's not so bad, having a little ghetto in you. I bet most of us around the table have had an abortion. Okay, let's just see how well I know you girls. Raise your hands if you have not had an abortion." Just then the waiter came and took drink orders.

"Sir," Eva motioned for the waiter, "would you take my order right away? I already know what I want and do not wish to wait for these thin girls to take all day long pondering the menu."

Out of the eight women at the table, five raised their hands.

"Well, two people at this table have had abortions," said Eva.

Another waiter came over and placed a basket with bread on the table.

"Ooh whee!" Eva looked the waiter over from head to toe. "I am going to have to start giving younger guys another look."

"Okay, now. Just because they only spanked the hand of those pretty blonde teachers messing with their students, don't think that you are going to get the same easy sweet treatment," said Shauna.

Meekly, girlfriend Renee, raised her hand. "Well, excuse me, but I haven't had an abortion. Thank you guys very much."

Shauna said, "Renee, nobody's counting you, girl. You don't even have a boyfriend. You're the youngest one here at the table. In fact, aren't you still a virgin at twenty-two?"

Everyone laughed.

"Yes, it's true. And I have my virginity certificate with the ten required signatures to verify its authenticity," said Renee giddily.

"If I were you, Renee, I would not go around bragging about being a virgin at the old age of twenty-two," said Eva.

"Twenty-two is not old," Renee countered. She is not giddy now.

"True. Twenty-two by itself is not old, but when you add a virginity to the mix, well, girlfriend, you need to know that a man is slow to mess with a twenty two-year-old virgin," said Eva, sampling french fries.

"How do you know that, Eva? You were not a virgin at twenty-two; you had your first child at sixteen," Pat said evenly.

Girlfriend Staff Sergeant Jawana McFadden, twenty-three, had recently returned from Iraq. She said, "I don't think a woman should rush her body to live up to a man's expectation or fit into his thinking to provide him satisfaction."

Eva finishing cutting her hamburger in two. "Are you saying that you're a virgin, too, Jawana?" she asked.

Jawana eyed Eva and offered icily, "I am not saying all of that."

Eva was not deterred by chill winds. She told Jawana, "I don't know if you can say very much to us girls at this table, Jawana, because you have been out of real civilization for over a year. We women in America are not trying to be like Iraqi women. Okay, sweetie?" Eva took Jawana's hand. "A year in Iraq is a long time, sweetie, to feel that you can just come and jump back on the same track where you left off. You have missed some steps while you were immersed in Iraqi culture."

"Some of what you just said might be true," said Jawana, "but I do not see how that supports your claim that a man would not want to involve himself with an intelligent twenty-two-year-old virgin. Am I to assume that you are trying to say that the substance of a relationship hinges on the man's libidinous proclivities?"

Eva looked across and down the table, as if hoping someone else would answer Jawana's question. Finding no taker, she said, "Girl, please look at all of those rap music and sex videos. Most of those girls in the videos are under eighteen. Need I say more?"

Jawana grew serious. "No, Eva, you don't need to say more unless you intend to make a point. But mostly those types of videos are made for and produced by men. Need I say more?" Jawana's cell phone rang. "You guys, excuse me for a moment," she said, getting up from the table.

Eva whispered to Shauna, "I know I don't know Jawana as well as you do, but I don't remember her being so high-hat, so self-important, before going to war. Maybe she is the type of soldier that Senator John Kerry made the botched joke about, 'If you are not smart, you'll get stuck in Iraq.'"

"That is hardly the case. Girl, Jawana was just about to enter law school when the military called her National Guard unit up," Shauna answered back. "The girl's a whip!"

At the other end of the table, Pat leaned forward. "Eva, I heard what you said about Jawana. She just places high values upon herself."

Eva flipped her hand. "Girl, you heard me way down there?"

"Shame on you," said Pat, shaking her head. "Girl, you do not know how to whisper. Jawana's priority is Jawana having what she wants out of life, and I don't believe she is only trying to become all that a man wants her to be. Jawana is trying to develop into someone she herself is pleased with."

"And I don't blame her," Regina chimed in. "These young sisters in their early twenties today are not like we were at their age. They are not doing a seventy/forty to make a relationship work."

"Please. These young sisters are worse today than we were at their age," said Eva.

Pat shook her head. "No, no, no. Our generation thought about babies and husbands before careers. A young black woman today is learning that it is not worth the sacrifice unless the man has himself already together—is on a path of a life he is developing for himself—and even then she recognizes that she has the big stake in her own destiny. Face it, Eva, our mamas didn't teach us that the first rule is self-preservation. They did not teach us how to maintain for long-lasting womanhood. Nor did they teach us emotional discipline: You don't put a man before doing for yourself first. We are just beginning to learn the life skills."

Shauna seconded, saying "Pat is right, Eva. And when you come from the projects, it is just hard to have high self-esteem. So all your investment in yourself is not so much about what you want for you, but the kind of man that you want to attract. There it is in a nutshell."

"Shauna, I am surprised that you have had an abortion," said Eva, as she reached for the basket of bread. "I would have thought that you had more self-esteem. I guess you have a little ghetto in you, too, huh? Does that attorney boyfriend of yours know about your ghetto side?"

All eyes were on Shauna. Everyone seemed truly surprised to know that about Shauna. She was thought to be the most worldly and sophisticated at the table. No moral judgment here I do not think, but I think that given the sophistication, people expected Shauna to use a different kind of birth control?

"What?" Shauna snapped. "It was a mistake that happened. I would not have another abortion because I know what to do now to protect myself. You guys need to keep in mind the fact that when it happened I was in my second year of college, and my parents were so very strict. My parents never told me anything about how not to get pregnant. And, of course, that was my first boyfriend in my sophomore year of college." Shauna swirled her straw around in her mouth, "If my parents knew then that I was having sex, they would have killed me—and I mean that like written word. My parents just said 'No sex. Keep your skirt down and legs closed.' They didn't even tell me condoms were an option," said Shauna.

"Didn't you take sex education classes in school?" asked Eva.

"No. I mean, I did, but there was no real reason to pay attention to that stuff then. My parents sent me to a private school, and nobody was having sex around me that I knew about. My parents just acted as if I was never going to have sex. But since I have learned better, I have not used abortion as a form of birth control. I made a mistake in college, and now I know better." Shauna tried to close the conversation about herself with a sip from her water and pressed lips.

The waiter brought over a tray and placed everyone's food on the table. He served Eva another batch of fries.

Renee was still focused on Shauna, pressed lips or no pressed lips. "If you accidentally got pregnant now, would you have an abortion?" Renee asked. No one could miss the anxiety in her voice.

"No," said Shauna. "I don't believe in abortion for myself anymore, but that does not mean I would want to see that law overturned, either. I am pro-abortion. I really think that freedom is the woman's choice for her body, and that should always be the case."

"Does E.J. know that you have had an abortion?" asked Eva.

"No. And I don't find a need to tell him either," said Shauna. Sad, Shauna looked at each woman around the table. "I guess I should admit the truth about my abortion. Look you guys, I was date raped. I had gone out with this friend on maybe three or four dates, but we never had sex. At least I didn't know that I had sex until I was two months pregnant. I remember having a drink with this guy. He was in college same as I was. And I had never had a drink of alcohol before. When I woke up that morning I found myself on the couch fully dressed. I felt funny all that day and the next but I thought it was a long hangover from the alcohol. I really beat myself after that, and felt that I did not use the better part of my judgment. I mean, people say that you have to watch your drink. I mean even if you go to the bathroom, take your drink; covering it up with a napkin does not stop a predator. The other thing I learned was that if you think you were drugged, you need to go to the emergency room and get a blood test within 24 hours to detect a date rape drug. Anyway, I got counseling. I..." Shauna began to choke up. She pulled out a tissue, and wiped her eyes. "I am really okay. I have forgiven myself and the situation. I have moved on to the better part of my existence. Sorry, but that was the reason for the lie."

A shift is felt; the conversation has taken a serious turn.

Folding her arms and leaning on the table, Renee said, "What happened to Shauna is really awful." A din of sympathetic consolations follows. "But, in general, I am anti-abortion. I would vote for the party that is anti-abortion. I really would. That's the kind of girl I am. I believe in abstinence, too, until I've gotten a ring on the finger. I work with a girls' organization, ages fourteen to eighteen, and I bring in mentors who talk to these girls about abstinence and reasons why they should wait until they are a little older before giving their bodies to anyone—before knowing the outcome for their future. I don't believe that you can tell a young girl to 'Just say no' to having sex when all of her friends might be doing that, but you have to tell her what could possibly happen when a young girl has sex too early in life. I tell my girls sex without love is definitely a step in the wrong direction." Six out of the eight women in the group did not want to have a law prohibiting abortions, and none other than Renee believed in abstinence. Most of these women were in their early thirties.

"Okay," said Joslin, sitting next to Renee. "I am just a little bit curious as to what you tell these young girls about love and sex? How will young girls understand when we at this table are just getting a grip on this thing called love? Really, how could these young girls know anything about love?"

Renee answered, "As I have said, I bring in mentors who share their views on why young girls should wait on sex until they are older and are mature enough to make decisions about their future."

"You do not get to decide if you are date raped or just straight dirty raped or if you are a preyed upon child," Shauna pitched. "You have to keep it real."

"I agree with that, and are your girls able to understand all of the complexities of love at their young and tender ages?" asked Eva, motioning to the waiter to remove some of the bread baskets from the table.

Renee explained, "My organization has a list of people whom we consider great mentors for our girls, and whenever I get a call that one of the mentors will be free to appear at our bi-monthly meetings, we take that opportunity and work it into our schedule."

Eva was impressed and commended the effort. "That's great because today it is hard to get real role models to interact with our young people. They don't really have time," she said.

"What fields do your mentors specialize in?" asked Shauna.

"From all walks of life—actors, politics, medicine, science, educators—you name it, and the field no doubt is on the list," Renee answered with satisfaction. "We have over one hundred celebrity names listed to participate. These girls are told different things from different guests, but key message is the same: 'Young girls, wait for the right time!'"

"See, you need me to come and talk to your group because I would break it down for them," said Eva as she summoned the waiter again.

"What would you tell them, Eva?" asked Renee.

"I would tell them straight up, you cannot be a princess, a queen and a harlot, all in one. If everyone in town knows about the secret you hold, then it's no good. I would ask your girls which one do they want to be when they grow up—a queen or a harlot? If they said queen, then I would show them how to walk the path that leads to queenship," Eva said.

Renee was not impressed. "A bit crude, but I get your point. If ever the organization gets in a crunch for a substitute speaker, we would make calls from our list first. But thank you for the offer," she said dismissively.

Eva said, "See, you and Shauna would like to dress up everything with a pretty spin, but sometimes you have to go straight to the point, and especially if you are going to talk to girls from the ghettoes."

Eva's comment did not sit well with Jawana who had returned to the table and had been listening attentively.

"I do not think that you have to teach down to the young just because they might be from the ghettoes. And it is not within their best interests to lower the standards of teaching. Do not underestimate these kids; they are very intelligent," Jawana said.

Toying with her fork, Pat counseled, "I would say if you do not have a nice ring on the finger, and we are not talking a promise of a ring, an agreed upon, pre-determined courtship period—when it starts and when it ends—then we cannot broach the other subject for discussion. If that's not happening, then we are talking about a Mickey D arrangement, I mean just driving through for the goodies—quickies any time of day or night, no need or reason to stay.

That is a 'hit it and run' type and we all know that hit and runs are illegal. I'd also tell them to stay away from the guys who just want to take them for a test drive. You know, the kind of guy who never has any intentions of buying a new car. He just likes to see how a new one runs every opportunity he gets."

Shauna got a word in. "Renee," she said, "I would like to talk to your young girls because I think more black women need to take the extra step and responsibility and become mentors to one another. And I hope you have Mary J. Blige on your list of role models. Every young girl could benefit from her story and what she sees as her purpose in life now. If its real, then she's been touched by an angel."

The eight women seemed to have forgotten that their luncheon meeting was to plan a bachelorette party for their two girlfriends. And so, they chatted on and on....

"...I wish more artists would take a hint from all of the things you pointed out, Renee, and to know that their music could touch the young in a way perhaps no other form of art could. But I get the feeling that a lot of music that black people listen to is off beat when it comes to helping to develop children and youth," Pat was saying.

"You can't just lump all black people together. Some black people. And you can't say that black people do this or that or are this or that like it's to the exclusion of other people. White, brown Native American and Asian youth might listen to more rap and hip-hop than all black people over forty-five. We get on others for doing this and we turn around and do the same thing. You know, there are different cultural norms within every race or group of people," Renee protested. "And we need to stop lumping black men together, just like we as black women do not want to be lumped together." A round of confirmations followed. "But speaking of the youth I am involved with," Renee continued, "these kids need a message to help them become more integrated into society so they can become productive as young people and grow into responsible enough citizens with equal access to opportunities."

"You know," said Pat, untangling her bracelets, "I still say I wish the young could somehow get the message of how hip-hop artists have been able to make business moves into the mainstream of

America. They know how to deal with ~~contracts, and these rappers~~ know about marketing. All I am saying is that somebody needs to write the story of how these rappers have been able to live the American dream far better than some had imagined. I wish the songs black kids listen to would help to foster a sense of self-worth, too, whereas our children would actually value the lives of other young black kids. If some of the music did that, perhaps it could cut down the violence many of these teens commit against one another."

Shauna placed her hand under her chin. "Now if you could count on musicians to be responsible that way, then it is worth calling them in as mentors," said Shauna. "But to sing and act one way, inciting drama, violence, advocating cop killing, disrespect of women, nasty language, getting arrested for publicity. Well, all that is just bad karma. Car chasing, looting, and lyrics suffering from an obviously limited vocabulary; the deplorable use of the 'N' word. All that stuff is just ear and mind poison and it is toxic for the young, black, white, brown and Asian, alike. I wonder whether Americans or people in the world period appreciate the extent to which hip-hoppers have been trendsetters? Look at the new words recognized in the dictionaries—'dis' has been in dictionaries for years now; the language, clothing, music, and even fine art have been influenced by a generation that some thought was just going to go away! But that generation is still here. And its influence is still here, too. I am saying all this to say that they can be of influence for betterment in all areas of youth growth and development."

"I couldn't say that any better myself," said Eva, as she reached to take some french fries off Shauna's plate.

Shauna slapped Eva's hand. "Girl, you better watch that weight piling up on you already. Too many black women are obese and are dying early deaths."

Eva gave Shauna the ugly eye, and sneered; her upper lip nearly kissed the end of her nose. "Anyway," Eva went on, not missing a beat or a french fry, "as I was saying before I was assailed by an uncalled-for attack, songs today use 'bitch' and 'ho' like they are saying 'hello.' Sadder is when young girls respond to these obscene greetings, if you can call them that. And with all of the cursing in music today, no way do I want my children, and I have two, anywhere near a stage with those sorts of performers. No way!"

Shauna shook her head, pointed her finger and said, "Worse than that stupidness is that radio announcer's inexcusable and deplorable remark on the airwaves. The fact that this white man could feel comfortable enough to actually call a prestigious college basketball team of mostly black women 'nappy-headed hoes' says there is a whole lot gone wrong with commercial ads and sponsorships for shows where such are said."

"Maybe he was less the problem—masking the real culprit," said Eva.

"Give me some skin on that," Shauna agreed. After Eva held her hand and the pair executed a perfect girly high five, Shauna added, "and until we fully discuss the shaded canvas of television sponsorship; anything else on the subject is flowery speech without a solution."

Eva said, "You are right and that is why you've gotta love Reverend Al Sharpton on this one. He rose to the occasion just perfectly to address the radio incident. Now I am not much on marching, but if I had been in the location where Rev Al was picketing I would have joined in and held a sign." Eva took a sip from her cup. "And something else, I won't be totally satisfied until everyone of those actors, comedians, rappers and musicians have changed their uncouth ways, too."

Regina, who had been silent for most of the evening, cautioned, "If you guys are waiting for some of these musicians and Hollywood to become responsible role model types, please breathe right now if you want to go on living. First of all, the entertainment industry, cut and dry, is into role playing and not role modeling. We are 'looking for love' in the wrong place there. Secondly, what makes you think these guys with prison skills, limited schooling, and a whole bunch of mama-baby-drama even possess any of the skills we would want the youth to have? You'd come out better by asking some of those artists to have an exorcism."

"Hey," Eva said, "I once heard a rapper respond to a black parent who asked the question, 'Well, what do you think we can do to get the rappers to stop singing so many bad songs to our kids?' The rapper responded, 'They are your kids. Rappers don't live at home with your kids to make them do anything and, therefore, it is your responsibility as a parent to make your own kids do what they need to do. Stop trying to put the blame on the rapper for a job you neglected to do as parents.' Needless to say, I thought the rapper was out of line with his remarks and suggested that parents not give their kids money to buy any more of his music."

"Now, Eva, I am going to have to side with the rappers on that one," Renee shot back. "It is first the parents' responsibility to monitor what goes on in the lives of their own children. How can you hold rappers responsible for the young people in society when the preachers or politicians can't do anything to bring about change? I know some rappers, and they are far from what you call celebrities. I think rappers are more genuine than most other type celebrities. And all I got to say is that the rappers did not turn society upside down. You need to blame the elected officials or the schools for not doing their jobs. The rappers are not the ones to blame." Renee's voice trembled. "Black parents won't make an impact if they stop buying rap music. In fact, over 75 percent of the rap music is purchased by white kids. So it's not like the artists are banking off of the monies from blacks, anyway. So you older folks should just get off of the rappers' case. Find the real culprits who are messing up young kids."

Shauna dropped her sandwich on her plate and jumped in. "But Renee, even though it is first the responsibility of parents, exactly what is the artist's responsibility in all of this? Don't think for one second that rap music is not having a negative effect on white kids, too. I have never seen such sleaziness coming from white women as I do today. So rap music is not just a factor relating to the low self-esteem being viewed of black women; the same is happening of white women, too."

"I am with you on that, Shauna," said Eva. "I think the difference may be in the degrees to which it affects blacks over whites, but the harm is upon both."

"How do you explain that, Eva?" asked Renee.

"Come on, Renee," said Eva. "If you want to go with the mindset of rappers, then you certainly have a lot more to learn. Rappers have rhythm, and that is as much credit as they get here. I would not send my child to a school that associated with a rapper whose message is in disrespectful lyrics. There is no way that kind of rapper can be seen as a role model."

Renee shrugged her shoulders. "I am just saying that since the rappers have so much power over society, maybe they should be the ones running for office or something."

"You are still young, Renee, and probably that's the reason you think the way that you do. You cannot dignify these rappers' behavior just because they have been given a mike," said Pat.

Renee picked up her soda and began sipping from her straw. "I listen to a lot of rap music, and I am not corrupt. So that means not all rap music is indecent. You guys are just getting too old and maybe rap music has eliminated your age group. I think Lil' Romeo and Lil' Bow Wow are fitting rappers, just to name a few. And sponsors are taking a long and different look at the rappers needed now to promote their products—they know society—is watching—and parents."

Pat leaned forward and looked around the table at the other women. "I am not too much out of the loop to know that Romeo and Bow Wow since becoming grown men have each dropped the Lil' from their name."

Renee put her hands over her mouth. "You're right. Neither of them use Lil' as names any more. You are definitely correct."

Shauna backed her chair away from the table. "It's time for the parents to stand up and speak up. Parents need to become more accountable because the future of their children is at stake. We can demand change from businesses to use integrity and scrutiny in their sponsorship of rappers, athletes and actors."

The group paid the tab, left a generous tip, and Eva made a comment that seemed—from yet another chorus of confirmation—to be a consensus: "Mothers and fathers need to take their children back. Take them away from all of the negativity and begin to set standards, goals, and expectations for their children. Our children belong to us, not to the violence in the street."

I am in Charlotte missing the closeness of my family. Everyone except Joey still lives in California. I haven't been myself lately, slipping deeper into a slump, questioning my purpose for being. I stopped going out as much and tried to work from home as much as possible. Though my hair had started to grow again in the spots where it had fallen out during the last several months, I continued to fret, just not as much. I reflected upon the conversation I had with Grandma during her visit to Charlotte. She said my hair loss was a way for me to focus on my life as a whole, and not just my vanity.

So I am trying to focus on me as the first step in sorting out my life. Questions like Who am I? Where did I come from? Who were my people way back when? haunted me. I keep trying to find ways to return myself to the time of black people's beginning in this country but in a way that did not conjure up slavery. Was that even possible? Could seeing a black psychologist help me? Could others who came along with my ancestors through the barbaric and holocaustic trade in humans, but were dropped off somewhere else, say the Caribbean, help me to see a different view?

I wonder if those who were of black and white mixture found life in America less of a struggle, with fewer conflicts with white society, than those who were not biracial, black and white. (Biracial? With all the mixing up through time, biracial has to be a politico-socio-economic term; surely it was not scientific.) I wonder if my best friend, Amy, who is mixed really has had life easier. My mind wonders and wanders endlessly. I remember a talk I had with Amy at her place about two years ago. Amy and I have always been honest with each other. We are like sisters. And that day, we spoke as sisters might:

Amy toyed with her hair, and spoke earnestly, "You know, Zemi, it is not that I mind the amount of black blood flowing through me. I really do not have a problem with that at all. But the low expectations that blacks have for themselves make me frightened to choose that as my race. Do you understand what I'm saying, Zemi?"

Amy sat on her bed while I continued looking through her closet.

"There is something about me that feels more white than black. Do you think that I am wrong to think that way, Zemi?"

As I walked out of Amy's closet, I stretched my neck, moving it from side to side. I felt a little tense although the tenseness has nothing to do with Amy's ruminations.

"Yeah Amy, I sense what you are saying. Sometimes I think that my folk have set the bar just too low. But unlike you, Amy, I don't have the luxury to choose to which race I belong."

Amy patted the bed and motioned for me to come and sit. "You are the only black female friend that I have. All the rest of them are white." Amy put her feet up on the bed. "You knew that about me already, and yet you never once questioned me."

Our conversation had shifted from benign girly talk to life consequence, heady matters.

"Amy, I didn't pick you for my friend because you are mixed. I adore you and accept all that you are. When I-I..."

Gently, Amy interrupted me. "I know that already. And I love you because you love me unconditionally. You don't have issues with me like some blacks do." Amy's face dropped. "It seems as though, well, black women and me just don't hit it off all that well."

I thought Amy was putting too much of the blame on the sisters.

"True, Amy, I don't have issues with you. When I look at you, I see someone that I share a lot in common with. We even wear each other's clothes." Teasingly I said, "What is interesting, too, is that we dance alike, both without soul, and we like to read many of the same books."

Amy smiled, "And don't forget, we are both intellectuals. We just share so much in common."

We gave each other a hand slap.

As I held Amy's hand, I said, "But still Amy, maybe it is you who has to do some cleaning out of the soul closet. In my opinion, I think that you are overly concerned with what you perceive to be issues that black women may have of you. But deeper than that, I don't think that you have allowed yourself an opportunity to know black women for yourself."

Amy reclaimed her hand. "How can you say that?"

Sometimes I do get just a bit disgusted with Amy. "Come on Amy, you didn't grow up with blacks in your circle. All the women that you had in your life growing up were your aunts on your mother's side, and all of their children were white, too. Everything that your mother did or belonged to was white-oriented."

Amy's face looked troubled. "Are you saying that was a bad thing that my mother did, the way she raised me?"

"Of course not. Your mother had to spend out of what she was given to make your life the best she could." I took a deep breath. "But the biggest issue is that you didn't have the opportunity of knowing the African American who was, indeed, your dad. I understand that. You don't know the black side of who you are. You just don't have a passion for the African American side as you hold for the Caucasian side of you. And until you examine those issues, then something in your spirit will remain adrift, searching for a part of you that you have never seen. Unattended to, that part of you will remain weak, if not broken, because it is not fed."

"How do you know that about me?" asked Amy with eyes open nearly as wide as her mouth..

"Because my Mother says that part of you is me."

We smiled weakly at one another, wondering what it all meant.

* * * * *

I did not know how Amy would take it. So what I could not tell Amy that day was everything my mother had said:

"Honey the part of that girl that is missing, that she is looking for, is you Zemi. For Amy, you represent that part of her as she sees herself: whole and well. But that is how she kids herself. And the problem is that the part she is missing probably is not as together as you are. If she stops settling for where she ends up all the time by ignoring these issues, and, instead, finds and deals with other aspects of herself, then she will also find that she needs to do a lot of work. The way it is now—is safe for her."

"Mother, how could you know all these things about Amy?" I asked.

"I know my children. And I know the people they spend time with. As a parent, I needed to know these things."

* * * * *

The phone finally stops ringing. I didn't know what to do with myself. I felt empty. Two weeks more have passed, and I have been in and out of sleep. I have lost ten pounds; I'm cooking not much to not at all. Then I went from sleeping too much to not being able to sleep at all. I began to have conversations with myself—a sign, too, that even solitude had gotten bored with me. Good for solitude, my soul needed it more than the lifeless layabout I had become. Perhaps, if solitude could heal my soul, then I would be healed also.

Time elapsed, but I could not tell you how, or what I did as time went by. I sunk to a low where all I could do was reach for what was higher. I could do no more than that, but at least I was no longer saying that God had abandoned me. And I was no longer at that place—where I was angry every time the light of day hit my eyes, where getting out of the bed was major. I had risen from that consciousness of hell. I always showered, ever since the cloud came; for I felt that if I did not at least wash, I knew I had given up, and whatever had come after me would win. So it might be three or four or five in the afternoon, but everyday I brushed my teeth, and showered, if nothing else. And I prayed, my heart to God's being was how. I could not utter a prayer out loud; the words would not come; the pain was in the way. A grief knot in the middle of my chest—dead center.

God must have heard me—or felt me. I had awakened early before dawn in my bed, or was I already awake? The last thing I remembered was a calm voice: "But you know the way." Why must the spirit give lessons and assignments in code? As if answering my thoughts, a louder voice spoke up, saying, "AIDS -YOUR WORK, A PART OF THE SOLUTION." That message was clearer than I wanted it to be. Why would I have to have anything to do with the AIDS pandemic other than giving a dollar here and there? Now how could I know what that message meant? It was more comfortable to listen to codes and riddles sent by spirit. That way I could figure as I pleased; that way I could sort out what was being said in a way I could ignore the message with a clear conscience and keep on doing whatever I was doing. Isn't that what people do? I got up and went into the bathroom.

Something good must have happened in the night, and that I could not ignore. I felt better, too. I looked different to myself. The image of what I saw in the mirror was hard to explain. But my face looked brighter, and no longer sagged with the weight of feeling badly. My eyes were willing to look at me.

I prepared the tub for a good, long soak. I don't remember the last time I've taken a tub bath. While bathing, I suddenly became aware of something else from my absence from a fully conscious being. A voice, and I cannot recall whether I heard this voice in a dream or semi-conscious state. It did not matter. The voice said, "Many Americans like to complain a lot, always playing the injured party. What do you suppose might happen if American people, all Americans, took charge of what God has placed in their hands— their own destiny?" But, for real, what did that message mean? I must have been hallucinating and without any medication.

Well, at least, the bath made me feel like a person again. I wanted for the first time in a while to look beautiful. So I slipped into a mint green, floor-length negligee with a sparkling silver V-line that extended to the waist. I relaxed in my bedroom, not in the bed this time, but on a small poufy couch that faced a view of tall and regal oak trees. When I looked towards the mountains, I could not believe what I was seeing: purple mountain majesties—just like in the song, *America the Beautiful,* and below the mountains spread the fruited plains, ready to be harvested. Katharine Lee Bates had to have seen what I am seeing right now, a manifestation of God's supreme love. I sipped a soothing cup of tea, and on the stereo played over and over, "A Love Supreme."

I began a letter to Zeth.

October 23

Charlotte, NC

Dear Zeth,

How is Power of Love? It has been a long time since I've seen him. I miss him—so much. I would like to come by and rub him some and hope that he has not forgotten my scent and taken on the scent of a new rider. Zeth, do you think that Power of Love misses me, needs me, is perhaps longing to see me? Since you are around him, Zeth, please tell me about his mood and what I have missed being away. If you wouldn't mind, please call to let me know when would be a good time to come and comfort him. I want to be in his life again....now I fear I will regret....

Ohhh! I took a deep breath. I could not write anything more. I stopped writing, crumpled up the letter, and missed the waste-basket in a half-hearted toss. Hurriedly, I moved into the living room. I paced back and forth, Grandma's words resonating with me: "Figure out what to do with that land. Don't just sit on it! Show Zeth that you know how to deal in spite of your youth. That will bring that man back to you in no time. He gave it to you to make a start of something. You are the youngest, but have had the advantage of combing through the experiences of your older siblings and your elders. Take and keep and use the wisdoms you have learned. And let your youth and good health move you quickly to the next level. It is said that fortune favors the swift and the bold. I do not know about that, but you, Zemi Navies, are favored by God."

If my family in California was an example, the next level was to own one's home—that's why it's called one's own home. For people of our means, having a deed to acres of land in California was a stretch so big that it had to be a dream or a lie. Accomplishing anything more than what our parents had done would be running our own businesses.

Something kept nudging me, and kept after me until I made a decision. The decision had to do with the land in Charlotte that Zeth had given to me. I made a phone call to Shauna and asked her to come down to Charlotte as soon as she could get there. I told her that I wanted to deed over to her some of the land Zeth had given me. I also had prepared a proposition for Shauna to consider once she arrived. For the next couple of days I mapped out what I wanted to do with some of the parcels of the land. I also planned my discussion with Shauna about the land that would involve a partnership with her, assuming she would come on board.

I picked up Shauna at CLT Airport. Right away, her demeanor seemed strange to me; she was too—composed? Borderline subdued, that's what it was. Nonetheless, she was dressed in trademark, It Girl, apparel, an aubergine knit pantsuit, a "must have" designer bag, and fine European boots.

"I am glad to see that you have come out from your slumber party of one," Shauna teased. Then, somberly, she eyed me and remarked: "Everyone in California misses you, Zemi." Touching my waist, Shauna observed, "You look nice and trim. A good weight for you, but just don't lose any more." Shouldering her carry-on bag, she told me, "You had me going when you talked about giving up some land. I didn't mind flying in to hear the finer details. It seems as though Grandma put some fire under you during her last visit."

I told her, "Yeah, it was Grandma and a whole lot of retrospection, too. I must concede that I had to give a lot of thought to get the meaning of what Grandma meant. Not just what she said, or the words she used. You know older people sometimes seem to talk in codes or riddles. Just like in those very old days, when they had to for survival—like singing out about a low-swinging chariot as the signal for fleeing from a slave plantation."

"Zemi, I think that after Grandma broke it down to us, we each needed to look at ourselves differently as black women and the direction we need to take for self-preservation. I know I have changed or at least am taking steps in that direction. Obviously, you have, too—if the moves you are making now are any indication. But I don't know what it is that Maria is doing; I haven't seen her much lately," Shauna answered.

I did not know what to say about Maria, so I said nothing. "It's about time I took you over to see the land," I told Shauna.

Shauna had a big grin on her face. I linked my arm through hers as we walked to the car. I was really glad that Shauna came down, and she did so on a moment's notice. That said a lot about our friendship.

"I presume Zeth is going to meet us at the land, or is that taking too much for granted?" asked Shauna.

"Ummm. Then you are presuming too much. This phase is not about Zeth and me. It is about you and me and a partnership."

"Say no more," said Shauna, shaking her head. "I got it!"

"Good."

As we pulled up to the land, Shauna pointed, saying, "Who is that guy?"

I looked in the direction she was pointing. "Oh, he must be the guy that Zeth sent to unlock the gates to the property."

"Well, that was nice of Zeth." Shauna stared out at the land, the part that she could see.

I turned to her and told her what was up. "Shauna. This is about our partnership—for the second time."

Shauna was scratching her arm. "I hope there are no mosquitoes out here."

"Shauna, it is late fall, cold and breezy, and you haven't even gotten out of the car."

"You are right. Maybe it is a subconscious thing I have about the South." Shauna lowered her window. "Oh, God, there's mud out there. I need to change out of my boots because they ain't made for walking over a single area of land, let alone five hundred."

"Don't trouble yourself. I am Johnny-on-the-spot!" I reached in the back seat for an extra pair of rubber boots, a jogging outfit, a light coat and some gloves.

"You go, Zemi. You are sounding and acting like a real Southern woman already. Don't trouble yourself," said Shauna mockingly.

I handed Shauna the change of clothes.

"I see that you thought of everything, so where do I change clothes?"

"Go right over there in those bushes. You are about to become real Southern."

"No, really, girl, where do I change?" Shauna rolled her eyes.

"Ah, Shauna, you can change right here in the car while I go and meet this guy. There is no one else on my five hundred acres. I hope he's the gatekeeper. I don't want to go over there and make a fool out of myself."

I walked over to the guy, who looked to be about sixty-five with frizzy gray hair. He wore coveralls, a handyman type. "Hello there," I said, forcing a Southern twang. "My name is Zemi Navies and this is my property a-and…."

"Oh, yes, ma'am." The man extended his hand. I removed my glove and accepted his firm handshake.

"Mr. Zeth said that you would be comin' by to see your land. I been gatekeeper fer this here land even 'fore Mr. Zeth's folk died. I know this five hundred acres of land better than anyone else 'cept fer Mr. Zeth. Hit ain't much he don't know about happenin's in the South. But this here is a special piece of land, more so than any of the other parcels that Mr. Zeth owns. This piece dat you standin' on is God's land. He done had me here protectin' hit fer the right people to be on this land. I know'd hit was time fer it to 'ventually open hitself up 'cause that is what God is ready fer."

"What is it that God is ready for, Mr. Gatekeeper?"

"A change! Anybody dat knows God would know dat, and anybody with eyes can see dat. And anybody with the will, will do dat."

Shauna joined us, newly garbed, work clothes, gloves and all. "Hello," she said with a smile as she extended her hand to the gatekeeper.

"Oh, yes, this is my friend Shauna, and I am sorry," I said, apologizing. "I didn't get your name."

"Aww. Don't worry about dat. Everybody round here jest call me Gatekeeper."

"The land… it's so plentiful," I said quietly.

"It oughta look that way," said the gatekeeper, nervously slapping a glove on his thigh. "It's five hundred acres."

I couldn't hold my excitement. "It is so green, so spacious, lush and rich. It is just heavenly. Oh, my God, look at the view. I am just so touched." I had seen the land twice before, but today's experience was so intense, almost too much for me. I became full after taking the first step onto this soil today.

Deep in thought was where I was when Shauna nudged me in the side.

"Miss Zemi, Miss Zemi," the gatekeeper was calling out to me.

The gatekeeper and Shauna were both looking at me expectantly. Shauna had to nudge me again before I got it.

I turned to the gatekeeper. "Okay then, Mr. Gatekeeper, where do we start?"

"Well, the first thang we want to do is make you feel lak the owner of this here property." He reached in his pocket and pulled out about twenty keys, all on one key ring, and handed them to me. "This here is your set of keys to everythin' 'round here, stable and some of the smaller houses on the land. I got the key to the big house. I keep that one in my truck. Mr. Zeth said if you wanted me to stick around, then I would, er, need to keep a set of keys on my person. But Mr. Zeth says it's 'cordin' to what you think about the idea of me stayin'."

"Well," I answered, "we can certainly talk about that at a later date. I am not prepared to make that decision right now." I considered a thing or two. "But tell me how much would it cost to keep you around to continue doing exactly what it is that you do now?" I became embarrassed by my apparent uneasiness with these questions.

The gatekeeper's laugh put me at ease. "Huh-uh. Mr. Zeth done paid me up pretty much fer the rest of my life. Mr. Zeth said if you don't want to keep me, then I can jest go on back to the ranch and do chores at his place. Shucks, I ain't no cost to you, Miss Zemi. I only work for Mr. Zeth, no matter what I do."

Shauna cut in. "Why, thank you, Mr. Gatekeeper. Zemi would be so honored to have you continue what it is that you do around here—and you hold on tightly to those keys now, Zemi."

"I lak you, Miss Shauna. You all right with me. Yep, I could tell right off the bat you know'd what's goin' on," the gatekeeper grinned, showcasing white teeth.

Shauna nodded. "You got that right, Mr. Gatekeeper. I do know what is going on."

"All righ', then let me go and pull up my Land Rover, so I can drive you pretty ladies all over the place. Whatever hit is that you want to see, I am the one to show ya." The gatekeeper stopped the Land Rover in front of the stable. "Now this here is the stable that Mr. Zeth had built fer Power of Love. Ain't hit jest 'bout the prettiest y'all ever done seen?" Mr. Gatekeeper asked as we walked through the stable.

I had been unable to put a lid on my feelings, and the tears just streamed down my face. What kind of guardian angel was Zeth? He does not talk to me, does not see me, yet he spared no expense to build such a beautiful stable—for me. It had just about everything that he has in his own stable. Now I felt obligated to really make the five hundred acres work. But what about Zeth's relationship with the other woman—Vickie?

We left the stable and headed to the SUV. "You all righ', Miss Zemi?" asked the gatekeeper, as we climbed back into the Land Rover.

"Ah, yeah," I said clearing my throat. "I think something must have gotten into my eyes," I fudged, and reached for my shades.

"Yep, the wind is kickin' up quite a bit out here," said the gatekeeper. He twirled a toothpick around in his mouth and seemed oblivious to my display of emotion. "Would you lak to see the big house now, Miss Zemi?"

"Yes we would," said Shauna, "but why do they call it the big house?"

"Well, hit's bigger'n all the other houses that sits on any of the acres."

"Who would have thought that to be the reason?" Shauna said.

"Here we go, Miss Zemi, this here hit is," the gatekeeper said, pulling up a long drive. "Yes, hit was here with Mr. Zeth's parents, righ' here where we stand."

"Are you saying this was Zeth's parents' home, Mr. Gatekeeper?" Shauna looked amazed.

"As plain as I can say hit."

"Gee, it looks like it is in great shape. I am so impressed," said Shauna.

"Hit looks jest as good inside, too," said the gatekeeper, nodding his head emphatically. "Come on, Miss Zemi, let me help you up these here steps."

When we reached the porch, I gasped. "Oh, my God! Look at the front doors. I have never seen doors like these. They are magnificent!" I touched the doors, rubbing my hands around the mirrored panels, and then gently patted the wood. "What kind of wood is this? I love this, absolutely. But Mr. Gatekeeper, why did Zeth let this piece of land go with his folks' home on it?"

"He let go of hit to you. Maybe he don't see dat as lettin' go," he answered as he took my hand and escorted me across the threshold, into this home.

Inside, Mr. Gatekeeper watched as Shauna and I marveled at the stately beauty of the interior.

"My goodness, look at all of the antiques in this home. Mr. Gatekeeper, are you sure Zeth wants me to have all of his family valuables that are inside here? I mean, these are priceless antiques."

"Reckon you must be priceless to him," said the Gatekeeper, rubbing a stubby beard.

"You know, Mr. Gatekeeper, I'm liking you already. I kind of think you know a whole lot of what is going on," said Shauna.

"I m...um... jest tryin' to make some sense to ya questions. Jest doin' my job."

The Gatekeeper took the rest of the afternoon to show us as much of the land that was possible to see in a day. Shauna saw a piece of land that faced a pond. Situation on the land were two quaint little houses, a pier and a barn. I could see that Shauna wanted that spot and would do almost anything to get it. She damn near was salivating. Before we left that day, we set up appointments with Mr. Gatekeeper for the rest of the week to see the remaining of the five hundred acres.

I was ecstatic. My land. Mine. This land is so far beyond what I had thought of it. It is my forty acres and a mule so many times over. I must do what it takes to develop it into all that it should be. Shauna was on fire, too. She was darting all over the place trying to see everything at once. I had known varieties of eye candy; but this was ambrosia for the soul for the goddest I was to discover within me? The fog from which I had emerged seemed so long ago. God is so good; if you only discover more of Him. I could let go of the goddest stuff. I would have to be content to see about those things at some time in the future.

Shauna and I agreed to meet in the family room after a shower and a nap. We had planned to go downtown around eight o'clock and dine at one of Charlotte's wonderful restaurants. But the day had overwhelmed us. By the end of it, Shauna and I were both so tired that we ended up crashing for the night. We skipped dinner and did not see each other until the following morning.

As I lay my head against my pillow that night, I ponder over the fact that I own something really big—five hundred acres and a stallion. And now the onus is upon me to do something really big with the land. And my prayer tonight is to be led by might, walk in faith, and to see what might come to God's glory. I thank Zeth, his family and his ancestors and include them in my prayers, and— hmmm— now I will sleep.

At the start of the next day, the words of Ms. Sheryl Lee Ralph about AIDS came to mind: "Redemption for us begins with a conversation; conversations with ourselves, our children and conversations with God." She also said that we couldn't shy away from the conversations and the actions that can save our lives. God had pressed this against my heart—a charge to do something about AIDS. I planned to take twenty-five acres and leverage them for partnerships. The average partnership was $100,000 paid up front, though partnerships would be with my family and maybe Amy. She is my best friend, next to Shauna, but Shauna is family anyway. All partnerships would fall under my parent company though I had not come up with a name yet. But the first partnership would be with Shauna. I proposed giving a deed of five acres to Shauna and leasing five of my own to develop on ten acres a GateKeepers AIDS Prevention and Healing Center—the Charlotte Headquarters. The effort would require that much of the ten acres be developed and leased for R&D, a private counseling center and a pharmacy.

Shauna would own 49 percent of the business and choose the name of the partnership, while the 51 percent ownership would be owned by the parent company. Should Shauna wish to sell any portion of her business, the contract will stipulate that she can sell no more than her five acres and all that stands on it, but the parent company would be entitled to the first bid at fair market value as determined by a third party. If Shauna's interest is sold, however, for whatever amount, the parent company would receive 30 percent of the sale proceeds. Shauna would be allowed to have her PR and event planning office building on location with no more than one acre allowed for administrative offices. The parent company has no obligation to that business whatsoever.

Shauna would be CEO and President of the partnership and responsible for its day-to-day operations. The board of trustees will be the 13-member governing board for the partnership with Shauna as chair and me as vice chair. Both companies would be responsible for securing and paying bank loans, should that be the route taken for financing. It is hoped that Ms. Ralph will be inclined to hold office as ambassador to the president of the non-profit side of the organization. It is further hoped that we will be able to open GateKeepers AIDS Prevention and Healing Centers throughout all the South since the South is the hardest hit area for blacks and AIDS; that is a plan for the future. Shauna would have to meet with Ms. Ralph to get approval for our intended eponymous tribute to her. We are optimistic that she will think that it is a wonderful project and an idea whose time has come.

Most of Shauna's dealings would be to make sure the for profit side of the company makes money to help support the non-profit side. She would also be responsible for procuring grants and donations. We would set up the non-profit side with government funds set aside for AIDS programs and, of course, we would lease out the ten acres of land and buildings which would be used for managing all efforts. The organization would have to sign a 15-year lease. For the non-profit portion, Shauna says she would anticipate very strong support from the NFL, NBA, and she holds great optimism that Burger King or Verizon will adopt this as a target program. Also, we will possibly seek platinum sponsorship from Wal-Mart. The options are serious and endless.

Shauna and I decided to leave home to discuss my proposal. She understood that everything was rough draft and would need the scrutinizing eyes of attorneys and consultants in business ventures, including non-profits. We had brunch at This Side of Heaven, a quaint restaurant in Charlotte which serves wonderful food. We collaborated to knock out as many kinks as we could here and there before consulting an attorney. I know that Shauna is going to make a fabulous partner; she raised questions about things I had overlooked, and had a lot of great ideas. More strategizing had to happen, and we would do that as we discussed plans and put things into place.

Shauna was absolutely overjoyed, too, over the prospects and especially over the idea of the two of us doing business together. We had not yet discussed which piece of land would be used for the AIDS project, and that decision needed to be made post haste. Before we left for the restaurant, I had placed a call to the gatekeeper earlier to find out how far the creek extended, and learned that it stretched over seventy-five percent of the property. Shauna had no knowledge of that fact. After leaving the restaurant, Shauna and I went to the five hundred acres. The gatekeeper was there as we expected. He was sitting on top the Land Rover, in freshly washed, crispy starched and ironed work clothes. But gatekeeper, himself, did not look so chirpy. At that time, I just thought he was feeling a bit down, and might perk up with a nice chat. But I was to learn later that it was a great deal more than what I thought.

"Hello, Mr. Gatekeeper, how are you today?" I asked cheerfully. "Oh, howdy, Miss Zemi. I-umm…fair to middlin' today. Fair to middlin'."

"Aww. What's the matter?"

"Oh, I don't know dat yet. I-umm…goin' to go and see the doctor tomorrow. Hit's a funny thin'. I don't usually get to feelin' so bad much. But I feel all righ' to take you pretty ladies around the property."

"Oh, no, that won't be necessary today, Mr. Gatekeeper," I said. "Shauna and I just want our feet to touch this soil today."

"Hi, Mr. Gatekeeper," said Shauna with a smile. "You have that Land Rover looking pretty spiffy today. Are you going to take that baby out on a date?"

"No, ma'am, Miss Shauna. I already done been on my date last night. But I got the Rover all shiny 'cause I got to go and pick up somethin' from Mr. Zeth, and since this is his truck even though I umm… the only one who drives hit, I always lak to keep hit shiny fer when he sees hit."

"All right, when you're riding in that Land Rover, don't let those young, pretty girls play that heart of yours," Shauna kidded with a smile and a wink.

Mr. Gatekeeper showed all thirty-two of his teeth.

We walked away, but when we reached the gate, Mr. Gate-keeper called out, "Oh, Miss Zemi, don't ferget that you gotta give this here place a name."

"Wow! I didn't know that I had to do that," I said.

"Yes, ma'am. Hit's kinda fer them city plannin' folk. But Mr. Zeth said a name is easy to come up with. He said in normal situations all a person need to do is walk the land every day and study them sur-vey maps of the land, he says, and feel what God gave you. Den a person sho' to come up with somethin' worthwhile."

"Zeth said that?" I asked.

"Yes, ma'am. Jest yesterday."

"Okay then, I will think on a name. And thank you so much, Mr. Gatekeeper."

Shauna and I exited through the gate and strolled along a flower-lined pathway.

"Girl, did you see that Viagra that Mr. Gatekeeper had on the dashboard?" asked Shauna. "No wonder he's not feeling too well. He ought to know that he cannot handle those young girls—at his age."

"Yeah, I hope he gets better. He has such a warm and caring spirit."

Shauna had twinkles in her eyes. She said, "You know that I am already all the way in, Zemi, 100 percent. But I have to ask you a question, and, well, if you say no, it will break my heart, but it has nothing to do with our partnership. I am already involved 100 per-cent as I stated. I do not like beating around the bush with my best friends. So, I really, I mean, I really would like to have my five acres where I saw the creek, or the pond if it's that. I know that is a lot to ask because if you had to sell some acres that would probably be what would sell first and for the most amount of money. But I would do anything to have my five acres on that spot. We can put the AIDS Center there, too, and I promise I will make the center all that you want it to be and that would be the incentive to make me climb all the way up Mount Kilimanjaro." Shauna offered me her most winning smile.

"I will make you proud and that's no joke. Truthfully, that piece feels so spiritual when I'm around it. I will probably have to uproot from California in order to make this partnership work its best. And that's a hard choice because of E.J." Shauna's smile faded and her face clouded when she spoke of E.J.

"Will you give me a moment to think about my answer?" I asked her.

"Take all the time you need," Shauna said gratefully. She turned to look out over the property while she buttoned up her coat against the chilly wind.

"Shauna, are you very clear on the notion that I will not seek any additional help from Zeth in any way to make this project work? I must prove myself on this. Are you comfortable with my decision?"

"Absolutely. If you had Zeth right now helping out, you would not have given up any acres to me in a partnership. And there would be no need for my expertise. But I don't come short either because my big black book lists black and white clients who could use such a tax write-off for our AIDS project. There are corporations, too, that I have worked with already. Don't underestimate your girl over here. I have been into event planning and PR for over a decade now, and I get the picture." Shauna went on, shaking her head, "But I just want you to know that I was paying attention to what Grandma told you about Zeth. Subject opened, subject closed."

If it was about Zeth, I could pass on the subject for now. I went elsewhere. "So what does E.J. think about all of this?"

"Well," said Shauna, "I can't quite figure it out, but E.J. is different. He's changed quite a bit."

"Changed how?"

"For instance, when I told him I was coming down here to work with you in a partnership, he was totally against it. He actually said he hated the idea and thought it was a bad thing to get involved in anything dealing with you. I didn't want to tell you because I didn't want you feeling down again about your relationship with your family, but he does influence my decision—up to a point. Zemi, I have never seen your brother so irate over anything like this before. And, frankly, it bothers me that he is so mean towards you, and I just don't understand why."

"Shauna, but how can you tell me that you are in all the way in this partnership when E.J. doesn't want you involved? I have moved on with my life, Shauna, and I cannot wait around for my family's forgiveness just because I decided to join the Republican Party. If they consider my change in political parties a sin, then I have to say that I know that some of them have done worse things."

Shauna's eyes dulled, and the light from them was gone, just like that.

"Zemi," she said, "this is just between us. I asked E.J. when he planned on marrying me. He answered by telling me that he's never given any thought about a specific date. He just figured it might happen someday on its own. Girl, I wanted to cry me Noah's flood—right there in his office. But guess what Ark saved my pitiful tail? I heard in my head Grandma's words about women always giving men the upper hand. So I waited until I returned home. And when I did, I dropped to the floor and boo-hooed like a baby. When I finally got off the floor and looked in the mirror, I could see that I looked like a prizefighter who surely must have lost. And my insides were all churned up. To'e up from the flo' up was sitting right next to woe is me. I mean I was *besides* myself. Truly. I was sitting one place feeling real bad, but could still see myself right next to me, looking real bad. Like I said—besides myself, girl. My whole soul was gone because that is what I had given to E.J., and when you lose your soul you will do just about anything."

Grief clouded Shauna's face now; she seemed to grow sadder as she spoke. "I couldn't sleep that night so I went over to E.J.'s house about one o'clock in the morning. I slept in his bed, and he stayed up on the couch whispering on the telephone much of the night. When I went into the bathroom, I saw a round trip airline ticket where he had flown nonstop on US Airways from San Francisco into Charlotte. I know he didn't come to visit you because you guys aren't talking now."

"Maybe he had a client in Charlotte."

"No. I know that was not the case, either." Shauna grabbed my hand and leaned forward. "Do you know that type of love, Zemi?"

I held Shauna by the shoulders and looked her straight in the face. "No, Shauna, I don't know that kind of love, but I do know that you will get over feeling this way."

We sat on a bench facing the pathway.

"It is like watching a loved one dying. It is just a matter of time before they are out of your life," Shauna said, wiping her tears. "E.J. was the most important thing in my life," she said, sobbing. "He came first above everything and everybody. He loved that I was that way for him, making him the most important person and putting him above my own life."

I then realized that this was a very fragile time in Shauna's life, but we had things to do and matters to accomplish. Maybe I should wait before letting her sign any business transaction papers. I needed to be sure that she was ready to work with an unburdened mind. What is the benefit to her loving E.J. when he does not want to love her the way she desires? I mean, call me young and dumb, but I held on to Grandma words, "Don't love nobody who don't love you—it is just another form of suicide, the killin' is just slower." Grandma said God created man and woman equally. But some women like to wallow in sundry seas of pity. Some women just can't seem to break that habit.

Grandma said that is why some men get away with treating women as if they are lower than dogs because some women don't know about putting a system in place for self-preservation. She told Maria and me never to be foolish for men because we were taught better. In her view, if the man has more money, that should not change the rule, but she also cautioned us not to marry a man who had less. She said there ought to be a law against two poor, unskilled people marrying because the only thing they can do together is to dig a hole.

The wind was blowing and I had fastened my coat. But the wind and cool air did not seem to bother Shauna. Her hat blew off, and I went to rescue it from the edge of the pond while she acted as if she hadn't noticed.

I returned Shauna's hat to her. The tears had dried up on her face, leaving her makeup streaked. "Why did E.J. take up so much of my time if he didn't want me?" she sniffled.

I really was not the one to give advice, but I gave it a try. "I think E.J. does love you, maybe more so then than now, but things change and people change and that could be what happened with you guys' relationship."

Shauna wiped her nose and snapped the top collar of her coat. "You have such a look on your face, Zemi. What is it?"

"Well, you know, you asked for your five acres to be on the parcel with the pond."

Shauna perked up. "Yes. Goodness, you made a decision already?"

"H-m-m. Yes and no. To be honest with you, Shauna, though you and I are close friends, I am just not sure if you can handle a partnership right now, being so broken up about E.J." I turned to look Shauna straight in the eyes. "I mean what if things get worse between you two? Really, it is like the partnership would be put on hold or something. I don't know if you can function without him."

Shauna took my hand, and spoke with a quiet resolve. "What if I told you that I would be willing to sell my house, move here to Charlotte and do whatever I needed to prove my sincerity to accomplish all that's written in the contract and more? I could still do my event planning from down here. Needless to say, I would welcome a change in scenery. If I did that, Zemi, would you give me the five acres by the pond? I love the cottages and with the building already standing, I could get started on the AIDS project right away."

"Okay I am sold. But I needed you to hear that type of commitment from yourself. The five acres by the pond are yours. I will have the deeds drawn up by the end of next week."

Shauna jumped up and shouted, "Oh, thank you, Jesus!" She balled her hands up and held them up as she screamed, "Yes! Yes! Yes!" Shauna gave me a bear hug. "This will be the best decision you will ever make about this land. Oh, thank you, Zemi! Thank you so much!"

"Shauna, you are welcome. And, oh yeah, I will draw up in the contract so that if you should decide to sell your five acres, the parent company has first bid."

I was glad to see Shauna so excited about the five acres she wanted so badly. I knew then that I had made the right decision. Shauna and I spent the rest of our time mapping out strategies on where to seek funding. Shauna took the lead right away. She said she had some ways of getting the building that was already standing on her acres renovated by improvising a few changes in décor.

This would immediately get the program up and operating, and in a better position before going to the bank.

Shauna closely read the information that Zeth had given me earlier on President Bush's speech to the National Urban League in Detroit where he emphasized minority entrepreneurship. Shauna's thinking process took another leap when she read in the President's speech that Small Business Administration loans to African Americans were up by 75 percent from last year. She knew right away that her company would not be denied the benefits of something that the government already has in place. There was just no reason not to make use of available funding programs.

I had suggested that we use E.J. as our attorney, but Shauna was against it. I ended up telephoning Zeth to ask for use of his attorney but was only able to leave a message. Zeth immediately e-mailed me and suggested I find a separate attorney of my own choosing. He said it was not a good idea for us to share the same attorney. Shauna had the names of a couple of attorney friends in California, but thought someone local would be better for real estate and business deals. I called Mr. Gatekeeper who gave me the names of two attorneys in the area, both of whom were familiar with the land.

Shauna went back to California to get things in order to make her move to the South. Through either e-mail or telephone conversations, I was hearing from Shauna at least seven or eight times a day. In one of her e-mails she asked that I be on the lookout for persons who could qualify for certain employment positions for the AIDS project. She already had in place a Ph.D. candidate who qualified as the director of the program and a person with an MBA for program development. We were on the lookout for qualified persons as an AIDS prevention project administrator, program associate, special project coordinator, administrative assistant, meeting planner, research assistant, a senior intern and five junior interns. I tried not to be frightened by the salaries these types of positions demanded, but with those employees alone, the company would be looking at a gigantic budget of approximately $900,000. That amount did not include miscellaneous staffing, Shauna's salary or mine, or insurance.

For a brief second the thought occurred that I, myself, could do at least four of those jobs, but where would I find the time? If I was going to run and develop five hundred acres from the standpoint of a CEO, I did not need to be bogged down in research. Besides, Shauna was skilled enough in many aspects of the business arena; the working principles are the same, just the level of doing business will have increased. In addition, Shauna has clients who are resourceful; she has surrounded herself with people in all walks of life; she has a plan, and the skills, discipline and passion to execute it. I must allow Shauna the freedom to exercise her creative abilities and fulfill her passion. I believe in Shauna. Bottom line.

* * * * *

Shauna returned to California to collect both her belongings and more of herself. When she left, I felt confidant that she was emotionally strong enough to do the job. I knew that things would still be tough for her, but tough did not rule her out. And that is because in the end, tougher would win the fight. Shauna was tougher; tougher than her dealings with my brother. And I would be pulling for her!

Alone now, I paid a visit to the five hundred acres. I walked and walked, covering as much ground as I could. This was my land! I removed my shoes to feel the dirt beneath my feet. Every place that the soles of my feet touched, God had given to me and even more, so much more. I wouldn't have even cared if someone was filming in secret. I bowed down, kissed the ground, hugged the trees, patted a lizard, caressed a flower, stroked a tree limb, dipped a toe in the creek, skipped stones across the water, danced, and when there was nothing else around for my hands or feet to touch, I threw my hands up in the air and shouted, "This land is my land!"

I returned home, in as much need of a bath as a toddler coaxed from a sandbox. But I would complete a woman's room. Candles flickered and the aromas of oils wafted throughout the house to the tunes of Miles Davis. I relaxed in the tub for a couple of hours, and went deeper and deeper, down into fathoms of mellow. I climbed out of the tub, cuddled a terry cloth robe around my body, and oiled myself down. My body and mind are soothed; I am capable only of sleep. Per chance to dream, and I did dream. In this dream I was caring for the aged, and the resources to do so were abundant, both hard earned and generously bestowed.

At dawn, I awoke to the whisper, "GateKeeper's Village." I lay still and permitted calm to surround, befriend me. My presence of mind was in the presence of God who made it plain to me: Gate-Keeper's Village, Inc., the name for land and the parent company. On this land, I would establish through discrete partnership management at least three key institutions to address matters close to my heart, but closer to the needs of my people. What would they be?

In due course, my plans would be disclosed, but I would not be like Joseph; I would not reveal my dream prematurely. I mean Joseph telling his hateful brothers about his coat of many colors was like walking straight into unknown territory, ghetto or suburban, or country, with a brand new fit, together with a new pair of high end shoes put out by a big baller sports gear endorser, and telling about your plans for your future. So, in time. In time. In time, I would speak. But I needed to give a few people some information on a need to know basis. Joseph needed to know about the need to know basis.

Maybe I got a promotion, I mean like a "life promotion." The Bible talk from Grandma I always figured went into one ear and out of the other; I did not figure that some of it actually stuck between my ears somewhere; I really was not trying to listen, especially on Sundays when in Grandma's house we could not listen to her record player or the radio (forget television on Sundays) unless it was a church worship service aired from someplace, and I wasn't understanding why she was listening to that in the afternoons when we had been to church already, and, as the youngest, I could tell her that. Grandma always used to say "Just keep on livin'." So now I sort of know what that means. Could it be the case that I am now having an experience to make me appreciate the tutelage Grandma gave me long ago? Whereas before I did not like the lessons or had no use for them, now I do? That is the way life goes for all of us, I guess.

Right away, I called Zeth and left a message on his voicemail, telling him the name I had chosen for the land, the estate. Then I called Mr. Gatekeeper and told him. He was so excited that he never stopped laughing, so I had to politely hang up on him—as I was laughing with him. I was certain Zeth would get the message about the new name; either from his voicemail or from Mr. Gatekeeper himself. When I telephoned Shauna in California to tell her the name I had chosen, she, too, started laughing. She told me it was an awesome name, for it stood for so much. And from a marketing point of view, she said that there were a lot of ways to play off the name. Amy was so wild about the name and everything that she told me she was coming down to check things out. I called Maria, and she agreed that the name had awesome potential and would be great for generating publicity. When I called Grandma, she said it sounded like God gave me an assignment.

The part I held on to for a while and did not reveal over the phone was my plan for GateKeeper's Village Senior Haven, a gated luxury community for senior citizens. The community would have everything—restaurant, clubhouse, golf course, billiard room, fitness center, spa, condos and beautiful homes. The layout was going to be magnificent with lush landscaping and the creek-like river already running through most of the property. A stunning waterfall would be a main feature.

I am remembering now a conversation I had long ago with a family friend named Miss Floretta. Miss Floretta seemed to be trying to build up her retirement coffers and was dead serious about it. When it seemed to me that she was obsessed about this money thing, I asked her why she was so intent about having money, and a lot of it at that. And she told me: *So when I am old, somebody in a nursing home won't be beatin' my ass.* My Mother and Grandma would never have to worry about any such beatings. Senior Haven will be built on this estate; it would be here inspired by and mainly for them!

In due and proper time, I let people see my vision about Senior Haven. I took steps to bring all projects together, and worked tirelessly, but I never tired. My passion for all of the work that was to be the fruit of this land, love and labor burned like an eternal flame. (Either that was the case or I was going nuts.)

Proceeds from the sale of my home in California were wired into my bank account. It was a good amount of money, too, thanks to the price of real estate property in California hitting unprecedented high and unheard of increases. Even though the market had softened, there was enough equity in my property to make a small killing. Geez, why are terms so violent? Cancel, cancel. Erase, erase. Let's just say that I made a lot of money selling my house. I had given Grandma power of attorney to handle the signing of all the papers. Now I was able to make some moves here and there. I was able to get a business plan done. I had a logo created and then had T-shirts and bumper stickers made up and sent them out to all of my friends and even my family. Zeth received the first T-shirt made and the first bumper sticker printed. I saw to that.

Mr. G passed out T-shirts and bumper stickers to folk in Charlotte using a list he helped me to create. Mr. G was very intelligent. His speech was not all that spiffy, but if he and Mr. Smart were at a meet and greet, Mr. Smart would be trying to glad hand and rub elbows with Mr. Gatekeeper. Same as me.

My best friend Amy is in Charlotte with me, but she cannot relate to my desire and passion to develop a gated community for seniors. Amy still speaks with her southern accent even though she has been in California for eight years now. She has been in Charlotte with me for only three days.

"Zemi, I know you love your mom and grandma a lot but with your being so young, I can't help but wonder why you couldn't create something for young people. I would have moved to the South to be with you and help out if you had something in mind for young people like me. What could old people possibly get out of such extravagance? This is just a waste of good land and precious time."

I was not in the mood for psychoanalyzing this mixed up friend of mine. Angrily, I said to her, "Amy, it's no more a waste of time than your quitting your job to head up a California College Students for Barack Obama for President Campaign."

Amy was stunned. "Excuse me???" she asked, her voice cracking.

Good, I thought, her ego was limping. Needs to.

"What is that all about anyway, Amy?" I held up my hand to Amy's face. "Ah, ha! Or is it possible that Obama has brought you to the realization that it's okay to be an African American?"

Amy flipped her hair out of her face. Amy's my best friend but why this attitude? Jealousy? Oh. She's talking.

"...I would think that you of all people, Zemi, would believe that it was time to have a black man as President of the United States. At least, E.J. thinks what I am doing is a good thing." Amy's face turned red. She turned from me and walked away, having told me that she was leaving.

Headed to pack her clothes, she yelled, "You know what, maybe E.J. was right about you, Zemi, when he said that you just don't process life and put things together all too well. I used to feel sorry for you when he talked about you that way. But I see what he means now."

I followed Amy to the bedroom. "What did E.J. say about me?"

"Forget it. You wouldn't understand anyway."

"Wh-wh-y would E.J. talk to you about me?" I pressed anxiously.

Amy kept packing and would not look at me. "It's just too hard being friends with you. E.J. told me it was a bad idea to come and visit you anyway. I wish I'd listened to him."

I was really sorry that I spoke to Amy that way. I'd never gotten that upset with her before. It's just that I've always supported Amy and thought she should be supportive of what's important to me. I am so sorry that Amy left Charlotte on such a bitter note. I will apologize to her the next time we talk.

Shauna thought my main reason for taking on this type of challenge, a senior citizens' gated community, was due to my overwhelming desire to have Mother and Grandma close to me. Although that was the utmost consideration, there were other reasons. Ishmael said that with more than 78 million baby boomers already over the age of fifty-five, many having stable income and sufficient good credit, his bank would be more than willing to finance such a sound and well thought out project. Baby boomers are looking for such a place to retire. He said this was a relatively safe investment while I got my feet wet in land development. He was my guide all the way in selecting the right people for me to work with. He suggested I bring Zeth in on the deal, but I just did not see that happening. Maybe I wanted Zeth to come in, but I don't believe that he would at this point.

I was hit with a barrage of Amy's questions about why a senior home by several of my other friends. (These questions were annoying, but not as upsetting to me as when Amy asked them. I expected

Amy to understand, and even if she did not, to support me.) "Why a senior citizens' community and why something so challenging?"

Nonetheless, I forged ahead on the project with creativity and enthusiasm. As the newer owner of the land, I felt compelled to do even greater things with the property than had already been done by Zeth's parents. The words GateKeeper's Village had inspired a promotional frenzy, some paid for, a lot free. The Charlotte newspaper did a big write up on the specs for the planned community. Initially, I was extremely concerned that the venture was being overexposed before it got sound footing, but Shauna assured me that there is no such thing as being overexposed.

She said, "Remember, the name came to you in the dark, and you, Zemi, are supposed to bring its meaning into the light."

Things began developing rapidly and smoothly, too. A force I could feel but not see had graced this venture. What else might explain the flow? On faith, I sent out invitations for the grand opening of the production studios. I had no knowledge in that arena whatsoever and no real passion for a production studio. Go figure. My spirits were in high gear. I was a vessel for a mission not entirely made privy to me, and on this belief, I was ready to forge every mountain, er—every proverbial stream. I found it amazing that I did not take the time anymore to question or overanalyze my actions or seek my family's approval. I was a different kind of person today; I was not playing it as safe, and I was thinking beyond waiting for somebody else setting me free! Huh? I never thought that way anyhow!!!

Imagine sending out invitations for a grand opening ceremony that was to take place in three months without a roadmap, blueprint or master plan? I knew the Creator had a master plan and that I was to put mind, soul, hands and feet to it. Surely, I could be made to look very foolish if it all came to naught. In that case, I would just write a book and tell my story. Everyone has one.

Today, I am spending the whole day at GateKeeper's Village, but in only one particular location—inside the home of Zeth's parents. The architecture is amazing. I went from room to room, upstairs and back down again. I craned my neck back, held out my arms, and gazed in amazement at the chandeliers and extraordinary beveled ceilings, as I twirled and twirled around. I touched the stones of the fireplaces and marveled at how the stones were arranged. For each room, the door handles and knobs boasted distinctive details. And every room showed off its individuality. The deep mahogany paneling surrounded an atmosphere of finery and wealth. And I felt a part of the ambience. Mr. Gatekeeper said the house was built in the mid-1800s. The improvements made sixty or seventy years ago increased total square footage of the house to 19,000.

This is it! It came through the mahogany walls and up from the floors, it sparkled from the chandeliers, and sounded with the turn of every doorknob. The message? Oh, I do hope I am right! Especially when I was slow to heed words whispered directly into my ears! And now I want to believe that walls, and wood and lights could speak? But did not the Lord say that He would be heard? Even if the rocks were to cry out? Yes! Ecstatic? I am! Call me crazy and I do not care, but this land was given to me for a reason—several in fact, and I do believe that I am in His will! If God is for me, then? Nothing else matters! Okay I know this is not how MBA 505 might have taught it! But what I have is greater than a Master or a doctorate. I have a greater understanding of the man, Zeth Higgenbottom! Zeth's spirit is to do the will of God—even without those degrees. This message: This is the home to Our Platform talk show, the beginning of GateKeeper's Village Production Studio! I knew Zeth would have to love the energy that his parents' home was providing for the platform for the voices of the unheard Americans.

I called Maria and asked her opinion of Our Platform as a possible title for a talk show. Maria was eager to be of assistance. She knew about the partnership I had developed with Shauna but had said nothing on the matter.

"Play around with the name Our Platform just a little bit more," Maria suggested. "Create a title that will be a magnet for your target audience," she added thoughtfully. "And certainly Our People's Voice does just that same thing, but it won't hurt to keep brainstorming until you have the right name, the name that will work."

"Maria, do you have any suggestions for a talk show name?" I wanted to pull Maria in more substantively. Without any hint to her, I had already made up my mind that I wanted a partnership with her, and that perhaps a talk show would be part of the plan.

"W-well from what I am hearing you want a title for the talk show, first off. You obviously want to tap into and present to an untapped group of people. There is no platform that welcomes or represents their views. So Our Platform is probably just the fit; it can be the stage for their voices and viewpoints, and evolve as the people evolve. Now, what that means to me is a format that does not need a lot of flash; the format needs to present the concerns of this silent segment of the public. Our Platform allows the audience and program guests to participate in a sort of raw voice format, and that just means without the guise of rehearsal, not fronting for any particular party or sponsor—thus far. But the real great thing about the audience base is not only are they disenfranchised, but they seek change...."

"Maria," I cautioned, "we must be careful. We cannot assume homogeneity either in the views of the un- and under- represented as those views exist now or as they develop in the future. All people need to eat, but everyone does not have the same diet. Ditto for views, other needs and priorities."

"That is so true, Zemi, but let me finish." Maria grew more and more animated as she spoke. "Our Platform is to move the audience from resignation and passivism in poverty and misery to activism for change. And the beginning is dialogue. So the persons invited to speak are key. The program has its agenda, and does not have time to accommodate people who just seek out others to promote their own stuff. As far as sponsors are concerned, the audience includes people yet to make up their minds and, of course, that happens with information given to process issues. In summation," Maria said, "Our Platform is to effect positive change in the lives of viewers."

I could hear Maria take a big gulp from the bottle of spring water she always had nearby. "Wow! Maria you sound more like the professor than actress."

I suddenly realized Maria's spiel might be another one of her finest moments in auditioning, but said, "Gee, Sis, for an impromptu question, you really gave a heartfelt response."

Earnestly, Maria confided, "Well, really Zemi, I must say that although I borrowed a few lines from this part I read for—I did not get the part, they picked a white actress, this girl straight out of drama school—I am feeling what you are talking about. I would have to give much more thought to a name, but Our People's Voices or something like it works. I don't know. Maybe you have a winner already. The more I say, Our Platform, the more I hear and say it out loud, the better it sounds. Just keep giving thought to what you want the talk show to accomplish. That is about the best advice I can give on a moment's notice."

Maria's tone was upbeat but philosophical. But again, I kept wondering if she'd been auditioning for her partnership role. After all, she did admit she "borrowed a few lines" from a script. Geez, why would she even admit that?

"Uumm, I will be finishing up my gig in about four weeks. Maybe then I could come down to Charlotte and be of some help."

I could be mistaken, but Maria seemed ever so humble, sincere even. She went on to explain how in her work she is a professional window dresser, how she is an expert in showcasing and selling, but how in this work, she would deal with real people and issues.

"You know, Zemi, this is very close to my field," she said in summary.

When Maria said those last words, I got it! This was close to Maria's field, I realized. So what if she took lines from a script? Maria was very intelligent, and if art can imitate life, then, for a lofty purpose, then why couldn't life imitate art? I think that happens anyhow, but too much for the worse; this talk show would be for the good. Maria may not have gotten the "art" part for which she read, but she might be just the ticket for the real life Our Platform.

"Okay, Sis, another call is coming through. Thanks so much and I'll call you real soon. Bye." I hung up quickly.

It was Shauna's first call of the day; they have dwindled from about eight to three calls a day.

"Hey, Miss CEO. How are you doing today down there in Southland?"

"Just like you are—on fire, sister, on fire!" I exclaimed. Maria had gotten me fired up again, script or no script.

"I can understand that," said Shauna eagerly. "Listen, I want to get your take on something. Have you checked your e-mail this morning?"

"No, I haven't."

"Could you do me a favor, please? I know you are busy, too, probably in the midst of something thunderous, but could you read the e-mail I sent to you and get back to me ASAP?"

"Sure, I will," I answered and hung up. The curiosity in my voice I knew was unmistakable, but I heard something else? Anticipation? Oh, I should just check my mail! I opened the email from Shauna and it read. The subject line was, Opening statement for invitations:

Finally, you and I seek an America that commits its wealth and expertise to helping those who suffer from this terrible disease. We believe that every person in the world bears the image of our Maker and is an individual of matchless value. And when we see the scourge of HIV/AIDS ravaging communities at home and abroad, we must not avert our eyes. Today, more than a million of our fellow Americans live with HIV, and more than half of all AIDS cases arise in the African American community. This disease is spreading fastest among African American women. And one of the reasons the disease is spreading so quickly is that many people don't realize they have the virus. And so we're going to lead a nationwide effort—and I want to work with the NAACP on this effort—to deliver rapid HIV/AIDS tests to millions of our fellow citizens. Congress needs to reform and reauthorize the Ryan White Act, and provide funding to states, so we can end the waiting lists for AIDS medications in this country—To Whom Much Is Given, Much is Required.

I telephoned Shauna immediately after reading the email.

"Did you read it already?" asked Shauna, high-spirited.

"You better know it."

"Don't have me guessing. What did you think?"

"I think the piece is worded beautifully—and expertly as well," I said.

"Well, first off," said Shauna, "I have to give President Bush most of the credit for that piece in the email. But now we want all of the presidential frontrunners, Obama, Hillary, Edward, Huckabee, Romney, and/or McCain, to focus on the plight of AIDS in the African American community; we want mainstream media to focus on the plight of Aids in the African American community, as well."

"That vision is so important to understand," I said, "and a really great piece to start off with for our project? The Oval office must make the AIDS issue a top priority."

"See," said Shauna, "when the President speaks, people listen. It makes the issue more important." "The part from President Bush was part of his first address at the NAACP Annual Convention. But let me tell you what I wanted to do. I am planning an event called Roll Call, and the theme is If I Care—Will You Help? Roll Call will host AIDS testing in Charlotte about two months from now."

"Do you think you are going to be able to have everything in place within a couple of months?"

"Sure! I am an event planner and last minute is also a part of my expertise; twenty-fours is a long time in event planning, and we get a lot done in just one day. I have already received okays from some NFL, NBA, and WNBA players from around the country who agreed to be tested in front of the cameras. The fanfare will be very similar to when Senator Barack Obama and his wife Michelle were tested for AIDS in Africa. The cameras were there to help bring about awareness of the spread of AIDS among both Africans and African Americans."

"Shauna, please tell me exactly how I can help out so I can get a head start because of everything else that's on my plate. But you know this project is most important to me."

Shauna was pleased with our conversation. I heard a lot of excitement and gratitude in her voice. She shared, "I have invited Ms. Sheryl Lee Ralph and Condoleezza Rice to be our guest speakers. Hopefully, we can get celebrities we respect to agree to be tested in a public forum. I have also asked Judge Joe Brown and Emmy award-winning journalist Harris Faulkner of Fox News Channel to serve as hosts of our daytime events held for the general public. They will be master and mistress of ceremonies for the evening affair for invited guests and corporate sponsors. I have to check my notes here. Let's see. Oh, we are asking Rev. Dr. J. Alfred Smith, Sr. to offer prayer."

"I hear that he is doing so much with AIDS projects."

"Yeah, he is heavily involved with AIDS programs. People do want to help, Zemi. Oakland is very vigilant with AIDS programs as are Pastor Smith and the Allen Temple Baptist Church AIDS Ministry. Dr. Robert Scott, a physician based in Oakland, has been on the battlefield with Allen Temple for years. And they are having phenomenal success with their programs."

"Yeah, that *is* impressive."

"Oh, oh, Zemi, and my good friend Ted Manning said that another way to enhance impact of the event would be to involve Bill Hunter, Executive Director of the National Basketball Players Association and Gene Upshaw, Executive Director of the National Football League Players Association because of their positions and influence. In addition, Ted says the two sports arenas are not only thunder-packed with African American men, but that many of these men are highly regarded celebrities of influence. Those guys are heavily involved with community projects."

I was very excited. "Wow! To pull this event off is big time," I told Shauna.

Shauna answered, "I was hoping you would like the idea."

"I am extremely happy with the idea, but what about the rappers? Why did you leave them out?"

"Please, Zemi," Shauna sighed deeply into the telephone. "I think we would be pushing it in that arena. The NFL and NBA would more than likely sponsor something altruistic in black communities; it would make them look good, but rappers do their own thing. They aren't really held accountable by anybody's standards or opinions. They are just not your benevolent types. I think that might be a hard group to recruit."

"But, Shauna, is it fair to embrace Roll Call, a charitable event that calls forth all types of celebrities to be accountable for AIDS projects, then jump to the conclusion that the rappers won't participate before you even ask? This event may be a defining moment for rappers to do some more good for their community. There is Diddy's 'Vote or Die' program and Russell Simmons and the Hip Hop Summit Action Network to consider. What about Ludacris? He's community conscience. And what about someone like Usher? Everybody is watching him. You just cannot leave people out on an issue so urgent as this."

Shauna was not hearing me. She fussed, "Zemi, there you go again, getting so analytical and high strung over something—over anything really."

This time I ignored her. To think that Shauna likes rap music, but she goes and stereotypes the people whose music she enjoys. The world will learn and not too soon that you cannot think "all" all the time. The world has shrunk, but our perspectives did not have to! Annoyed, I told Shauna, "The rappers must be seen as being as responsible as anyone else who has a public stage. The rappers need to keep watch over this epidemic, too. Their lyrics can be the needed message for this precise time in the lives of African American people—all people for that matter. Not so fast, girlfriend! You cannot just throw away a group that has the listening ears of so many young people. Amy is having a lot of success with rappers showing up to speak at her California College Students for Barack Obama for President Campaign events. Shauna, you should not judge them. Black women are dying, black men are dying, and black babies are born infected."

"I know that Zemi," said Shauna.

"Then call on the rappers. Call them out! It is their onus, too, to help black women and black men, especially down here in the South, to better ward off this disease. Personally, I think they will answer the call. Most certainly," I said, convincing myself as much as I was trying to win over Shauna.

"Oh, yeah." Shauna was skeptical still; I did not win her yet. "What makes you so sure, Zemi?" she asks.

"Because I believe that rappers and hip hoppers are called, too, to be gatekeepers. Their music has been around for decades now. Can you imagine how many artists and their fans are approaching and have reached middle age? I believe these younger artists are just biding their time. The smart ones know that it is just a matter of time before they must pour out God's message. God's way will take center stage. After all, it really is God's stage and His alone. Any voice, any ear, any rhyme or rhythm, any rap or tap of any artist is a gift from God. Speaking of tappers, the late greats knew that. Did you know that William Robinson gave up perhaps more charity concerts than perhaps any musician in his day? And during the Great Depression, William..."

"Excuse me, who?" Shauna asked.

"His stage name was 'Bojangles,' but, as I was saying, Mr. Robinson would see a family cast on the street along with their furniture and personal effects. He would pay the back rent, and then hire out-of-work men to move the family back into their apartment. Bill Robinson was a serious and committed man. He and other late greats. The greats still with us know. Any future greats will also know, and act on that knowledge now."

* * * * *

OUR PLATFORM: To say it was a challenge to find a niche in the talk show arena is an understatement. The idea was not to mimic established talk shows or their hosts. In fact, I don't know if I should be the one to host Our Platform. Perhaps that concern will be addressed further down the road. Our Platform is not about any individual or personality. The show concerns systemic causes of appalling conditions left lingering within the communities of a people who have become the lesser of the choice between saving an animal's life and the lives of human beings. Our Platform is not a talk show for the edification of sundry needy egos in politics, entertainment, government or even religion and business. It will definitely not be a talk show for those who wish to compromise the needs of one people to secure the loyalty base of another. Our Platform is not for those who wanted to show off their bling-blings as a symbol of acceptance, bearing yet a false status passport. It is not a freak show to display the debauchery of lewd and lascivious lifestyles for high ratings at the expense of tormenting and confusing further the minds of our young. It is not a show for idiocy, buffoonery, lampooning or comedic relief. It is not a stage for those who wish to take advantage of the most unfortunate groups of people.

Instead, Our Platform offers uninformed, underexposed, poor and black people an opportunity to talk to mainstream America in a rare, (almost "raw") format—to make them listen. Our talk show will demonstrate through unconventional methods the under performance of government. It will expose how the opportunity of public education for all is no longer a priority of our national government. It will take the time to lay open Hollywood's detriment to the psyche of all Americans and show how some actors and actresses are used to sustain the deluge of negativity.

Our talk show will provide a forum for people of this country to talk to each other; to have conversations about what concerns them. (We are talking about topics such as "Black women as positive role models.") We need more shows like that. Our show will encourage American people to see one another heart to heart. This will place the onus on those looking to internalize their observations and consider changes in personal outlook and actions to effect positive change. Such actions might, in sum, be what President Bush relates to as compassion, a compassion that could help American people to exemplify the good of a superpower. On the stage of Our Platform will be real people and real circumstances without staged affect or ornamentation. This will enable us to capture more succinctly the essence of conversations from voices that must be heard. Our stage will allow people who for all intent and purposes have been mute to speak openly and earnestly and be heard by all of America. And so, the dialogue begins.

This is Zemi Navies' (my) "stream of conscious version" of my vision for Our Platform. Of course, it will be tweaked and re-tweaked with the input of other team members and the media host and experts we anticipate bringing on board!

* * * * *

Only a month and a half away before GateKeeper's Village Production Studio was to celebrate its grand opening and the company was taking a nontraditional (circuitous?) route to establishing a financial portfolio. Portfolio, profile, whatever. Hmmm. Power? Potential? Presidency? Hmmm. Through the proverbial grapevine, I heard that another power word has been buzzing around inside Maria's head for several months: Partnership. Even though I had not spoken a word about a partnership to her. She must have felt the time was near because I heard that she was thinking about putting her house in California on the market.

Shauna has a new friend now. I guess he was the balm she needed to soothe the pain of ending her almost ten-year relationship with E.J. Anyway, Shauna's new friend is a financial adviser and was able to assist Shauna in acquiring capital financing, $500,000 for each $100,000 she was able to raise and put on deposit. I raised $275,000; a $100,000 loan came from Shauna, her partnership compensation for the first year, and $175,000 out of the money from the sale of my home in California. (Trying to be prudent about things—ha!—I banked nearly all of the proceeds from the sale of my home.)

Oh, Maria. (There is so much to do right now. Truly.) I had not discussed a partnership with Maria earlier because I felt she exuded such a whimsical Hollywood persona. Business never appeared to be either her forte or interest. I was concerned about whether she was intense enough and could inspire the confidence of the people we would need to have behind us. See, Maria was always anticipating or looking for the next gig; it was just hard to know if she would dedicate herself to running a business, something not nearly as sexy as the acting for which she demonstrated such a strong passion. Plus, Amy has always said that she finds it difficult for blacks to work well with family in business. But how could she know? I still had Maria to consider. I was not quite sure what Maria would bring to the table right away, other than at least another $100,000 from the sale of her home. But the money was on the table—I could see it and feel Maria's energy; she was a racehorse chomping at the bit.

Acting roles in Hollywood for black women seemed to have all but dried up. And the roles that black women appear in seem much too insubstantial to consider serious. A lot of black actresses have resorted to playing other than what the masses want to see projected across the screen—such as lesbians, prostitutes and such comedic roles that they don't draw much of a crowd as some of them might have in the past. Although Maria is a talented and skilled actress, her dream of co-starring opposite a black man in a top notch film was so implausible. I think long ago she shoved that dream all the way to the back in a file labeled, "Deferred." Black women in Hollywood do not make any real money compared to your highest paid white actresses. Staggering Hollywood payouts (the $25 million bracket) go first to white male actors. Only a minuscule number of black male actors are in that club. There are some white females in the $15 to $25 million pay scale. But black women just can't seem to command comparable opportunities and pay.

Procrastination is not an option. I call Maria and talk partnership. Within three weeks I am picking her up from CLT Airport. She looks different; her attire expresses individuality, but stated sophistication, and with no doubt. She seems tired (probably jet lag) but eager; youthful, but mature. We talked about the studio on the drive to the land. For some reason, she was not so La La Land-like. Perhaps because of the change in the color of her hair. She had worn it red for so long that I'd forgotten she was born with black hair. Oh! She cut her hair! She had gone from long to short. I am impressed, but kept that close to the vest.

Once we arrived, Maria appeared taken by everything. But strangely, the gatekeeper was not on the land. Maria and I sat down on my favorite bench. She commended Zeth and I picked a hint of apology in her voice.

"My hat's off to Zeth," Maria said earnestly. "I misjudged Zeth, as well as the value of the five hundred acres he gave you, just because it was land located in the South. I have expressed such ignorant and stereotypical views of the South that I hope I have not jeopardized any real future here. I know that we are on as far as the partnership; I guess I just want you to forget the things I said, Zemi."

I had to communicate my concerns to Maria about whether or not she could do the South for the long term and make a successful go of things. I was trying not to show reservations regarding her capabilities and hoped my face would not betray me. But my sister has always been able to mystify me.

"Maria, look, this is the biggest endeavor of my life. Needless to say, I have taken on a lot for a woman so young, but feel I need to put whimsical aspirations aside now to emulate our elders and ancestors, to build institutions. Since I have youth, it will be an asset because I can trade on health, well-being and strength to see the projects through. So my youth will not be a distraction or liability."

"So true," said Maria.

"Maria, you are family, and we were taught always to love family, and sometimes the word love must be accompanied by a demonstration of that love. And, yes, there is such a thing as unconditional love, but even with that type of love, I would think some level of trust must be there. Dad's love extended beyond just his immediate family. He took on the whole African American race as family. Mother says his love for black people was, in fact, his overdose."

Maria fidgeted nervously.

"You see, Maria, this land isn't just about my success. It is something more. You know the old saying, 'He that possesses freedom from guilt may open his eyes to see the vision now and with an obedient mind will understand the way to lead.' So y-you…."

Maria interrupted me and looked me squarely in the face. She took my hand. "Zemi, I know you have concerns about my abilities in certain areas, and you are right to hold such reservations about me. But harboring uncertainties about me is not the way to begin a partnership. I have somewhere to go to in life, too. And besides that, Dad didn't give just you all the brains, in spite of your conceit."

We both smiled. Maria let go of my hand and patted my cheek.

"I was the older sister. I had to establish my position as such. When we were growing up, Mom and Dad always told me to watch out for my baby sister, and I was to make sure you did the right thing. You became my responsibility. I always saw myself as the one who had to keep you in your place so I got my respect, and you would do what I told you to do. But the bottom line is Mom and Dad believed in and trusted my abilities. When they had other things to do, you were the precious cargo they left with me, not E.J., Rodney or Joey, but *me*. And look at yourself, honey. I did a damn good job with that responsibility, too."

"Look, Big Sister," I said twirling my glove. "Don't go too far out there, overpricing your tail. But you did do all right." Our laughter brought levity; our sisterly connection was stronger instantly.

"I guess what I wanted to say, Zemi, is that I don't have the energy chasing Hollywood to make them see my talent as an African American woman who can really act if given the opportunity. And though I recognize my gift, it was never meant to be Hollywood's harvest. It took me a while to know that. But I am ready to rise above expectations and make a name for myself with my own endeavors. And with all that said, Zemi, hopefully, now you have become the enlightened one." My sister gave me one of her dazzling smiles.

I hugged Maria. "I have, Maria. And I might add, that was your greatest performance ever. You have convinced me."

Later that day, Maria went over the partnership business plan. Changes were made to sweeten the deal for her company. Maria wanted the five acres containing four cottages and two bigger buildings situated between GateKeeper's Village Production Studio and the spa. I was okay with the request since her 49 percent share had no ties to the acreage where the spa was located or where Zeth's parents' home was situated. At the end of the day, both of us felt like winners. Maria became CEO and the executive producer and host of Our Platform.

Maria and I met weekly in my office to collaborate on themes for potential talk shows. I was there for whatever she might need, but I knew she was in the batter's box, not I, and I felt confident that she would hit a home run. Maria stayed with me while her cottage was being designed in a style similar to Shauna's. They both used the same company, Lance Owens & Company of Charlotte, mainly because Mr. Owens, the owner of the company, demonstrated his intuitiveness, respected and abided by the desires of his clients, but at the same time could introduce ways to enhance their plans. Mr. Owens' company was a business successfully run by a black family. So there, Amy! Their company had masterfully transformed Zeth's parents' home into the elegant and well-appointed GateKeeper's Village Production Studio. Here is how that went. Mr. Owens had a theme in mind that he thought would draw out the beauty of the estate. The theme would convey, though subtly, the connection of a people to North Carolina. (He also owned a mansion on the lake in the Sail View suburbs and thought that I should visit his property in order to get more ideas and a better vision for Zeth's parents' estate.) Mr. Owens came out to the estate to sketch my concept so that we both could see my ideas as I saw them. He was a master at his craft and liked for his clients to be intimately involved with the planning to ensure the desired outcome.

The improvements embellished the ambience, opening up space here and there but retaining the original atmosphere characteristics of the main house and the small cottages. Authentic ebony statues were well placed at focal points within the 19,000 square-foot mansion. A bronze plaque telling the history of the estate accompanied each statue. Mr. Owens' fastidious taste and selections bestowed upon GateKeeper's Village Production Studio an awe-inspiring museum effect. African masks and huge drums placed by Mr. Owens on the generous landing between the ground and second floors doubled as décor and conversation pieces alike. The motif of the window treatments and wallpaper thread together African and African American themes. Mr. Owens' professionalism and work were outstanding, and I am so pleased.

The interior of the estate was nearly complete, but I had to wait for a message, namely, what to include as the final signature touch. And it came. The message. Sepia-toned and black and white photographs of the Higgenbottom Family, including mid-nineteenth century daguerreotypes, were reframed and hung on the wall of the long staircase. (One was Zeth's baby picture; he looked into the camera daring it to doubt him.) But the centerpiece? I had a picture of Zeth's parents turned into a painting, and hosted its unveiling. The unveiling of the framed portrait was well attended; people went "ooh" and "aah" all about. The portrait was placed in the foyer of the home, where people upon entering could meet the ancestral gatekeepers of this grand estate. The true Gatekeepers of the Village. During the unveiling, my soul soared! A spirit was there. And it embraced me. After the ceremony, I stole away to the foyer and looked up at Zeth's parents. My eyes welled as they spoke to me and said, "Well done, Zemi. Well done." I knew the day, too, would come when Zeth would be pleased and he, too, would speak those same words.

Maria worked assiduously, most of the time getting no more than four hours of sleep a night. She watched all kinds of talk shows and particularly liked the format of Hannity and Colmes of Fox News. Maria was ready to start the talk show, but the sound stage in the studio had unanticipated design defects and probably would not be ready by the scheduled date.

Maria now seems aloof, almost distant. I just thought she had developed some intensity to help her prove whatever she thought she had to prove. So, I let her be; after all, I did have enough to do.

This afternoon, Maria calls Shauna and me and requests an unscheduled meeting in her cottage. Maria could have had the meeting at the studio made available for her use and Shauna's at anytime. They both have keys and each has a small office inside the studio. But Maria's cottage was extremely nice. Mr. Owens had done a really great job. (From time to time I noticed when he went to Maria's cottage in the late afternoons.)

Maria had salad and crispy dipped garlic bread ready in a bowl and glasses of spiked casaba juice prepared for us. It was nice to see Maria entertaining for a change. Is that what she was doing? In any case, she was definitely feeling in charge of her own space. Mine and Shauna's, too? The food was quite tasty, and the brief respite from our micro rat race was refreshing. This was awesome. We were doing it!

"Hey, y'all," Maria said in a mock, exaggerated Southern accent, "since I am an official resident of the South I might as well blend in."

Shauna's face went to matter-of-fact look. "I am anxious to know what the meeting is about," Shauna says. "Seems to me the smarter thing would be not to blend in that way but rather to stand out. I am beginning to realize that a lot of people here in the South were born elsewhere."

"Yes," Maria agrees, "you are probably correct about that, especially when I think about the demographic research I just acquired." Maria reached behind her chair and handed Shauna a thick booklet on demographics and breakdowns about North Carolina. "Here. I think when you take a look inside you just might find information useful to incorporate into your proposal and grant writing. On an even more serious note though, I have given careful thought to the idea that I should be the first of the partnership out there in the public's eye with the talk show, er... ahead of you guys." Maria paused. There was a long silence.

"Uh-huh," Shauna acknowledges, sipping her juice. "And?" she asks.

"Well," said Maria, "I thought this would be the best way to introduce the upcoming AIDS testing to take place here at GateKeeper's Village." Maria handed us an outline. Her confidence was surfacing big-time. "A presentation of the history of the land would help to introduce our work, including the studio and, likewise, the AIDS center. And, Zemi, here is where your passion comes in. The talk show topics would encompass many of the topics you feel strongly about. I am thinking of how you are always talking about how women of African descent in America should join forces for a New Black South and for self-empowerment throughout the country."

"That was summed up nicely," I said.

"Well, of course, it all makes sense to do the introduction of each partnership and at the same time introduce each of us as individual personalities. Within the framework of Our Platform, all of this ties in as being the way to establish other platforms for the voices of African Americans, no matter which class of blacks; through Our Platform their voices can be heard, loudly and clearly. And I will talk more about that as we go along. But what we want to do is to get the public involved immediately; we want the public to participate, to be enthusiastic about what we are doing. In the trade, this is called creating the buzz scenarios. Are you guys following so far?" asked Maria.

"So far I am with you, Maria," said Shauna, "and also I would just like to interject by saying that your marketing strategy has widespread appeal and presents guidelines for possible next steps."

"I guess the main effort and pitch is to focus on what happens in the lives of African Americans for public interest stories," I said.

"You are right," said Maria.

Maria was drawing us in; she was getting us to see ourselves as a part of her vision. I was happy to see that Maria was able to realize her ideals through GateKeeper's Village.

"This might be an afterthought, but I guess that just about any aspect of African American life can be noted and discussed on Our Platform. We can explore much and still remain on task. In a way, we could be the grapevine of information for targeted audiences; the ideas presented by the show might springboard positive actions in their communities," said Shauna.

"Exactly," injected Maria, whose mind and body seem to run off of sheer drive and hunger. "We will be the agents of change."

I was very slow to speak. "Okay, I am confused about two things. First, is the hype of Our Platform that it is the cutting edge think tank for connecting the mindsets of blacks in America? Is this our first task?"

Maria shook her head, and bit her bottom lip.

"It is a first task in that it presents simultaneously all the other projects taking place. Almost for right now anyway, every single thing is interdependent in that we have to feed off of each other for the success and completion of all that is at stake or this moment won't grandstand," she explained, although I still did not quite get it. Was this from Maria or more "borrowed lines"? I knew that Maria wanted to make sure that both Shauna and I were accepting of our roles, but make no mistake about it: Our Platform was Maria; she was definitely the one for center stage. I was very happy about Maria taking the lead in that format.

"Certainly we each have our own spin," said Maria. "But Our Platform will extend a public invitation to the open house of the studio and AIDS center. We will also arouse melodrama around the Who's Who list of North Carolinians and, really, our guest list will extend from around the country. All of these agenda items are the sparks and flames to ignite the kickoff for so much of what we are doing at first," said Maria.

"Let's not forget to include word of mouth as a strategy for disseminating information about who and what we are," I said.

"Word of mouth is an important piece of advertisement, no doubt, and we will take advantage of that whenever and wherever that is happening. But we must be proactive, too, in generating excitement about our noble efforts right here in Charlotte. The key is that we present what we want out there on our projects as the first public release of information, and let word of mouth pick up from there—so the right words get out there from the right mouths. Our Platform will be the primary forum used for our projects to become public interest stories. And then advertisers and sponsors will follow the hot trail—the way a man follows the scent of a woman," laughed Maria.

"Maria," I smiled, "you've just got to throw a man in there somewhere, don't you?"

"Catch this, Zemi. I am just being what God made my nature to be," Maria said smugly. "Therefore, it is my nature to always want to have men around me. Sometimes girlfriends and sisters can be so routine," she said. Using her forefinger to stress each syllable, she added, "Women can become mo not o nee. And that ain't working for my a-nat-o-mee." Making an exclamatory point, she set her glass down on "mee."

Shauna chuckled and observed, "There is nothing wrong with having men around when you have it that way."

"Now, Shauna," said Maria, moving on, "I understand that you do have some key athletes from the NFL who will recruit other athletes to participate in the AIDS event. Their participation either through sponsorship and/or getting filmed taking an AIDS tests will be just remarkable. Since you are the event planner for everything we do, we need to arrange a time for those guys to do some cameo appearances to tell people why they decided to participate in the GateKeepers AIDS Prevention and Healing Center. We will make that a big story, seeing such together young guys in a sports arena taking the test, now that's big! Your company will also need to make sure that the sponsors who advertise on the talk show are on board for the day and night events." Maria stopped briefly and consulted her notes. "I created the opportunity to talk to and interview spokespersons for sponsoring companies. Some companies are going all out by allowing their employees who want to volunteer to take the AIDS test to leave work for a couple of hours to be tested. And we will consult legal counsel to make sure we are in compliance with the Privacy Act regarding information gathered from people who agree to the tests."

I glanced at the materials and noticed something. Something I did not like. "Whoa, Maria," I said, taken aback. What is she doing? I had just noticed the date at the bottom page of the outline. "Whoa," I repeated, waving my outline, and I knew I had a frown on my face, and hoped it was all I needed. "Maria, have you forgotten that the studio is not going to be ready for the scheduled date, yet you are making all of these plans?"

"Oh, I forgot to explain something. I am getting ahead of myself here." Maria spoke in a hurry. Car salesman-like?

"Maria," said Shauna passing Maria a glass of water, "calm down. You are pacing ahead like a sho' 'nuf hustler, talking like this is Three Card Monte and Zemi and I have to find the hidden card. Are you the same Maria I once knew in California?"

"You know I am not capable of scamming you guys, Shauna. But I am sorry, you guys," Maria apologized. "I just cannot turn off my engine. But I will try to slow down some. Now, Zemi, I know that we do not have the studio ready yet, but it is too risky to wait two more months before we can work from the studio. Now what I did was, I…gee…" Maria removed her sweater and fanned her face.

"Are you all right?" Shauna asked.

"Yes, I am. As I was saying, my marketing agent, Albert U. Greene… well, we have become close, and he has worked out a deal with one of his clients whereby Our Platform can use his luxury motor home to host the talk show on the road, I mean, just locally—around Charlotte. If you look on the third page of your outline, you will see photos of the inside of the motor home along with the contract information. But, get this, his client is going to let us use the luxury motor home almost for free. All we have to do is pay the insurance on it for two months and give the client free advertising as a sponsor. Those types of luxury motor homes are the bomb! They range from $250,000 to $400,000 to purchase. Albert said that he thinks this one is in the $400,000 range and that the owner only uses it whenever he's lucky enough to be in town on Sundays to catch home games of the Panthers." I was stunned.

"Zemi, you look as if you just turned off a scary movie."

"Maybe because this feels like Halloween and I don't know yet if it is a trick or a treat. I mean, it is quite a stretch to try to fathom Our Platform telecast from a motor home."

"I'm with you on that, Zemi," Shauna piped in. She was frowning, too, looking like she had just eaten something that tasted real nasty.

Maria resorted to preachy. "Look, guys, it's time to get this show on the road and literally, too. You guys need to be a little bit more imaginative," she fussed, adding, "envision what a moment like this could present. To me it almost seems to be in divine order."

Now she was imagining herself a goddess? I swallowed; I felt like puking. "Maria, I wish there was some shred of hope in that statement. How do you get to something so way off base?" I asked her.

"Look, Zemi," she snapped.

I hear defiance?

"Zemi," she was saying, "the people here in Charlotte don't know who we are. They don't even know we exist," she replied. She got up and adjusted the ringer on her cell phone.

"I think perhaps we all should turn off our cells off, you, too Maria," I said. It was a comment and not a suggestion, and judging from the faces, they got it. We needed to talk, and without interruption. Maria was mute to that and was still trying to explain what sounded to me like what Daddy would have called a wild goose chase.

"So, to start off, we need to make such an impact in the communities that we'll capture the true essence of our audience employing a human interest type of approach. We don't want to frighten them off with matters so heady and grave. So, for the first two months of the show, we really get to mingle with the people. No one has to know that our studio isn't ready yet. Really, this luxury motor home makes a statement. I, for one, would not be ashamed to cruise around the communities in something so vogue. Black folk have always been about setting trends. Besides, I think that the real folk would love to see us pulling up in their neighborhood to talk just to them. We come with compassion to our own. It's okay, Zemi. This will work. Rest your fears. I know how to handle this one." Maria closed her notebook shut, as if to say the discussion was over.

I folded my arms and huffed, "Oh, so that is how you come to it being divine? Now I see the light." If only saliva were sarcasm, my words would be suitably coated. Nasty? Well, I am thinking that I hope this will not get nasty.

Maria held up a sheet of paper. "I went to see the luxury motor home the other day," said Maria. "That bad boy was perfect in every detail, style and oozed power. It was designed with your total pleasure in mind. It is good for driving on the open roads and high-ways. Everything about the luxury motor home says, 'Spoil your-self.'"

"Maria," I tried to reason, "do you think we should look like we are basking in luxury? What philanthropists would want to give their money for that? And in some of these communities, the people are downright poor. Give it some serious consideration in light of our purpose and goals. Should 'fabulous' be our image? I mean are we trying to look like some storybook royalty parading before sub-jects of the kingdom, and that is exactly what comes to mind. My mind, at least. If we put it out like that we would be like the naked emperor, only clothed, but people could see right through us. We would be no better than the people we say are just fronting for lead-ership. Think about that, would you?"

"Now Zemi, you need sponsors and advertisers to help you make things happen. Right now we have to bring things to the peo-ple and the poorer communities at that. We must spend out of what we have at hand. You want to let people know that you can do well at doing business in the South. If you start looking poor and acting poor around these people, then you will lose any platform that has been created. If you're not doing any better than poor people, then why should they think that you know what works? My dear, sweet, young and highly educated sister, you cannot explain everything that works in life from an intellectual standpoint, at least not with the audience we are going after. Why do you think rappers have such influence over so many? It is because they show to tell. Folks are worn out with people telling them that money isn't everything. I told you this was not just any old motor home. This type of luxury motor home is a gift from God. You don't have to hide God's bless-ings," said Maria.

Shauna agreed with Maria on this point.

Two against one, I'm feeling.

"I am thinking the same way, Maria. If God gave it to us, let's roll with it," said Shauna. "And if we should get a flat somewhere down the road, God will just have to pump it up again."

Annoyed, I reminded Shauna, "God is God all by Himself and He has to do nothing he does not please to do. And as Grandma said a guy named Fosdick said, God is not some cosmic bellhop. So let's be careful. And we are not trying to look like prosperity gospel hawkers, complete with wheels. Nobody is going to accuse our companies of carpet bagging through town, luxury wheels or no."

Both Maria and Shauna looked and waited for a definitive response.

"But I do agree to hear this through," I said begrudgingly.

"Okay, Zemi. We hear you don't we Shauna? Since I am an actress, I have pretended to be a lot of things in that arena so I would not have to pretend in real life. As it is in real life, I am never going to pretend that I am poor, ignorant or not freed." Maria spoke earnestly. "Zemi, I see us reaching out to a culture where people's aspirations are perhaps undeveloped, but definitely unmined. I see us reaching out to our people who are rootless, but still they seek hope from God, and, Zemi, we are a part of that hope, just presented by something tangible to help them to see their way out. Black people hurt and I can feel the pain. There are some people out there who really don't know how much black people suffer inside," said Maria. "I mean. My goodness. So much pain." Maria took another sip of water.

Maria could hardly contain her melodrama. Acting again? Must be something divine.

Continuing, she said, "Those people who are unable to see the inside of people do nothing. Do they get a free pass to walk away without being accountable? I don't know the answer to that. But you do have some people who do know what it's like to hurt from the inside out because they have experienced suffering for themselves. Still, it is easier for them to walk away than to kick in some humanity that might help them to act. I've been there. I learned what it is like to try so hard to identify with other groups when I was in Hollywood. The harder you tried, even to a point of giving up your soul, the more Hollywood despised that which you tried becoming. It seems to me that all three of us should identify with God's abundance and not deny it, and definitely we should not reaffirm a spirit of poverty and helplessness as so many others choose to do, even those called to help the less fortunate."

Reticently, I gave in. "Okay, I'll be a team player. I just hope that I am exercising the better part of my judgment. I'll roll with the punches."

"No, baby," said Maria. "You will roll with style, I can promise you that. Let me tell you all about this motor home. Look on your outline; it's all there. The interior is exquisite and is incredibly spacious. The interior height is seven feet, and it has mirrored ceilings, expansive double-pane windows and halogen lights throughout. It has stunningly coordinated colors and fabrics in the coach from the inviting living area to a private spacious bedroom with a king-size bed. It has granite tile floors and a granite shower, a slide out granite table, a camera monitoring system, an electric fireplace, a dinette, leather sofa, workstation, and entertainment center. Plus it has surround sound, a 40-inch, high definition television, satellite radio, multiplex lighting, stainless steel residential refrigerator and freezer, stainless steel microwave and convection oven. It has a stacked washer and dryer, dishwasher, power awning, outside entertainment center with slide out TV and stereo, a second king-size bed, a sofa bed with air mattress, a safe, and an electric commode— and, of course, it's fully air conditioned."

"Okay, Maria, we get the picture," I said.

"I just wanted you guys to know that we can make this work," Maria said, and smiled. Sincerely?

* * * * *

I got extremely busy; in fact we all did. Shauna was busy talent scouting for persons who have experience in managing AIDS support centers and wellness programs. Maria was traveling a lot, interviewing possible co-hosts for Our Platform. Unfortunately, I was stuck up in a macro level, at least for the moment. My company included paperwork and reports and figures and accountants and lawyers and insurance people and licensing and permit people. This was definitely not the sexy part; and, weeks later, I was glad to crawl out from a miasma of considering this and thinking over that.

Shauna and I received an email from Maria that read:

Zemi and Shauna,

I think I might have found the perfect co-host: the very talented Laurel Swopes; I am sure you might have heard of her. Anyway you will meet her soon enough. I am doing some trial runs with her on the road and will have a better idea of how she works out when I return.

See you soon,
Maria

A week went by and no Maria. No calls. No answers to her cell. No returned messages. Inspiring confidence? Not mine. Finally, we received a second email from her:

Zemi and Shauna,

We have taken the show up and down the coast of the Carolinas. Many of our productions worked. With different pitches, we have successfully marshaled the concerns of the people, and from that Laurel and I have formed a proposed framework for Our Platform to implement once in studio.

See you soon,
Maria

Shauna and I had not yet met Maria's co-host; the only thing we were told was her name, Laurel Swopes. Maria said she wanted someone the opposite of herself, but Maria said she had to change quickly and take on the role of a host from the Independent Party. Laurel was a die-hard Democrat and would not stray from that for any reason. Maria said that it was important that her co-host looked African American, a look like Harris Faulkner of Fox News. She did not want to give her audience the impression of what Hollywood had passed on to other directors and producers—that black women had to look European or Caucasoid in order to have a viable future with a network. The masses of African American women certainly do not look mixed. Our Platform would like to see the darker hue presented along with black women of other skin tones so that a complete picture of African American female beauty is offered.

Maria gave Shauna and me a syllabus of the format and content for Our Platform. The beginning part was from a historical perspective. Shauna was concerned that since a first-glance presentation of Our Platform was from a luxury motor home, she strongly hoped the substance of the program is what people would see. Shauna also expressed concern that Maria might lose her audience with so much serious data. Maria felt she needed to convince Shauna that, although she was new to the talk show arena, she, nevertheless, had surrounded herself with knowledgeable and experienced mentors.

Maria's marketing agent, Albert Greene, was also a marketing agent for Laurel Swopes, and he alone was the reason for her co-host position with Maria. Albert Greene felt the two women co-hosts would strike quite an attractive image and build a following, an audience that eagerly anticipated the next show featuring two beautiful headstrong women with contrasting views. Usually, on talk shows women pretend to get along, but Albert Greene had said he knew that these two women would get along like oil and water—and that was the intent anyway.

At my urging, Maria scheduled an appointment for Shauna to meet with Maria and Laurel Swopes; the meeting was scheduled to take place at Ms. Swopes' office at VL Satellite Radio in a prime real estate location in Charlotte. For some reason, Maria seemed hesitant about Shauna's meeting Laurel so soon. But I felt that if the three women were to work together, a synergy needed to be formed earlier than later; that way, Shauna—who has been in on everything from the beginning—would not be joining the other two as though she were crashing a party. Grandma did "learn me" something! I would attend the meeting mainly to stay informed, for my edification.

Shauna, Maria and I were all dressed to the nines. But the impression we made paled in comparison to that of Ms. Swopes. Ms. Swopes looked like she had stepped out of a 5th Avenue display window. She came salon-dressed and her coif professionally finished to the last soft and lovely lock. That Maria was in awe of Laurel Swopes should have been no surprise; we should have gathered as much from the emails and telephone conversations.

"Shauna Anderson, Ms. Laurel Swopes," said Maria, moving to the side, as she introduced them.

Shauna looked stunned. "Hello," Shauna said, extending her hand to Ms. Swopes. I thought a bit half-heartedly. "...I believe we've met you before," Shauna added. "Your name...It was at-tt...." Shauna stopped mid-sentence.

"Odd," Ms. Swopes remarked shaking Shauna's hand. "Usually I don't forget a face."

"And this is Zemi Navies," Maria continued.

"I am very pleased to meet you. I want to thank you personally for this fabulous opportunity and joining our meeting."

"I am just sitting in," I explained, "—to receive a lesson from the three of you on the art of promotion—and, you are very welcome. And thank you for joining our team." I smiled, hoping Ms. Swope wouldn't expect much input from me.

Ms. Swope smiled generously, showing gorgeous cosmetically finished teeth. "I am glad to meet you both. Please have a seat," she invited. Extending a smooth, brown arm at the end of which was a baby-smooth hand and a set of natural, long nails any woman of style would covet, Ms. Swope waved to overstuffed chairs facing her spacious, executive desk. Not a thing on the desk, clearly a power statement. On the credenza behind her was a library of the trade, and a gold gilded name plate that read Laurel V. Swope in fancy lettering.

"This is really a beautiful office," said Shauna, a bit nervously. She said to Ms. Swope, "You look so familiar," Shauna suggested.

"Well, I am kind of a public figure, so that does not surprise me. But thank you for the compliment to my office. It was done by designer Lance Owens & Company."

Shauna was probably afraid to say that she had used the same designer. Maria did not speak up, either. Before seeing Ms. Swope's office, both Maria and Shauna thought Mr. Owens had made their offices extraordinary. The difference was stark; this office was higher than one cut above. Truly, what you end up with is what your money could buy, and obviously Ms. Laurel wrote a bigger check for her exquisitely-appointed digs. Maria was still standing, captivated by the museum quality fine art that graced the walls.

"Why don't you sit here, Maria?" Ms. Swope indicated a chair next to Shauna. "Would any of you like something to drink...or perhaps a Danish or chocolate croissant?" she offered.

"Ooh, a chocolate croissant sounds good, and I'll have some blended tea," said Shauna.

I was wishing Shauna had not said, "Ooh." She has no reason to be that impressed. Giddy is not sophisticate. Yes, sophisticate. No "d".

"I'll just have tea," said Maria.

"I would like a sparkling water with a twist of lime and just a hint of bitters. Thank you much," I answered with a smile. I needed to let her know I had been somewhere; to have her wonder whether my office was every bit of this. I hoped those two would not look at me as if I were out of character, and do you know they did?

But Ms. Swope was on the phone summoning someone. "José, come in, please," she was saying.

"Yes, Miss Swopes." A young, lithe Latino appeared almost instantly.

Well, we know she's single, but then it could be Jose's ESL. "Jose, would you go to the café and...ah...get two chocolate croissants and two blended teas, a bottle of sparkling water with a wedge of lime, lemon if they do not have lime, and ask Lolita to make me a cappuccino. She knows how I like it."

"Yes, Miss Swopes."

Ms. Swopes looked over to me. "Zemi, I do not think the café would have bitters...."

"Of course," I answered innocently. "Then lime or lemon it is! Perfect, and thank you."

Ms. Swopes dismissed the young man with a subtle, but understood gestures and he left as quickly as he appeared.

She sat erect in her chair. "So, Shauna," Ms. Swopes, said. "I understand that you are a little uneasy with the proposed content and format for Our Platform." Ms. Swope swivelled her chair slightly toward Shauna. A challenge move, understated, but still a challenge. "I would like to take the time to help you get acquainted with some of the formalities around this radio station, to offer some firsthand knowledge of how things operate. I assure you, Shauna, I certainly know what I am doing. And there are others who believe that, too. I have been in the business for fifteen years. A radio station would not pay an African American woman $45 million not to know. And whatever I don't know, you will never realize because I am resourceful enough to get matters done the way things need doing." She spoke with authority, confidence—resolve? Would things have to be her way?

Just then José entered. He placed our drinks on a pullout tray beneath the wet bar and served us.

Shauna pulled her chair closer to the desk. She was uneasy now. Shauna knew that Ms. Swopes could speed up the success for her and for Maria's event planning business, now headquartered in Charlotte. She believed this woman could bring success to their business all over the country if she chose to do so. Earlier, Shauna had stated to Maria that black women did not believe in helping other black women climb the ladder. She stated that she obtained most of her contacts and referrals from white people recommending her business as opposed to other blacks. She also felt that blacks bicker and dicker too much over pricing, always wanting to pay reduced rates for top-of the-line services. (When pressed by Maria, Shauna had to concede that whites were the same way, especially in this economy.)

Shauna was smooth. She had successfully played one clever card by urging me to get Maria to introduce her to Ms. Swopes sooner, under a guise to which I was privy—Shauna's need to be clear on program formatting, a natural. Now Shauna needed to help make sure everything was clear to all the players. I listened quietly to see how she'd bring that off.

"Miss Swopes," Shauna began.

"Yes?" Ms. Swopes answered quickly. There was no offer to call her by "Laurel," but this was the South and not California. Besides, "Laurel" and "Maria" had gotten to know one another already and hadn't I spent a whole afternoon with Mrs. Williams with no suggestion of being a tad less than formal? Ms. Swopes it is.

"...I would like to begin by saying." Shauna was saying, "I was uneasy about the presentation of the content, not so much the format itself. Secondly, I had no knowledge that you had come aboard.

You don't know how good it is now, knowing that we do have someone with your expertise on board."

Ms. Swopes' eyes glowed with appreciation. She was too accustomed to being lauded.

"I guess my anxiety was centered around a concern about how the targeted audience would receive what is being presented. Perhaps I would have helped things along had I articulated more hope rather than fear about Our Platform. My hope is that our folk will be able to identify with and embrace our message. Otherwise, Our Platform might as well be like those news stations out there that are of no interest to many black people. Our Platform should fill the void created by stations that offer programs of little relevance to the lives of blacks. Our folk have pretty much overdosed on the ghastly tallies of a bad day in the 'hood, the day's killings and the drug headliners. That information is presented like it is as ordinary as the weather. I didn't know if you and Maria had taken those things into consideration, that's all," Shauna said, mildly.

"There are so many fluctuating circumstances in the lives of black folk that to be able to know which variable to speak to on any given day to me is such a colossal task," said Maria. "But with Ms. Swopes' skills, I feel most confident about our platform now."

"I definitely agree with what you said a moment ago, Shauna, and very much with Maria—that we have a colossal task at hand," said Ms. Swopes. "But here's the thing, businesses and advertisers have already developed a profile of the different characteristics within African Americans. And with each subset of African Americans, the media and advertisers have figured out how to reach people; they have it down to a science. They know the message that must be given and how to attain what they seek. This is what media and advertisers do, not just for black people, but for all demographic groups. You would be surprised of the demographics they have on people and communities and their habits. The moves of black people are no different than other groups: predictable. And when people's moves are predictable they are more easily manipulated," said Ms. Swopes.

Maria chipped in, "I am so glad you pointed that out. Earlier, Shauna expressed that she thought we may lose our folk because

Our Platform was too moralistic and that perhaps we should add a touch of comedy or melodrama." Maria handed her cup to Ms. Swopes, nodding her appreciation for a refill. "Shauna was also concerned that the programming included too much data and too many fine details."

Maria remained standing while stirring sugar in her tea. "But here is my take. There is nothing that needs to be made funny or comical on Our Platform. Our folk are in a crisis, and my position with Our Platform as a co-host is to help blacks come up with stratagems for change. I would like to at least try to undo some of the catastrophic damages that Hollywood and TV have helped cause. Right now, the mentality of the American viewer is horrific, and that included *all* Americans—just addicted to idiocy. So to reach our viewers on real issues, we need to lay off the diet of the really stupid comedy found on television."

"I have to agree with you, Maria," Ms. Swopes said. "And not to stray too far from the issue at hand, but the art of acting is just about lost, and inane so-called entertainment is in its place. There are too many ridiculous, unimaginative roles and black actors have more than their fair share."

I nodded in agreement, and said, "I agree, however I also have a concern. I am concerned that in some respects that when we address the needs, concerns and challenges of black people, that there is a suggestion that other people do not have those same issues. If we say, black people catch colds in the winter, we certainly are not saying others do not. Perhaps while others catch colds, both prevention and remedies are more readily available. I want to make certain that we are all on the same page in the subtle messages sent, too. I think we might agree that black people have a disproportionate amount of these issues, on the one hand, and on the other hand, black people lack disproportionately access, resources, capital and resolution tools, and that is why we are here, we meaning Gate-Keeper."

This time, the others, Ms. Swopes, too, nodded in agreement. Sometimes the unstated must be stated. Things get that complicated.

"The onus is great but enough to make us all accountable," said Shauna.

"Shauna," said Maria, "hopefully, your mind has been put at ease. I am convinced of our abilities to convey and present the concerns to folk in a fashion that is digestible. I do not believe that Laurel and I are so far removed that we cannot get the message across."

Ms. Swopes nodded as she leaned back in her tall chair. "See, Shauna," Ms. Swopes looked at Shauna and then leaned forward, "if people are getting an overdose of foolishness, then there is nowhere to go but up, nothing to do, but build. Our Platform allows businesses and sponsors to put their stamp on something of integrity. Businesses will become much more accountable for the types of programs they sponsor as the public awakens and insists upon corporate integrity and accountability. In Parenthood 101, that may be interpreted to mean that you cut down on the cartoon watching; the toons played now are not the ones played in our parents' time; today's toons are violent, have sexual innuendo and all of that. The viewing public has a role, too. And that is the real message to get across."

"Do you really see blacks having that much of a role to play in this format?" Shauna asked.

"Most definitely," said Ms. Swopes. "Blacks cannot afford to sit by while the same rot is telecast and aired, the same degrading images and buffoonery."

Both Shauna and Maria seemed pensive after Ms. Swopes' last remark. Shauna was most likely surprised that Laurel Swopes spoke in such a fashion. Shauna always thought that when folk acquire the kind of money that Ms. Swopes earns and are in that type of arena, it usually means not too much is said or done to buck an exploitative system. We decided at last to move forward and stay true to our original agenda, to develop a substantive program of topics, questions and potential answers, with input from the listeners. We would address real issues, and any comedy at all would not be programmed, but could be spontaneous, and, more likely than not, would be much needed relief from sordid matters and situations. How did hip hop artist Lauryn Hill put it? *"Fantasy is what people want, but reality is what they need."*

* * * * *

Since Laurel Swopes is known around the country, Maria figured by using Laurel Swopes' name as a producer and host of Our Platform, the show would certainly get the attention of sponsors. Maria Navies and Laurel Swopes went everywhere presenting synopses of their findings: There are many class and other demographic differences among African Americans, yet the one thing the majority of blacks agree upon is voting Democratic. Our economic differences stem from accessibility to jobs and a proper income. People of a lower class have less access because they are less educated, trained, skilled, or not from moneyed backgrounds. As in other races, all well to do blacks do not necessarily have degrees or advanced degrees, but those with degrees are able to have a better quality of life and definitely have more choices for generating income than persons without degrees, as a general rule. Blacks of all classes generally agree that having a college education improves lifestyle and career choices. Many who are productive and have done well or even gotten rich are not necessarily highly educated. For the most part, the "American Dream" is legend; education and training do not guarantee a decent livelihood. Nor does working hard. Not to say well being is a crapshoot, but luck, fortune, opportunity and blessings seem to weigh in big. Still, it is definitely a case of being more damned if you do not have the skills.

Disadvantaged blacks must deal with the fact that often those persons charged with trying to make them better prepared for life expect them to fail. Disadvantaged blacks must wrestle with trying to find a means of living, welfare dependency and the stigma that comes with it (even though tons of white folks are on welfare, corporations, too), increasing crime in their communities, etc. But just because middle and upper-class blacks are going to school and working and have skills really doesn't mean that they are free of problems. Though the middle and upper classes aren't grappling with survival issues (beyond trying to survive to maintain or improve status quo), they nevertheless have to deal with racism at high-quality educational institutions, attaining positions for which they are qualified or even immensely qualified, racism in corporate

America, and educating their children in such a way that the kids do not end up confused if they attend predominantly white schools.

Black parents did not have to deal with the smoking issue as much as white parents, but seems everyone has to address sex and drugs. Middle class blacks also have to deal with the disdain of bene-fiting from a program that is just giving qualified persons a chance to get in the door then prove themselves. They have to compete with white privilege, that is, white affirmative action which is an American tradition that is expected to be around for a minute or two. Blacks have to deal with constantly having to work twice as hard in school and the work place just to prove they had a right to be there in the first place. White privilege includes a tradition of ex-tending opportunities to the mediocre—if they are white. So non-white people do not enjoy an equal opportunity to mediocrity. (Not to say anyone should aspire to doing just so-so.)

As to relationships and family make up, the differences are there again. We see the lower class blacks shortening the generational gaps by mothers becoming younger and younger with multiple children, more abusive relationships, more single-parent homes without fathers, more of the men in jail, and even that list goes on. The middle-and upper-class blacks have other issues that surround the women, always having to compete with white, Asian and even brown women for their men, especially as the men climb higher up the success ladder. Or black women, especially now, have to follow the trend of higher-class black men by dating people of other races. Some black women have become more appealing to Hispanic men, although some have what might be a "citizenship relationship." And the black middle class finds that its getting smaller, too.

There is also the issue of still being the first to go when downsiz-ing occurs, and when trying to find another job, being the first to be told they are either underqualified or overqualified. There are also issues of identity crisis that have hit middle-class blacks hard; one can't be sure on which day they will identify with race and on which day they will identify with class.

But still, as mentioned before, even with all of our differences, the one thing we can seem to agree on is, for the most part, the black vote has been a Democratic vote. You know it is a farcical thing, not the idea that blacks switched to Democrats, but the idea that black folk have remained Democrats. Laurel Swopes is a Democrat, Maria Navies is an Independent; yet neither of them is saying whether blacks should keep voting Democrat or switch to Republican or Independent. What they are saying is that the vote, your vote, should be carefully weighed before it is cast.

Routine can be boring, whether it concerns the bad or benign. The problem is that habits can be numbing. If something starts off as beneficial for all parties involved and becomes a routine, it can be a problem, simply because neither life nor time is stagnant. When we do a good thing and it becomes routine, it is still important to go back and re-examine whether what we are doing is still constructive or beneficial. The problem is that blacks are not re-examining where there votes are placed; they do not re-examine reasons that influenced them to vote a certain way in or for a certain party in the beginning. This is pretty much the trend for Americans—getting stuck. We just get accustomed to doing the same thing, and that's the end of that.

Instead of analyzing a situation to effect change, people become anesthetized in apathy or mindless hope eternal. That is not faith; faith presumes consideration of the matter at hand.

Above, it is said that some blacks actually analyze to make the choice for the Democratic Party in the first place. Actually, this might be overly generous. See, to a large extent, the Democratic Party has actually inherited the black vote. One can only wonder how many black people vote Democrat because their mother and father did. Black people might not follow their parents to church or heaven, but, if we get to the polls, we surely will vote the way they did.

In any event, routines are scary, and people don't realize how scary they can become, especially if a lot is at stake. It is a very dangerous thing when decisions are made without feeling and critical analysis. It is like being in the same job where you learn to do it with your eyes closed. The challenge isn't there, and the passion is gone as well. It is like being in a bad relationship in which neither person will leave because they have become accustomed to being together, or being in a relationship that is bad in the sense that neither party is getting the maximum benefits from the relationship. Nor is anyone happy. Routine in voting is no different. And there are credible arguments that this same type of pathology characterizes black Americans and the Democrats.

The right to vote should not be taken lightly by anyone, especially by African Americans, and neither should candidates take the black vote for granted. White people, and only white males, were the only people who counted at the time our country was founded. Blacks were not counted as whole human beings, according to the Constitution. Voting was a right that African Americans did not have during slavery. It is a right that was not protected by segregation and racist polling and votary intimidation practices law until President Lyndon Johnson signed the Voting Rights Act of 1965. There were African Americans who died for the right to vote (and in Africa and so many places in the world, throngs have sacrificed their lives for this freedom), a right that many of us either take for granted or might as well be taking for granted. For too many, voting has become a little-considered, perfunctory practice, if we do in fact take the time to cast a vote. Laurel Swopes and Maria remain uncertain of which is worse, not voting at all or voting without critical analysis of what you're voting for and who will be affected. It seems like different sides of the same coin because the whole idea behind voting is to attempt to bring about change for the better and to have a voice in what goes on around you.

What we found lacking with many African Americans was any real knowledge of the past history of their great-grandfathers and great grandmothers as members of the Republican Party then, and why today the Democratic Party can safely assume the votes of more recent generations of blacks. Our Platform finds we must have a history of which political party African Americans have followed and why in order to consider if African Americans should remain with the Democratic Party presently or if an opportunity to switch should be seized. Laurel and Maria are not kidding themselves, for they know that the task at hand is not a walk in the park and that there is a lot of history to be covered. Our Platform is not a history talk show and the hosts are not historians, but we enjoy the benefit of participation by political, social and psychological experts, persons who have the ability to render socio-economic, political and scientific analyses electoral trends and party affiliation.

As co-hosts of Our Platform, Maria and Laurel believe that every eligible African American should vote. Presuming it is within the interests of black people to continue to vote as a group, which should stand as the party for African Americans for 2008-2012? Our Platform will deal with the following topics:

1. Should blacks and browns consider going to a third party?

2. Do African Americans and Latinos really have the same voting issues?

3. If blacks and browns form coalitions, what would be the issues to unite on?

4. Do corporations and sponsors have a responsibility to promote positive images on television?

5. Will same-sex-marriage affect black and brown families? How?

6. Is illegal immigration a main issue for you? If so how?

7. Are the Catholic Church and black church impacting the role of black and brown women as leaders?

8. Does an artist have an obligation to his or her community or racial group? If so discuss in regards to blacks in entertainment and black people.

9. Are Civil Rights organizations relevant to today's youths?

10. What would make black and brown Democrats stay with the Democratic Party?

11. What would make blacks and browns leave the Democratic Party?

12. Should Katrina be a top priority for 2008 presidential candidates?

13. Does Hollywood show enough diversity on television?

14. Discuss the relative influence and progress of white women and black males in politics.

15. Which party do you think will deal more with public education, health care and AIDS Programs for African Americans?

16. Do blacks still need affirmative action? Do women?

17. How has affirmative action benefitted white women? Do they still need it?

18. What would the Republican Party need to do to get an appreciable increase in African American votes?

19. Do you believe blacks can shape the results of the 2008 election? In what way?

20. Does the media have a role in the portrayal of blacks? If yes, in what way?

These are issues with which the black public can grapple, and Our Platform is a vehicle for the necessary dialogue that must occur. Maria and Laurel expected such topics to catapult Our Platform into the center ring. They had guest speakers lined up from all across the country to lead discussions—both noted and unknown guests. We have asked participants to rank the topics according to their priorities. Number 19 is the topic that viewers wanted to debate first. With that question, Our Platform and GateKeeper's Village shifted into high gear. Again, I became very, very busy. I just hoped that I was not getting so busy that I had missed something important. Maria and Shauna were quite busy too.

9

The weather was perfect and every detail attended to. Hundreds showed up for the groundbreaking of Gate-Keeper's Village, a luxury gated community for senior citizens. It was also the grand opening of Our Platform and the GateKeepers AIDS Prevention and Healing Center. Shauna's production of Roll Call, a marketing strategy to encourage AIDS testing, took center stage over the other segments of the event. And people took AIDS tests, too. Shauna is still beaming. She had just returned from seeing E.J. in California, and she thinks they might be getting back together. They even talked about marriage. He is the only man Shauna has ever loved. Shauna took the AIDS test, too, though she could not put it together why E.J. would not come down to the grand opening. She believes it has to do with me. Maybe he is still upset that I've become a Republican. Maria's marketing agent, Albert Greene, missed taking the AIDS test because his flight was delayed. By the time he showed up, events taking place at the different venues were wrapping up. But Maria was still happy he still showed up. Maria and Albert see a lot of each other. I understand Laurel Swopes, Maria's co-host for Our Platform, dated him two years ago. But I am happy for Maria. I think she has finally found the man of her dreams, and they make an adorable couple. Her fling with the house designer and her engagement to the Mexican seem to be something from days of old.

Zeth showed up at the grand opening. Gosh! Oh, my! Does he look handsome! He's coming in now. But, he's not alone? Who's hand is he holding over the threshold? I can't see…. Laurel Swopes is coming in… and….its her hand Zeth's got and now she is on his arm? Zeth is dating Laurel? Did they meet here? On the property Zeth gave me? *My* property? And *GateKeeper* gave her a job and boosted her career? My heart fell into my stomach; this picture is making me sick.

The two of them arrived just minutes too late to take the AIDS tests. It took more than I had to hold it together while they greeted me. I called her by Ms. Swopes, but she interrupted me and waved that same lovely brown arm to which was attached an expertly manicured hand–only now I was not coveting some damned finger nails. Then she said, "Oh! Do call me Vickie, Zemi. 'Ms. Swopes' and 'Laurel' are for business and the office. 'Vickie' is what close friends and family call me, for Victoria, my middle name." *Laurel is Vickie? That Vickie? I am sicker now.* She giggles, then she gushes, "my Daddy said that Victoria is a queen's name." I wanted to go for an Oscar. I really did. With my best Scarlett O'Hara drawl I wanted to say, "Oh? You mean your daddy did not think you worthy of a royal first name?" Instead, I offered the smile of a shrew. "Do call me Zemi Navies, that's Dr. Zemi Navies to you and your kind." I managed even to smile at Zeth and turned and left them standing there, vowing to consign this mess to the morrow, to the future, where Scarlett tossed all of her troubles.

* * * * *

Yes. No one had bothered to tell me about Laurel Victoria Swopes and the 411 on her many affairs. Maria knew all the time that this was the same Vickie that Zeth was seeing. How could she have allowed Vickie to become her co-host of Our Platform, a business venture that I got started for Maria? Shauna knew also; she had met the woman! She had said not a word but became best friends with Vickie. But why did they invite Zeth to come, knowing he was dating Vickie, Laurel or whatever she fronted for? In the back of my mind, I was hoping that Zeth would come—but not with another woman. And he came with *her*???? A woman who has what the world calls, "grace," but she has no mercy? I remember what Grandma would say from the Bible: That the Lord requires three things of us, to walk humbly, to do justice and to love mercy. If she is without mercy, then she is without grace, I figure. She is a nullification unto herself. I remembered when Shauna first came to visit me in Charlotte and told me of the woman Zeth was seeing, but I don't think she gave me a last name for the woman. I feel stupid, deceived. Everyone knew but me. I wanted to strike back at everyone, but for now I held back—though at the moment I was not in the state of mind to let vengeance be the Lord's alone. I needed a piece of the action! I had a chance to talk to Zeth for a while; Shauna had taken Vickie to see her office. Strangely, I didn't feel any deception on Zeth's part. Because of inertia on my part, I mean, wasn't I unresponsive to his romantic overtures? And to his hints about marriage? Zeth did what a man had to do. It is not that I am overlooking any of his faults now, no way; it's just that I understand. I had an opportunity to grab him and didn't. I don't know if it's too late, but I am hoping that the offer is not behind us. Us? How could I dare think "us," when he came to my event with that trollop?

Grandma said a woman has to know when to bait, trap and catch a man. Perhaps it is time for me to use some bait and trap on Zeth. But did I want Zeth? Or was I merely coveting, or reacting to a bruised ego and public derision? Did I want to show those who had betrayed me that I, Zemi Navies, wins at the end of the day? Is my pride rolling out before a red carpet, luring me to trip, then to fall? If I could not appreciate this man when I was all alone with him and he was all into me, then what made my eyesight so much better when I saw him holding someone else?

Could he have heard my thoughts? Zeth walked up to me with both hands in his pockets. "My, my, Zemi," he says with a smile. His eyes caught hold of mine and held all of me. And as I am trapped (wasn't he supposed to be the prey?), he says quietly, "Girl, I don't know what to say. I guess I ought to start off by sayin' that I'm extremely proud of what you've done with the land so far."

I returned his smile, and invoice mellifluous, asked, "Dear Zeth. Do you really like how everything is coming together? I was hoping that the color treatments and refurbishments in your parents' home would all be to your liking." I put my hand on Zeth's chin. "Thank you so much for your foresight," I told him (sweetly).

"Why, what do you mean, Zemi?"

"This vision today is because of what I believe you saw in me. You knew me better than I knew myself." I linked my arm into Zeth's. "I wanted you to be proud of me. I didn't want to let you down or myself down, and I wanted you to feel the presence of your parents with every footstep that you took in this home—the home you grew up in."

Zeth lowered his head and tapped his foot, "Ah, Zemi, this here land is your spot now. But, of course, if my parents were alive today to see all of this, they'd be proud, too, with all you have done to this house and to the land."

"Here, let's go this way," I suggested, and led him toward the spa and fitness center (that, by the way, I now operated with a couple of NFL athletes).

Politely, Zeth disengaged his arm from mine.

"What's wrong, Zeth?"

He looked wounded. "Zemi, what makes you think somethin's wron'?"

"Because I know you. Because I now feel what you felt before, when you were in love with me," I told him, looking at the ground.

"Look, Zemi," Zeth said firmly, "the spa and everythin' is great, but you act as if you can just waltz back into those feelin's that I held for you a lon' time ago. It's just not that way today."

We both stood still and for a moment were both mute, too. Then I folded my arms, and asked him. "Zeth, please be honest with me. Are you in love with Vickie Swopes?"

Now Zeth folded his arms. "I can't answer that question. Besides, Zemi, you have no right to ask me such a question."

"Fair enough. Do I have the right to ask if you are still in love with me?"

"For whatever reason you need to know, well, the answer is yes. Not only am I still in love with you, I'll always be in love with you," he answered, his face, pained. He turned to walk away.

I pulled his arm and gently coaxed him to turn and face me. To see me. "Zeth, how do you know that you still love me?"

He shook his head and said, "Because not bein' able to have you is a constant pain. It's a pain that sometimes feels like I would imagine a lion would feel with a dagger ripped through its heart. It's greater than any prolonged sufferin' I have ever experienced." He looked at me with tenderness, but his eyes were red. "For your sake, I hope you never have to experience this kind of torment."

I held out my arms to this beautiful man. "Zeth, my sweet darling. I made a mistake."

Zeth's voice choked with emotion. "Sometimes you have to live with consequences from mistakes you make."

I turned away. I wanted to cry, but I just would not. Not if I could help it, I thought, trying to wipe away the tears.

Zeth turned me to face him this time. "Oh, my Zemi." He kissed me, and kissed my face, my tears. First gently, then a hungered kiss. My knees trembled. I thought I could feel the earth moving under me; I could feel Zeth's love. From the corner of my eye, I saw Vickie Swopes and Shauna coming in our direction. But Zeth kept kissing me as if he didn't mind if the whole world, Vickie, included, could see.

"Zeth," I whispered, "why would you make me feel this way if our relationship has ended?"

Zeth smiled, and stroked my face. "Silly girl, you held the keys to open up heaven, but I guess there were some thin's those high-end books just couldn't teach you, huh, Puddin'?"

* * * * *

Today is Wednesday, a month and a half later. This was my special spa day. Usually, I treat myself to the works. When I entered from the far end of the spa, I saw Shauna and Maria in the Jacuzzi, but they didn't notice me. I felt like intruding on them but hesitated. They were talking so loudly that their voices carried throughout the spa. I stayed quiet and listened in on their conversation. At first, I felt guilty, as if I were spying, but the more I heard from their conversation, the less guilty I felt. I saw that Shauna had started crying.

"We were wrong, Maria, the way we treated Zemi." Shauna wiped her eyes. "We treated her as though she had no feelings. We were girlfriends and we were sisters. Did we do that to Zemi because of her youth?"

"I felt bad for Zemi, too. I just didn't know how to tell her about Zeth and Vickie. I placed more value on being friends with Vickie, no matter the pain to my own blood sister. I mean, I like being with Vickie. I like the feel of being around the movers and shakers, people with all the bling-bling. I just got caught up. It felt like Hollywood again," Maria admitted. "And," she added, "I just thought that Zemi would get over it."

I thought to myself, how fake Maria is, even with Shauna. If it was not for the partnership that bonded us, and, biological sisters or not, Maria would have been an all-out deceiver without the cloak. But I could believe this part: where Maria admitted that she could care more about the bling-bling than a sibling!

Shauna's voice echoed across the spa. "I was getting used to the glitzy lifestyle myself. Got to hand it to the sister, though, Vickie was on her job. She opened an awful lot of doors for us, doors that you and I would still be knocking on had it not been for her. She let us into her world. It was a wealthy world. I love being in that type of energy. But you know, what I don't like is what we did to Zemi."

Maria made circles in the water with her hands. "I mean I feel bad about what we did to Zemi, but I don't know if it was all of what you are making it out to be, Shauna. Exactly what do you think we did to her that makes us so bad?" asked Maria.

I sank to the floor; I went on listening to Maria and Shauna discuss me as if I did not matter to them at all—as if I were too young to have real feelings.

Shauna scissor-kicked her legs back and forth in the water, as she rested her elbows on the side of the pool. "I feel bad that we did not think Zemi deserved to be there with us. When I asked Zemi for my acres on the parcels with the lake, she agreed. And she put her heart and soul into that land so that Zeth would be proud of her. And the truth is that she gave us our start in this venture," said Shauna.

"I agree. It made Zemi so proud that she could do something for her big sister. But Shauna, sometimes it hurts even more to have to be the one to break bad news. Do you know what I mean?" asked Maria. "The funniest thing of all is that Vickie knew the whole time that Zeth had been with Zemi before, yet she said nothing of the matter. And then she came with Zeth to the grand opening." Sweat trailed down Maria's face. "Now that was unfeeling. Shauna, how do you suppose she found out about Zeth and Zemi?" Maria asked.

"Is that a trick question? Are you kidding? Zeth was so in love with Zemi that he could never hide that fact. Though Zeth and Zemi are not together, Vickie knows in her heart that he loves Zemi and maybe only her. But, girl, life can just be so full of irony, twists and turns. Zemi might try and act as though she is not hurting, but I know she's feeling like she got Cupid's arrow, only I think the arrow must have been poisoned. When E.J. and I were separated, I was crushed, and that's why I jumped at Zemi's offer to come to Charlotte. I was sinking and she threw me a life saver, a sweet one at that. And I promised her that I would not leave. And now E.J. and I are talking marriage. Maybe he will move to Charlotte."

"Do me a favor, Shauna. Don't count on E.J. so much to do the right thing. He's just another man with men's issues, and might not have room enough to make you a priority. Maybe you are better off without him," said Maria.

"Girl, are you envious of me and your brother?" Shauna's voice grew loud. "Now really, Maria, why are you putting out so much negativity? Did you just hear what I said? I am never going to give E.J. up. Never. Call me stupid, but I'll be another Hillary Clinton, standing by her man."

"Now that is the real definition of love," said Maria.

"What is?"

"Stupid. Stupid is the definition of that kind of love."

"Oh, well, so is life. Tra-la-la."

"I don't know if many women are the way you, Hillary, Vanessa and Kim are today. I don't think that is an appropriate message to send out to young women."

"What message are you referring to?" Shauna snapped.

"That every time a man farts, a woman is there to smell it. I am damn near allergic to flatulence, at least from other people!"

Shauna threw up her hands. "How gross! Please stay serious, Maria. Look at what Hillary received for what you considered stupid—a seat in the Senate and with the promise of the big house. And look at what Vanessa has, a $4 million ring, and, well, I don't know what Kim has received, but I know that it is more than what you and I have put together."

"Hummm. I don't know about all that you're saying." Maria shook her head. "Hillary might have to get at the back of the line with black folk and wait with us on that big house promise. If we get our forty acres and a mule, then Hillary will be your president after next."

Shauna seemed to jump at the chance to change the subject. "Are you saying that you would not vote for Hillary as the next president?"

"Nope."

"Why not? She was very instrumental in the success of President Clinton."

"Hillary represents the old ways of Congress," said Maria. "Frankly, I would be too afraid that she would sweep too many incidents under the rug like she did with Gennifer Flowers and the rest of the coquettes in Clinton's harem. She might be too much in denial that we are at war whether we want to be or not. The American people want change and feel the Iraq War is disastrous. I am not for war and don't suppose that too many sensible people are, but America is over there in Iraq now, and this is no time to play hide-and-go-run. I just don't have a comfortable feeling about her being capable to handle those Iraqis and keep them in place, off of our soil." Maria moved to the second step in the spa. "Hillary couldn't run her own house. She talked badly about Barack and his experience. But her eight-year experience as first lady wasn't enough; she couldn't keep Bill in place, and I believe that's enough said."

"What about Barack Obama?" Shauna prodded.

"Do you really need to ask? Everybody wants Obama in the Oval Office. And I don't pay attention to conjured up polls claiming to show more black women supporting Hillary over black males who support Obama," Maria said, rubbing sweat over her face. "That man wouldn't even have to run and I would vote for him. He represents change, the new way for America. Maybe he keeps hope alive. I believe many young people would come to the table and vote for Barack."

"Maria," said Shauna as she splashed water on her shoulders, "you can't just vote for a person based on how they look."

"You are absolutely right, Shauna, and all joking aside, Barack Hussein Obama has the most going on to run for the Democratic Party. And it won't hurt to have a pretty face in the Oval office matched up with intellect."

"Would you vote for Condoleezza against Barack, being that you are for women taking greater leadership roles?" asked Shauna.

"First off, that might be rushing America, having both presidential nominees be African American. Get real, Shauna. But dealing with it theoretically, Barack has my vote over Condi. Barack is the better suited candidate, bar none."

"But really, why him over Condoleezza?"

"Because in my heart I am a Democrat. I want them to reclaim national leadership, and I think Obama would get just about every black person's vote who wasn't a Democrat," Maria declared.

"Well, if Condoleezza was the only black running, without a thought she would have my vote because on the personal side of things, I think that she is qualified," said Shauna.

"Yuk. I don't get the right vibes from Condoleezza. She is too much of a mouthpiece for Bush." Maria poked her toes up through the surface of the water, admiring her pedicure.

"Oooooh. You are a bad girl, Maria. You are an Independent co-host on Our Platform, and besides that, your whole damn synopsis talks about you as an Independent and the Republican agenda versus the Democratic agenda presented by Vickie. Now how are you going to act that way around black people? To say the least, both Zemi and Vickie have fallen for the okey-dokey regarding you as an Independent, Maria," said Shauna.

"They will never know," Maria said with a dimpled grin. "I'm an actress. My role is to make the scenario relevant and convincing. And that is what will make the audience tune in and the sponsors pleased. Look at Hannity and Colmes. It's the opposites attract scheme. Both of those guys are very knowledgeable and astute. They appear well-bred, charming, courteous, not egotistical or conceited, and they each appear to be enamored with the party they serve. And that is what they want us to think. But those big boys might get off the air, and they might not even be that nice or loyal. My job is to please. For all I know, Vickie could be pretending about being a devout Democrat."

"Would you vote for Al if he ran for president again?" Shauna returned to the national political scene—it was a safe distraction.

"Which Al? Gore or Sharpton?" Maria asked.

"I am talking now about Sharpton," Shauna clarified.

"I didn't vote for Al Sharpton the first time he ran for president because he didn't convince me that he believed he could win. Taking up my time for Al Sharpton to get paid a nickel for effort from the Democratic Party is my idea of a joke gone sour. Black folk are not going for something so not worth the time in '08."

Shauna wiped water from her face. "What are you trying to say, Maria? Do you think Al should just stay out of the voting ring, come 2008, and not split the black vote between Obama and himself?"

"I am saying that I am going to fit this type of conversation into my topics and format somehow. I like how these types of questions are drawn out. They will get folk excited. It makes me feel more like I am acting, especially when I have to examine the liberals. Shucks, by the time the '08 election rolls around, there is no telling who might be a presidential nominee. For all we know, Michael Bloomberg might be sporting himself on a ticket. Then I might have to be recognized as an Independent, for real."

"What about handsome Barack?"

"He will still be handsome. And when I go inside that little booth, it will be just me and Barack."

"Well, now, girl," said Shauna, "that's what I was trying to get you and Vickie to understand earlier. Your stage just seemed too didactic at first for blacks to really get into a political groove. But I am glad that you two have tweaked the presentation so that it worked out."

"I knew that at the time, but then Vickie was all caught up about her image and notoriety. She had more influence. Her participation brought the sponsors in. And without sponsors you don't have a show, no matter how good your content."

"I know that's right. Vickie worked it out, girl, didn't she? I am so proud of her. You and I should maybe take her to the islands or somewhere maybe for a couple of days." Shauna unwrapped the towel from her head and shook out her hair.

"Hey, I'll make reservations for next week. We will take her to Barbados and stay at the Sandy Lane Resort. You know they have those fine dark, dark men in Barbados."

I got up off the floor. I didn't hear any more. At that moment, I hated Shauna and Maria both. I walked away, knowing my eyes were swollen even though I'd fought to hold back the tears.

* * * * *

What a pleasant surprise! Zeth called. He was on his way over with something to tell me. I wondered if he wanted to tell me that he and Vickie Swopes were no longer a couple. Maybe she saw us kissing and got upset. I rambled through my closet to find something hot and sexy to put on. I changed clothes a third time to a cashmere, mauve-colored V-neck pants outfit. I met Zeth at my office.

"You look beautiful, Zemi." Zeth looked me over as if he were reading a map to a treasure hunt. "So how have you been doin', Zemi?" Zeth bit his lip. "I meant to say doing. How have you been doing? I promised myself that I was going to stop chopping off the g's to my words. You can correct me on that if you like. I wouldn't mind you helping me out with my faults." Zeth studied his parents' picture. "That frame must have cost you a pretty penny," he said, touching it gently.

"It did." I took in the picture, too. "Yes, it did, but I had to find the very best to pay tribute to your parents. You are blessed, Zeth. I also know what it's like to have wonderful, solid parents who lived for a better day for their children, more so than they lived for themselves."

"Yep. I guess we were both lucky that way to have great parents. I miss them sometimes, Zemi. I don't have much of a family left with most of my relatives being so old and feeble."

"You know, in this house, Zeth, sometimes your parents talk to me."

Zeth stared at me. Saying nothing, he waited for my next word.

"They tell me things about you."

"Oh, yeah. Like what?"

"Well," I said, with a smile as I took Zeth hands, "that you deserve a good woman in your life."

"Is that right? Did they have a particular good woman in mind?"

"Yep. Me."

"Is that right?"

"They said you should take care of me, protect me and love me forever."

"Is that right?"

"Straight up," I said.

Zeth turned and place his hands on my shoulders and, answered, "Well, did you tell my parents that I tried to take care of you from the first day I laid eyes on you?"

"I did tell them that, and they said for you to try harder."

"Is that righ'? Try harder how?"

"Well, your parents said that you are well-bred and that you already know how to court a woman. All you have to do is to do it the best way you know how, and that will be good enough."

"Do you think I'm good enough fer you, Zemi?"

"Oh, my goodness, Zeth! If I waited for anyone better, I would be waiting for an eternity."

That got a wide grin out of him. He asked, more seriously now, "You really want me, huh, girl?"

"Like water wants wet."

Zeth rubbed my arms gently; his eyes filled. "I can tell you got it bad fer me, girl. Do you really, really want me now, Zemi?"

"I do."

"Girl, that sounds like an answer to a marriage proposal, and I ain't even asked you yet," said Zeth.

"Hmmm, that's strange," I said.

"What is?" Zeth was frowning.

"I thought I heard something."

"Heard what?"

"I thought I heard you ask me to marry you."

"If you heard that, then what was the answer you heard to the question?"

"Yes! I would marry you right this second."

"Okay, girl, you can't play with my feelings like that. You'll mess around and give me a heart attack."

I grinned coyly and said, "I promise whatever I give you, you will love it."

"Will you give me some little Zeths and little Zemis?"

"Every time it rains."

"Let's see. Since you are in a giving mood, what else can I get from you?"

"I have already wished for your every desire."

"Get out of here. Are you saying that you know what my desires are without me first telling you?"

"I was created just to slake your thirst," I said with a grin and the eyes of a novice vamp (which I was truly, but I had studied well).

"Will you move into the ranch home with me?"

"As soon as we are married."

"Then, shucks, I now pronounce us man and wife. I just became a preacher blessedly called."

"Awww. With that kind of marriage, you are never going to get the real thing."

"Hmm. I already know it ain't nothing like the real thing because I ain't never had the real thing. That's what's been missing. Is it worth waiting for the real thing with you, Zemi?"

"If you had the real thing already, Zeth, you would never have had to ask the question."

"Will you marry me, Zemi?"

There was a very long silence. The earth shook.

I asked, "Did you feel it too, Zeth?"

* * * * *

Zeth called me when he got back to Asheville. Mr. Gatekeeper was in the last throes of death. He had AIDS. The really sad part is he doesn't know from whom he contracted the virus or to whom he might have given the virus. He told Zeth that at sixty-nine he only dated young women over twenty-one and under thirty-five. He never gave AIDS a thought. The story was that when these erectile dysfunction drugs hit the market, the gatekeeper went to town. There are a lot of stories about older men and these drugs. They will go to a physician other than their own and lie like there's no tomorrow about no heart this and no blood pressure that to get these drugs. So older women are getting infected more, too. The E.D. drugs these old guys are taking, for sure; many of them boast that if they have to die in the saddle just to get that feeling again, then so be it. But they never thought for once about AIDS; I mean this was a generation of men that knew nothing about wearing a condom, and then they are to learn at 69? We would see the kindly old man creep in and out and every now and then he would make a side remark about a lady friend; we had no idea he was creeping out to his death. And I liked the gatekeeper, and I didn't know what to say or think. Mr. GateKeeper's death would not be in vain; GateKeeper's village would see to that!

I know how responsible Zeth feels for the man, who was like a family member. I went to Asheville to be there for Zeth. Weeks, ago, I had received a letter in the mail on the results of my AIDS test, but had not taken the time to open it. I was cleared. I started to call Shauna and Maria to tell them about the gatekeeper, but then hung up the phone. I had told Zeth how I felt deceived by Shauna and Maria and how they made the choice to have Vickie Swopes' friendship over mine. I could tell that Zeth was a bit concerned about how his dating Vickie Swopes might have affected us. He asked if I felt he had deceived me. I was not so sure I should answer that question.

Maybe I don't want Zeth to feel as though he has been granted a total dispensation. Maria and E.J. say that I don't have any game, but I wanted my life to be as uncomplicated as possible without denying me opportunities to learn, to grow. I could grow just fine without the disruption and heartache of being involved with a man who either wanted someone else more or who had someone else.

I had not been answering my cell phone. Shauna left a message on Zeth's home phone, saying that it was urgent that I call her right away. She called five times. Finally, Zeth urged me to call her. Just as I picked up the telephone, Zeth's doorbell rang.

Zeth opened the door, and Shauna burst in.

"Shauna, what's the matter?" My hands began to tremble. I thought maybe something had happened to someone in my family.

Maybe Grandma was sick or E.J. "What are you doing here, Shauna? It's late. What's wrong?"

"Let's take her into the great room," said Zeth. "Izabelle," he turned to the lady who ran the house, "we could use some tea."

Zeth took Shauna by the elbow and led her to an overstuffed chair in the great room. "Here, Shauna, sit down right here." Shauna had been crying. Her eyes were swollen, her hair in disarray. It was thirty degrees outside, and Shauna had on a pair of sneakers, a short-sleeved blouse and a skirt that stopped mid-calf.

Something awful—had happened. What?

Zeth wrapped a thick quilt around Shauna and turned on the fireplace. "Here, Shauna," Zeth held up a cup of tea to Shauna's trembling lips. "Drink some tea. Tell us somethin' now. You can talk to us. Ain't nothin' in the world that bad that we can't fix."

"I am so sorry, Zemi, about what I did to you," Shauna said, wiping her nose; her shoulders shook with her sobbing. "It was wrong, I wanted to come to you and tell you about Vickie Swopes, but I didn't know how to tell you. Maria admitted that she was wrong, too. She thought you might want us to stop talking to Vickie, but she was bringing in big accounts so Maria kept quiet, too. We both said nothing. I feel so ashamed of what I have done to our friendship. Zemi, please forgive me, please. I am asking because I need you not to hate me. Please don't hate me."

"Come on, now" Zeth consoled, "It might not have been a very smart move, but Zemi doesn't hate you, Shauna. She's not that type of person." Zeth got her to take another sip of tea.

My face burned, and my tongue sharpened. "Zeth, don't ever do that again!" I told him.

"Do what, Puddin'?" He looked befuddled. He was *not* to be saying these things to Shauna.

"Don't make light of what Shauna did to me. She hurt me, so, Zeth, don't say how I feel if you don't truly know." I turned away. "Good night, it is late. I am going to bed." I walked out of the great room, and they could probably hear my feet pounding the stairs. Even so, I could hear Zeth's words to Shauna.

"Excuse me, Shauna. Make yourself comfortable," said Zeth. "I have to go and tend to my spoiled little girl upstairs first. I'll be back shortly."

Zeth entered the room. "I guess I owe you an apology. You were right. I had no right to try and butter up her feelings at the cost of your feelings. Please forgive me. I always like for a guest to feel comfortable in my home, no matter who it is. That's just a part of me, and I know you know that about me, too. So I meant you no harm. But I-I know better than to do somethin' that stupid again." Zeth took his fingers and parted my lips. "Will you forgive me, Zemi?"

This man knew how to cool my anger.

"You know," Zeth went on, "I am the one who made Pluto burst and fall from the sky. I could make another burst if you let me."

I hesitated. "Okay, I'll let you."

"You will, Puddin'? When?"

"When you put Pluto back into the sky as a planet. I liked Pluto."

"Zemi, are you really going to make me wait?"

I stroked Zeth's nose with one finger. "You are spoiled, Zeth. When you don't get your way with me you call me Zemi, but when you think of me as a precious thought, you call me Puddin'. Do I have a Dr. Jekyll and Mr. Hyde on my hands?"

"Would you like for me to just call you Puddin'?"

"I will answer to whatever you call me because it all sounds so sweet."

"Do you wanna know why I call you Puddin'?"

"Is it going to make me?"

"Make you what?"

"You know."

"No, I don't know. You have to show me what you are talkin' about."

"You want me to show you what?"

"Awww girl, you are sounding like Rumplestiltskin up here. Do you mind if I go back downstairs and check on Shauna?"

"No, I don't mind."

As Zeth was leaving the room, I called out to him. "Zeth?" He turned his head. "Yes, Puddin'?"

"I love you."

"You know, Puddin', on second thought, your girlfriend down-stairs, she'll probably be all right until in the morning." Zeth started twirling his hand around. "Ha, ha, my sweetie, would you like fer me to stay up here and show you some compassion? Your girlfriend doesn't really look that bad after all."

I tenderly blew Zeth a kiss.

He closed the door.

Only minutes after he left, from downstairs I heard, "No! No! No!"

Screaming! I flew from the bed.

"Zemi, get down here," Zeth was yelling.

I get to the great room in time to see Shauna jump up from the chair. She sank to the floor, and with her arms wrapped around her-self as she lay in a fetal position, Shauna cried with the shrill of a wounded animal. The sound pricked my skin. What is she saying? What? What? My eyes well up and a knot of pain swells inside my chest. I look from Shauna to Zeth where I find no comfort; his face is twisted in agony and pity.

"I don't want to die! Please, God, don't let me die." Shauna keeps screaming.

"Zeth, Shauna, what's going on?" I shout. I rush over to Shauna and shake her by the shoulders.

"What is the matter? What is it, Zeth?"

"I don't know, Zemi." Zeth took his hands out of his pockets. "Izabelle told me that she'd be here tomorrow because of Gate-keeper's death. When Shauna heard that Gatekeeper was dead, she just started screamin' and cryin', and now she won't stop screamin'. What's wrong with her, Zemi?"

"Shauna, listen to me. Stand up." I looked to Zeth. "Zeth, please stand her up and get her back into the chair."

Once Shauna is in the chair, I place my hands on her shaking shoulders, and then I held her.

She was hysterical. "Zeth, please pour another cup of tea for her and then get a couple of face cloths and wring them out in hot wa-ter."

"Here, Shauna, drink your tea. You're not going to die."

Zeth returns and I sponge Shauna's tear-stained face. "There, how does that feel?" "Shauna, just calm down. I am here for you, and you are not going to die."

Zeth stood by.

"How do you know I am not going to die? Gatekeeper did. He died. Zeth just told me."

"Shauna, Gatekeeper had AIDS. That's what he died from —AIDS. I cared for Gatekeeper, too, and so did Zeth, but you have to learn to handle death without going into a frenzy to cause yourself more hurt. Okay, Shauna?"

"You don't get it do you, Zemi?" asked Shauna.

"Get what?"

"I didn't know it could happen to me." Shauna started crying again. "I didn't sleep around. I was only with one man for ten years. Why did God let it happen to me? I was the good girl."

"Shauna, you are scaring me," I said, trying to stay calm. "I don't know what you're talking about."

Zeth put his hands on my shoulder. "Zemi, I think Shauna is trying to tell us that ah…" He could not say it. Zeth went mute.

"I tested HIV positive. I have AIDS. Your best friend has AIDS."

I put my hands over my ears and shook my head. "Naw, Shauna, not you. Not you, Shauna! You're my girl. We kick it together, remember. I would know if you had AIDS." I put my head in Shauna's lap. "You don't look like you have AIDS. No, Shauna, it can't be so. How did you get it? Who did you get it from?" I lifted my head and screamed at the top of my lungs. "Oh, God, no! E.J. has it, too. He gave you AIDS. Is that what you are trying to tell me—that everyone around me that I love has AIDS?"

"Puddin', come on now. We need you to be strong right now fer Shauna." Zeth put his arm around my waist.

I stroked Shauna's forehead and rested her head on my shoulder. "Come on, you guys," I said. "We are probably worried about nothing. You know our AIDS clinic probably didn't have the right testing equipment to be accurate. And you know the people who did the testing were sent to us as volunteers, so you know you don't get the best when it's free. They were probably…." My voice trailed off.

Zeth's face beads of moisture and he's in and out of dialect. "Shauna," Zeth said, "I want you to know that Zemi and I are going to do everythin' we can to help you pull through this disease."

"Does E.J. know about this?" I asked.

"No. He probably doesn't know because he has never taken an AIDS test. I haven't told anyone because I feel so dirty. Like I did something so wrong. Zeth, I am not a dirty woman. Tell him, Zemi. For ten years I have been with no one other than E.J."

"Come on, Shauna, we both know that you are a very clean woman. But from now on we have to work out a plan to get you back healthy again. Does that sound like really good news to you, Shauna?" asked Zeth.

"Will you be there for me, Zemi? Because I am so scared. I am so scared." Shauna's voice shook, her lips trembled, her eyes fearful. She was scared.

"I'm scared, too, Shauna, but we will lick this thing together, and Zeth is here to help out, too, aren't you, Zeth?"

"Wherever you are, Zemi, I am right there on the front line with you. But one of the first things we must do is talk to E.J. You have to tell him, Shauna," said Zeth. "And maybe that way we can get a better handle on this thing and calm a few nerves along the way."

"When did you find out, Shauna?" I asked.

"The testing service sent me a letter and then made a telephone call. I made an appointment to see the doctor. I didn't think it was anything serious. I didn't think the AIDS virus. E.J. and I had been talking marriage. That was the thing I wanted most from him, and we even talked about having two children. But now where does that leave us? My life is ...." Her voice broke, she sobbed again.

Shauna stayed overnight and was able to get a restful sleep. Last night, when we spoke with E.J. he asked Shauna not to tell Mom, Grandma or any of the family members that she had AIDS. She told him that I knew already. E.J. was terrified. He believed that Shauna had not been with another man, but he must now confess his own infidelity and search for the one who might have given him AIDS. It was hard for E.J. to imagine that he could have AIDS. There were no noticeable signs. Not yet.

This morning, Shauna and I drove to the stable, hoping to relieve some stress and to help her gain enough composure to meet E.J.

When Shauna saw my horse, Power of Love, for the first time, she said that his name was as beautiful as the horse. She rubbed his flank and spoke his name softly over and over.

I nudged Shauna's elbow. "Go ahead, Shauna, sit on him. He's a very calm horse."

Shauna put both hands to her cheeks and let out a deep sigh, "Zemi, he is gorgeous and all that, but my energy is so messed up...I wouldn't want to put that type energy into Power of Love." She declined, shaking her head. "Uh-uh. Now is not the time. I can barely concentrate. I might get up on Power of Love and tell him to go when I need to stay put."

I wanted, in vain, to elevate Shauna's spirits. "Oh, stop being such a chicken." I shook Shauna's shoulders. "Be a big girl!"

Shauna put her arms around my waist. "Come on. This is a tough moment. I don't know what to expect from E.J."

I lay Shauna's head on my shoulders. I was weeping inside but could not let her see my sorrow. My best friend was hurting and could possibly be dying. "Shauna, you have every right to be nervous, but if ever it was the real thing between you and E.J., then now would be the time to know."

My cell phone rang. "That was Zeth," I said, pocketing the phone in my jeans. "He said E.J. will be at the ranch in just a few minutes."

Shauna was disturbed, I could clearly see.

"Well, I just hope I have enough courage to deal with him now," she said.

"Oh, sure you do," I said, hoping that my words would bear out.

We were walking to the car when Shauna stopped. She said, "Look, Zemi, you go on. I need a little time to myself before I see E.J."

"Okay, I understand. But take this." I handed Shauna my cell phone. "Call the ranch phone to let me know when you're ready, and I'll come and get you." I looked back at her and assured her. "I love you, Shauna. Remember we will fight this thing."

* * * * *

I arrived at the ranch house only minutes before E.J. rang the doorbell. He gave Zeth a hug and thanked him for taking care of Shauna. Zeth invited E.J. to stay at the ranch, too, until Shauna was ready to go to her own house.

E.J. came into the great room. I stood with my hands clenched on the arms of the couch. E.J. and I stared nervously at each other, and neither of us said anything. Zeth held up a hand. "Well, uh, can I get anybody anything? How about something for you, E.J.?"

"Naw, man, I'm cool," said E.J. He walked over to me and took one of my hands from the arm of the couch and held it to his chest. "Would you please forgive me, Zemi? I was wrong to treat you the way I did. I couldn't control you anymore. You had your own thoughts and ideas. I was the family attorney but thought that you had abandoned me and didn't need me for advice anymore. I guess I could not accept that my baby sister had finally become her own woman."

Tears rolled down my face. "I missed you, E.J. I'm so glad to see you." With my other hand I wiped my eyes clumsily. "You know that you are still my favorite brother."

"How long do you plan on staying in Asheville?" asked Zeth.

"As long as it takes," E.J. said, draping his suit coat on the back of a chair. "Man, I am in big trouble. I mean, I gave the woman I love a disease that could kill her. I am responsible for that. If she dies, Zeth, I won't be able to live, knowing she didn't deserve that kind of love, if you can call it that. Do you know that this was the only woman who really cared about my happiness? I came first in her life, yet I am the first one to hurt her. We were planning on getting married in a couple of months. We even decided to have two children. That's what I wanted, a girl and a boy. It's not like she and I were bad people." E.J. rubbed his bald head.

"What do I do, Zeth? I am an attorney. I am the one who's usually giving the advice." He pounded his hand on the table. "But now my life has sunk to an unknowable bottom and I don't know what to do. I mean, can Shauna still live a life with something like this? Man, I never caught anything from a woman before. I always prided myself on knowing how to choose the women I was with."

"Well, the first thing we are going to do is have you tested. I have a doctor friend and he will see you today," Zeth told him. Zeth seemed to have friends all over Charlotte.

"Man, if Shauna has AIDS, I am the one who gave it to her. There is no doubt about that. It's unfathomable for me to ever think of Shauna being with another man. She belonged to me already. That had been established." E.J. kept pacing around the room. "I didn't have to do anything else to earn her respect or love. I took her for granted because I knew her heart and how pure it was. I tell you, Zeth, I am going to go crazy. I can't live with what I have done to her."

Zeth had his hands in and out of his pockets and kept hunching his shoulders. "It seems like never the right time to say this, but I don't know if it ever will be, given the present circumstance. But your sister and me, well we are courtin'."

I wasn't ready to discuss Zeth's and my engagement with E.J. at this point, so I politely interrupted. "E.J., if you'd like to see Shauna, she's at the stable. I can drive you over there."

Ignoring me, E.J. stopped pacing and said nastily to Zeth, "Wait a minute, Zeth. Man, what the hell? Does courting mean a license to play over my sister?"

I now noticed that both E.J. and Zeth were of equal height and weight. E.J. dared to look at Zeth up and down. "You think I don't know about you and Vickie Swopes?" E.J. said in a raised, angered voice.

"Hold on a minute!" Zeth raised his usually calm voice. "This here ain't no courtroom. This here's my home. And you don't come into my home and disrespect me. I don't know how y'all fancy boys handle your business in California, but down here in the South, we don't back away from business. Now, I have told your sister about Vickie and me. Besides, I was with Vickie only after Zemi refused me."

"Exactly what did you tell my sister, Zeth? Did you tell her that you and Vicki had sexual relations?" asked E.J.

Just then I sat back down on the couch, a bit stunned. How dare the two of them discuss me as if I were not even present! There were certain things that I knew about Zeth and Vickie already, but I was not ready to hear Zeth give his defense in front of E.J. I did not like the discomfort of appearing naïve and immature in E.J.'s eyes.

"Come out of the courtroom, man." Zeth frowned and balled up his fists as he turned his back. "Don't question me, man. Zemi and me are tryin' to make things work between us. We don't need your law degree to do forensics on our relationship."

"We both cheated and we both got caught up in a woman's web," said E.J. I sat on the couch unable to comprehend what E.J. was saying. What could he have meant by that? I am frightened. Things sound so ugly. Hives are erupting on my arms; this is making me ill.

"Don't get me tied up into your habits, E.J. I never cheated on Zemi." Zeth started pacing around the sofa. "Zemi refused my proposal of marriage a while back. I have loved Zemi since the day I laid eyes on her. It was Zemi who was the one unsure. I knew Vickie several years before I even met Zemi, and we were on and off. Vickie's beautiful and a woman in every way that a man could want a woman to be. But Vickie liked bein' with a lot of men at the same time. She was too much in love with herself to give herself to any one man. When I met Zemi, I was through with Vickie. Now I knew Vickie loved me, but I also knew she liked to make a whole bunch of other men feel like she loved them, too, so I was never serious about her. Our involvement was only casual dates here and there. I wanted to make Zemi want me, and I knew that if she saw me with Vickie, she would get jealous. I am trying to get Zemi's mind off of Vickie, and now you want to raise her up again." Zeth stopped and took a breath. "E.J.," he asked, "who told you about me and Vickie?"

"Zeth, I am sorry, man. I'm so tense that I don't know if I am going or coming. Really, I'm sorry. I am the one who has messed up and here I am, pointing a finger."

Zeth bent his head, slightly, his hands in his pockets. "I'm sorry too, E.J. I don't like guests being uncomfortable in my home. But you still didn't answer my question. Who told you that I was seeing Vickie?"

"You really don't know, do you?" E.J. asked.

"If you mean that I don't know who told you, then I guess not."

"It was Vickie. Vickie told me about you two," said E.J.

Zeth hit his palm with his fist. "It was you! You were the fellow that she was seein' from California. Oh, man! Oh, Jesus, no! E.J., you've got to be straight up with me. If you have AIDS, do you know who might have infected you?"

"It had to be Vickie Swopes. She is the only one I have been seeing over the last year and a half besides Shauna."

"Are you being straight with me? This is no time for games, man!"

"If I have the AIDS virus, then I am a hundred percent sure about her."

I got up from the couch and looked over at Zeth. I had fire in my eyes, and felt my soul had charred. I left the great room, but as I walked away could hear Zeth. His voice rose and he spoke crazily. "Oh, Jesus. Zemi and Shauna are going to be so upset. I know Zemi will become enraged. She doesn't tolerate any nonsense in her life." Zeth's voice was trembling. "She'll leave me."

I could barely stand to hear him speak. With a tear-strewn face, I stood outside the great room, and listened to the rest, hoping that all of this was not my comeuppance for ill-placed faith and foolhardy actions.

"Not my baby sister, Oh, God, please don't let my baby sister have it. It will just kill Mama." E.J. shook his head sadly. "Damn, one person can wipe out a whole village."

"I don't know if I have the disease," said Zeth, "but I know that Zemi does not have the AIDS virus."

"How can you be so sure about Zemi?" E.J. asked eagerly.

Zeth cleared his throat. "Because Zemi and I never had sexual relations, and your sister is a virgin."

E.J. threw up his hands. "What? You mean Zemi never did it, and you are going to marry my sister and you don't know that part about her? Well, now ain't that about a new kind of love?"

I went on into the kitchen into which their voices carried. E.J.'s and Zeth's voices were somewhat overshadowed by my fervent prayer and praise to God that I was able to remain mindful of HIS ways. I continued to pray as they spoke.

"From the situation that we both might be in, it sounds like hers is the better type of love. Shucks, I get excited just the way Zemi teases me to let me know she knows what to do. But I guess you don't want to hear that, with her bein' your sister and all."

When I approached the entry to the great room, I heard E.J. say, "No. It's okay." He clasped his hands as if to pray, tears rolling down his face. Then he took Zeth's hand. "Zeth, talk to me that way because you're telling me my baby sister does not have AIDS. Oh, God, thank you for sparing her from this." E.J. fell to his knees. "Man, we all thought that Zemi was square, but she seems to be handling herself much better than the rest of us."

"E.J., you might want to think about your sister Maria instead of Zemi," said Zeth.

"What do you mean, 'think about Maria'?"

"Well, I am not saying that she has anything, but her marketing agent...well, they are a pretty heavy couple in Charlotte."

"And? This ain't no time for you to be slow in speech, Zeth. What are you saying about Maria?"

"Your sister Maria has been with someone. Listen, man, Maria and Vickie have the same marketin' agent. He had been dating Vickie Swopes for about a year and a half before he started datin' Maria. But maybe Vickie did not have AIDS then if, indeed, she has it now...I just don't know, E.J."

"Are you pretty solid that this marketing agent has been with Vickie?" asked E.J.

"More certain than what I knew of you and Vickie."

"This just seems too unreal." E.J. wiped the sweat from his hands onto his pants. "My fiancée has AIDS, I gave it to her and now my sister might have it from the guy who dated the woman who gave it to me. And right now I can't think straight enough, but I don't know if when I had a brief encounter with Amy, it was before or after I met Vickie. Amy was a virgin. Please, I hope I have not ruined Amy's life, too. Zemi will never respect me again. Life is a bitch—and then you die."

My friend Amy. How could E.J.? Please God, not my friend Amy.

"It doesn't have to be that way, E.J. If we have AIDS, we will fight it with treatment. Some people die because they won't get tested and then have no reason to get treated. I've got something to fight fer, something to live fer now that Zemi said yes to my proposal."

Now Zeth started crying. "She said that she would marry me and have my babies every time it rained. I want those babies she promised me, and I am not gonna let any disease steal my dreams and life away from under me without a good fight. Do you hear me, E.J.? Are you going to fight with me, brother?"

"I am going to share that attitude with you, Zeth. I want a life with Shauna. I promised her a family and I owe her that."

"You think Zemi might leave me?"

"Why should she?" E.J. slapped Zeth's back. "It is all right, man. Zemi doesn't have it."

"But what if I have the virus or something?"

"Come on. Zemi is a sensible girl. I don't think you have to worry."

"That's exactly why I am worried. Zemi is too sensible when it comes to doin' the right thing," said Zeth.

"Man, Zeth, but who would have thought that something so sweet looking as a Vickie Swopes was walking around with a weapon of mass destruction?"

"Come on, man." Zeth put his arm around E.J.'s shoulders. "Let's go to the stable and get your woman. She really needs you now more than ever."

E.J. rubbed his head. "Let the truth be told, I need her. Oh, man, Zeth." E.J. sat down. "Jesus, help us all." He got up and looked out the window. "You think that Shauna is real angry with me? I mean, she has every right to be. But I swear I did not intend to hurt her that way." E.J. began to weep again. "Oh, Jesus…Oh, God, my family really needs you now."

EPILOGUE

Those who were involved with this AIDS predicament—E.J., Shauna, Maria, Zeth and Zemi—went to visit Zeth's doctor friend. This situation was bigger than any family matter that Zemi's family had ever come up against. Zemi's family was broken and had to find its way back to family unity—the love—the way it used to be. These AIDS consequences were more severe to Zemi's family than what she could take responsibility to handle or solve. Through guidance from Grandma's pastor, the whole family stayed in constant prayer.

Out of the family, the situation hit Shauna and E.J. the hardest. Both of them had the AIDS virus, HIV, but did not yet have AIDS. In Zeth's home that evening and that next day everyone jumped straight to the conclusion that testing positive for the virus meant AIDS, and all were thinking AIDS, even though medically and scientifically they knew better. Shauna was told that the risk of having children born with the AIDS virus was extremely great and that she should consider adopting children if she wished to experience motherhood. She and E.J. got married right away and adopted twin boys. Shauna, Chairperson of the GateKeepers AIDS Prevention and Healing Center, has taken its message around the country on speaking circuits. Often E.J. tours with his wife, and contributes his legal knowledge to keep the center in compliance with applicable laws and regulations. His other time is spent obtaining funds to further exploratory research on AIDS. E.J. and Shauna said that they are forever determined that the AIDS Center will stay committed to its founding principle—"Our doors will always be open to anyone who needs help."

The Center that Shauna and E.J. run owes much of the organization's success to the many spokespersons and professional athletes who have loaned their names and given money and time to the continued progress of the Center's goal and mission. Rappers also answered Gatekeeper's Roll Call in huge numbers. Many entertainers and artists, of other music genres and varying art forms, people of varying ethnicities, followed the rappers and hip hoppers through the door. Tremendous public relations efforts have brought out rappers who have given free concerts to raise awareness and even become board members. In addition, rappers have reached out to their fan bases to make known the risks of AIDS to us all. In its day to day operations, the Center keeps communities aware of AIDS and STDs and prevention and treatment. The Center prides itself on its ability to raise funds to help minimal income patients get the treatment necessary and to alleviate some of the frustrations that come along with living with AIDS and HIV. AIDS can touch each of us individually.

Vickie Swopes learned that she had been dating a married, bisexual man. Vickie had infected at least five other men who came forward. A year later, Vickie Swopes died from AIDS. She donated a large amount of her wealth to the GateKeepers AIDS Prevention and Healing Center. The Center is becoming more and more philanthropic throughout the South. Through generous real property endowments, the Center's outreach efforts so far have helped to establish AIDS centers in Mobile and Tuskegee, Alabama, as well Atlanta and Augusta, Georgia. In North Carolina, the Center has gone beyond Charlotte to Asheville, Raleigh, Winston-Salem and Greensboro.

Maria's marketing agent did not have the AIDS virus. He and Maria were engaged to marry, but they decided there was no more love between the two of them. She was free of the virus herself. Maria is dating a politician now, so she is often seen on the political scene. As long as it is a stage is what Zemi thinks of Maria.

Lately, Zemi mused, 'Our Platform is enjoying critical acclaim. Maria leads the show now with a Latina as co-host. Several times the show has been broadcast from minimal income neighborhoods and communities. The audience is largely black and Latino. Funny thing about where we are now with our brown siblings, as Maria calls them. By having dialogue with Latinos through the show, we have come to understand many of the issues that face them. Like black people, they do not all think or feel the same things. And as Latinos focus primarily on their issues, we feel black people must focus primarily on theirs. We submit that most black people would conclude that they would not be welcomed if they crossed the border to the South—or any international border for that matter and worked jobs that the people in those countries would otherwise have. Does history pretty much show that the only time a people are guaranteed an all out welcome by people in a foreign country as labor is if they are brought there as slaves? Well, perhaps Red Cross and maybe UN workers are welcomed, but something like a tsunami or war has to strike first? And, well, it has to be work no one else can or will do? Where are the answers? What are the questions? And there should be plenty. Until we have some answers every statement we make should end with a question mark. We need to know that we do not know. If anyone knew, wouldn't it all be fixed and people would just get along? Wouldn't we be clothed and fed and healthy? Has the world really gotten exponentially duller with exponentially greater knowledge? Well, Our Platform says we have to talk about all these things. And today our focus is the things all people need to talk about. AIDS and HIV. Denial is death, but owning up can mean life. The guest speakers on Our Platform are from all walks of life. Politicians—all ethnicities, Independent, Republican and Democrat—find Our Platform their greatest stage to address the American people. Call-ins to the show are at a record high.'

Actress Maria remains an Independent (at least, in the public's eyes). The talk show has become the largest home front from which minority women's voices and views are now heard.

Joey remains single. He and Natasha have a healthy son. Ishmael remains a Muslim but orthodox.

Amy has succeeded, at least by the Census Bureau and in many other arenas, in being classified a white. For her sake, it is hoped she is right, too. God had spared Zeth from the AIDS and HIV and rewarded Zemi for her abstinence. Married now, Zeth and Zemi are blessed with children from two single births and a set of triplets.

Zeth once asked of Zemi, "Had I been infected with the AIDS virus would you still have married me?"

Zemi answered, "Give thanks that you would never have to know the answer."

Through Zemi's tireless efforts and with Zeth's support wherever needed, a very successful AIDS Prevention and Healing Center was also opened in Liberia. Zemi's fondness for Liberia's President Ellen Johnson-Sirleaf has fueled her enhanced commitment to establish Monrovia, Liberia as a sister city of Atlanta, Georgia, Charlotte, North Carolina, and Oakland, California in hopes of helping to establish dual citizenship for the citizens of Liberia. Zemi had another dream. She is on course to open a state-of-the art, resort-like Writer's Palace in Liberia. The Writer's Palace is Zemi's vision for developing a film production concern out of Liberia—a gateway for open dialogue between Africans and African Americans. A Writer's Palace is already in operation from the GateKeeper's Village. Many young authors and speech writers have sprung from this effort.

The GateKeeper's Village and its many real estate developments have become the blue-blood signature for Zemi. Next to Zeth and her children, though, there is nothing that fills Zemi's heart more than the architectural majesty of the luxury gated community for senior citizens. Mother and Grandma are now proud owners and residents in the gated GateKeeper's Village for Senior Citizens.

Zemi and Zeth have both become much more astute politically, but are still contemplating which political party to join. As a family, they both want to serve within the same party. They are working assiduously within minimal income communities to help influence the results for the 2008 election.

AFTERWORD

It is my sincerest hope that Americans will begin a serious dialogue on all the topics we need to discuss to mend this nation. We live in a historical time when an African American counts among the front runners for the candidate the Democratic Party will choose to run for President of the United States of America. Even today, many blacks will say that they would not expect to see such strides in their lifetimes. So, congratulations are in order for Senator Barack Obama, his wife, Michelle Obama, their family, and all the persons who have come thus far with them by faith and much work, indeed! Even in the gloomiest of times, a spark of light will show, and lift spirits and such is manifesting as I pen these words. Congratulations are due to Senator Hillary Rodham Clinton, for she, too, has ushered in some history as the female front runner for the Democratic Party's slate for the Presidency. These historical events are occurring when so much hangs in the balance, and so much healing must take place. But is this not how it has happened throughout history—when during the times we are most tried, then emerge the new, the dynamic, the inspiring leaders to usher in a new age? And, as we speak of cures, we must remember our home in this universe: as 2007 Nobelist Al Gore makes clear, it is imperative that we tend to our Earth, for even it is very sick.

While fact and data are blended in this book, the story, after all, is fiction. While I do not profess any expertise in the various disciplines which might best address the issues raised in the book (or even best determine the issues that need to be raised), I can wield a long handled spoon and stir the pot, tossing this or that into the mix. Of course, no one would want to digest the resulting "stew" in a

465

literal sense, but to address, digest and process substantive changes for the better we must. If we do not, we perhaps would much prefer a shaded canvas over our world and lives, as to feast our eyes on the grotesque in the tomorrow not prepared for today in wisdom, strength, and truth is not what we are prepared to do. (Is today not our tomorrow of yesterday?) And such tragedy, a grimmer tomorrow, would be unnecessary as we possess the wherewithal to be loyal stewards over our collective destiny and the world (and Earth) that we leave for our progeny. So, if it is too late for us to dream, perhaps we might act, if not for ourselves, then for the sake of posterity—future generations. To the winner of the U.S. Presidential election this fall goes a lot of work, in deed, but as the late President John F. Kennedy made plain, every American must roll our sleeves! May God bless and keep us all.

Isis I

January 2008

Contact Information for Author:
www.isisprivatestock.com
Email: isis@isisprivatestock.com